PLEASURE HOUSE
by
Scarlet Darkwood

Pleasure House
Copyright © 2015 by Scarlet Darkwood
All rights reserved.

This book is an erotic, adult novel intended for readers 18 years of age and older. Contents and scenes in this book are graphic and not suitable for those younger or for those with weak sensibilities. Please note that the scenes in this book are for fantasy stimulation, and by no means meant to suggest that people in real life conduct themselves in the manner of the characters: Please practice safe sex! No part of this book may be reproduced or retrieved by any means, electronic, mechanical, or otherwise, without written permission from the author. All characters and activities in this book are fictitious, and any similarities to those alive or deceased are purely coincidental.

Text and Cover Design: Rebecca Poole
(Dreams2Media)
Photo Credit: depositphotos
First Printing: 2012

Acknowledgments

I'd like to extend a warm thanks of appreciation to those who helped me with this book: Rebecca Poole, for her reliability and creative mind in creating an awesome cover for this book; Vicki Sly for her proofreading skills; Shelly Lazar for her marketing assistance and support; Nymph Du Pave, who so graciously took time out of her busy schedule to read through the manuscript and offer her seasoned experience and opinions (www.nymphdupave.wordpress.com); my editor, Mírakel Mayoral, whose insight helped this book become a better story; Jessica West, who is supportive in every way. I'd also like to thank my beta readers, and you know who you are, for your time and energy too. Most of all, I'd like to thank my dear spouse who supported me the whole time, and even took his time to read through the manuscript. Without all of your help, *Pleasure House* wouldn't exist.

Chapter 1

COOL AIR from the room brushed against her pink, exposed flesh. The morning sun peeked through the window, spreading strands of light on the bed where Rose lay naked. Between a pair of youthful thighs, a carnal fire raged as she relived each sensual scene from the night before. A throbbing ache kept taunting every sensitive nerve within her pelvic region, its flaming fingers holding her prisoner with a choking grip. No amount of shifting or repositioning alleviated the searing discomfort.

She still felt his hands, firm and sure, on her flesh, his fingers working sensitive areas with an intensity that had driven her mad. She reached up to squeeze a nipple, hoping to mimic the way he'd first aroused her senses. The pinch sent thrills radiating all the way down to a dripping sex, but still there was no relief. If they'd been left alone longer, perhaps in a different place, free from any possible disturbance, what then? Would they have …? A slender finger trailed over the hard, tiny knot nestled within her cleft and lingered, teasing the sensitive area until a series of spasms erupted. She pressed her shapely buttocks deeper into the bed and closed her eyes, prepared and ready to penetrate her dark, hidden passage with a pair of steady, delicate fingers. She took a deep breath, opening her thighs wide ...

* * *

Her eyes flew open and she let out a shout of surprise. Horrified, she discovered a man by the bed.

"So this is what you've been up to lately? Your mother and I have been wondering why you spend so much time in your room. Now we know. This is the last straw."

"Father!" Red-faced and flustered, Rose tried in vain to cover herself. "What…? When…? How come …? How did you get in here? I thought I locked the door."

He glanced around, spying a robe hanging on the edge of a chair. "Put this on for heaven's sake. Get up right now and get dressed immediately because we're taking a little trip this afternoon." His eyes flashed with irritation.

"A trip? Where are we going?"

"Your mother and I have talked at length, and we think sending you to The House will be a good thing. Maybe they'll be able to fix whatever craziness is going on inside your head, because we can't help you here. This running around to parties in short dresses, staying out late, and now finding you here, doing …" He ran his fingers through his hair. "This is unacceptable behavior. Nice girls don't act this way, and don't think we haven't figured out what goes on when you're out with other men. Call them friends all you want, but I know better."

"But … Father …!" Rose took a few deep breaths, trying to calm herself. How she hated the injustice! Answering to her parents all the time had finally taken its toll. "This isn't fair. I'm not doing—" His words rang in her ears. The more she thought about this situation, the invasion of privacy, the angrier she became. She sat up and glared at him. "How dare you come barging in on me. You know what, you don't own me. You may be my father, but I'm a grown woman, twenty years old. I'll do what I please, thank you very much." With courage in full swing, she stood up and looked him straight in the eye. "Besides, you can't make me do anything against my will, so there."

His face burned bright red, eyes bulging. "In this day and age, when we aren't allowed to drink, when church people go around minding everybody else's business, I do own you. You're my daughter, you're unmarried, and if you don't do what I say, I'll make sure you do it. And if I have to, I'll have you arrested on grounds of insanity." His lips curled into a sneer. "Don't push me, dear girl, because I won't think twice about it. No daughter of mine conducts herself in a lewd manner, embarrassing herself and this family."

"I'm not going anywhere!" In anger, Rose bolted forward, pushing him aside. Just as she reached the hallway and started down the stairs, he grabbed her arm, pulling her back into the room. "Enough! I need you dressed and downstairs in five minutes, or I'll drag you out just as you are." His hot breath filled her ear. "You dare pull a stunt like running away, and I'll get the authorities. Give it up, dear. You'll not win this battle. Not by a long shot." As he uttered this last threat, he turned on his heels and left the room, his footsteps echoing in the hallway as he tramped down the stairs.

Rose started to follow him so she could give him more of a piece of her mind, but decided against it. Sitting back on the bed, she curled her hands around her knees to think. Maybe she could quickly dress, make a run for it. There were friends who'd surely help if she wanted a life away from home. Call the authorities. Send her to The House. The mere suggestion infuriated her even more.

In minutes, however, she considered reality: people were picked up by the authorities and sent to The House all the time. It happened. She'd heard the stories, but never thought much about them. If situations didn't affect her directly, she usually didn't care.

At the touch of a warm hand on her back, Rose jumped. Her mother sat on the bed next to her.

"There, there, dear, you'll be all right, I'm sure."

"I didn't hear you come in." Rose sniffed.

Rose's mother sighed. "We know this seems harsh, but your father and I think you'll benefit a great deal from treatment. It's just not proper for young ladies like yourself to be so engrossed in ways of the flesh. We don't want you behaving in a questionable manner. Keep acting like this, and you'll never find a suitable husband."

"Oh, mother, women aren't much different from men. How come they have the freedom to do anything they want, while we pretty much have no rights and are treated like property? I want control of my own life. When I do decide to marry, I want an equal partnership, not someone telling me what to do and how to do it."

"Darling, you're a young woman, and your father and I are aware of how young people think these days. Such thoughts!

Women need to know their place, and they need the protection and guidance of someone strong."

"What nonsense. Women aren't weak, brainless people. You know that." Rose leaned closer to her mother. "Don't you ever want to tell Father what to do? Let him know you're the boss sometimes? Even just a little?"

Her mother's face flushed a light pink. "Rose no matter what young women are saying and trying to change right now, we have roles, and one of them is certainly not conducting oneself like a common streetwalker. If you ask me, you're falling prey to some of the horrible fashion trends. Your father's right. Why, some of the dresses you're beginning to wear are just a little too short for my taste! No wonder men want just one thing when they see you."

Rose sniffled again; tears filled her eyes. "This is terrible! Do you think he'd really go so far as to have me arrested?"

"I wouldn't try anything rash. No one wants to get involved in such private matters."

Rose held her head in her hands and sobbed harder. "Oh, Mother, I've heard rumors about The House. Only crazy people go there. No matter what you think about me, I'm not crazy. I just want the freedom to explore things on my own and make my own decisions in life. I'm sick and tired of being told what to do. I want to call the shots for a change."

"Darling, you'll be fine, and no, we don't think you're crazy, either. You just have some problems we need to fix."

Rose scowled. "Problems? Why do I have a problem? There's nothing wrong with me. Have you forgotten how you and Father felt when you were first in love? Did you think you had a problem because of the way you felt inside?"

Her mother shrank back. "I think we've had enough of this conversation. And if you want to settle the way you feel inside, a good man would cure that right away. Especially if he's your husband."

Grimacing, Rose took in a deep breath. "I've heard

strange stories about people who go to The House, and I'm scared they'll hurt me. If I promise to be good, will you and Father reconsider?"

"No, dear, our minds are made up. And don't believe everything you hear. The House is the perfect place to help you get better. Here, let's get you packed up and ready to go. Your father is waiting for us."

Rose sniffed one last time before she pulled herself off the bed and plodded to the closet. Each article of clothing she put on created a certain agony within her, drawing her closer to an unknown fate. Heartbroken and dejected, she pulled out her travel bag while her mother retrieved some undergarments from the chest of drawers. As Rose packed, a personal war waged deep inside. She knew arguing with her parents served no purpose. Nowhere else offered her a safe harbor if she decided to run away and hide. Would she ever see her home again? What if her parents wanted to rid themselves of her and abandon her at The House? She'd heard stories about people entering that place, and not ever leaving.

Should she include a small memento, a trinket of some sort to remember the life she was leaving? One perusal over her small dressing table, and she decided against it, unsure which of her possessions would be the best to choose. She merely tossed in a couple of dresses, matching stockings, and an extra pair of shoes. Her mother added a few toiletries, a silver brush and comb. Forlorn and near tears, Rose scanned her room once again to make sure she'd taken everything she might need. At last she turned to her mother. "I guess I'm ready."

"You'll be fine, dear." Rose's mother put an arm around her daughter's shoulder as they headed down the stairs.

When Rose reached the bottom of the steps, her eyes roved over her surroundings, trying to store each detail in her memory before leaving. Her eyes fell on the large grandfather clock in the hallway, its *ticktock* sounds rolling over her ears as if counting down the minutes before the delivery of a death sentence. She spied the sitting room where her parents spent hours together, her mother mending clothes, her father reading. Located at the back of the hall was the kitchen, where she often slipped out the back door and into their lovely flower garden. How she'd miss that place most of all, choosing to spend much of her time enjoying the colors, smells, and the fresh air. Now the possibility of never returning home again filled her with great sadness, its heaviness in her chest threatening to crush her with its weight.

She gave her mother one last look. "You won't forget me, will you?"

Her mother kissed her on the forehead. "Oh, goodness, no, dear. How on earth did you come up with such a notion? Just be good and do everything you're told to do, and you'll be fine. Come on. Your father will be waiting in the car."

*   *   *

The House, located deep in the countryside on the outskirts of town, remained somewhat shrouded in mystery, hidden by towering walls and spacious grounds, keeping itself at arm's length from the general community. True enough, snippets of stories surrounding The House and its activities floated about, their scant, elusive details falling into the occasional listening ear. Whether or not those narratives contained an ounce of truth, only the inhabitants of The House knew for sure.

As Rose and her father made their way to the edge of town, the scenery changed from orderly neighborhoods and quaint merchant shops on the town square, to country life and its sprawling, rolling green meadows and various native animal life. An occasional deer perked up its head and watched with curiosity as they continued down the long, winding road that headed toward The House. Under different circumstances, Rose might have enjoyed this ride, but today feelings of dread held her captive, their sinister threads entwining around every fiber of her being.

"We don't have much farther to go." Rose's father tried

to appear calm, engaging in small talk, but she rebuffed his efforts. "Oh, come now, Rose, don't be so angry at me. I know I came down hard on you, but I care about you. Your mother cares about you. We're doing this for your own good." Attempts to comfort her with words of consolation won him nothing more than an upturned nose and a sniff, as she merely turned her head away and ignored his comments.

Her father proceeded down a road that wound through a dim forest. The trees opened and spread their branches high and wide to the sun-filled sky, just as a young girl who opens and lifts her nether regions to her lover. Small streams trickled over stones scattered about. As they rounded a bend in the road, Rose saw the high stone walls surrounding the grounds. Their heights barred any attempts at escape and, likewise, any glimpses of activity within the grounds.

*   *   *

When they neared The House, her brave front crumbled, and her heart began to pound. "Father, are the stories I've heard about this place true?"

"What stories are you talking about?"

"Stories of strange goings-on and such."

Rose's father sighed and pursed his lips. "Well, now you have me stumped. Let's see now, do I know of any stories about this place?" He became silent a moment and then continued, "Yes, as a matter of fact, I *do* know a couple of stories. I'd forgotten them because it's been some time."

"So, tell me about them. I want to know."

"Do you remember Mrs. Starnsby, who lived in the old Victorian home in the historical district?"

"Yes, what about her?"

"If I remember, she became sullen and irritable over time. I guess living alone in such a big house would make anybody lonely, and subject to fits of depression. At any rate, not even her physician could determine the reason for her change in behavior, so he sent her to The House to see if they could help. Let me tell you, when she came back home, she had a smile on her face and a spring in her step. We couldn't figure out what happened, but she did end up marrying old Mr. Wisenburg, a widower who lived two blocks down from her place. They now have quite an exciting marriage from what I hear. He once told a friend of mine that marrying Thelma Starnsby was the best thing he'd ever done in his life."

"Interesting. The House cured her that much?"

"I guess so. Oh, and there's the story of Willie Strumpkin. You know him, don't you?"

"Yes. He's rather shy and awkward, isn't he?" Rose shuddered. "Personally, I find him a bit creepy, and a big bore, too."

"Not anymore. His family decided they'd had enough of his dull and listless ways. They knew he'd never catch a good wife at the rate he was going. They sent him to The House for treatment, and he came back a changed man. He soon married Lulu Carnwell."

"That bossy, demanding thing?" Rose glanced at her father in surprise. "I can't imagine anyone wanting her."

"Apparently Willie took quite a fancy to her. Once they married, she became meek as a lamb, and from what I hear, he's had not one bit of trouble out of her. They get along quite well."

"As hopeful as these stories sound, I'm still not convinced. How can you and Mother be so heartless, sending me to a place like this?"

"Your mother and I are not being heartless, Rose. Please try to see this from our point of view."

"Why don't you see it from my point of view?" She caught her sharp tone and dropped her head. Thoughts of another heated argument exhausted her.

Rose's father continued staring at the road ahead, and after a few minutes, he reached over and laid his hand on top of hers. "I do see this from your point of view, and all I can tell you is, please, don't be scared. I've heard good reports about this place, and you'll benefit."

As they rounded a turn in the road, she now glimpsed the rooftop on the building, but gained no more clues as to what lurked inside. Everything mocked her, daring her to enter. At last they stopped at a gated entrance, and a uniformed guard came out smiling.

"Yes, Sir, may I help you?"

"My daughter needs to be admitted here. Is there someone who can help us with this?"

"Absolutely, Sir." The guard nodded. "Please pass through the gate, and when you reach the end of the drive, you may proceed up the steps to the main door. All you need to do is knock, and someone will let you in. I'll notify the steward and tell him you're coming."

With a loud squeak, the iron gates opened.

*   *   *

Rose caught her breath. The House, built like an impenetrable castle, sat on a sprawling front lawn, both showing off majesty and grace like a queen greeting her subjects. She craned her neck and gazed at the amazing structure of towers, tall windows, and striking eaves and dormers. The architecture, strong and solid, maintained an orderly front on the outside, but in her imagination, she envisioned labyrinthine corridors inside leading to unknown places. The immaculate lawns flourished with sculpted gardens and scroll pathways, peppered with the occasional bronze statue or fountain. A place this beautiful on the outside must be good on the inside. Perhaps she'd reached the safe haven she sought.

"Well, Rose," her father said, as they reached the end of the drive, "we have arrived." They walked up the large, stone steps to a menacing iron door. He turned to her one last time. "Just make sure you mind your manners." He grasped the heavy door knocker and rapped on the monstrosity while Rose craned her neck upward. She caught the view of the most curious sign above the door. The script made her heart sink as she read the words, "Abandon Hope, All Who Enter Here." How unusual. Why would a facility place such a sign over its main entrance? Besides, this phrase rang a bell. Where had she seen it before? In horror, she shuddered as she remembered. According to Dante's writings, this script announced the entrance to Hell! Fear gripped her once again, and her body began to tremble. What would happen to her here? She still felt uncertain with her father's brief stories of this place. No one had ever told her personally of their experience at The House. What if her father had just told her those things only to appease her?

Within a few moments, a handsome man in smart attire greeted them. "Good afternoon. The guard informed me of your arrival. I understand you wish to discuss the subject of your daughter's admission." He offered his visitors a warm smile.

"Yes ..." Rose's father began. He hesitated a moment and looked the young man up and down with a light frown. "I need to bring my daughter here for help. To whom do I speak regarding admission here?"

"My name is John," replied the man in a silky voice, "and I'm the steward here. I'm the one to whom you'll be speaking. Please come inside and we can discuss this more." He moved aside and opened the door wider. Rose, astonished, studied the man's attire in more detail. On his tall, well-built frame, he wore a white shirt with a bow tie. Black trousers hugged his lean hips and muscular buttocks, and between a set of toned thighs, he held a bulge that made the interior of her loins swell and moisten. A pair of shiny, black shoes completed his outfit with a flourish. So engrossed she became in checking out his fine physique as she passed through the door, she stumbled over the last step, plunging headlong into her father in a most ungraceful manner.

"Watch your step, Miss!" John cautioned.

Rose caught a glimpse of her father's disapproving scowl, and blushed at her awkwardness.

John reached forward, caught her soft, shapely arm, and helped her regain balance. The touch of his hand sent waves of electricity through her, and her stomach lurched with a certain nervousness. Touched as she was by his charm and drawn in by his inviting eyes, her face flushed a soft pink. The sight of this man stirred in her a deep spark of attraction she didn't quite understand. John smiled at her, and shut the door with a loud bang.

Wide-eyed, Rose stepped over the beautiful, tiled floors of a spacious lobby and landed her eyes on the most stunning marble staircase that traveled upwards to unknown regions of the building. Somewhere in the distance, she heard the sounds of mirthful laughter. She eyed the magnificent marble statues of Diana and Venus on either side of the staircase landing, their scantily clad figures causing her to nearly blush. Their outstretched arms seemed to invite her in.

A magnificent crystal chandelier put the crowning glory on the whole room, its lustrous prisms flashing rainbows of color against the high, pale yellow walls and white ceiling. Rose marveled at the various oil portraits of ladies and gentlemen gracing the walls. Their facial expressions hinted of mischief, and the clothing on the women in the paintings seemed to push the boundaries of decency, revealing a little too much bosom. Likewise, the crotches of the gentlemen appeared rather inflated. Despite the casual hints of naughtiness that caught her eye, this room struck her as the most beautiful she'd ever seen.

John led the small party down the left hallway to his office. From behind, Rose admired his gorgeous sable hair, the medium-length soft waves falling carelessly around his head, occasional wisps blowing in the air as he walked. His neatly trimmed mustache, full and soft, gave him a more dignified and mature air, and a mouth full of immaculate, straight, white teeth gleamed when he smiled. The sight of him took her breath away. Much to her surprise, she experienced a strong urge to kiss his soft mouth and feel his mustache tickle the skin beneath her nose. John turned around and glanced at his visitors. As he grinned, Rose's heart fluttered.

After they reached the office, he showed his guests into two elegant armchairs before seating himself in a throne-sized chair behind a large, ornate desk. With a businesslike air, he reached inside the desk and brought out some forms and a pen.

"Your name, please," he requested, glancing in her father's direction.

"I'm Samuel Barweather, and this is my daughter Rose."

"Thank you. And why does she need to be admitted to our facility?"

Mr. Barweather sat up and cleared his throat, uncertain how to begin. "Well, um … you see … Rose, as of late, has been engaged in some curious behavior. This morning I found her in her room doing some rather … um … well …"

Breaking off from further formalities, his sentences began falling in a torrent from his lips. "Her mother and I didn't raise her this way, and we need her to be cured of wanting to spend long hours in her room behind closed doors, doing god knows what to herself while she's in there. We suspect she's been hard at it for quite some time, but we finally got to the bottom of it this morning. I caught her red-handed. This is all abominable, I say." He shook his head and rubbed his chin in frustration.

John sank back in his chair and eyed both of them for a moment, mulling over Mr. Barweather's concerns before answering. "I think I understand quite well what you're saying, Mr. Barweather." John nodded at the father, a sober look on his face. He rested his hands on the desk and tapped his fingertips together for a moment longer before he sat up straight in his chair. "To sum up what you are most likely trying to say here is that Rose, blossoming into womanhood, has a newfound need to explore certain parts of her nature, and at this point in time, her behavior is causing you great distress. You find her actions most inappropriate, and you wish for us to assist her in dealing with these."

"Exactly!" Mr. Barweather tapped his hand with enthusiasm on the arm of the chair. "Well spoken like a wise man. I'm sure you have a good handle on situations such as these. I've heard nothing but good things about this place. But I must say, Mr. … um … John … that I'm a little concerned about leaving Rose. I just don't want her treatment and experience here to be her undoing, that's all. And from what I've seen so far, I just have my …"

"Oh, you needn't be concerned about leaving Rose under our care." John smiled.

"Well, it's just that these young people today, especially the women, are getting such ludicrous ideas into their heads. Nonetheless, I admit I feel a little guilty, like I'm feeding her to the lions by bringing her here. Is this a common problem?"

John folded his hands together, maintaining composure. "Mr. Barweather, please let me first say that I completely understand your concern. It seems we're in a flux of social change right now. A new type of patient is emerging, those who are preoccupied in learning more about their body, if you know what I mean. Women are demanding more rights than ever before, and they're slowly winning, too. However, we understand the importance of proper behavior and helping people function well not only in society, but their personal relationships as well."

Mr. Barweather narrowed his eyes and nodded. "All I can say is she needs to be cured of this insatiable … What would you call it …? Lust! That's it!" He cried out again and gave the chair arm another resounding thwack. "So you think you can help her?"

"I assure you, plenty of family and friends like yourself have brought their loved ones here with the same problem. Trust me when I say we're more than adept at dealing with all types of people, especially those concerning … um … carnal matters."

*   *   *

John smiled and sank back in his chair again. He quietly studied the girl who sat before him, her face covered with a rather glum expression. A soft smile crept over his face. Young, limited in her experience in the ways of the flesh, she presented as a most perfect candidate for The House. Her figure showed off a lean and graceful frame, with just the right height. A crown of champagne-colored hair framed her pleasing face, and fell in soft ringlets about her shoulders. Her full, luscious mouth made him salivate. Her breasts, not large enough to be vulgar, but small enough to maintain their nice round shape, perched on top of a delicate chest. No doubt those sweet mounds sported a nice pair of ripe, sweet, succulent nipples to throw into the bargain. Virginal, he wasn't sure, but he didn't obsess too much over this issue. He knew time revealed all secrets.

"Well, I've made my decision," Mr. Barweather said, after pondering the situation a few moments. "I'll leave Rose here with you, if you promise to teach her a thing or two, if you know what I mean."

"Trust me, Mr. Barweather, Rose will be in the finest hands and taught well. You needn't worry yourself too much." John gave a smile of approval. "If you'll just place your signature on these documents, we can begin."

With a quick flourish of the pen, Mr. Barweather signed the paperwork. "Well, Rose, this is good-bye." He turned and put his arms around his daughter, giving her a hug and kissing her on the cheek. "Please know that your mother and I love you, and we want the very best for you. You'll be fine here."

"Yes, Father, I'm sure I will." She managed a wan smile.

After escorting Mr. Barweather out of the building, John returned to the office within moments. He brushed his hand over her shoulder. "Well, Rose, your treatment is about to begin, but there is one more piece of business we need to address. And this issue surrounds confidentiality." He stepped behind the desk and pulled out a piece of paper from one of the drawers and retrieved a pen. She leaned over to read the writing as he pushed the document toward her. "You see, we take our privacy here at The House seriously, and we have only our new admissions sign this particular sheet."

"I see. Father never saw this?" She lifted her face and met his stare. Her expression showed panic. While she continued reading the white sheet on the desk, he sensed chaos filling her mind. She shook her head with a frown.

He came around from behind the desk and stood next to her. "You seem a little confused, so let me see if I can clarify a few things for you. First of all, the treatment here at The House is unique, and we prefer to keep our activities hidden from public knowledge. We find that the community, in general, tends to repress certain emotions and behaviors. You, on the other hand, will be addressing those emotions and behaviors. You'll learn things here no one else does."

"Is that why I've heard very little about this place? I mean, people seem almost reluctant to talk. Perhaps it's because they signed this document?"

"Precisely. And if you've read everything, you'll see that we will silence those who talk."

"Yes, but you don't say how, exactly." She put the paper back on his desk and folded her hands in her lap. "I'm unclear why such secrecy is necessary."

He knelt down next to her, his eyes holding hers with a steady, pleading gaze. "While I can't reveal our methods to you at this time, I'm hoping you can surely understand our position. You're in need of assistance and we can help you. So will you be willing to put your signature right here on this line?" He tapped his finger on the specified area. Maintaining his stare, he handed her the pen.

"What if I don't sign? What if I just got up and left, right now? My parents are gone. You can't stop me." Her eyes remained fixed on his.

John swallowed hard. "I really don't recommend you do that. You won't get far, and if you don't sign this form, then we'll have other plans for you. And you don't want that. Trust me on this."

"It seems no matter how much I try coming up with ways to get out of this, I can't seem to. Everyone keeps telling me the same thing as you. Don't people ever say no, leave here when they feel like it, go start a new life for themselves?"

Returning the stare, John replied, "Most people actually like it here."

Stunned, Rose sat for a few seconds, digesting his words. She eyed his tapping finger and took up the pen. "The House is a treatment facility after all, and the issue of silence makes sense. Besides, for some strange reason, I have this uncanny sense that you're telling me the truth. Very well, I'll sign." With a quick scribble, she placed her signature on the form. "I guess I've sealed my own fate, haven't I?"

John swiped up the paper, and placed it back in the desk. "You won't regret anything, I assure you. As a female admit under our care, you will not only learn roles of submission, you'll also learn how to dominate and command. Within these walls, you learn a new freedom that will serve you well outside these walls. Do you understand me?"

Rose narrowed her eyes. What exactly do you mean by dominate and command?"

John smiled. "You'll see soon enough."

He came out from behind the desk once again. "Your attendant will go over the rules in more detail. If you need anything, please ask one of us, and we'll be only too glad to help. But first, our policy here mandates that each admit undergo a physical examination by our House physician, Dr. James, before we commence treatment. Once this part of the admission process is complete, you'll meet your attendant, who will finalize the last half."

"Dr. James? I have to see a doctor?" Rose's questioning eyes bounced between John's face and the floor.

"Yes, we must make sure you're fit to participate safely in our setting." John gazed a moment at her face, viewing the fear and confusion playing into her eyes. "There's nothing to fear. Dr. James is gentle and very kind."

"It's just that …" She cleared her throat, struggling to find her words. "I've never really been examined by a doctor before. I've been lucky, being so healthy and all. I don't get sick very often, and resting in bed for a day or so usually works wonders for me."

"Excellent to hear." John patted her on the back. "Yes, it seems time in bed does wonders for one's vitality and disposition, doesn't it?" He gave her a long, hard look, overcome by a carnal desire so strong that it threatened to derail his sense of professionalism.

"Before we go," Rose said, "I have one thing I cannot get out of my mind. I hope you can answer my question."

"Yes, dear, what do you want to know?"

"What does the sign over the outside entrance to this place really mean?"

"The sign over the main entrance?" John stared at her a moment, caught off guard by the question. Overcome with an emotion of tenderness—and dispensing with any propriety he had left—he placed his hands around her tiny waist and pulled her into his arms. "Rose, the sign means you must abandon all hope of ever quenching the primal desires contained deep inside you. You were born with them—they comprise your most basic nature—and they are part of who you are. We're all made that way. Our goal here is to help you explore these desires in depth and appreciate their raw beauty. In the end, you'll know yourself better than anyone."

Her innocent face worked a certain charm over him, and her lips, pink and full, broke down his last bit of restraint. He leaned over her and, with a gentle lift of her face, gave her the softest kiss, caressing the depths of her mouth with his tongue, tasting her sweetness. His hand wandered down the side of her neck, worked its way inside her blouse, and surrounded a warm, plump breast. His cool, slender fingers grasped and stroked the peak on top with a firm rhythm. He liked the way she yielded to his touch, the way she shivered in his embrace, the way her sighs sent a scorching heat flaring throughout his body, the way her cleft teased him as he pressed hard against her. Her presence stirred something deep within his soul, left him a little unsure and uneasy, awakening a certain ache in his heart. Though women of all types had passed through these doors, this girl held an allure, grabbed his attention, and he found himself at a loss for the reason. If only this moment could last a little longer … He shook off the notion as mere lust.

"We need to go." He smiled, wrapped her arm around his, and led her out of the office. They passed the marble staircase and continued to a room near the end of the hall.

*   *   *

When they passed through the door, a distinguished-looking man came out from behind a large wooden desk and walked over to greet them. "Well! Who do we have here?"

"Dr. James, this is Rose Barweather, our new admit. I informed her that we always begin the admission process with an exam."

"Absolutely." He beamed at the girl before him. "We want to make sure you're fit, safe, and sound." He reached out and took Rose's hand between his. A warm smile lit his strong, handsome face, and his eyes sparkled with mirth. Strands of gray throughout his hair suggested a man of more advanced years. Rose liked his reassuring manner in an instant.

"I'll leave the two of you alone. Rose, you'll be in good hands." John smiled, bowed his head a little, and turned out of the office.

"Come this way." Dr. James took her arm and led the way to the exam room.

Rose eyed the numerous cabinets and drawers lining the wall and wondered what they held inside. The vision of the exam table in the middle of the room filled her with anxiety, and the thoughts of lying there, not knowing what to expect, made her feel self-conscious. Dr. James shut the door behind them, and headed to one corner of the room where he began searching through the drawers. When he finished gathering up his supplies, he returned to the table.

"Now, Rose, I'll need you to remove your clothes, and we'll get started."

She stared up at him a moment, frozen with fear and embarrassment.

"Have you never undergone a physical examination before?" he asked, placing his hand on her shoulder, hoping to reassure her.

She shook her head, a heated blush creeping over her soft cheeks.

He smiled down at her, his eyes shining with new energy. "There's nothing to worry about. I'll tell you what you need to do, and I won't hurt you, I promise."

Rose nodded and moved toward a chair, where she removed every stitch of clothing until she stood before the doctor, naked and shaking.

"Here, let me help you get on the table." When he finished assisting her up, he positioned her on her back and pulled out a pair of stirrups at the opposite end. "Now, put your heels in these." After situating her feet, he spread her legs apart. "There, that's good." He returned to her side and smoothed her hair back from her forehead. "Don't be scared. This won't take long at all."

Rose took a deep breath, trying to calm herself, giving him a weak smile.

*   *   *

Dr. James stood beside her and gazed at her fresh form for a moment, his eyes beginning to burn with lust. With a calm façade, yet eager hands, he enclosed his fingers around one of her breasts and began squeezing and pressing the flesh in a methodical, circular pattern, ending with a pinch of her nipple. Yes, he liked nothing better than wrapping his hands around a pair of beautiful orbs, plucking the pink tips, feeling the spring of skin beneath the pads of his fingers. He liked the sound of involuntary sighs escaping her lips even better, a confirmation that each caress and pinch was sending lightning bolts of pleasure down to her loins.

He moved to the stool at the end of the table, slipped on a pair of gloves, and situated himself between her open legs, peered at the gaping cleft in front of him, the wet flesh tucked inside awaiting his touch. He shifted his position on the stool. These exams always put his restraint to the test, and viewing such a specimen of beauty splayed out before him, he had to battle the urge to plunge himself inside her. He inhaled a few deep breaths. Experience had taught him to curb his carnal appetite and wait for more opportune times to satisfy his masculine cravings. And they always came—as did he!

He began by spreading her apart, taking her fleshy, small lips between his fingers and massaging each one. She smiled and closed her eyes. His fingers found her clit and ensnared the protuberant knot with a gentle grasp. Large clits on female admits always soared his lust to exorbitant heights, and hers proved noteworthy as he squeezed and tugged, causing her to writhe.

"There, that's good, Rose," he said with approval. "I'm just testing different areas of your body to determine how you respond. You're doing quite well." The gleam in his eye brightened as he watched her struggle to anchor her hips to the table. Rose dug her head into the small pillow under her head, closed her eyes, and clenched her teeth.

Dr. James reached for an item nearby. "Good. Now I need to have a look inside." He inserted a couple of thick, soft fingers, and Rose's eyes flew open at the shock of cold, hard metal hitting her skin. "Take a few deep breaths for me." He advanced the speculum and, after opening the blades, shined a small light inside her body. He remarked, "Yes, everything looks good so far. Okay, this part may feel a little strange to you, so don't be alarmed." The doctor removed the speculum and inserted a finger inside her rectum, inspecting the walls hidden within her backside.

Rose gave a little jump, but once she recovered, the expression on her face showed him she liked the sensations of his fingers against her flesh.

"Everything still seems fine." Dr. James removed his hands, pulling off the gloves he'd donned earlier. He assisted

Rose to a sitting position and helped her down from the table. "I'll let you get dressed again, and one of our staff will show you to your room. Don't get too comfortable, though. When you've completed the last half of our admission procedure, your attendant will show you to your permanent room. And just remember, if you need anything else, please feel free to come to me … anytime." He gave her arm a quick, reassuring pat and left the room.

*   *   *

Rose retrieved her clothes from the chair and began to dress, relieved to have some solitude for the moment. The examination still left her a little breathless. She'd never heard of doctor visits like this one, but her loins continued to thrill with approval. As soon as she donned the last piece of clothing, a knock sounded at the door, followed by the entrance of an attractive female wearing a short, black dress. The fitted garment showed off every curve and muscle of her well-proportioned figure. Her auburn, bobbed hair fell neatly over her ears and rested against her face. Though the lady's attire seemed rather unusual, the luminous brown eyes and warm smile glowing from her satiny face put Rose at ease.

"Hello, Miss Barweather, I'm Delores. I'll be the one assisting you until you meet your attendant." Delores walked up to Rose and put her arm around her shoulders. "If you'll follow me, I'll show you to your room."

"Will I have to wait too long before I meet my attendant?" Rose gave her a weak smile, trying to hide her impatience. "And I left my travel bag in the office. Can I go back and get it?"

"Don't you worry about a thing. John's already taken care of your bag. Actually, you won't need the items you brought from home. We provide everything for you here at The House. Come, let's go this way." Delores led Rose out of the office and turned left down the hall. As they walked, they turned down other hallways until they reached a room.

Delores opened the door and allowed Rose to pass through first. "This is where you'll remain for the rest of the day. We have books for your reading entertainment, the bed is comfortable, and you can also enjoy our garden. It's quite lovely." She pointed to a door on the opposite side of the room. "Here let me show you." Rose followed behind and when she stepped out the door, her spirits lifted upon seeing rows of colorful flowers. Their sweet scent filled her nose, and she took in a deep breath. Overhead the sun blazed from the cornflower-blue sky, and in the middle of all the scenery, a large stone fountain entertained the birds bathing in its cascading water.

"You're right, Delores, this is lovely." Rose surveyed everything around her and spied an iron gate at the far end. "Is that gate open? Can one go out onto the grounds?"

"That gate remains locked, but this area is pretty large. You should have ample room to amuse yourself. For now, you'll eat your meals in your room, or you can eat out here. We have tables and benches."

"Okay." Rose eyed a couple of scenic spots.

Delores turned back and headed inside the room. "Relax and make yourself comfortable. I'll be checking on you every couple of hours or so." Giving Rose one last, bright smile, she slipped through the door leading into the hall and disappeared into the depths of The House.

Left to her own devices, Rose investigated her surroundings in more detail. The bed appeared comfortable, draped with a soft, white coverlet, topped by two large, fluffy pillows. Another small room caught her attention, and she discovered the porcelain sink, toilet, and tub housed inside. A nightstand with a lamp stood by the bed, and a chair rested in a corner of the room next to a small bookcase filled with a nice assortment of reading material. But the garden called out to her, and she slipped outside once again into the warm sunshine.

After taking her time, wondering from pot to flower bed to each climbing vine, sniffing flowers and hearing the birds splash in the fountain, she ambled over to the far side of the garden, toward the iron gate. She peered out through the bars and viewed the woods in the distance. A sudden, overwhelming sense of confinement made her catch her breath, and for a brief moment, she wanted nothing more than to break out of the enclosed garden and make a run for the shadowy depths of the forest.

She distracted herself by studying a small bronze statue of a rabbit peeking out from a cluster of pansies situated in a flower bed next to the gate. Stooping down for a closer look, she fondled the soft petals, running her hand over the crevices of the statue. A rustle outside the gate startled her, and she bolted upright to a standing position. She clamped a hand over her mouth, stifling a scream.

Through the bars, a man peered at her with glinting black eyes. His face remained expressionless, but his eyes burned, lively and bright, like a panther eyeing its prey. Clothed in nothing but black trousers, his rippling chest muscles seemed to dance in the sunlight, and he sported an equally strong pair of muscular thighs. His head showed off black hair, shaved close to the scalp, and a full mustache lined the top of his lips. A small, silver-colored earring hung in his left ear. Rose stepped away from the gate, taken aback by his presence. The man stared at her a few seconds longer before he turned away, leaving her alone once again.

Gathering enough bravery, she went to the gate once again and peered out, turning her head in the direction she saw him leave, wondering if he still lurked somewhere nearby. Only the branches of the trees moved in the wind, and somewhere in the distance, an owl hooted lonely, haunting cries. A light, cool breeze ruffled her hair, and she shivered, thinking—hoping—the encounter with the strange man was just a mere dream and nothing more. She turned her head toward the sky, catching the sun as it hung over the horizon, ready to retire for the evening. Had she spent all day out here? Without a timepiece, the passing of the hours slipped away, barely noticed.

* * *

"Oh!" Rose let out a scream at the touch of a hand on her shoulder. She turned around, slow and easy, fearing the hand just might belong to the man she saw a few moments earlier.

"I'm so sorry, Miss Barweather." Delores hesitated a moment. "I didn't mean to scare you. It's time for dinner. You must be hungry."

"Yes, I guess I am." Rose tried to smile and appear calm.

"Are you okay? You look like you've seen a ghost."

"I'm fine, really." Rose smoothed out her skirt and fidgeted with her hair.

Delores glanced up at the sky. "Since it's getting dark out here, you may just want to eat inside your room tonight."

Rose followed Delores back into the room and shut the back door behind her, giving the lock one last turn for good measure.

"If you'll just have a seat by the bookcase, I'll bring in your tray."

Rose seated herself as Delores stepped out to the hallway, returning with a small tray.

"Here you are. Take your time, and I'll pick this up in a while."

When Delores shut the door, she lifted the cover and began eating, savoring the juicy chunks of vegetables and picking at pieces of the roast resting in a pleasant-tasting brown sauce. Within moments, nothing remained before her but an empty plate. She swallowed the last drops of water from a crystal glass and finally pushed the tray aside. For the first time, she didn't know what to do next. The night had just begun, and going to bed this early was out of the question. Was she allowed out of her room? Delores didn't tell her she had to remain there; but she didn't tell her, either, that she had the freedom to go exploring. The only choice of entertainment left was reading, and the bookcase provided ample opportunities for that.

She reached over and picked up a red, leather-bound book

and read the title, *The Pearl*. Interesting! The thoughts of reading about pretty jewelry or hidden treasure seemed exciting to her, but excitement soon turned to shock. Her eyes scanned the paragraphs, over and over again, and she tried in vain to believe the words on the pages were other than what she actually read. She closed the book and put it down, shaking her head in disbelief. Was this book about nothing more than sexual encounters? How strange. Her body began to grow warm, and the dull ache between her thighs flared up again, just as it had done earlier that morning.

Her eyes fell on the bathroom door. A cool bath would do her body good. She made her way into the simple room and stripped off her clothes. While soaking in the tub, she caressed sensitive parts of her flesh, rubbing and tweaking different areas. She closed her eyes, feeling her internal fire rage once again. As her hand trailed between her thighs, an image of John flashed through her mind. How would his lips feel, teasing her nether regions? She imagined his fingers slipping inside her. Unable to dismiss the images, she worked the pleasure knot at the top of her sex, not stopping until rolling waves filled her pelvic region. Thoughts of his hands on her sent her hips jerking even harder. She opened her eyes and blinked, refocusing her vision. So much for cooling off! Disgusted with herself, she climbed out of the tub and dried off.

A white cotton nightgown had been placed on the bed, and she slipped it on over her head, smelling the freshly laundered fabric. She retrieved *The Pearl*, slipped into bed, and read for a long while, devouring every page, before turning out the light. Though fatigue had her in its grip, sleep did not come easy, and the subject matter she had read continued to taunt her, doing nothing to calm her carnal ache. Why would a facility like this one have such an unconventional book available for people to read? And the staff here seemed too oddly dressed. What would happen to her here? At this moment, she wished for home more than ever, longing for familiar surroundings and the closeness of family and friends. After a few tosses and turns, she allowed herself to fall asleep.

* * *

"Good morning!" Delores sang out, shaking Rose gently on the shoulder. "Did you sleep well? Sometimes that's hard to do when you're in a strange place."

Rose shielded her eyes from the sun, a little dazed, as Delores opened the shades. "Yes, I finally did doze off." She yawned and rubbed her eyes. "What will I be doing today?"

"You'll still need to stay here until I take you to meet your attendant." Delores placed the breakfast tray next to the chair. "I see you've been reading. Your selection is quite interesting, don't you think?"

"Um … yes … I've never read anything quite like it before."

Delores moved closer, lowering her voice. "To be perfectly frank with you, I think you'll find your treatment here quite unique, but most effective. I suggest you pay close attention to that book." She gave Rose a wink and left the room.

Ignoring Delores's comment, Rose got dressed and prepared to spend another day alone, reading and wandering throughout the garden. When she finally grew tired of being outside, she returned to her room for a nap. During the late afternoon, Delores returned.

"Miss Barweather, it's time to complete the admission process with your attendant. Are you ready?"

Rose got up from the bed and nodded.

"Good. Please come with me."

Filled with a mixture of excitement and nervousness, she followed Delores until they reached a large wooden door.

Delores turned to her and said, "All you need to do right now is wait for your attendant. Do you have any questions before I go?"

Rose shook her head.

"Good. I hope you enjoy your stay here." Delores opened

the door and allowed Rose to pass into the room.

* * *

A cozy ambience pervaded the room. Along the right side of the doorway, Rose located a tapestry bench and sat down, making herself more comfortable. Upon surveying her surroundings, the simple beauty calmed her nerves. She liked this room. Plush, wine-colored carpet covered the floor, and a fire glowed in the fireplace. A carved, black-lacquered cupboard with numerous drawers stood in the left corner. Across from her, a simple writing desk with a chair rested against the wall. A solitary window allowed golden streaks from the sun to steal through, adding a warm sheen to the room. From the ceiling hung a chandelier wrought of iron, topped with a set of clear, glass hurricane shades.

Seized with curiosity as to its purpose, she stared at the most unusual piece of furniture in the room: a waist-high bench, showing off four Queen Anne-style legs and a plump red-print cushion on top.

A rustle at the door ended her solitude as a handsome young man, near her age, entered the room. Tall and lean, with sculpted muscles rippling over a wide chest, his torso ended in lean hips plastered with tight, black trousers. He didn't wear shoes. Rich espresso-brown hair covered his head with a cropped neatness, and his boyish face housed two deep pools of cobalt blue. His lips carried an easy smile. When he faced her, he stopped short, staring at her in surprise. The smile faded. Rose stood frozen in amazement.

"Rose?" A puzzled expression covered the man's face.

"Thomas?" Astonished, Rose stared back.

"Oh, my goodness!" His eyes lit up, flashing lightning bolts of blue. "This is a surprise. John told me I had a new admission and gave me only your first name."

"It's been—quite a while, now. How long has it been?" Rose relaxed a little at the sight of her old friend.

"I think it's been a few years. But tell me something, because I'm dying to know." Thomas moved in close to her and whispered, "Did your mother ever forgive us for playing doctor that time when we were little?"

She chuckled, remembering the look of surprise on her mother's face. Little did he know, the memory of that playtime still burned in her mind. "She forgave us—and didn't tell Father." Her eyes locked with his. "Though nothing happened, he still wouldn't have liked it. We did some of the funniest things when we were little, especially when we were bored."

"Rose, I can still remember everything as if it were yesterday. We've had some fun times, haven't we?" He stood back and took in her whole frame. "But look at you. You're just beautiful."

She blushed under his gaze. "You're not so bad yourself."

He took a deep breath. "We'll have time to catch up later. Let's go ahead and get started. First, I'll go over the rules, so don't be too overwhelmed. During your stay, I will be your attendant, the one responsible for your total care, safety, comfort, and overall nourishment. I'll supervise and administer most all of your treatment here at The House. You must obey my orders completely and without question. Please let me know any time you experience severe pain or discomfort. Participation in community activities is mandatory, unless there is a reason why you can't. Harm no one, and no one will harm you. All things that you see and experience here are confidential." He looked her squarely in the eyes and paused a moment before continuing. "The last rule, the most important one, is that we can't have secrets between us. This ensures the best for you and allows me to perform my job. Think you can do this?"

"I think so." Rose nodded. "You seem to have a lot of rules, though."

"There are quite a few. But don't forget, I'll be with you. Any other questions before we begin?"

"No, I think I'm fine for now."

"Good. We'll have plenty of activities, so I guarantee we won't be bored like when we were young." He smiled and shut the door, turning a key in the lock. "I just want to make sure everything's in order so we can get through this without a hitch."

Rose observed with interest while he prepared for the intake procedure. He strode over to the window across the room and pulled the soft green velvet drapes closed, blocking out the sun. From the cupboard, he retrieved some supplies, which he placed within easy reach beside the bench. At last he approached the desk and pulled out some paperwork, a wooden clipboard, and a pen.

"Come over here." Thomas returned, took her hand, and led her to the bench in front of the fireplace.

She stood waiting, her heart pounding.

"I need you to strip." His eyes met hers with a solemn look.

"Excuse me? She stood speechless, stunned at such a request. "Why do I have to do that?"

"I'm sorry, this is part of the admission process here at The House. Everything will make better sense in a minute."

*　*　*

She turned her head away and stared into the fireplace, hoping her gaze on the flames would bring some sensible answers. "What exactly are we going to do here?" The epiphany hit her full force. The plaque over the main entrance of The House, the peculiar portraits on the lobby walls, John's advances, and Thomas's attire, all started connecting together like pieces to a bizarre puzzle. Then she remembered Delores's words regarding *The Pearl: 'I suggest you pay close attention to that book.'* Though the idea made her squirm somewhat, a part of her found the whole prospective experience exciting in a twisted sort of way. Besides, the fullness hidden beneath his trousers had caught her attention the minute he'd walked into the room. If anyone could help with her dilemma at home, Thomas could. In an instant, she sensed her life moving forward in the most unusual way. If John spoke the truth, she might just end up with what she'd been wanting. Still, the reality of it all scared her. Baring herself, opening herself up set off an avalanche of nerves, and if Thomas hadn't locked the door, she'd have made a run for it for sure. She turned back to him, face flushed. "I'm sorry. Everything's happening so fast."

*   *   *

Thomas pulled her close to him. "Rose," he said in a kind voice, "I know things seem strange right now, and you're a bit uncomfortable. "But you know what, I was in your position not long ago. I know what you're feeling inside. I know what it's like hiding in the dark, trying to satisfy myself."

Rose stared back at him in amazement.

"It's time to make that gnawing ache go away. More than anything, it's time to stop feeling guilty about everything, trying to hide, trying to act like your urges don't exist. Do you agree with that, at least?"

"Won't disagree." She grinned.

"Good. Let me help you." He reached up and began unbuttoning her blouse, which soon displayed a fine, sweet pair of breasts, plump and round, with full pink nipples standing erect.

Unprepared for the beautiful vision he had unveiled in front of him, he caught his breath. The firelight reflected a delicate, but striking, figure, and viewing the young girl, fresh and timid, only made his desire hotter. The idea of having his companion back once again thrilled him to the marrow. Playtimes would be different from this point forward. He reached to unfasten the buttons on her skirt, removing it from her waist, followed by the extrication of shoes and stockings. Eyes blazing in lusty anticipation, he beheld the silky, sheer undergarments, revealing soft curves underneath. His loins stirred; a heavy sensation gathered between his thighs. He wanted to taste her, feel every inch of ivory flesh in every way imaginable, and most of all, slip himself inside, creating a complete, perfect union. In silence, he held her close for a few moments longer, trying to collect his thoughts on how to proceed. Unlike his experience with others in the past, a familiarity existed between them, and he preferred handling this particular interview in a softer manner, using delicacy, patience, and a gentle hand, rather than force his will without care or thought.

Thomas took her head in his hands and gave her a reassuring kiss before assisting her onto the bench. He placed her in a supine position, knees bent. Now for those undergarments! He hooked his fingers on either side of her waist, catching the silky fabric.

Rose lifted her hips to accommodate their removal. Thomas sighed as he viewed his friend before him. Her vulnerability brought out his power, and he loved having total control; but at the same time, tenderness filled his heart. He wanted to help her discover the depths of her own sexuality, guiding and teaching her in the art of lovemaking as she surrendered to each sensation. He guided her hips to the edge of the bench and spread her legs apart, eyeing the glistening parts between her thighs.

"Oh, no you don't." Thomas intervened as she clamped her hands over her breasts. "No hiding when you're with me." He caught her arms and stretched them back over her head. From under the bench, he grasped a pair of cuffs and snapped them around her wrists, securing her in place. "Sorry, Rose, these only serve as a reminder to stay still. I need you in this position unless I move you."

She said nothing, but nonetheless strained at the cuffs, embarrassed.

"Don't be scared; we're alone. I'll get the chair by the desk, and we'll continue." He placed the chair beside her, sat down, and took up his clipboard and pen. "I have some standard questions we ask all our new admits. Your answers help us understand your history and your needs. It also helps us plan your lessons."

Rose nodded.

"First tell me a little bit about some of your physical experiences. I need you to go into detail because we need to know this."

"Well," she sighed, "I'm not sure where to start."

"You can start with your first experience and go from there."

"I really haven't experienced a great deal. Not as much as you might think. I have to confess, though, our doctor episode started everything. For me it was like an awakening of some kind, rather difficult to explain. When I saw both of us unclothed for the first time, I realized the difference between boys and girls, and I've been intrigued ever since. Of course as I grew older, encounters with boys became more frequent. I became more curious, and they sure didn't try to stop anything." She stopped and remained silent.

"What did these encounters involve?"

Silence.

"What happened during these moments you're talking about?" He pressed on, refusing to let her off the hook.

She licked her lips. "Mainly just touching each other. At times we kissed. Never anything beyond that, though."

"Nothing more? Are you sure you're telling me everything?"

"As hard as it may be for you to believe, I'm telling you the truth. I don't have much more to tell you."

Thomas beamed in triumph. "So you're still a virgin? You've never allowed a man inside you?"

"I've never gone that far with anyone. So yes. The most I've done is help a male friend relieve himself with my hand."

"What's kept you from going further?" Thomas considered her story rather unusual. He understood all too well the power of physical arousal and how sensual urges robbed people of their self-control.

Rose hesitated a moment before she answered. "I'm not

sure. I think it's because I'm not ready, or maybe I'm waiting for the right time, some magical moment I think exists. I may be fooling myself, though. Maybe such a time doesn't exist after all."

Thomas remained silent, blood running hot as he viewed the curves of her body, a mature woman. She was ripe for tasting, and the minutes—seconds—ticked away. Scribbling fast, he noted her information on his clipboard, clearing his throat for the next question. "Rose, can you tell me exactly what prompted your father to bring you here? I mean, let's be honest with each other, he must have believed your admission might serve a good purpose, don't you think?"

"I don't know. Who can figure parents out, anyway? They think I'm some shameless hussy, so what else can I do? I tried reasoning with him, even told him to leave me alone. He threatened arrest. I'm here, so I guess we'll make the best of the situation. That's really the gist of it, and all you need to know. You can add that to your clipboard of information, if you like."

His handsome face clouded, and he frowned at her a moment. "Rose, you're not getting out of this interview, and I expect you to talk to me about the events leading to your admission. I need every detail you can remember. Don't leave anything to the imagination. Actually, I'll understand better if you show me what you did. And explain your feelings, too."

"What?" Her face blanched. "I don't see how going into this type of detail, and showing you, has much to do with my being here!"

"Everything we talk about affects you being here," he insisted. "Now, I'm going to ask you one more time to please show me what you were doing before you arrived. I want to see, and I want every accompanying detail you can add."

She pursed her lips, collected her thoughts, and began her story. "Well, I had nothing to do this morning, so I went up to my bedroom and closed the door. As I lay on my bed, I started thinking about my last encounter with a young friend, which happened about three nights ago. I attended a party, and a male friend of mine and I had been talking for a bit, about nothing important, and our conversation came to a lull. He had been giving me strange looks for a while, anyway, and suddenly he suggested we go outside to be alone.

"We decided to sneak over to a grove of trees located some distance away from the house. This gave us some privacy and decreased the chances of anyone finding us. Once we were there, he started kissing me, and I felt my body heating up. Before long, he started sticking his hand inside my dress.

"I tried to push him away and told him to stop. I didn't want anyone catching us. Of course, he insisted, and finally cupped one of my breasts. He started playing with it, smacking lightly and then squeezing my nipple. I liked the way it made me feel. He pulled me closer and managed to slip his hand inside my skirt. His fingers worked their way between my legs, and before long, my lower abdomen became racked with uncontrollable spasms. I pressed against him to keep from jerking so hard. The next thing I knew he had unfastened his trousers and begged me to touch him, to finish him off. Of course I wanted to, so I took the head of his shaft in my hand and started rubbing the velvety skin between my fingertips—you men have very silky tips, you know that, Thomas?" Rose paused.

Thomas looked at her with a raised eyebrow and chuckled, shaking his head. "Nice to know. Please continue your story."

"Anyway, I continued to take his tip between my thumb and index finger. The shape reminded me of a smooth mushroom cap, and I found this little ridge right under the head where my fingers rested comfortably. I kept on squeezing and rubbing and stroking, until he suddenly tensed up and shot out a white milky stream all over the ground. I must admit watching him unload was rather exciting. Anyway, just as he finished, we heard someone calling for us. Alarmed, we tried to fix ourselves up and arrange our clothing as if nothing out of the ordinary had happened. We headed back to the house, acting cool and casual, as if we'd simply decided to go for a walk and a catch a breath of fresh air. And there you have it, my full story."

"Very good." Thomas complimented her. "But, did remembering this event relate to your behavior when you were in your room this morning?"

"Yes, this is why I told you the story. When I thought about the party, a queer sort of ache throbbed between my legs, and I needed relief from this pain. I undressed and lay naked on my bed. Though I wanted relief, I rather enjoyed the pain too. So I decided to close my eyes and let my body talk. I felt my breasts tingling, so I reached up and started to run my hands over my skin, tracing the shape. I squeezed my nipples, and the pinch only made the ache worse. I trailed my hand down between my breasts and on to my belly button. What a curious little area, a fun place to dip your finger, but a bit uncomfortable as well. You want to rub a little, and yet you don't. Anyway, the burning between my legs became the most troubling. I spread my legs open and felt the air hit my skin as I exposed myself. My crotch ached so hard, especially one little location right …" She stopped, unsure how to proceed next.

"Show me." Thomas leaned over her, ready to see where she pointed. His face flushed as he prepared himself for a view her most intimate parts. She lifted one of her hands and touched right below the center of her pubic bone. Thomas placed his finger on her mound and gently spread the lips open for a better look. He touched the spot lightly where Rose had indicated, feeling the hard little knot beneath his fingertip.

She gave a short gasp, "Oh, that's the place, Thomas. Please rub it again, please. It hurts so bad."

He obliged, caressing the little hidden bump at the top of her slit. At his touch, she opened her legs, allowing his fingers better access. As a soft whimper escaped her lips, a burst of heat ripped through him. How he wanted to invade her without thought of consequence or discretion. He avoided temptation, and removed his hand, saving her relief for a later time. "That's your clitoris."

"Yes." Rose took a deep breath and frowned.

Smiling, Thomas scribbled furiously on his clipboard.

"That's fine. Go on with your story."

"Laying there on my bed, I started rubbing my … er … my clitoris. I'll just call it 'clit.'"

At this last statement, Thomas let out a loud laugh. "Fine by me."

"Anyway," Rose said, her voice becoming more animated, "I continued rubbing, and all of a sudden, waves started to roll deep inside me, and oh, I felt so good! My hips jerked as I kept rubbing, sort of like an uncontrollable reflex. The whole thing was incredible. I reached down further ran my fingers all around inside myself. I was all thick and wet down there, and my fluids swished over my fingers when I moved them. I was enjoying myself, when Father came in. And you know the rest." She glanced over at Thomas as he added more information on his paper. "I hope this is good enough information for you."

He sat, face turned down, a light sweat over his forehead. Rose's narrative had stirred the hot coals of lust, and the bulge between his thighs grew fuller and harder. Desperate to keep his own throbbing at bay, he wrote with furious strokes on the clipboard, pretending to look over his notes with a studious air, lest his shaft erupt in a carnal explosion.

Satisfied his notes contained complete information, he cleared his throat, put away the clipboard, and prepared for the last half of the exam. This was the moment he'd been anticipating, and his stomach clenched with excitement and a twinge of anxiety. Though he adored breaking in virgins, this particular one resting on the bench in front of him required care, and he wished to make judicious choices. He arose from the chair, stepped to the end of the bench, and reached down to open a wooden box containing a small variety of glass phalluses in variable sizes, along with some lubrication.

"Rose, this part of the exam becomes pretty invasive, which means I'm going to insert some objects inside you, so please, don't be nervous. I'll try not to hurt you." He rattled through the box and made a selection. "Here is what I'll be using."

She craned her neck to view the object. "I've never seen one of those before … well … only a real one, if you know what I mean. And why do you need to …?"

"I need to know the largest size your cute little muff can hold." With a twinkle in his eye, he patted the outside of her thigh. Thomas sensed the trust building between them as he watched her open her thighs, her body ready for the next level of sexual initiation. "Okay, I'm ready. Lie still, and I'll try to be as easy as I can. I'm starting with the smallest one first." He applied a generous amount of lubrication and, with gentle fingers, spread her lips apart, located her internal opening, and slid the glassy device little by little, proceeding with care to avoid causing pain. His heart pounded, eager for her response. Rose gave a tiny jump. She sighed, shifted her body, and took several deep breaths. He moved the phallus back and forth and asked, "Are you okay?" He rubbed the outside of her thigh.

"I'm good. It's snug, but not too bad. I've never had anything inside me before, so I'll have to get used to everything."

"True enough. Do you think you can handle the next size up?"

"There's a next size?" Rose tried to lift her head. "How many are in that box? This one I have inside works fine for me."

"I have at least six, and I know you can hold a larger size whether or not you believe me. You won't be able to hold the sixth one, I know for sure. Since your body is being filled for the first time, the smallest phallus fits you well. Let's at least try the second one so you can be stretched open more. My goal is for you to hold the third one, but we need to go easy and get your body more acclimated." He removed the first phallus with a light tug.

"I have the second one in my hand. Ready? Here I go. Take a deep breath for me."

"Oh! You're right … much tighter, and … oh!" Rose winced. "This hurts a whole lot more. It stings." Even so, she opened her thighs a little wider.

"Take some slow, easy breaths," he instructed. After a few seconds, Thomas wiggled and pushed in the remainder of the phallus as far as it would go, resisting the urge to push further. He knew these proceedings needed to be handled with patience and ease. "There, is that okay for you?"

"Ow, please don't go any further. Please don't hurt me." She started to pant a little.

"I've gone as far as I can with this one, so don't worry." He reached up a spare hand and rubbed her lower abdomen, hoping to soothe her body and her nerves. "Pretty tight this time, yeah?"

"Much tighter. Can you move it a little to help loosen everything?" As Thomas twisted and manipulated the phallus, her slippery walls yielded.

"That's a little better. Thank you," she said, between breaths.

After a few moments, Thomas said, "Let's try the third one, and I think we'll be done. We won't be able to go higher." One last rattle from the box, and Thomas announced, "Get ready because this one is much bigger. I'll try to go easy."

Rose let out a small whimper, trying to stifle a shout. "Ow!" She twitched her hips. "Please go slower. I feel like I'm going to be ripped apart!"

In the firelight, Thomas caught the glimpse of tears welling up in her eyes and stopped pushing, permitting her a brief recovery period. He gained no pleasure in causing his partner pain, though several of his comrades contained such a sadistic streak, taking any opportunity available to make their admits squirm. He gazed at her. "I bet you didn't imagine your body being this tight, did you? It hurts at first, but after you've been entered a few times, you'll enjoy yourself. I promise." He bent over and placed a soft kiss on her lips and ran his fingers through her hair.

"You're right. I never guessed this would be so painful. The way I overheard people talking about it, I just thought everything went in nice and easy."

"Don't feel bad. I think most of us believe that at first." He smiled down at her. "Let's try to get this one in, and then we'll be done." Rose gritted her teeth and sucked in her breath one last time before giving him the cue to continue. With another twist and a push, he allowed the phallus to rest at the point where his hand met resistance.

He sighed with relief, pleased with her progress. "We're done. I'm going to leave this one in for a few minutes so you can adjust." He leaned over her head and stroked her hair. With a sweep of his finger, he caressed her face, wiping off a small lingering tear near her eye. "You did a great job," he whispered in her ear.

"You really think so?"

"Yes, you did, sweetheart." As he studied her face, his eyes beamed with pride. Along with his ability to break her inhibitions, she showed great promise in learning how to become a skilled lover. Unable to resist, he placed a tiny kiss on the top of each nipple and continued to taste her sweet skin, his tongue traveling over her tummy and ending in the tiny dip of her navel. Her laughter signaled to him her mounting trust, which he desperately needed to earn.

Once again he made his way to the end of the bench. While supporting the phallus in one hand, he placed a finger from the other hand on her clit and began massaging in rhythmic circles. Silence filled the room. Thomas shot a glance toward Rose's face. Beneath his hands, her thighs opened, ready for his touch. His eyes glazed with lust as he continued to rub, slow and easy. A faint groan of ecstasy slipped from her lips. In his hands, the phallus began to move, echoing the spasms of relief deep in her loins. Excellent, she was now ready for the next step.

A knock at the door shattered the mood. Thomas stopped, frowning at the intrusion. Answer the door or ignore it? It could be important. He sped to the door, twisted the key, and peeped around the edge.

John entered the room holding a large tray, which he placed on top of the desk. Thomas moved over to Rose as she tried in vain to wriggle off the bench. He pushed her back down. "We're not done yet, and I need to you stay still," he said firmly.

"Oh, Thomas—" she gasped. "Please … no … This is too embarrassing …"

"Sh-h-h, don't worry about him. He's perfectly safe, and it's not like he's never seen an unclothed woman before."

"Why does he have to see *me*?" Tears welled up in her eyes.

"Take it easy. I'm here, okay? But let's get you situated again." He replaced her legs on either side of the bench, baring her open so nothing remained hidden. He stood behind her head and cupped his hands around her chin in a soft grip. Cuffed and stretched out, her body showcased a set of heaving breasts and a moist gap. "John, why don't you come here and have a look at Rose? Tell me what you think. She's quite lovely, isn't she?"

*   *   *

John, heart racing and lust building, stifled a smile as he strode to the opposite side of the bench from Thomas. From this position he viewed Rose in her entire nakedness, her thighs spread open just enough to tease him. Her breasts, pert and round, heaved with discomfort and fear. He sensed her modesty and felt a twinge of compassion. Being exposed in such a manner for the first time must be a shock to someone as fresh as herself. He'd seen this many times before. Without warning, a searing sting of envy welled up inside his heart, and he almost resented Thomas for a second. Startled by his own emotions, he merely said, "Yes, I agree, she's quite lovely. How did she do?"

"She handled the interview well. We were able to fit her with the third one."

"I see." Standing between her open legs, he leaned down over her face and peered into her eyes. A personal war brewed inside. If he wanted to, his position as steward allowed him to supersede Thomas and physically take her first, Thomas being powerless to refuse. Somehow he found such a decision, made on a whim, unsuitable for the moment, and he fought off his building desire by making the more prudent decision to allow Thomas full reign at this point in time. He reached down and softly caressed one of her breasts with a finger. Rose shivered at his touch. With a small tug, John removed the phallus. His fingers touched her flesh, and like one separating the petals away from the heart of a flower, he gently inserted two of his fingers deep inside.

*　*　*

The shock from his touch produced a surge of self-consciousness, and Rose writhed in embarrassment, trying to remove herself from his exploring fingers.

Thomas leaned over her face. "Don't even think of moving!"

In a desperate attempt to compose herself, she took some deep breaths and swallowed hard. Using every bit of her will, she tried to relax as John continued to massage her inside walls with his fingers. In the firelight, his charcoal eyes sparkled like a million diamonds. Hypnotized by their magnetic pull, she disregarded everyone and everything else around her for just a brief moment, choosing to forget her current position, exposed and vulnerable, under someone else's command. However, the persistent work of John's hands created a fullness between her thighs, setting off a strong desire for relief. With an upward turn of his fingers, he continued grazing that certain sweet spot, until his magic touch unleashed strong contractions of pleasure. Her walls clamped down on his fingers and her moisture poured in torrents. "Very good." He glanced up at Thomas. "Yes, I think she'll do quite well here."

Thomas moved over to John, and whispered in his ear. John nodded in approval. In vain, Rose tried to catch their conversation, but instead viewed Thomas reaching down beside the bench to retrieve some unknown object. Her heart began to pound again. Thomas unsnapped his trousers, while John stepped to the opposite side of the bench, wrapping his soft hands around Rose's cheeks.

He leaned down. "Don't panic. You'll be fine."

Her wide eyes met Thomas's thick, hard shaft supporting a large, engorged bulb, full and ready to explode. The vision before her announced the body of a mature man, leaving little doubt regarding his intentions. He placed a generous amount of lubrication on his entire length, paying special attention to the head. He situated himself between her legs and prepared to enter.

He bent over her and whispered, "Okay, Rose, this is our final step. I'll be easy. Just hang in there with me."

Rose took a deep breath, preparing to grant him entry. She knew the leap from young girl to young woman loomed before her, and by submitting to him, she would be forever changed. The finality of it all both scared and excited her, but her desire to undergo the transformation remained solid. His hands reached around her hips with a firm grip, while he aimed his pink tip at her tender orifice. She tensed at his touch. To her surprise, the phalluses paled in comparison to the warmth, force, and energy of a man making his entrance. Her interior cried out in resistance as he pushed inside with a slow, steady force, slipping through until he touched the end. Her body yielded; she stifled a cry. A smarting sting announced her initiation to womanhood. She stared up and noted the strange, intense pleasure on Thomas's face. His eyes glittered in the firelight; the sounds of his breathing filled her ears with soft, hot, rhythmic, wordless whispers, each breath matching his smooth thrusts. He leaned over her and took her in his arms. His chest, damp with perspiration, pressed against hers with such a weight that she feared he'd smother her. With gliding undulations and an occasional small twist of his hips, he continued until he shot out a thick, streaming, cream into her dark core.

The warm pulse deep in her interior set off strong contractions of approval. She relaxed and caught her breath; her whole body tingled with excitement. The veil had been lifted, and a new knowledge gained. Thomas rested his cheek against hers.

Their friendship was now consummated.

Chapter 2

"EXCELLENT," JOHN SAID, "both of you have completed the final step of this admission process. I, on the other hand, will retire for the evening and leave you alone. The kitchens have now closed, so I've left dinner on the desk. No doubt, you two will enjoy dining in here by the firelight." He smiled at Rose. "I'm sure I'll be seeing you around." He gave her a soft kiss on the cheek before heading toward the door.

* * *

Rose watched as Thomas returned to the cupboard again and pulled out a small body shawl from one of the lower drawers. "Here, you can wrap this around you if you'd like to maintain a little modesty."

"How pretty." She fingered the delicate fabric and wrapped the material around her slender physique.

Thomas returned the examination bench in front of the cabinet while Rose busied herself collecting the plates from the writing desk. She joined Thomas on the floor in front of the warm flames.

"I'm so hungry."

She whisked the tops from the dishes, uncovering a modest array of delectable edibles. Rose stared at the food for a second, a little confused by the presentation, which was nothing like what she'd experienced at mealtimes thus far. The first thing she observed was the absence of utensils. Both plates held small morsels of food resting on thin, flat bread. In a small wicker basket lay more bread, each one rolled up like little scrolls. Upon closer inspection, the food appeared to be finely cut vegetables, tiny slices of spiced meat, and course-ground legumes. The last item she spied was a glass bowl of fresh fruit accompanied by a condiment dish filled with a white, thick cream. Two glasses of spiced tea stood next to each plate.

Thomas picked up one of the rolls of bread from the

basket, pinching off a tiny morsel after unwinding it. "Here's how we eat a meal like this one." With the tiny piece of bread, he reached into one of the meaty piles and scooped up a small bite. Rose opened her mouth as he brought his hand toward her, accepting the tasty morsel from his fingers. Stricken with a playful notion, she did the same, and placed a savory bundle in his mouth. As she picked up another bite for herself, some of the sauce dripped down her lips, which Thomas removed with a skillful flick of his tongue. Rose let out a giggle and fell back, clapping her hands.

"Do I make a good napkin?" he laughed.

"I think so—and a good fork—and spoon. I see The House doesn't believe in using knives, forks, or spoons during mealtimes."

"True, but don't you think it's more romantic this way?" he asked, half serious, half amused.

"It is." She nodded in agreement. By this time, her fingers were covered in the light brown sauce smothering the protein they consumed. Thomas took one of her fingers deep in his mouth and licked it clean.

She gasped at the strange sensation, her eyes sparkling. "Oh, that felt so …"

"You'll find the fingers are highly sensitive." Thomas licked all her fingers clean. Rose giggled and grabbed his hands, proceeding to imitate his gesture. Thus they continued enjoying their meal together in the glow of the firelight, nourishing one another, and getting reacquainted.

*   *   *

After they ate, Thomas stretched out on his back. Rose curled up beside him and ran her fingers through his hair. "Thomas, tell me how you got here."

Thomas turned his head in her direction and thought for a few moments before answering. "Remember you mentioned earlier that our doctor episode sparked your sensual curiosity?

Needless to say, I experienced the same thing. Like you, my encounters since then were similar. However, a couple of years ago, I lost my virginity to an older woman who was a friend of my parents'. One day she told them she needed someone to help fix things around the house, and they gladly sent me. Though she was older, I found her attractive, and I had fun talking to her. One thing led to another, and our conversation turned to the subject of sex. One day when we were alone, she suggested we go up to her bedroom, that she wanted to show me something. Once we entered the room, she pulled me over to the bed, where she undressed me. I know I must have seemed a little awkward, so she took her time, coaxing me to relax and enjoy myself. I followed her into bed, and from there, she initiated me into manhood."

"So what kind of things did she do? And tell me every detail because I want to know too." Rose placed a soft kiss on his ear.

Thomas continued staring at the ceiling, and recounted his story. "After we got into bed, she cupped my sac in her hands and started massaging. What a sensation! But she wasn't done by any means. The next thing I knew, she started sucking and licking me with her tongue, at which point I became hard. Her mouth worked wonders on me. Next, her hands landed between my legs. Starting with my head, she rubbed and stroked around the ridge—like you did with your male friend. As for my cock, she ran her hand up and down the full length, applying a light pressure with her fingers.

"By this time, my fluids were bubbling and starting to rise. I heated up, breaking into a mild sweat. Never before had my body been so stimulated, and this lady knew she had me. I wasn't sure how long I'd hold out because at this point, I ached so hard. Her eyes blazed down at me in satisfaction as I let her have her way with me. The more she sensed my desperation, the harder she teased. Driving me further to distraction, she placed the tip of her tongue inside the little opening at the top of my head and licked with rapid, flicking strokes.

"With that little tongue lashing inside, I nearly exploded right then, but I kept hanging on. She opened her mouth and swallowed my entire cock, sucking and licking the opening at the head, and then over the entire shaft. With more licking and teasing, I shot a load in her mouth. She swallowed every drop, too, sucking at me without batting an eyelash. What an amazing experience it is to have, your body full and at a breaking point, to empty yourself totally and completely into someone else." He became quiet for just a moment, lost in thought.

"What else did she do, Thomas?" Rose prodded. "Don't hold back. I like your story." Not only her ears had perked up during his narrative, so had her loins, a hard throb permeating her clit. She stretched out on her side, propped herself up with one arm, and ran her fingers over his cheek and down the side of his neck. He remained silent. She reached over to trace the outer rim of his ear and whispered, "Tell me, what else did she do? I want to know."

He continued, "Needless to say, I was well spent and required several minutes to rest my body. But she wasted no time with her teachings. In a swift move, she straddled my hips and placed one of her breasts in my mouth. I could feel the fullness of her nipple with my tongue, and so I just licked the flesh for a bit, flicking and feeling its plump smoothness. Temptation crawled over me, and I wanted to taste her more, so I bit down on it softly with my teeth, not wanting to hurt her. To my surprise, she giggled a little, and with more encouragement from her, I began to suck. The harder I went at her, the more she moaned. I know now her body needed release because she writhed her hips and, taking my hand, placed my finger on the precious pink button between her legs. Oh, she possessed such a sweet little clit. I decided I wanted to make her come as hard as I had, so I managed to coax it back out, nice and stiff.

"As soon as I touched the smooth, slippery tip, her hips jerked a bit. I stayed right on the hot spot, not giving up, rubbing more. Little by little, her clit hardened, and I simply continued stroking her with my finger. She started grinding her hips harder against my hand, letting out a moan every now and then. Her lips fell on mine as her fingers wound themselves around my hair, and I tasted the sweetness of her mouth. The way she pulled and grabbed me, I knew her loins burned the way mine had earlier. I discovered I loved the way she depended on me for her pleasure and release. For sure, I aimed to please her.

"I was fascinated by her, fingering all her parts, rubbing over every fold until my fingers slid further inside, where I felt her fluids, thick and warm. As I grazed my fingers over her walls, I inhaled her scent, which filled me with an urge to taste her like she had tasted me earlier. I sprang up and flipped her over.

"She knew what I wanted to do, and her body desired me even more. Once she landed on her back, her thighs sprang open, bringing everything into full view. What else could I do at this point? With nothing left to the imagination, her gaping crotch and heaving breasts excited me even more. Without hesitation, I dipped my fingers back into her dripping slit and, parting the moist lips, began to taste her, sweet and thick, lapping at her with my tongue. I remembered well how she responded to the attention I gave her clit the first time, so I found it and sucked hard for a few minutes. She let out a small moan. Before I could think, she guided me on my back, her breathing hard and fast in my ears.

"In the meantime, I had recovered, and the fluids swirled inside me, ready to shoot out again. With unrelenting strokes, she teased my sac again with her fingers. At this point, straddling my hips, she opened her legs and mounted me, gliding on in one smooth move. She radiated warmth like a tiny heater, raising my temperature to the boiling point. The ache inside me became unbearable, my shaft hard, ready to explode. I begged her to ride me hard. With a toss of her head, and another shift of her hips, she did what I asked, clenching me like her life depended on it. Before long, I unloaded everything I had inside, while she responded back with an orgasmic burst. In the end, we held each other until she signaled the end of our lovemaking. I got dressed, and she gave me one last sweet kiss, before we said good-bye."

"So was that it?" Rose's voice filled with urgency. "And you still haven't told me how you arrived here."

Thomas turned over and faced her. "That was our last time together. Now, I must say she used to work here—before we met, of course. On her suggestion, I sought a position here because I wanted to learn more about some of the activities we'd done in her bedroom. When an opening became available, I applied, and here I am."

"Do you like it here? And how do you enjoy your work when you're dealing with so many people over time?"

*   *   *

Thomas returned to his supine position. Resting his hands behind his head, he answered thoughtfully, "I do like it here. I enjoy helping people learn more about themselves, and each person is unique. Various women want different things. They all have their own perspective, and I enjoy exploring and sharing each experience with them."

He fell silent, appearing to contemplate his last words. Not wanting to break the silence with more questions, Rose studied him in the firelight, watching his chest rise and fall in time with his gentle breathing. His story had encouraged her own lust, and she wondered if her ability to make him come matched those of her predecessor.

Time to find out. Without a word, she ran her finger down the length of each ripple on his chest, feeling his smooth skin against her fingertip. But he said nothing, ignoring her attempts at seduction. She tried again, this time caressing the tiny tips of his nipples. Still no reaction.

Perplexed, she studied this situation, trying to determine her next step. She knew asking him what was wrong was not the answer. Her eyes wandered down to his trousers. In the glow of the firelight, the huge bulge between his thighs taunted her.

Pure lust burned within her, along with a determination to command and conquer his body. With her long nails, she grazed the top of the material, attempting to tease out some kind of amorous response. He remained staring at the ceiling, oblivious to her advances. By this time, desperation mounted, her frustration growing stronger.

She stopped a moment, considering her next plan of action. Overtaken by a surge of confidence, she sat up, straddled his knees, and unsnapped his trousers. She drew back the front panel and beheld the vision before her. Unable to resist, she reached down to squeeze one of the spongy balls hidden inside his sac, intrigued by the springy texture beneath her fingertips. But the shapely, plump tip perched on top of a stiff cock cried out to her the loudest. Spying the opening at the top, she dropped her head and lapped at the slit, tasting the pool of salty moisture. She opened her mouth, encasing him, the tip of her tongue sliding over the swollen veins with hot, rhythmic strokes.

Thomas stifled a gasp and reached up to run his fingers through her long tresses, wrapping her golden locks around his hands. She moved over him harder and faster, mercilessly teasing his taut flesh. He closed his eyes and ground his back into the velvety carpet. Rose, pleased with her success so far, enjoyed the idea of making him sink deeper into carnal bliss, his hips tensing with each pass of her roving tongue. His hands gripped her hair like the reigns of a fine horse. With a shudder, he released warm, thick, jets inside her mouth. To her dismay, Thomas's sensual story still left her ill-prepared for the shock her taste buds now received. Unsure how palatable she found the taste and texture resting on her tongue, she froze, paralyzed with a bout of indecision, before gulping down his slippery, pearly emissions. In a desperate attempt to appear casual, she shook her head, pretending to fluff the waves in her hair as she took some deep breaths to clear her throat. Success at last. What a tease. Apparently she'd passed another lesson.

Thomas let out a soft chuckle and stroked her hair. "I applaud you, Rose. You were amazing," he whispered. She freed herself from the body shawl and stretched herself out on top of him, her moist cleft cradling his soft tip between her folds. Her head rested on his chest, and his heart pounded out a quiet rhythm in her ear. Together they lay for several minutes in silence, basking in the glow from the fire.

Finally he spoke. "Not quite what you expected?" He enfolded her in his arms and ran his fingers between her shoulder blades.

"Um … well … no, not exactly." She lifted up her head to answer. "But not bad."

"Smart move. It shows me you can take initiative, and you have a willing spirit. You'll need those qualities wherever you are." He pulled her face over his and she slipped her tongue into his mouth. She explored the moist walls and grazed against his firm teeth. He tasted good, soft and warm.

When the kiss ended, Thomas said, "You'll be experiencing some very interesting things while you're here." His eyes shone up at her. "If I know you like I think I do, you'll enjoy yourself." He reached up and smoothed back a wayward lock of hair straying over one of her eyes. "We're done down here, so it's time we head upstairs." Rose crawled off and stood up, while Thomas replaced the front panel of his trousers back to its proper position.

"I don't know how much this covers me up, being so sheer and all. Is this appropriate to wear upstairs?" She adjusted the shawl around her body, craning her neck from one side to the other for a better view. "How do I look?"

"You're fine. We just want you to have some semblance of covering. Let's go." He took her arm in his and led her out of the room and down the long hallway back to the staircase. As they neared the end, a man walked in their direction. Rose's pulse quickened. She noted the exchange of cold nods between him and Thomas when he came near them; she caught the leer he gave her as he brushed past her. Though she dared not turn around, she sensed the burning stare of his dark eyes on the back of her scantily-clad figure.

She shivered, loosening her grip from Thomas's arm so she could wrap the body shawl around her tighter. With a whisper, she asked Thomas, "Who is that man? He was the one who kept staring at me behind the garden gate … when I slept here last night."

Thomas stopped a moment and turned to her, his eyes filled with alarm. "You've seen him before?"

"Yes. I was wandering around in the garden outside my room, and he stood on the other side of the gate in the wall … just giving me that odd stare. He never said anything, but he finally left."

Frowning, Thomas said, "That's Joe, one of the attendants here." He turned his head back down the hallway and continued walking, saying nothing more.

"Well, do you know more about him? Do you like him?"

"Let's just say Joe and I have our differences in taste and style. I'll leave it at that for now. We can talk more about it later."

*   *   *

When they reached the top landing of the staircase, Thomas led Rose to the left and up the remaining flight of stairs. After backtracking down a short hallway, they reached a plain black, metal door. He turned the latch and ushered her into a long hallway lined on both sides with numerous rooms. She turned her head up and admired the decorative ceiling lights illuminating the area in a rosy glow. Like the lobby down below, she found the mosaic patterns on the tiled floor artful and attractive. As they walked, she came to a halt, stunned by one singular, fleeting observation.

"What's wrong?" Thomas turned to face her. "Is there something you wanted to see?"

"Um … why are there no doors to these rooms?"

"Oh, that …" He paused a moment. "I meant to tell you earlier, but I didn't want to alarm you, either. You see, none of the rooms here on the upper wards have doors."

"Oh." Rose, surprised and a little taken aback, blinked at

Thomas as his announcement hit home. "This means you can see everything …"

"Yes, you can see everything people are doing. You can hear everything people are doing. If you ever take a notion, you can join in on what people are doing."

"Why is that?" Her voice rang with uncertainty. "All this sounds a little strange to me."

He shrugged. "Those are House rules, and from what I've been told, have been in place since the beginning. Don't worry about the lack of privacy. You'll get used to it. Besides, we don't judge people around here. Nobody will think you're bad or odd. And, yes, you'll learn to be an exhibitionist as well a voyeur."

"An 'exhibitionist' or 'voyeur'? Oh, dear, I never would have thought about such a thing." Her eyes darted all around her, uncertainty building at the prospect of being on constant display.

He placed a hand on her shoulder. "Don't worry about anything. I'll take care of you. Let's keep going. Our room is near the end of the hall. And feel free to stop and look at anything you find interesting. It's the custom here, you know."

Rose walked, taking her time, paying attention to detail as she and Thomas moved down the long hallway. The rooms appeared comfortable, furnished with a bed that held two people, a nightstand adorned with a decorative lamp, soft carpet covering the floors, and a chest of drawers containing various sundry items. Each room also contained a small sink and running water. She heard sounds of kissing, an occasional soft moan, a flirty giggle, and attendants and their admits whispering secrets or terms of endearment into each others' ears. Each couple seemed lost in their own world, engaged in various acts of carnal activity.

In one room, a male rippled his fingers through the gaping sex of the female reclining beside him. With gentle movements, he spread her nether lips apart and dropped his mouth down on her clit, sucking with a long, hard draw. She arched her back, closed her eyes, and let out a low moan, as an occasional twitch escaped her hips.

Rose paused in the doorway of another room containing a couple engaged in lovemaking, their bodies entwined in a most unusual position. As the male sat on the bed, a young lady sat on his lap with her legs wrapped around his waist. She fell back over the edge of the bed in a backward position, while he held her wrists to keep her from falling all the way over. With his cock buried deep inside her, he smiled as his movements brought her to orgasm.

"Oh, goodness, I think I would have fallen all the way over and landed on my head, if I'd been in her position," Rose whispered to Thomas.

"I agree it's an interesting position. Quite fun, and no, you wouldn't fall on your head. I wouldn't let you." Thomas smiled, rubbing her shoulder.

Rose peeked into another room and observed a couple on the floor. The male, resting on his stomach, placed his legs on either side of his female partner as she reclined under him, supine, her head in the opposite direction of his. She pushed up against him, her face drawn up in obvious pleasure, and undulated her hips.

"Now that's an unusual position," Thomas grinned.

As they progressed, a section of the hall opened up off to the side to reveal walls lined with cabinets. A chandelier, suspended by a heavy, iron chain, lit up a large, semi-round desk situated in the middle of area. Two staff members, one male and one female, looked up from their work and smiled as she and Thomas approached.

"Rose, this is our supply area for the floor. If you, or I need anything for our activities, we come here, tell the staff what we need, and they can help."

Thomas nodded in affirmation to his fellow staffers, and continued down the remainder of the hallway. But an activity of great interest caught Rose's eyes, and she curbed her steps into the doorway to get a better view.

*   *   *

A female knelt in front of a handsome, young blond-haired male and engrossed herself in securing him in a belt-like device. The lady, attractive and wearing her short, black hair cropped close to her face, wore a leather brassiere and a matching short bottom. Fishnet stockings hugged her long, shapely legs, and her stilettos seemed to lift her more heavenward. Her makeup, showing off flawless, porcelain skin, blood red lips, and dark-lined eyes, created a striking, diabolical look.

"I need you to stand perfectly still, and don't move unless I tell you to." As she barked out these instructions, she stood her charge in front of her.

A work of pure art, his body showcased muscular arms, buttocks, and thighs. His physique appeared shaven, his skin glowed smooth and clean. As he stood there totally naked in front of her, she retrieved some lubrication to slather on the limp flesh between his legs, rubbing, stroking, and arousing him just a little. With slow, gentle fingers, she worked his sac, one ball at a time, through a ring on the belt, followed by his shaft. She pushed the ring snugly against his body and finished by buckling a strap, attached to the top of the ring, around his waist.

"You look perky. How does that feel so far?" She squeezed and massaged his tip with a playful thumb and forefinger.

"Very good, Mistress." He sighed, enjoying the device and, even more, the attention from his lady.

"Good," she answered. She looked him squarely in the eye, and a smile played across her face. She lowered her eyes to take in the view between his thighs, and she licked her lips. The man's cockhead had bloomed within her grasp, and he began struggling to contain himself.

At this moment, they looked up and spied Rose and Thomas standing in the doorway. They smiled, undaunted by their visitors, and continued their task. As the lady stood up, she grasped the remaining strap, which hung from the bottom of the ring.

"Spread your legs," she told him. She passed the strap through and caught the end with her right hand. Rose stared as the lady inserted the flared end of a shiny, steel bulb into a slot inside the strap.

"Now lean over and put both hands on the bed. Spread your legs wide apart," she ordered the gentleman, pushing his back lightly with one of her hands. Before inserting the bulb, she covered the end with lubrication and gave his backside a firm swat. "Here I go." Standing to one side of his hips, allowing Thomas and Rose a clear view of the proceedings, she spread his buttocks open with one hand and prepared to enter the steel bulb into the man's anus with the other. As the cold steel brushed his skin, the man gave a little jump. With a gentle push and a few twists, she attempted to work the steel into his body. The young man started to whimper in pain.

"I know this one is large, so I need you to relax a little so I can get this plug in easier." With a frown she continued pushing and twisting, gaining some success in its passage. "Oh, come on, I know your little girlie bottom can take it. You're just clenching too tightly, that's all. Spread your legs wider and relax." She gave his buttocks another firm swat and continued pressing harder. The man's legs quivered, his pain and stress level obvious to Rose as she watched with an uneasy interest.

The young man cried out, "You're splitting me apart. I don't think I can do this."

"Take some deep breaths for me," she said. "We'll go slow, but you'll hold what I give you, I guarantee it."

Allowing her charge a brief reprieve, she released one of her hands from behind and reached around his waist, taking up his tip between her fingers. He sighed as she rubbed the silky flesh, taking a moment to play in the tiny slit at the top. His breathing became deep and rapid in response to her gentle touches. Without word or warning, her fingers pushed the remainder of the plug inside his hidden walls. He let out a gasp followed by a groan. She finished buckling the strap to the back side of the belt and gave one of his buttocks a firm squeeze.

"Turn around now. We're all done." Reaching between his thighs, she grasped all of him in her hands and pulled him closer to her. Her eyes narrowed, filled with a lusty gleam. With a purring voice and a sultry smile on her face she praised him. "You were really good, very brave."

"Thank you, Mistress," the man said through clenched teeth, wincing on occasion as he moved.

She indicated for him to turn around, and surveyed her handiwork. Her handsome charge, fully plugged and harnessed, was ready to do her bidding. As she gave a little tug on the back strap, the young man caught his breath and closed his eyes a moment.

"Walk across the room once and come back to me," she commanded, giving his buttocks a quick, sharp smack with her hand. He complied. "Now pull and adjust your belt a little to make sure everything really fits right." His face drew up in pleasure as his movements wiggled the plug. The mistress, seeing she still had an audience, turned to her man. "I think you need a quick reward for being so good, don't you agree?" she asked him in a coy tone.

"Whatever you wish, Mistress." The man lowered his head in submission, trying his best to conceal his anticipation.

She studied him for a moment, deciding her next plan of action. "I think your little cock could use some milking, don't you?"

"As you wish, Mistress."

"I know those little balls of yours are about to burst, aren't they?"

"If you say so, Mistress."

"I'm really hungry, and I want you to feed me. I want everything your little cock has to offer. I want to suck you hard and suck you dry. Would you like that? Do you want your cock sucked hard and dry?"

"If that's what you wish, Mistress," replied the young man, his eyes flashing a look of internal lust and anticipation.

"Come here, then." She knelt down in front of him. "Feed me hard, and feed me good." She swatted him again on his buttocks. "No skimping, either."

The man offered himself to her, as she swallowed him to his hilt. Holding on to his hips with both hands, she sucked hard and long, before releasing him, pinching his buttocks as she withdrew from his length. Her tongue now began flicking over his tip. As she tugged softly on the strap behind him, he let out a small moan, his eyes closed in bliss.

She stopped, glanced up, and continued, "Don't come until I tell you to. Do you understand me?"

The young man gritted his teeth. "Yes, Mistress. As you wish."

With a groan, he strained to contain himself while she squeezed and massaged the full sac between his legs. She ran her tongue around the ridge of his head. The man threw his head back, closed his eyes, and clenched his jaw.

She popped his buttocks again. "No cheating. Hold it in." Again she focused on the slit at the top of his engorged tip, working her tongue with more persistence into his opening.

The man broke down and begged. "Please … Mistress …"

With narrowed eyes, she answered, "I'll take pity on you this one time. You were a good boy, after all. So go ahead." With her permission, he held her head in his hands and released thick jets of semen. The lady quickly swallowed him again, drawing hard, as he continued to climax down her throat. He finished with a gasp and slumped his head and shoulders down with fatigue, his breathing deep and labored. As she withdrew herself, she lifted a dainty finger to wipe off a drop of his lust which had escaped her mouth.

"What a good boy." She stood up and rewarded him with a kiss on the lips. "But you'll still wear this harness until I remove it from you."

*　*　*

"C'mon, let's go." Thomas took Rose's arm, pulling her away from the doorway.

After they made their way past a few more rooms, a hallway cropped up on their right.

"Rose, down that hallway are the tub and shower rooms where we'll be going in a few minutes." They kept walking until he stopped and led her into a room. "This is our place where we'll spend most our time when we're not engaged in other community activities. We nap, sleep, play, and eat breakfast in here."

"We eat breakfast in here? Why is that?" Rose thought the idea rather romantic.

"The House staff believes in starting off the morning in a nice, gentle manner. You'll find people keeping rather odd hours here, and morning meals in the rooms are much easier on everyone. Also, we do have a dining room on this ward where we eat lunch and dinner. It's in one of the rooms just before the common room at the end of the hall."

"Are we ever allowed outside?" She began fearing herself in jail, or prison.

"Oh, yes, you're free to wander the grounds. Some of our events will be held outside, as a matter of fact. So don't worry, you're not trapped in here all the time."

"Good to know." She liked her surroundings and examined everything with great attention. Her feet sank as she walked across the plush, wine-color carpeted floor. The nightstand by the bed, like the other rooms, held a simple decorative lamp, its fluted globe casting a soft glow throughout the room. She spied a small counter with a sink in one corner, and along the wall next to it, a wooden chest of drawers. A simple, cream coverlet adorned the bed, finished off by two fluffy pillows on top. Upon closer inspection, Rose noted leather straps and cuff-like rings attached to the ironwork of both the head and foot railings.

"Thomas, what are these things?" She held up one of the cuffs in her hand.

"What?" Thomas turned from the drawers. "Oh, those. Um … I wouldn't worry about them right now. They're there in case …" He frowned a little. Wishing to change the subject, he turned back to the open drawer.

"What are you getting out of there, Thomas?" She crossed the room and stood beside him, peeping over his shoulder.

He let out a sigh and smiled. "Glad you asked. I'm getting things out for our bath."

"Our bath?" Her face filled with surprise. "What exactly do you mean by *our* bath?"

"Just what I said, our bath. We like being clean around here, you know!" He winked at her and resumed his task.

"We take our baths … er … um … together?"

"Yes, Rose, we do. Will that be a problem for you?" He stopped a moment and faced her once again. "We'll be doing a lot of things together, you and me. Just so you know ahead of time, you'll also be doing things with others, too." He lifted her chin and placed a soft, reassuring kiss on her lips. "Now let's go take *our* bath. You need to relax a bit. You're awfully tense." He gathered up the supplies, and they left the room, re-tracing their steps back down the hallways.

*   *   *

Rose glanced from one side of the hall to the other, noting the tub rooms as she passed, a few of them occupied by attendants and their admits. Together they soaked in comfort, some busied themselves washing, and others appeared engrossed in sensual activities she could not identify.

Thomas selected a vacant room at the end of the hall. Rose liked this room, too. She rubbed her foot over the tiled floors, which mimicked the other hallways, and spotted the large picture window in the middle of the wall across from the entrance. On the right side of the window rested the tub—a long porcelain bowl supported by heavy brass claw feet. An iron screen with bars running in crisscross patterns stood on the left side of the window, and other than a small drain in the floor, nothing else stood behind this unusual screen.

What an odd piece of equipment to have in here. What was it used for? Her eyes moved to the left side of the room, where tall, white cabinets hugged the wall. Behind their glass doors lay an assortment of colorful bottles containing various oils and powders. Underneath the top cabinets, the ample counter held an eye-watering collection of large apothecary jars filled with dried herbs. Drawers and more cabinets below held sundry supplies. A beautiful leather divan lined the right-hand wall, and at its head sat a small, wooden table.

She turned her eyes up and admired the simple brass chandelier hanging from the ceiling, its white globes emitting a soft light throughout the room. What a pretty place to bathe—and with Thomas, too. She liked the idea already.

Thomas strode over to the tub and turned the knobs. Sounds of splashing water echoed throughout the room like a waterfall cascading over rocks. He ran his hands through the water to test the temperature. Satisfied, he shut the faucets off after several minutes. Other than the occasional drip of the faucet, the room thundered with silence once again. With a plop, Thomas tossed a small bag into the water.

"What's that?" Rose turned and viewed the tub, intrigued.

"It's what we call an herbal bath infusion. Our jars on the counter over there contain a nice selection of herbs. We can create all kinds of blends when we want to. I created a blend from a personal, secret formula. That's why I brought the bag from our room."

"What's in it?" Rose, eyes sparkling, moved closer to the tub and peeked.

"Um, I can't tell you that. Then my formula wouldn't be a secret anymore." He blew her a kiss, and pinched her cheek.

"Oh, you." She stuck her tongue out at him. "Fine, then, don't tell me. Probably some silly hocus-pocus stuff you've made up, anyway."

"Trust me, Rose. No silly magic stuff here. I know what I'm doing. You'll enjoy yourself, I'm sure. Come on, let's get undressed."

Rose stood there a moment, hesitating to remove the body shawl, her last vestige of security. For the first time she wondered what had happened with her clothing. Suddenly, the memory of her home and the outside world she left behind seemed nothing more than a dream.

Thomas removed his trousers, and stood there before her, totally naked. "Are you going to join me or just stand there?" He started to laugh. "C'mon Rose, loosen up a little." With a quick jerk of his hands, the shawl disappeared from her body, and the two stood naked together. She lifted her hands, attempting to cover her breasts, but he chuckled, pulling her hands away. "Rose, you're fine—really you are. Let's get in before the water gets cold." He helped her into the tub and, climbing in behind her, seated himself first.

With a gentle tug from Thomas's arms, she sat down and guided herself between his legs. Thomas wrapped his arms around her while she snuggled back against his chest. She sighed. The warm water flowing over her body calmed her nerves. Thomas held her close and placed a soft kiss on her cheek. "Do you like this?" he whispered in her ear.

She nodded. Never in her wildest dreams had she imagined bathing with a man. She liked resting here with Thomas, leaning against him, his arms around her.

He hugged her tighter splashing water over the upper parts of her body, allowing her a little time to settle down. After several minutes, his hands cupped her breasts, squeezing and massaging each one. Rose sank down lower into the water, draping her legs over and around his. She felt the full impact of the warm water coursing over her body, and her arousal heightened even more.

"Are you feeling more relaxed?" Thomas caressed the little bump hidden at the top of her sex, moving his fingertip in a circular rhythm. On occasion, he slipped in a finger.

"I love it when you do that, Thomas. And to answer your question, yes, I'm fine—more than fine …" Rose closed her eyes and pressed her head harder against his chest. The warmth of the water, along with his fingers, took their toll on her sensitive areas. Inside, her core rolled with spasms of relief; her hips jerked. Thomas's fingers worked faster. She squeezed her eyes shut for a moment. As her lust mounted, so began her advances. She sat up, flipped herself over onto all fours, and grasped the flesh between his legs with her own warm, delicate fingers. Thomas shot out of the water and sat on the rim of the tub, his eyes blazing. Rose knelt in front and swallowed the fullness of his pink tip, licking at the ridge around the head of the shaft. Thomas closed his eyes and threw his head back. His thighs began to quiver, and he cupped her head between his hands for support. With tender strokes, her fingers massaged his sac. After a few moments, his muscles tightened. Without faltering, as if she engaged in this sort of activity all the time, she succeeded in his release.

He let out a soft groan, feeding her the last drop. "Much improved."

"I'm not sure what's going on, but I don't seem to be myself." She rubbed her head a little and blinked her eyes, attempting to clear her vision.

"Do you think it's something in the water?"

Then she remembered. "Thomas, you're a wicked one." So he hadn't been kidding with her, after all. She splashed a handful of water at him. He laughed and seated himself back down into the tub. He pulled her into his arms and rested his chin over her head.

"I warned you it wasn't silly magic. Will you believe me from now on when I tell you something?"

"Are you going to keep rubbing it in?" She turned and gave him a playful scowl.

"Yeah, I might just do that." He kissed her again on the cheek before reaching for the soap and two cloths. "Let's finish up now." For the next several minutes, each one busied themselves applying a healthy dose of lather, scrubbing away without a care.

"Here, Thomas, I'll get your back if you get mine." She reached for the soap. With care, she rubbed the cloth over his back, admiring the muscles and curves. His buttocks glistened with water, and she grabbed each shapely one with a firm squeeze. He turned around and returned the favor, mimicking everything she'd done to him.

"Hand me the nozzle, will you?" he pointed to the opposite end of the tub. "Now stand still."

"Oh, this water feels so good. The soap smelled nice, too. Is that another one of your concoctions?" She took a moment to admire his chest as rivulets of water cascaded down, accenting each muscular ripple.

"Sorry, I don't make soap. Hand me that towel." After he dried off himself and Rose, he helped her out of the tub. "We're done with this part," Thomas said.

"What do you mean by 'this part'? There's more?"

"Oh, you know, there's always more." He laughed and snapped her smooth buttocks with one end of his damp towel.

"Why does that not surprise me? I should have known better than to ask."

"Your life here will be so much easier if you accept everything I say without question, you know that?" He crossed over to the cabinets, pulled out a sheet and an amber bottle, then made his way over to the divan.

"You dream big, don't you, Thomas?"

"Any chance of that dream coming true?"

"H-m-m … nope."

He sighed and shook his head. "I guess a man can dream, can't he?"

She laughed and strolled over to where he stood. "You'd like that, wouldn't you?"

"Oh, yes, I would. But I think every man likes his woman to accept and obey everything he says."

"So I'm your woman now?" She stood with her hands on her hips, tapping her toes against the floor.

"You are while you're here, so don't forget. I may have to share you at times, but you're still mine." He finished covering the divan with the sheet and placed the amber bottle on the small table.

She glanced from him to the divan and back again. "What are you doing?"

"You'll see." He patted the sheet. "Here, lie down … on your tummy." Rose crawled on and spread herself out with a small grunt. "I'd like to try an herbal oil on you. I think you'll like it." He sat down beside her, opened the bottle, and poured some of the contents in his hands. She turned her head back to him and narrowed her eyes. "Will it make me feel strange, or do crazy things?"

"Of course." He laughed. "Doesn't everything we use around here make you crazy? Actually, this oil contains no aphrodisiac qualities, though we have ones that do. You'll like the way it feels, and smells."

"I see." She rested her head back down and closed her eyes.

* * *

As she lay in front of him, Thomas admired her smooth back and nicely shaped buttocks. He rubbed his hands together and began massaging with long, firm strokes, starting with the back of her neck. His hands developed their own rhythm, up and down, as they coursed over her shoulders and ended on her back. Her skin, like fine velvet, kissed the pads of his fingers as he traced out her curves, kneading, pinching, and pressing her supple flesh between his fingers.

Rose sank deeper into the divan, letting out a soft moan of satisfaction. "You're right, Thomas, I like the oil. It smells good, too, just like you said."

"Good. Now flip over." He poured more oil into his hands and began rubbing her cheekbones. As he stroked over her face, she lifted up her chin. She closed her eyes with a contented smile.

"If I were a cat, I'd be purring right now." She interrupted the mood with a giggle. With quick, rolling vibrations of her tongue, she managed a successful attempt at imitating a cat's purr.

"Are you my little kitty?" Thomas grinned, amused at her humor.

"Oh, yes, I'll be the best little kitty in the world for you, Thomas."

"Really? Will you obey me and do everything I tell you to do without question, if you're going to be my best kitty?"

Her eyes popped open and she shot up, giving him an incredulous look. She thought a moment and wrinkled her nose. "No, I don't think I can do that." She shook her head and collapsed back down on the divan. "On second thought, I don't think I'll be a very good kitty after all. I think I'll just be a naughty one instead. It's more fun that way."

"Then I'll have to spank my naughty little pussy for being such a bad girl." Thomas gave her a quick, sharp swat on the outside of her thigh, leaving a lingering sting.

"Ow!" She rubbed the reddened area. "Oh, Thomas, you wouldn't do that, would you?"

He tweaked a nipple. "Oh, I might. I like my kitties well-behaved."

"You know kitties aren't that way." She performed a feline stretch, a demure smile across her face. "But I'll try to be extra good for you, anyway."

Thomas laughed and re-oiled his hands. He reached over and cupped one of her breasts, pressing and working his thumbs and fingers into the soft flesh. As he pinched and rubbed the plump nipple softly between his thumb and forefinger, she let out a small moan and ground her hips into the divan.

He continued working the oil over the rest of her body with smooth, even strokes until he reached her pelvic region. At that point, he pushed her thighs apart. "Open up for me." Between his fingers he took up each large lip and then the small ones, squeezing with a soft, rhythmic pressure. Rose remained quiet, eyes closed, her breathing deep but regular.

With the pads of two fingers, he rubbed her clit in both clockwise and counterclockwise directions. She opened her thighs wider. Thomas smiled. Taking the slippery knot between his fingers, he applied a gentle squeeze and quickly let go. Beneath his hands, he felt her hips twitch ever so slightly. He then slipped two fingers deep inside, and turning up his hand, he moved them against her walls with slow, forward-moving strokes. Rose sighed and arched her hips. He finished the session by inserting one well-oiled digit deep into her backside, employing the same stroking movements. Rose opened her eyes, blinked a few times, and took some deep breaths; but she remained silent.

"We're done now." He gave each nipple a tiny kiss.

"What kind of massage was that? And you didn't even try to …"

"Yes, I know." He smiled down at her. This 'rubdown,' as you call it, is an ancient technique used to achieve total connection. Not just the physical, if you know what I mean."

"Hey, Thomas, what about you? Don't you deserve a special massage, too?" She smiled, fluttering her eyelashes a little.

"Oh, don't worry about me right now. Let's go. We need to get back. Here, we'll need to wrap these around us." He picked up two dry towels from one of the cabinets and tossed her one.

*　*　*

Rose followed Thomas's lead and removed her towel once they reached their room. He wrapped his arms around her. "Now, that wasn't so bad, was it?" He smiled and kissed her lips.

"I'll have to get used to it. I'm not used to bathing with people. I liked the massage for sure."

Thomas turned toward the bed, pulling her along with him. "Here, help me turn the cover down."

"These are really nice. Soft, too." She ran her hands over the fibers of white linen.

"We have nice things here. Let's get into bed." Thomas, wasting no time, climbed in and nestled himself under the covers.

She stood there for a moment lost in thought. So much had changed since she left home. Her whole world had transformed in the blink of an eye. The old saying "be careful what you wish for" rang loud and true. Her internal urges had nearly gotten the better of her, and now here she was, in a place where these urges and a willingness to learn more about them ruled the day. Her father had warned she'd lose the battle. Inside she smiled, feeling rather smug. Little would he ever know he'd prepared her for winning the war.

"Rose, are you joining me, or are you just going to stand there? Did you want to sleep on the floor or something?"

"I've never slept with anyone before," she said softly. "I mean, spend a whole night in bed." She thought a moment longer. "Thomas, did you ever dream we'd find ourselves in this situation? I don't think I ever thought about the possibility of our ever being together like this. I think it's going to take a while for it to all sink in. It's like we started something in our lives much too early, before we were ready, filled with curiosity and totally unaware of the consequences an internal awakening brings. Because that's what it was like, something we couldn't explain, couldn't understand. We'd started on a path destined for a certain future, and were forced to stop while our bodies and minds ripened. Now we've met on that path once more, where everything's as it should be and no one to stop us."

"What a beautiful way of looking at it, Rose. You're right. I guess I've never thought about it much, either. We were so young, and as we got older, I guess we just went our separate ways, that's all. We haven't seen a lot of each other over the last several years, you know. And you're right. Here we are again, still curious, but this time unstoppable. The internal awakening makes sense. We're ready for it, ready for the full force of it, with all its reckless beauty.

"

"That's true." Rose smiled at him.

"I will say this, had your mother not intervened, I'm not sure what we would have done during our game. Probably not much of anything. But things are different now. Trust me when I say we'll be playing doctor to the utmost while you're here. After all, we're in a special hospital setting designed to treat a specific set of issues. Look at this place as an asylum, a safe haven for sensual exploration, though that's not how we present The House to the general public."

"I'll say. I can't imagine Father agreeing to ever send me to a place like this if he'd known differently." She stifled a giggle. "Now I'm glad he didn't know."

Thomas patted his hand down against the covers. "Let's talk more in bed. Get on in here." Rose crawled in beside him. He fluffed the covers about her and snuggled up close. "So what do you think now?"

"I'll be fine, really I will."

Thomas reached over with a finger and began caressing a nipple. She looked over at him and smiled, sinking her head deeper into her pillow. Thomas's hand moved over her stomach, and the gentle motions of his palm against her skin set off a wave of drowsiness.

"I have a question." She forced her eyes open.

"What, sweetheart?"

"How do people end up here at The House? I know Father brought me … because he thought I had a problem. But I don't think there's anything wrong with me, do you?"

"No, of course not. Your body's blossoming and maturing, and now you're experiencing the feelings and sensations you described earlier. I'm here to help you explore all of that. You're not abnormal or strange."

"But do the other admits here have these same problems? And how did they get here? Did someone drop them off and leave them, too?"

"Everyone must be signed in and pass the examination

process before they can enjoy the privileges of The House. They can be escorted here by a family member, friend, or other relative who knows them well. In your case, your father signed you in. And yes, the other admits have similar issues as yourself. They, like you, have been brought here by someone who thought they would benefit from our treatment. A person rarely will be admitted here on their own accord, because most people don't want to admit they need help."

"Has anyone ever been turned away or failed the intake exam?"

Thomas wrinkled his brow in thought. "We don't turn away many people. I can't recall a time when I've not recommended admitting someone, but I've heard some stories about sending away unsuitable candidates on rare occasions."

"What happens if someone isn't allowed in here? And what happens if they tell people what happened to them once they leave?"

At that question, Thomas bolted upright in bed and gave her a hard look. "Trust me, no one who has failed the intake process ever revealed what happened. Do you remember the contract you signed with John?"

She nodded. "Yes, and I found the whole thing confusing. How do you make someone keep their mouth shut? The form never spelled out what the consequences are."

He took her hands in his. "Listen to me. I didn't tell you this before, but while we're on the subject, there is something you need to know. The House is divided into two sides. When you and I came up the staircase, I led you to one side—our side—where we address emotions and needs of a carnal nature. The other side of The House contains residents who are truly mad and deranged. They're seldom let out, but when they are, they have enclosed areas where they can at least enjoy the light of day for a little while. The patients there never mingle with us. You'll never see them."

Her eyes widened. "You're not serious are you?"

"I'm not lying, Rose. If anyone fails the entrance exam and

retaliates by notifying people in the town, the directors here will declare that person insane. The offender will be brought back and locked away on the other side of The House, never to be seen or heard from again by family or friends."

"You mean they're put away for good?"

"Yes, they are. We cannot have outsiders interfering in our business. We serve a special population that benefits from our treatment methods. Besides, some of the higher-ups in authority actually support us—in secret. Some of them have even been admits here."

"How odd—and how cruel at the same time." Rose rolled her head back and forth on the pillow in disbelief. "Anyway, tell me this, how do you all determine if someone is not a good fit?"

"From what I've heard the person fights back verbally, or with their body. In other words, they simply do not, or cannot, submit themselves willingly to our examination. Their whole essence, or nature, fights back, if you can understand what I'm trying to say."

"I can understand reluctance on their part," Rose shrugged. "That examination is pretty intense, Thomas. I'll admit it's not for everyone."

"Yes, true enough." Thomas continued, "But let's use you as an example. There were moments when you weren't ready to perform or answer everything I asked, but I was able to coax you, and you gave in." He smiled at her. "There were moments, too, when you enjoyed yourself, but at no time did you fight against me, nor did I have to struggle with you. Our knowing each other, coupled with your body being ripe and ready, helped you, no doubt."

"True." Her fingers managed to locate the cockhead between his legs, and she stroked him gently, feeling the softness against her fingers. He closed his eyes as she swirled her fingertip in the pool of moisture gathered at the top. "Have you ever had an admit you didn't like?"

He thought again for a few moments, opened his eyes, and

answered, "No, I've liked all the admits I've had. Rather, we were able to get along, you might say. People have different levels of connections, and there have been some admits I connected to easier than others."

"What happens if an attendant and admit don't get along?"

"Well, that really doesn't happen, or not often, anyway. John is pretty good at reading people, and has a good idea who'll be the best attendant for a particular admit. If there's a problem, we'd put the admit with someone more suitable."

"That's good to know." Rose nodded in approval. She fell silent a moment, trying to think of other questions she wanted to ask, but her eyes were growing heavy, and her mind tumbled in a blur.

Thomas watched her and smiled. "Sweetheart, you've had a long day, not to mention an adventuresome one. You need some sleep. I'll answer your other questions later." He leaned over her and kissed her.

"Good-night, Thomas." She smiled and entwined her fingers around his. Sleeping next to her friend became more comfortable with each passing minute. Soon this would become a sweet routine, something she'd look forward to each night. Weary and exhausted, she fell into a deep sleep filled with strange dreams.

Chapter 3

THE SUN THROUGH THE WINDOW awakened Rose with a gentle hand. She stirred, somewhat confused. Why was she not in her own bed at home, in familiar surroundings? Between her thighs she felt the most arousing sensations. Then she remembered.

Thomas rested between her thighs, nursing her hidden bits with a gentle, sucking rhythm. On occasion, he rubbed and flicked the tip of his tongue against her highly sensitive clit. Thickness gathered within her sex. She stirred again. His slipped in his fingers, stroking over the slippery walls, and commanded an internal release. She closed her eyes, sank back into the soft sheets, falling prey to a deep, strong, silent, internal climax, revealed only by the reflexive jerking of her hips.

"I take it you slept well?" He popped his head up, and smiled with a sly grin.

"Yes, somewhat, I guess. Not bad for being away from home and sharing a bed with someone for the first time."

He pulled himself up and placed a soft kiss on her lips. She spied an early-morning erection bobbing between his legs. The palm of her hand moved over his firm belly, over his pubic bone, and she caught his thickness between her fingers. For a moment she played with the sweet, smooth head on top, caressing the velvety flesh. While she stared up at the handsome man in front of her, the ache in her clit pounded harder. Unable to contain her lust, she stretched out and spread her thighs open further. His skin felt smooth and warm under her palms.

Thomas, ready with a stiff cock, positioned himself and pressed against her entrance. "I'll go easy," he whispered. He slid in with smooth, gliding movements and buried himself deep inside her. She winced a little, still sensitive from the day before. He continued with slow, gentle undulations, persuading her walls to loosen up and accept each thrust. Her initial discomfort soon gave way to pleasure as he worked himself back and forth against her firm, internal grip. His tip continued teasing her hidden sweet spot, causing her to arch her hips in delight. With steadfast movements he finally released his fluids, and with a soft gasp, he filled her with a pearly warmth. With one last shudder, he sighed and sank down on the bed, cradling her in his arms.

"What a way to wake up, huh?" He kissed the tip of her nose.

She smiled over at him and ran her fingers through his hair. "I like it." She leaned over to kiss his ear.

"Breakfast is served." A handsome, well-sculpted male, carrying two trays in his arms, entered their room. An easy smile played across his face. "And where will you partake of this lovely meal?"

"We'll be partaking here on the floor, if you please." Thomas jested in turn as the staff member placed the trays on the floor.

"Enjoy your meal." He gave a simple nod of his head before striding out of the room.

Thomas removed the tops and slid a tray over to Rose, who eyed the contents with eager anticipation. Her stomach rumbled with hunger, and she salivated as she spied succulent fruit, tiny sausage links, and bite-sized quiche tartlets filled with ham, broccoli, and cheese. She began to pick off morsels of food and pop them into her mouth, consuming everything with the speed of a starved street urchin. An embarrassed flush lit up her face, and she paused before taking another bite. Thomas had been staring at her with a mix of amusement and disbelief.

"Do we not feed you well enough? By the look of you, one would think we kept you starved."

"I'm sorry for my bad manners." She lifted a hand to hide her mouth. After she swallowed, she sat back and took a deep breath, his comments serving a well-meant cue to slow down and savor the meal.

"Much better. Take your time and relax. No need to hurry." He smiled and snared a tasty tartlet from his plate. "I thought I'd give you a quick tour of The House after we finish here. What do you think about that, Rose? Would you like to visit some of the other wards?"

If the others floors proved to be as interesting as the one she was on, of course! The opportunity to prowl new hallways and rooms, giving her voyeuristic animal a little exercise, suited her fine. "Sounds good to me. Are they much different from this one?"

He gazed at her in thought, taking the opportunity to savor and swallow the tart he had popped into his mouth, before answering. He nodded. "Yes, they are different. I think you'll be exposed to more than you bargained for, but such is life. If you ask me, you'll receive quite an education."

"What kind of education?"

"Trust me when I say beware of the difference." He leaned over to lick off a drop of juice lingering on the side of her plump, full lips. With a giggle, she flinched as his warm, wet tongue tickled her flesh.

When they finished their breakfast, Thomas walked over to the chest of drawers and pulled out two articles of clothing. "Here, put this on." He handed Rose a simple dress, which she put on without delay. The red cotton material hugged her body, showing off firm breasts, a tiny waist, and curvy hips. She grabbed the two straps at the top, reached behind her neck, and tied them into a tight, neat bow.

"Why are we wearing these clothes?" Rose ran her fingers over the material. "And you're wearing the same trousers as you did yesterday."

"The difference is they are clean, so no, I'm not wearing the same trousers as yesterday. Besides, House rules say we wear some form of clothing, unless an event requires we don't. The other exception to this is mealtimes."

"You mean House rules dictate no nudity? Why? And why are meals an exception?"

"Mealtimes are different, that's all. As for the no-nudity policy, the directors of The House believe in leaving something for the imagination, and everyone running around naked would defeat the purpose, don't you think?"

"I guess I can see their point."

"Yes, I think so, too. I mean, catching the girlish curves outlined by a tight dress—"

"Or tight slacks fitting over the fullness of a man's privates," Rose chimed in, a sparkle creeping in her eye.

"You get it." Thomas chuckled. "And I'm sure you've wondered about the design of the clothing. The way we can unsnap or push up the clothing helps us take care of business without a lot of fuss. Also, if you didn't realize this earlier, once we unsnap our trousers, we can extend the panel all the way back so our entire pelvic region is exposed, both front and rear. Pretty neat, isn't it?"

"The design's creative, but look how short this dress is on me. I'm barely covered." Distracted, she turned her head down and inspected her new wardrobe, trying hard to imagine how she must appear to others, with the bottom of her dress hitting only several inches below her hips.

"Again, you look fine. Come on. I think we're ready to head on out of here and go visit the other wards." Thomas took her hand and pulled her out of their room. They turned left and headed down to the end of the hallway, where they found themselves in front of a heavy, wooden door with elaborate, ornate carvings.

*   *   *

This door granted passage to the back wards. Thomas reached out, turned a scrolled, brass latch, and ushered Rose into the adjoining hallway before closing the door behind them. As she peered down the hall, the decor didn't appear much different from her own ward. Just as Thomas had mentioned, however, the various activities within the rooms made her eyes widen and her mouth gape open. Thomas glanced over, appraising her reactions, the corners of his mouth twitching into a small grin.

"Didn't I warn you earlier? Not quite what you expected, eh?"

"You can say that again." As they walked, Rose realized

that even the wildest imaginings failed miserably in preparing her for the activities she witnessed within these open rooms.

They stopped in the entrance of one room and watched while two females engaged themselves in a position that appeared much like the yin/yang symbol she'd seen in old books written on spirituality. They seemed so engrossed in their lovemaking, with their faces buried in the other's sex. While their fingers busied themselves in spreading each other open, pink tongues flashed as they explored each other with great care. Rose drew back a little, blushing.

After a few minutes, the girl on the bottom pumped her hips in short, furious jerks as an orgasm overtook her body. "Oh, yeah, keep working it. Yes, keep going—work that clit. Harder! Faster!"

The girl on top, finished with her task, looked up at the ceiling for a brief moment and stopped her work on the one below, giving her partner ample opportunity to finish her off. She closed her eyes, opened her mouth, and let out a string of soft moans before her hips shuddered with relief. Once her spasms subsided, she tumbled onto the bed, and both girls broke out in merry laughter.

"God, we're good, aren't we?" The girl who climaxed first laughed. She reached up to smooth a lock of hair from her partner's face, who responded with an affirmative deep kiss on the lips. So engrossed they were in their own pleasure, neither paid attention to their new visitors.

Rose tugged on Thomas's arm, and they progressed down the hall until she stopped in the doorway of a room near the end. She shook her head and blinked twice to make sure she wasn't dreaming while she watched the play between the occupants.

"Ow—be gentle. I've never used one of these before." A slender female with long, corn silk-colored hair positioned herself over another female who held a blue, double-end phallus in her hands.

The girl wielding the bright toy let out a giggle, shaking

her sprawling, obsidian curls over the pillow trapped under her head. "Here, let me help you get this in," she said, "and then we can do each other at the same time." She took the phallus in one hand and spread open the glistening, feminine slit looming above her with the other, sinking in the short, bulbed end deep inside. The glossy blue tip disappeared as the recipient pumped her hips and glided on, situating herself with a satisfied sigh of pleasure as the full, smooth head filled her up. "Yeah, that's good. Oh, so nice and tight inside." Her shiny mane flowed behind her, as she threw her head back with a moan and undulated her hips with a slow, steady motion. "This thing hits me in just the right place."

"Ready? Let's go, then, because my pussy's hot and dripping wet for this thing." Impatient, the girl with dark curls positioned herself to receive the longer part of the phallus. She spread her legs open wide and let out a gasp. "Oh God … slow … nice … easy!" Her face lit up in an ecstatic smile, as her crotch opened to swallow the longer end of the phallus to the hilt. Her throat unleashed staccato gasps as the slick appendage glided within her. Both girls let out vocalizations unique to their experience, and the unison of both served only to fuel the fiery tension in the other. Within a few moments, the hip action of the girl on top succeeded in bringing out a strong climax for both parties.

Rose stepped back and turned to leave, ready to continue on with their tour. Turning from the doorway and taking a left turn, they headed down the remainder of the hall until another large door greeted them. For the first time, the carvings in the wood caught her attention. Enticed by burning curiosity, she lingered before the wooden monstrosity for closer inspection. A vague recognition crept into her mind, and with lightning speed, her brain comprehended the work before her. Memories ran amok as visions of rooms on the wards flashed before her, reminding her once again of other inhabitants who imitated these exact positions. How clever and creative this artist proved himself, availing the use of doors to illustrate man's primal urges with blatant, unabashed candor. Had she missed these carvings on the first door? She shook her head in disbelief and looked up at Thomas, hoping he could tell her more about this art work.

"I don't know the artist who did the work on the doors, but I'm told the carvings were inspired from reliefs etched in the stones and trim work found in temples from far away lands." Thomas gazed up and ran a finger over one of the figures. "Pretty impressive, isn't it?"

"I'll say. These male figures sport some pretty big ..." Rose's fingers traced the outline of a large, portly phallus standing at attention between the legs of one of the carved men. One scene showed a group of men and women engaged in oral sex, while another showcased homosexual acts.

"Well, enough with these. Let's move on." Thomas opened the door and led Rose into another adjoining hallway. In the distance, she heard male voices. Some gave off shouts of laughter, others released moans of ecstasy. At that moment, she deduced that if the previous ward housed females, this ward held the males and all their sexual antics and appetites.

"Thomas, is this ward going to be what I think it is?" She wanted to confirm the logic behind her thinking.

"What do you think you'll see here?" Thomas glanced at her with a solemn face. "Well ..." Rose swallowed, nervous. Her eyes wandered over the tile-work in the floor, following the repetitive pattern to the end of the hallway. "I think it will be like the last ward, but with men instead of women."

"Correct."

As she continued surveying the floor, the length seemed to ramble on forever. For some strange reason, fatigue had set in, and the idea of continuing this tour unnerved her. She found herself desperate, eager to leave and return to her own ward.

"You know what, Thomas, I've seen enough. I mean, how different can all this be, anyway? Maybe we can go back to our room for a nap?"

Thomas stood his ground, shaking his head. "House protocol dictates that all new admits visit each ward." He rubbed her arm in sympathy. "I'm sure all of this is overwhelming for you, but we'll be done soon. You need exposure to this ward so you can round out your experience here at The House. When we're finished, we can do whatever you want." He smiled at her as he smoothed back a few strands of hair.

His caresses and reasoning had little effect on her disposition, irritability growing with each passing second. She remembered her agreement to follow the rules, so this, too, must be endured. Rose narrowed her eyes and let out a sigh. "Fine, let's get this over with." Thomas slipped his arm through hers, and they began their trek down the hall.

Visions of male admits with their attendants greeted Rose from every room as she caught glimpses of them kissing and embracing. She stopped in the doorway of one room and viewed the couple within. Her eyes widened at the scene. Bent over the bed, a handsome, young male, legs spread apart, twitched his hips at intervals as his partner attempted to impale his backside with a phallus.

"Quit moving so much." Another attractive male stood behind him and laughed, stopping long enough to place a sound smack on the buttocks of his partner.

"I can't help it. That stuff you put inside me earlier is driving me crazy. Hurry up, would you?" His complaining stopped as his rear cheeks received another sharp blow from the attacker behind.

"Just hold still a minute, and I'll give you relief soon enough." The gentleman grasped the scrolled end of the phallus and inserted it with a smooth, swift push, burying it fully inside the young man's body.

"Oh, yes. Keep going. Don't stop." The prone man gasped as the phallus glided back and forth, relieving him of the irritant previously instilled inside him.

"There, you like this? Stand up a minute."

The man, following instructions, removed himself from the bed and stood erect, his eyes closed, as the phallus continued to graze against his anal walls. "Oh, I can feel one coming on." He closed his eyes, and his thigh muscles tightened. An erection soon formed between his legs, and his pink tip stood proudly at the top of a hard cock. "Keep going, Eric. Oh, this feels so good." Eric placed his arm around his partner's waist to steady him, and with a few more passes of the phallus, the man released his emissions onto the floor.

Rose turned from the doorway in silence and continued on to another room, Thomas close at her heels. The suspension of legs in straps, however, caught her attention, and she peered through a new doorway. Her mouth fell open, and glancing up, she caught Thomas's eye. He smiled and focused his attention back to the occupants in the room.

A male with short pecan-colored hair lay supine in the bed, his legs held apart and elevated by leather straps hanging from an overhead bar. A black blindfold covered his eyes, and inside his anus rested a plug with wires attached to the end. Rose's eyebrows lifted in surprise when she discovered the other end of the wires connected to a black box controlled by a gentleman with sandy, wavy hair.

"Are you ready, Rick?" The man with the box had his finger on a switch, and once he acknowledged an affirmative nod from the other, a soft click resounded.

"Oh!" Rick threw his head back and gasped. "God, this is great." He gritted his teeth, and dug his head into the pillow."

"You like this thing? Makes your ass hum inside, doesn't it?" His partner grinned. "Or even better, I bet you like the way it makes your dick hard."

Rose watched as Rick grabbed the stiff erection between his thighs and worked the cockhead into a frenzy. In a few moments, he shot out a milky stream of semen, which landed in a thick puddle on his stomach. His partner, toting a full hard-on topped by a shapely head, shut off the black box and moved toward Rick's mouth. He inserted himself, grunting with relief as Rick's strong oral movements finished him off.

Rose stepped back from the door way and strolled down the hall. "Thomas, how does The House come up with these devices? I mean, I've never heard any of our friends talk about using these things. And we all talk. You know that."

Thomas put his arm around her. "First of all, I don't think we all share what really goes on behind closed doors, no matter how close we are as friends. Let me point out, however, that The House has hired staff dedicated solely to experimenting and coming up with new ways to enhance sexual pleasure. Much of what you see here is several years, maybe decades, before its time. We have the capacity for creating special instruments you won't find outside these walls. These are proprietary secrets of The House, and we guard them with utmost care."

Rose nodded, turning her head toward the sound of moans coming from a room down the hall. She grabbed Thomas's arm and sped toward the doorway. Flashes of metal caused her to screech to a halt, and Thomas, close behind, had to veer in order to avoid crashing into her. In horror, she viewed the scene. A young man was pulling a thick, heavy chain from the buttocks of another, who knelt on his hands and knees on the floor. As Rose craned her neck, she caught sight of ejaculate spilling from the man's cock, falling in a milky puddle on the floor.

Without another word, she whirled around in the doorway and rushed back to the large, ornate door. "I'm done here, Thomas." Her brow furrowed with determination. "I don't care what you say, I've seen enough."

Thomas smiled as he caught up to her. "Yes, but we have one more ward, and then we'll be finished."

*   *   *

The sounds of music and talking greeted their ears as they entered a ward situated on another floor of The House.

"Are they having a party or what? And how come we weren't invited?" Upon hearing the merriment, Rose's mood lifted.

Thomas laughed. "I think you'll find this ward the most interesting of all. The admits and attendants here are unique, to say the least, but I think you'll like them."

Unlike the other wards, the rooms here sat empty. In the common room at the end of the hallway, the sound of tinkling instruments and pounding drums provided a backdrop to an assortment of vocal talent. This room mimicked a guest drawing room where well-dressed attendants and admits occupied the various brocade sofas and sumptuous velvet armchairs scattered about. With a carefree air, they reclined back on puffy pillows. Rose heard the buzz of voices as each shared intimate secrets with the other and laughed at an occasional bit of humor. Artwork decorated the mauve-painted walls, along with the occasional gilt mirror accented by crystal lamps on each side.

At the back of the room, others gathered around a large dining table filled with silver trays of food and crystal goblets of water. A sparkling, elegant chandelier hung from above. In one corner of the room stood a large, decorative screen covered with scenes of lovers engaged in various sexual acts. A group of musicians played, an assortment of drums, flutes, and other unidentified tinkling items, while men in tight loincloths danced in time to the music, swinging their hips and waving their arms, stepping left and right in a lively rhythmic pattern. A sheen of perspiration illuminated their facial features, showing off glittering eyes and luscious lips painted with bright cosmetics.

Rose turned to Thomas in amazement. "Why are these ladies wearing such formal dresses? And their hair—their jewelry ..." Her eyes roamed the various figures sporting colorful ball gowns, glittering jewels, and coifed hair. "They don't dress or act like we do. Why?"

"There's a reason for their ..." Thomas turned to the sound of rustling skirts behind them. A striking woman in a flowing, emerald green gown sidled up and interlaced her arm through his. Her deep cinnamon-colored hair, arranged in an elegant upsweep, glistened with jewels interspersed throughout thick tresses. A large, sparkling diamond choker rested on her bosom.

"Hola, Señor Tomás. Won't you come join us at the table?

Perhaps you and *la bonita* can help us enjoy the food and drink. It's all quite divine."

"Ah, Isabelle, how could we refuse such an invitation from someone as lovely as yourself?" Thomas bowed and kissed the lady's hand. She waved a hand for Thomas and Rose to follow her. When they reached the table, Thomas pulled out a chair for Rose. Isabelle sat down close beside her.

"What, Tomás, are you leaving already?" Isabelle arched a dark set of brows above a pair of brilliant olive-green eyes. Thomas nodded, and her lips feigned a delicate, pretty pout.

"No offense, my sweet Isabelle, but I see someone I haven't spoken to in a while. Could you please help entertain Rose for me?" His ingratiating smile met with laughter.

"Ah, yes, we will take care of *la bonita*. She's safe with us." Isabelle blew him a kiss and motioned for him to take his leave. She turned and took Rose's hand within her own. "You are new here? I haven't seen you before."

"Yes, I came yesterday."

Isabelle leaned in close and whispered, "Quite an interesting place here, *La Casa*, no?" Rose caught the scent of patchouli and amber from her hair, and a heavy, ornate earring brushed against her cheek.

She sat back a little and looked at Isabelle with a grin. "Yes, The House is the most interesting place I've ever experienced."

"Ah, but you are still young, and have much to taste in life."

"Somehow I expect I'll taste more here than what life will ever offer me out there."

Isabelle threw her head back and let out a melodious, throaty laugh. Her white teeth flashed in the light. "True enough, as you will soon learn." Her laughter faded and she bowed her head in respectful acknowledgement as someone passed by. Rose caught sight of a lady clothed in a cherry red gown, whose gathered train trailed behind her like a cat's tail with every slow, easy, deliberate step she took. A matching head scarf covered most of her hair and hung with an elegant drape down the back of her neck. Rose shook her head, thinking this whole scene merely a dream.

She studied the face, the hands, size and girth of the fingers. Where she lived there had been rumors that a male neighbor liked dressing in women's clothing. The gossip about his private life ran fast and furious. If she thought hard enough, imagining him dressed like one of these ladies, he just might bear a striking resemblance. Though Rose thought him a nice enough man when she spoke to him on occasion, everyone else thought him odd. She turned back to Isabelle in silence.

"*Querida*," she said, "you seem troubled. Is there something wrong?"

"Isabelle, is it me or my imagination? But several of the women here seem rather unusual to me."

"Oh? How do you mean?" Rose watched as Isabelle reached for the tiniest banana she'd ever seen. With deft fingers she stripped the fruit from its thick sheath and plunged the top into a sliver pot of chocolate simmering over a small blue flame. She caught Rose's eye.

Rose licked her lips, unsure how to present her observation. "Well, they seem so beautiful … powerful … strong … I can't quite put my finger on it."

"Would you like a chocolate?" Isabelle pointed to a crystal vase housing a collection of long-stemmed confections. Rose, in absent compliance, reached over and plucked out what appeared to be a floral bud on a stem. She peeled off the red paper covering and started to pop the treat between her teeth, but stopped short and clapped her hand over her mouth to stifle a laugh.

"Now this is the most interesting chocolate I've ever seen. It looks like the head of a man's …"

Isabelle chuckled. "And it's filled just like a man's …"

Rose raised her eyebrows at Isabelle in surprise and paused. She turned her eyes back to the treat before her.

"Please, go ahead and taste. It's quite good." Isabelle

pushed Rose's hand gently toward her mouth.

Rose poked her tongue at the top of the bud and broke through the chocolate. A thick, rich cream oozed out and covered her tongue. "M-m-m, vanilla—with a hint of clove." She smiled and smacked her lips a little to savor the taste. Her tongue flicked around the bud as white, milky drops began running over the edge. To her chagrin, she glanced up to catch a pair of eyes staring at her from a corner of the room. Lit with an intense gleam, their beams of light burned and melted through her core like the hot flames of a torch. The lady in red scrutinized her movements with intense interest, and as Rose flushed with embarrassment, a small grin twitched at the corner of her cerise-painted lips.

"Who is that woman? And why is she looking at me like that?"

Isabelle, amused by the whole scene, said nothing, but coursed the tip of her tongue over her chocolate-covered delicacy and caressed off the sweet droplets running down its length.

* * *

"Come, you dance with us."

"What?" Rose jumped, startled by the arrival of a young, handsome man who had bustled to her side. With a quick, wandering eye, she scanned his physique and made out the plump bulge beneath the loincloth he wore around his hips. His heaving chest showed off worthy sets of ripples, and colorful cosmetics highlighted his eyelids, cheeks, and lips. "I've never danced much before. I really don't know how to do this."

He ignored her protests, caught her up by the arm, and pulled her toward the group of dancers. "It's easy. Submit to my lead, follow me, and I will show you what you need to do. Don't think. Just do."

They stationed themselves at the end of a line of dancers in progress, their feet stepping in time to an ardent beat. Rose found the dance patterns easy, picked up her pace with more enthusiasm as her confidence increased, and surrendered to the partnership. The music pounded in her ears, and after several minutes, the rhythm and movement of the dance intoxicated her. Her partner took her hand in his and pulled her a few steps to the right, then pushed her a few steps to the left. He raised his hand, and Rose took the liberty of performing a dainty, little twirl—right into the arms of the lady in red.

"Oh, I'm so …!" Rose locked onto a pair of bright eyes, their piercing glint soulful and penetrating. She studied the face before her, the well-formed nose, and the strong, square jaw line which curved down to a nice, rounded chin. Like many of the others in the room, certain facial features bore evidence of the skillful application of cosmetics. Both hands, though neatly manicured, exuded a certain force between their widths, but she marveled most at the strength of the arms wrapped around her waist. Within their embrace, she became overwhelmed by an intense energy, a radiating heat that threatened to suffocate her, and the scent of bergamot and myrrh made her swoon. Rose gave a small cry of surprise as the figure scooped her up and, with quick, graceful steps, moved toward the opposite corner of the room. Once situated behind the privacy of the screen, he placed Rose on a large, soft cushion. The lady in red loomed over her as if to consume her very being.

A surge of panic set in, and she writhed to get away from the stronghold of muscular thighs locked in position on either side of her hips, held fast by the weight over her. "Please, let me …!"

"Sh-h-h, *silencio*. Quiet, please, *amor*. No need to be afraid."

The soft, sultry voice made Rose stop and blink her eyes in amazement. "You're—"

"I am Ramón. And yes, I am …"

"… A man! But you're so beautiful …" She stared, unable to remove her eyes, his beauty taking her breath away.

"Thank you, *amor*. You are most kind, but I think you are the beautiful one, *la hermosa*." Rose's heart quickened; the hard bulge between his thighs pressed harder against her sex.

Without thinking, Rose reached up and moved her finger across the fabric of Ramón's gown, her brows knit together, perplexed. "You … you like women … even though you wear …?"

"I adore not only women, but everything associated with female beauty. I love silky fabric against my skin, the touch of cold metal and sparkling gems around my neck. With cosmetics, I can transform myself and be one as beautiful as yourself, even if only for just a moment in time. In this way, I honor and pay tribute to the power and beauty and strength of the woman."

Rose pondered his words in silence. Meanwhile, from the chestnut-colored depths of Ramón's eyes, a quiet hunger surged. In lusty anticipation, he licked his lips with a glossy tongue and peered into Rose's face. "Allow me to immerse myself in your beauty, taste your divine sweetness." Rose shifted under his weight, aroused by his declarations and eloquent request. The hidden place between her thighs responded with an outpouring of hot, thick moisture, and she tried in vain to open herself up to this strange person who wielded power over her. Ramón's thighs held her fast.

"You're allowed." With a serene smile, she reached behind her neck, untied the straps of her dress, and threw her arms behind her head. Ramón eyed her heaving chest with approval and hooked his fingers at the top, slipping the fabric down. A pair of soft, heaving breasts greeted his eyes, and he licked his lips again, salivating for the bobbing, pink flesh on top.

The music in the background thumped out a hypnotizing rhythm, loud and clear, and Rose found herself lulled into a relaxed, open state of mind and body. "Yes, *amor*," Ramón said softly, "just lie back and give your body over to the music. Let the sensations carry you away." He leaned over and captured one of her pink nipples between his lips, and ran his tongue over the firm flesh. Soon his strong sucking movements extracted a cry from her throat. Filled with a strong desire to taste his lips, she caught his head between her hands and pulled his face over hers. Her wet, pink tongue sank into the depths of his mouth, and traced over the slippery ridges, flicked over the hard curvatures of his magnificent, white teeth. His thumb and forefinger grabbed her other full peak, and the gentle squeezing and tugging set off an uncontrollable ache blaring inside her core.

In urgency she caught the fabric of Ramón's dress and managed to free the skirts beneath him. Her fingers wound their way up between his thighs, brushing against the hard bulge struggling to break free from the satin bindings. She pulled away the lace band and dipped her hand inside. Moisture from his engorged head met her fingers with a slippery warmth as she fluttered over his velvety flesh and stroked across the pronounced veins along his cock. He stopped reciprocating her kisses, and, with a moan, broke free from her grip. Like opening the pages of a closed book, he grasped each one of Rose's thighs and spread her open, viewing her with a smile. Within her carnal pages, he seemed to read wet words of hot lust.

A thick pool bubbled within her cleft, and with a neat, manicured red nail, he dipped in, gently grazing the top of her clit. Rose gasped; her hips jerked in response.

"Now I taste," he whispered. "Give yourself over to me."

She nodded, and closed her eyes in submission. "Yes, please ... taste now." Ramón reached down to separate her folds. Moving his tongue in smooth flourishes, he swirled his soft, pink tip in the pool at her entrance, and caressed her firm, sensitive clit until the strong ache between her thighs turned into an eruption of spasms.

"You're a very good girl." A warmth from his eyes radiated over her. He ran his hands through her hair, pausing to twirl one of her satin locks around his finger. "A most delicious girl—*sabrosa*." With a sigh, he drew her face up to his and placed a soft kiss on her lips.

"Ramón, I'm sure you're most delicious yourself."

"Does your body long to taste mine, *amor*?"

Rose nodded. In fact, her body ached to swallow him whole. The face of a strong, handsome man peeked through all the cosmetic trappings, and his easy manner and seductive words held her captive in their powerful clutches. Her fingers teased his cock and the full, pink cockhead on top. "Will you honor and pay tribute to your masculine side and fill me with your beauty and majesty?"

"Ah, *mi amada*, my beloved, nothing would please me more." He moved and fluffed his skirts while Rose slipped off the satin undergarments, freeing the potential power and fury hidden underneath.

"Thank, you. Now I taste …" Rose smiled, stretching her thighs open. With a willing sigh, she received his full length. With a gentle strength, his arms cradled her close against his chest, while his hips rolled with a cadence in tandem with the music. He pounded against her, sliding in and out, creating an internal vibration in her that nearly drove her mad. Her walls clenched him with determination; her core ached. Ending in a crescendo of thrusts, he issued streams of warmth inside her. Her arms stretched around his broad frame, hugging the hard muscles in his back, a rather comical contrast to the soft ruffles fluttering against her cheek.

*　*　*

"So I see you two have met."

Ramón turned and viewed the new visitor behind him. "*Señor, Tomás*, this is your little prize?"

"Yes, and I see you've pretty much stolen her," Thomas narrowed his eyes, teasing.

"I would keep her for myself if I could, but I'd be no match against your endeavors to stop me."

Thomas shook his head. "Oh, I doubt that, Ramón. You're a worthy opponent. You merely flatter me."

Ramón stood up and assisted Rose from the cushion. "She's quite a sweet flower and wise beyond her years. I'm sure you will train her well." He turned to Rose and kissed her hand. "*Amor*, the pleasure was all mine, but I commend you to the one who brought you here. I hope to see you again." He bowed low, flowed past Thomas, and disappeared behind the screen, losing himself in the sea of guests. Rose pulled up her dress and retied the straps.

"Well, did you find this ward more palatable?" Thomas beamed at her with pride. "Looks like you made quite an impression. And I might add Ramón is not one who pleases easily."

"A most interesting man. I liked him, strange ways and all." She wrapped her arm around him. "You can bring me here anytime you want."

Chapter 4

THE SUN SPREAD RAYS of warmth over the grounds of The House, and soft breezes blew careless breaths throughout the forest. Sculpted gardens and scrolled pathways beckoned the onlooker to approach and lose themselves in a maze of twists and turns, while bronze statues struck majestic poses amid flowing fountains. A colorful carnival of flowers tumbled in playful abundance in their beds, and stepping stones, dressed in their characteristic matrices, glinted in the sun. Everyone at The House knew the mystique of the grounds, filled with dense forests, soft emerald coverlets of moss, and flirty flowers peppering hidden coves and lining edges of bubbling brooks. Somewhere in the primeval depths, a waterfall cascaded from a rocky cliff and splashed down to an ice-cold pool below.

Inside The House, everyone buzzed with excitement. Today was the day for the monthly game of Hide and Seek. Everyone waited with eager anticipation, because this game signaled a time for lusty romps outdoors and an opportunity to engage in free play with someone different. Morning arrived with only a few hours before the game commenced, and Rose found the whole ordeal rather intriguing. She wanted more details.

"So what is this game like? Do you play the same way we did when we were young?"

Thomas took a sip of coffee. "Somewhat, but it's considerably different from how you and I used to play." He smiled and wiped off a stray droplet from his mouth with a finger. "Basically, admits will have fifteen minutes to hide. The property is big, and you need ample time to explore and find your hiding place. Admits are the ones who are tagged by the attendants, and base, contrary to our games of youth, is never safe. If you run to base, you will be picked up by an attendant and led to participate in the game. Nobody is spared."

She glanced over in curiosity. "Does that mean you can be tagged by any attendant? I mean, if every one of us is playing at the same time, and we don't know someone—"

He laughed. "If you're concerned about being picked up

by … a female, in your case, you needn't worry so much. We actually have that issue worked out, because we respect gender preferences. Armbands will identify preferences, as well as who are admits and who are attendants. Attendants wear armbands on their right arm, while admits wear them on the left. Same-sex preferences will wear a multi-colored band, those willing to engage in both sexes will wear two armbands, yellow and multi-colored, while opposite sex players will wear yellow."

"Interesting." Rose stroked her chin in thought. "What sorts of things happen? I know it's a game, but there must be more to it than what you've told me so far."

"Yeah, you're right. Basically you are subject to the whims of the attendant who tags you. Unless a request causes harm or can kill you, never refuse to do what they ask."

"What happens if you do refuse?" Rose flashed him a concerned look.

"I don't think there's any danger of an admit refusing an attendant. I hope you don't go against an attendant's wishes. We have strong, dominating staff members who can find all sorts of punishments if you turn them down. And there's one more thing. No House attire."

Rose widened her eyes. "What do you mean no House attire?"

"Just what I told you, no House attire. Female attendants wear loincloths and tops, and males wear loincloths. But admits wear nothing, though you can wear something decorative, such as jewelry."

"Ugh!" Rose grimaced. "I hate the idea of wearing nothing."

"Don't worry, sweetheart, I'll make sure you're decked out well enough." Thomas curled up on the bed and pulled Rose into his arms. In a comforting gesture, he ran his fingers through her hair and placed a quick kiss on her lips.

Rose sighed. "So all in all, this means you and I may not be together in this game?

"No, I'll tag someone else. You need to meet some other

people, Rose."

"I guess you're right. It's not like I haven't mixed with others here, but you're always with me. That's what makes things so much easier."

"Trust me, you'll be fine with any attendant who tags you. We're all trained, and we all know many of the same things. I promise you'll have fun. Tonight we'll be back together again, anyway, so don't worry."

Rose looked at him and smiled and reached up to rub a finger against his cheek. She loved the moments they rested and snuggled together. The warmth of his body lulled her into a deeper daze, and his arms, strong and protective, wrapped around her like a fortress. In slow, delicious strokes, his fingers now moved over her stomach, up between her breasts, and trailed over at last to squeeze a nipple. The full weight of her head dropped against his chest, and she closed her eyes and tried to remember the past, back when she and Thomas lived in another world. In vain she tried to view the mental snapshots floating through her mind: their childhood playtimes, their fights, their shy moments of forgiveness … and then all over again. Her brief time at The House had broken and discarded that old innocence, making everything else from the past seem like a dream.

*   *   *

"It's time to get ready, Rose." Thomas's lips tickled her ear with a soft whisper.

"What?" Rose squinted up and rubbed her eyes. She sat up with a start, a little disoriented. "Did I doze off?"

"Yes, I think we both napped a little, but we need to get ready. Let's go." He led a yawning Rose to the tub room, where they performed what was becoming their customary bath ritual. When they finished, he said, "That's it, I think we're done here. Let's get back to our room so I can dry your hair and finish getting you ready."

He proved quite handy with a comb and hair pins, as he

lifted her luxurious locks into a sophisticated upsweep, pinning in shimmering crystal drops into several golden curls dancing on her head. "Now for the finishing touches." He walked over to the chest of drawers. After a few seconds of rattles and swishes, he brought out a box filled with glinting jewelry. Around her neck he fastened a bib of glistening crystal drops, which landed in a thick cascade between her fine, shapely breasts. Around her waist, he added a large silver chain dripping with longer chains of crystal drops, barely enough to cover her front and the cleavage of her buttocks.

Thomas stood back, admiring his breathtaking handiwork. "You look absolutely radiant!" The afternoon sun stole through the window and caught the crystalline facets, setting off her slender figure in blazing rainbows of glory. He prayed in silence for her selection by someone worthy of a diamond princess, someone able to provide a most unique experience. Thomas glanced at the clock on the wall and grabbed his loincloth and armbands.

He snapped his fingers. "You know what, I nearly forgot. I have one more item left for you." He scurried to the drawer, pulled out another crystal item, and sped back over to Rose. On a ring attached to the back of her bib necklace, he hooked a jeweled leash.

"Oh, Thomas, how embarrassing. Do you really see me as a dog?" She smacked him on the arm. "Well, I must admit you're the sweetest pet around, wouldn't you agree?" He patted her on the head. "Actually, I'd make you walk on all fours and bark a little, but no one could see your jewelry. I didn't go to all this trouble for nothing."

She rolled her eyes and laughed again. "Well, I feel silly enough."

The clock chimed upon the appointed hour. "It's time. Let's go," Thomas pulled her along.

*   *   *

Outside in the courtyard, the air buzzed with excitement.

Animated conversations included last-minute instructions from attendants to their admits or suggestions on the best places to hide. Like a carnal mutual admiration society, bright eyes strolled from one to another. Though many wore adornments, Thomas swelled with pride, assured that his admit stood out above all the rest, sparkling and beautiful, like a prime champagne ready for tasting by the best connoisseur.

Pride turned into immediate dismay. He caught Joe staring at Rose, licking the bottom of his lips with a cold, calculating stare. The discovery made Thomas's stomach lurch and his heart pound. While Joe himself didn't present an immediate problem, his penchant for blood and pain did. In Thomas's opinion, this man's sexual preference didn't suit Rose. Though Joe was bound by ethics to cause no harm, and to only engage in these practices with an appropriate, willing partner, the knowledge of this did nothing to keep Thomas's throat from going dry from panic. In this game, all partners were new, and he wondered how much Joe might be willing to tone down his urges. Thomas stared out into the distance, trying to rack his brain for a way to intervene.

"Okay, admits, the game is about to begin. Be careful, and most of all, have fun. Everybody ready?" John, as master of ceremonies, prepared to sound off the battle cry. Everyone stopped their conversations in mid-sentence, and Rose gave Thomas a quick kiss.

"Just be careful," he said. Rose nodded, her eyes bright, and she ran and scrambled into place with the other admits at the edge of the courtyard. John raised his hand. The sound of a whistle split the air, followed by the command of "Go!"

In a mad dash, the admits thundered for the forest. Rose turned to blow Thomas one last kiss before she ran, like a shooting star, into the dimness of the forest. Thomas sighed and shook his head, overwhelmed with helplessness. Joe stood a few paces in front of him, eyes narrowed deep in thought, and stroked his chin.

"God, I'm worried about her." John peered into the distance. "Did you see the way Joe looked at her?"

Thomas jerked around to face him. "You and me both. Joe knows every inch of these grounds and where every move will land you. These woods are dense, but there are places where the sun shines through. With those crystals she's wearing, he'll find her." He shook his head and looked at John with pleading eyes. "I didn't realize her jewelry could be her undoing. Isn't there anything we can do?"

John shaded his eyes from the sun and peered off into the distance. All the admits had made it somewhere into the woods. All who remained in the courtyard were attendants chatting in congenial tones, biding their time. "Thomas, you know the rules. We'll just have to leave everything to fate. Joe is bound by House ethics, and I've never received any complaints about him from an admit."

"Are you sure his admits aren't too scared to tell someone?" Thomas gave a small laugh.

John grinned. "I think you and I may be overreacting a bit. Our tastes are different to his, and face it, we just want to protect her, that's all. Maybe she'll get tagged by someone else." He faced Thomas and patted him on the shoulder. "You did a great job with her, by the way. I wish I was playing this game today. I'd tag her myself."

"No rule says you can't." Thomas smiled at John and raised his eyebrows, hopeful.

"This event has no place for stewards, Thomas, but I feel your pain. Really I do."

"Well, you can't blame a guy for trying, can you?"

John shook his head; a light smile crossed his lips. "I think she'll be fine." He left Thomas and returned to his podium. "All right, attendants," he shouted, "time to find your new admit. Ready, go!" All the attendants ran toward the woods, scattering in different directions. Thomas made a start, but John stopped him. "Thomas, remember, you can't pick your own admit, so don't go try to find her first."

"Yeah, I hear you." Thomas hung his head in despair. Deep in his heart, he knew rules could be broken, and if necessary, he would protect Rose at all costs.

*   *   *

Rose immersed herself in the scenery as she ran over leafy trails, captivated by the beauty of the woods. The crunch of the ground beneath her feet and the fresh air in her face infused her with a sense of raw energy and vitality, and she wanted to run forever.

Today marked her first time outside The House since her arrival, and she intended to make the most of it. Though she preferred a leisurely stroll, she knew the rules, and one of the rules said she needed a hiding place. Her plan included a hidden stakeout post where she could slink out and at least appear available for the first attendant who seemed nice and safe enough.

A noise in the distance caught her attention. She stopped, turned her ear, and listened. Her eyes lit up. The waterfall! Concerns with the game vanished, and she sped through the woods until she arrived at a pool surrounded by rocks. Her eyes followed the stony cliff to a cleft where water ran from deep within the earth and tumbled into the pool below. She scanned the hills leading up to the top from either side, where one could cross from one side of the forest to the other over the falls. Quite interesting. Several feet away from the top, she spied trees once again. The forest must continue from that tree line. Lost in thought, she stood, swarmed by rays of sunlight, cooled by mist from the water. Enough with daydreams. She needed to continue with the game.

"Tag, I've got you." A male voice boomed in her ear. A pair of rough, strong arms grabbed her from behind and enveloped her in an iron grip. Rose, startled, caught the glimpse of a pair of attractive, neatly groomed, hands about her waist, but the flash of a silver claw-like cover over the tip of one finger frightened her. As he loosened his grasp, she turned around and faced her captor. The sight filled her with dread, and her heart sank. The strange man she'd seen behind the gate upon her arrival stood before her, eyes gleaming, his mouth twisted into an evil grin. She hadn't liked the look of this attendant then, nor did she like him now. She tried her best to break free.

"Oh, you're not going anywhere." His eyes blazed with lust. "I've had my eye on you for quite a while, and you're mine for the afternoon." Joe, like a seasoned chess player, had calculated her every move with stunning accuracy, and now he intended to have her. Before she protested further, he scooped her up in his arms and placed her on a patch of green moss.

Rose trembled in fear. "Please, don't hurt me." She gasped as tears welled up in her eyes.

Joe leered down at her, eyes gleaming as she pleaded for mercy. The more the tears came, the more satisfied he seemed. "You know what, I've got a big cock. Know what I'd love to do with it? I'd like nothing better than to pump it right into that tight little pussy of yours, that's what." He forced two strong fingers between her legs, pressed in deep, and shoved them in and out with rapid force. She writhed in pain under his touch and struggled to free herself. But his arms held her fast. He forced himself on her again and sunk his tongue into her mouth in an attempt to steal a kiss, but she bit down in a heat of fear and fury.

"Ah-h!" He cried out in pain and jerked his tongue free. He glared down at her; an evil gleam filled his eyes. "So I see you're into pain, are you? Well, luckily for you I've come prepared." He raised his hand, brought down the silver claw, and with one slash, grazed her skin with its sharp point. She winced in pain as the cold metal sliced her skin. An aggravating sting filled her arm; droplets of blood seeped from the wound.

She let out a blood-curdling scream and made a quick lunge for his face with her hands, barely missing his eyes. Joe raised his hands, warding her off. Rose, finding an opportunity for escape, sprang up and made a run for the hill to the top of the falls.

*   *   *

Thomas stopped dead in his tracks. Where did that scream come from? The sound echoed off the rocks and bounced back to his ears. In his gut, he sensed something amiss. He often heard screams during this game, but they were usually accompanied by laughter or fun shouts of protests, but not this time. Perhaps an admit was running away from an attendant? Filled with panic, he ran to the edge of the woods and concealed himself behind a large tree. He strained his eyes over the other side of the falls just in time to catch Rose running up the hill, with Joe hard at her heels. His heart sank; the ill omen had come true at last. He cursed under his breath in dismay. Had he been that close to them this whole time?

"Don't you run away from me! Come back here, you!" Joe shouted, determined not to lose her. "You know the rules."

"Dear god, please run!" Thomas mumbled and clenched his fists, his heart racing.

Rose ran hard, but she finally made her way, tripping and sliding, to the top above the falls. Joe, several yards away, came bounding after her, fast and furious. She ran to the edge of the cliff, peered over, and then glanced back at him. She peered over again, and bent her knees, preparing for a jump into the icy cold water below. Thomas felt his blood go cold. *Oh, god, no! Please don't jump!* He wanted to shout, but like one caught in a bad nightmare, his voice was struck mute. Paralyzed, he stared, glued to the ground, forced to watch the scene before him.

Joe stopped a moment, uncertain. "Don't you try to bluff me," he shouted. You don't have the nerve to jump. It's a long way down, so give it up and get back here."

"Get away from me!" Rose screamed back at him. "I don't want you. Go find somebody else."

Joe pressed on anyway. "I'll get you yet. I tagged you first so you're mine."

"I'll jump. If you don't think I will, just watch me." She positioned herself one more time.

Thomas's horror had reached its height, but when he saw a flashing red flame out of the corner of his eye, he threw up both fists in triumph. Yes! Rose would now enjoy the afternoon with a more suitable partner. Satisfied, he left in search for an admit to play with.

*   *   *

"Tag, you're mine." A male voice filled her ear. "Let's back away from here before you get hurt." The voice behind her whispered, and another pair of arms, more kind than the first ones, gently pulled her back from the edge.

"Daren, let her go. She's mine!" Joe shouted, and moved faster toward them.

"I've got her, Joe. She's not yours anymore. Back off."

Joe stopped short. "The rules say she's mine. I tagged her first, and I'll have her, damn it." He stamped his foot in anger.

"The rules don't address an admit getting away. She's rightfully mine now, and I have no intention of giving her up."

Joe's eyes flashed with anger, and he clenched his fists tighter. "That's not fair, I tell you!"

"You don't have her, and I do. It's that simple. Now get out of here. You've caused enough trouble."

Joe glared at them, seething. "You're an ass, Daren. You can have your pampered crystal bitch. I don't care." He spat on the ground and, giving them one last hard look, turned around and made his way back into the woods.

Daren merely smiled and turned Rose around to face him. She gasped. He backed away, a concerned look on his face. She continued staring at him, the most striking creature she'd ever seen. Before her stood a handsome young man, tall and well-sculpted. His face, like smooth marble, was set with soft pink lips and sparkling amber eyes, the color of rich ale; his smile showed off straight, white teeth. But the most striking feature was his hair, blazing red like the flames of a fire out of control. Cut short, its thick, full body rested neatly around his head. The bulge beneath his loincloth spurred her curiosity.

"Don't mind him. Are you okay?" His face showed

concern. "You nearly had a bad end there. I was worried about you. I'm Daren, in case you didn't catch the name."

"I'm Rose. Yes, I think I'll be okay now. I didn't like him. I've seen him before, and he scares me."

"Doesn't surprise me. Joe isn't for everyone."

"Why is he allowed to work here?"

"Every staff member goes through an intense interview before they're hired, and directors of The House know that certain people will want attendants like Joe. He fills a need, and believe it or not, he's quite competent at what he does." Daren smiled and put his arm around her. "But personally, I have a hunch you and I are much more suitable together than you and Joe. I was up at the top here, and I saw he had tagged you. I was coming down to help, but you got away."

"How come I didn't see you, then?" Rose viewed him with curiosity.

"When I saw you running up, I hid again to see what would happen." He looked at her with a warm smile.

Rose glanced down at her arm, still stinging where Joe's silver claw had made its impression. She checked the scratch and discovered the bleeding had mostly stopped.

"Let's get back down to the water's edge, and I'll help you with your arm." Daren chuckled and picked up the jeweled leash hanging from Rose's collar. "I must say you're quite dazzling in those crystals. This leash is great. I love it." With a light tug, he pulled her toward him. "Come, my tender pet. This afternoon is ours." Filled with relief and a new sense of adventure, she followed him back down the same hill she'd fought so hard to climb just minutes earlier, thankful the tides had turned in her favor.

*   *   *

When they reached the bottom of the hill, Daren led her to a mossy spot under a large old tree. They were a few yards from the pool, and the cool air and mist from the water soothed her skin. Daren helped her down and took a moment to examine her arm.

"Wow, he scratched you good, didn't he? Hmm … doesn't look too deep, though. Luckily, it appears to be on the surface." He pulled off a leather bag he carried over his shoulder and reached inside, pulling out a few packets of cleanser. With tender care, he cleaned her arm. "There, I think that should do it for now." He grinned at her and pushed back a strand of hair hanging loosely around her face.

"What do you have in that bag?" Rose stared at him with curiosity.

"Not much." He shrugged. "I usually carry some basic items for times of trouble … or … fun. The rest is my secret." He gave her a sly smile and patted the bag. "You know what, though, all this excitement has made me hungry. What about you?"

"Unfortunately, as you can see, I don't have any food with me." She held out empty hands.

"Here's where my trusty bag comes in handy." He patted the soft leather with a smile. "Now let's think about all this for a minute. You see, I had the wonderful fortune of tagging and rescuing one as lovely as yourself, which means you are now obligated to me. Would you agree?"

"I think so." She nodded. She liked Daren, but his comment instilled a certain discomfort. What did he mean by her being obligated? By her standards, obligations were best avoided.

"Good, then we have an agreement. You are bound to me, to do my bidding, since I rescued you from that horrible ogre." He laughed, reached inside his bag and pulled out a spike with a ring on the end and a small mallet. With a few loud raps, he hammered the spike into the ground.

"There, it's in there tight. Now, I need you to lie down. Here, let me help you take all this off first." He removed the jewelry and placed the sparkling costume in his leather bag. Rose stood totally naked, embarrassed, and vulnerable. She moved her hands from her top to her bottom, unsure what area to hide first. "What's the matter? You seem nervous."

She blushed. "I just feel so naked without something on."

"Well, let's face it, you are naked, but I won't hold it against you." With a teasing smile, he pointed to the ground. Rose, in obedience, dropped down and stretched out. "Give me your arms." Daren took her arms and placed them over her head. He tied her wrists together and attached them to the ring on the spike. "Good. No chance of your getting away from me. I know how you like to run." He reached in his bag one more time and pulled out a blindfold.

"Um, do we really need to use this?" She pouted. "I hate not being able to see."

"Really? I'm so sorry to hear that. But, yes, we really do need to use this." He chuckled and slipped the covering over her eyes. "By the way, as part of your obligation to me, how about we have an agreement?"

"What's that?" Rose liked his jovial mood, which spread a relaxing effect over her.

"Let's agree you won't question me when I tell you to do something. Is that clear?"

"Yes, Master." She used the sultriest voice possible, struggling hard not to laugh.

"Ah, master, is it? I like that. Now just lie back and give yourself over to me. You're mine, remember?"

Rose heard him rummage through the bag. She jumped. Something cold and wet moved in circles on one of her nipples. A few seconds later, a soft, warm tongue licked and sucked the same place. An ache spread throughout her pelvic region. Daren held another wet item to her lips. She reached out her tongue and licked the sweet juice. With a gentle push, he placed the rest of the treat in her mouth. She recognized the taste of fruit, a piece of melon, a grape, and then a strawberry.

"This is good, Daren." She licked her lips. "I didn't realize I was so hungry."

Daren said nothing, but Rose felt his soft lips on hers, as he slipped his tongue deep into her mouth. He hooked his hands behind her knees, pulled them up, and spread her thighs apart. The warm air brushed against her skin, teasing her with a wispy tongue. The thickness between her legs grew stronger; she tried to anticipate his next move. She gasped at the sensation of a cold substance dripping between her legs. The tickle made her twitch.

"Oh, god, Daren, that's cold. What is it?"

"Sh-h-h. You'll see."

She wriggled as the contents trickled down between her legs and over her anus. Daren grazed an unidentified object over her clit, swirled it into the pool between her legs, and placed the morsel into her mouth. Rose now understood her crotch served as a vessel for the condiment covering the fruit he placed in her mouth. She licked her lips and enjoyed the sweet, creamy flavor. He fed her a few more pieces of fruit and then he stopped. Her heart skipped a beat. Warm and soft, his mouth came down on her, licking at the cream with firm strokes. The flicks of his tongue hit her clit, stoking the storm building inside her. He scooped up one of her soft, small lips with his tongue and sucked softly, followed by soft easy strokes into each wet, sweet fold.

She sighed, strained her thighs further apart. "You feel so good, Daren." He took his time, lapping at her entrance, pushing his tongue is as far as he could. Then he worked his way up back up over her clit. Filled with a new sense of urgency, she hoped her release came soon. But he lingered over sensitive areas of her flesh, unconcerned with neither time nor her need for satisfaction. Just as her loins prepared for orgasm, he stopped. "Oh, Daren—please don't stop!"

He neither moved nor spoke.

She sighed and dug her heels into the ground, trying to drown her frustration.

"Impatient, are we?" Daren removed the blindfold. Wincing from the blinding shock of sunlight, she turned her head. "I'm sorry, the sun's pretty bright, isn't it?"

He positioned himself above her and shaded her eyes from the glare. She blinked. God, he was beautiful! He kissed her again. Her tongue teased the inside of his mouth and tasted the lingering sweetness from the fruit and confection. The hardness under his loincloth announced the need for its own release, and she opened her legs wide again, inviting him in. He glanced at the spike, reached over, and with a flick of his wrists, released the bindings around her hands. Rose lifted the loincloth and placed her hands around his hips for support while he lodged his full pink tip inside her.

In one swift push, he slipped inside her. She pressed her head hard against the ground and gasped. His smooth entrance wracked her whole body, awakening the old ache within her. He placed a soft kiss on her neck, then on her earlobe. Rose took his head in her hands, guided his face over hers, and lavished a soft, deep kiss on his lips. She ran her delicate fingers through the glowing red locks of his hair, traced the outline of his shapely ears, and then hugged him close to her. His heart pounded against her chest, alive, vital. With quick undulations, his hips glided, his full cock lost within her tight walls. She gave off a small moan, accepting each thrust with a smile. He moved faster, his breaths filling her ears like the rush of wind. The muscles in her backside clenched, and the fullness in her core grew heavier, a sweet pleasure pain. With a soft groan, he released a rich stream of lust. He smiled down at her before smothering her with another deep kiss.

*   *   *

He reclined back on the moss and stared up at the sky. Rose, meanwhile, admired the cockhead that topped his shaft, its pretty shape, the soft pink color. She wanted nothing more than to savor its taste, run her tongue over its silky flesh, play at the opening with her tongue and coax out the creamy treat hidden inside.

Her cheeks flushed. Daren had turned his head and caught her staring, but said nothing. A soft smile crept across his face, and his eyes glazed, as though lost in a dream. He flipped over on his side and reached out his hand. Rose stretched out and relaxed as his fingers grasped the pink flesh of one of her nipples. The breeze whispered all around, and she relished the warmth, along with the cotton-soft movements of Daren's hands and the occasional sharp pinch from his fingers. The sounds of the waterfall hummed a lulling tune beside them.

Daren broke the silence. "Rose, have you ever drunk from the waters of life?"

"Huh? Um … the waters of life?" Curious, she turned her head at him, her eyebrow arched over a questioning eye.

"Yes, the waters of life."

"No, I can't say that I have. I've heard of the Fountain of Youth. Come to think of it, I may have heard about the water of life mentioned in other teachings, too, but I don't remember. What are you talking about, exactly?"

"Several years ago, I traveled with my family to a faraway land. While I was there I learned from an ancient teaching that one could achieve health and vitality by drinking occasionally from the waters of life. The stories say they are nourishing and healthy." "Oh, that's interesting. I've really never heard of such a thing. And where would these waters be, I might ask?"

"Actually they say these waters reside deep in the belly."

"Deep in the belly? How odd. What do you mean?"

"Deep in the belly, Rose. Literally, deep within the belly."

"Of a human being? In us?" She sat up in surprise. He sat up too. They faced each other, locked together in a long stare.

He continued. "Yes, Rose, deep within ourselves." He paused a moment as she stared back at him in silence. His golden eyes flashed with an intense sparkle. "When I brought you down here, you agreed to do whatever I asked, remember? I said you were to do as I say without question."

"Yes, Daren, I remember. What do you want?" She became a little concerned, her voice filled with urgency. Where was this conversation leading, and what on earth did he want from her? Surely it couldn't be too bad.

"Rose, I want us to partake of the waters of life, here and now."

She raised her eyebrows, her mouth fell open. "Oh, and how do we do that?"

"I'll show you. Stand up."

Rose, stunned beyond belief, sat there and stared at him, unable to move. "Daren, do we really have to?" His request made her uneasy, and she suddenly wanted to run.

"You heard what I said." His voice rang out, steady, determined. "I need you to stand up. Now. Do what I say. Without question."

"Okay, Daren. But please don't get cross with me."

"I'm not getting cross, but when I tell you to do something, I need you to do it." He softened. "Now place your feet apart just a little, like this …" He planted a foot between her feet and pushed her legs apart. "There, that's good." He knelt down before her and placed one hand around her buttocks and one hand on her lower abdomen. "Are you feeling a little full, Rose?" he said, pressing in .

She winced, taken aback by discomfort and the question he put before her. But she knew he expected a truthful answer. "Yes, Daren, I am." The consumption of juicy fruit and the passing of time had taken its toll on her. Her blood turned cold; her face turned pale. The realization of what was about to happen dawned on her. Oh, lord, he surely wasn't serious, was he? She grimaced and braced herself. Daren's fingers slipped inside her. With gentle strokes of his soft, wet tongue against her clit, he worked up a throbbing ache between her thighs. Her knees weakened and she placed her hands around his head for support. She closed her eyes, ready for a strong climax. A few more circles of his tongue, and his persistence paid off. Her thighs quivered, and her interior burst into waves of hard spasms. All that remained was a burning, nagging urge, a desire for relief of a different kind.

"Now I need you to release yourself." His voice was calm, collected. "You'll need to use some discipline and control when you do this because I want every drop from you. Do you hear me? Every drop. Now go."

Rose felt his fingers spread her open. A light heat warmed her skin as his mouth moved in position in a tight fit over her flesh. She gritted her teeth. With a skillful tongue, he located the other tiny hidden orifice, the entrance to her internal fountain; and his tiny flicks and probing elicited a light peppery sting. Her heart pounded. Unnerved, she stood, paralyzed. One thing for sure, she didn't want to make him angry or displease him in any way, but one main question lingered. Would she be able to relax her body enough to give him what he wanted? The gushing sounds from the waterfall seemed to grow louder, intensify the burning in her lower abdomen.

An idea popped into her head. What if she used the sound of the falls for assistance with the task at hand? If Daren wanted water, then she must be his waterfall and release her fluids, like Mother Earth released hers. With a new resolve, she firmed up her grip on either side of his head for support and prepared herself. *Good, this may be easy after all.* She closed her eyes, immersed herself in the sounds of falling water, and commanded her muscles to relax. With a light muscular push, she released a small stream into his mouth, and she felt his lips and tongue move against her with a sucking rhythm. She stopped and allowed him to get his breath. Though her bottom burned in protest, she now understood the need for control, lest he drown in her fluids. She let out another stream, and then another. She heard him swallow as she poured herself out to him little by little, until her golden pool ran dry.

"I'm done, Daren." She relaxed with relief. He gave his tongue one last sweep at her opening before he removed his mouth.

He looked up at her and smiled. "It wasn't too bad, was it? You actually did a good job. Many people can't control themselves well. It's hard."

"I can see why. I'm surprised I was able to do it."

"Now it's your turn, Rose." He stood up. "Are you ready?"

"Oh, I guess so," she said. Her face clouded. Now the tables had turned. Uneasiness set in, and she wondered if she would lose her nerve.

"Look, Rose, I saw you staring at me a few minutes ago, with a hungry look in your eyes. I can give you what you want. Now get down on your knees like I did, and we'll begin."

Rose stalled a moment. His request pushed this game to the extremes. For a moment she regretted not staying with Joe. How crazy could he really be? Surely not any worse than this. But didn't doctors in olden times actually taste the fluids of a patient to determine a certain illness? She thought a history lesson taught that fact. She glanced up at Daren, hoping he'd change his mind, but the look he gave her indicated that she was not getting out of this situation.

She took a deep breath and sighed. He reached out his arms and, placing them on either side of her shoulders, firmly but gently, pushed her to her knees. His head rose before her, ready for tasting. Yes, true enough, she had wanted him earlier, but her original intent had now turned into something different, something altogether strange. He slowly guided himself into her open mouth, ready to release the libation his body was about to offer. She stroked the full, silky tip with her tongue, tracing its shape.

"Are you ready?" He ran his fingers through her hair.

She stroked one of his buttocks with her finger to indicate she was indeed ready. A warm stream trickled into her mouth as he let down his pelvic contents. He stopped a moment, just as she had done for him a few moments ago. He allowed her a few seconds to become familiar with the taste of his fluids. The taste was salty, not much different from salt water. Perhaps a very slight tinge of a lemony tang, though she sensed other properties that were a little difficult to describe. All in all, not too bad, not bad at all. Perhaps she could handle this. He continued again; she swallowed. Cupping his scrotum with her hands, Rose finally settled herself down to such a degree that he was able to produce a controlled, steady stream. Like one drinking from a golden fountain, she consumed the contents released from deep inside his belly. She swallowed without ceasing, without really tasting anymore. His fluids merged with her body. They were hers now, just as she was contained within him.

He stopped. "I'm done, now," he whispered softly, stroking her hair with his fingers. "You are amazing. I've never had anyone take to this quite like you did."

"It wasn't as bad as I thought it would be." She grinned up at him. "This has to be the weirdest thing I've ever done. I had to put myself totally into it, try not to think too hard, if you know what I mean."

"I do know what you mean." He pulled her back up to a standing position and hugged her close to him, smelling the sweet fragrance of her hair.

* * *

"Hey, buddy!" A shout sounded from the woods. Thomas and his tagged admit emerged and walked towards them.

Daren smiled and waved.

"Do you mind if we join you?" Thomas sidled up to his friend.

"Not at all." Daren cocked his head. "And who is this lovely lady you have here?"

"This is Daria." Thomas gave the girl a quick kiss on her full, pink lips. A rather striking young girl, her athletic figure held a head of glossy, straight black hair that curled under her chin. A few soft freckles played beneath her dark eyes, and below perched a cute button nose. Like the other admits, she wore nothing, except a metal pendant on a black leather cord secured tightly about her slender throat. The most striking feature about her consisted of two small silver rings, each piercing a nipple. When she turned in certain directions, the sun struck the metallic surfaces, shooting off flashes of steely fire. "So you two haven't tried out the water and gone for a swim?" Thomas angled his head toward the waterfall.

"Are you kidding? That water is freezing!" Daren

shivered. "Even on a warm day like today, I don't particularly care to be cold. But you know what, there is a hot spring located here on the grounds. Let's go there instead."

"Great idea, Daren." Thomas's eyes brightened. "I completely forgot about that."

"There's a hot spring here? Nobody ever told me." Rose tugged on Daren's arm. "That sounds like fun. I want to go."

"Oh, yes," he said, "the water comes from deep inside the earth and picks up minerals from the rocks as it flows through the ground. They say the waters have healing properties as a result. Most of us just like to soak and relax there. It helps get your body in the mood, if you know what I mean." He winked at Rose as he put his arm around her waist.

"Well, what are you waiting for? Lead the way," Thomas waved an arm forward. Daren move ahead and found the trail leading to the spring. They all followed, winding deeper into the forest.

"So what makes the water hot?" Daria picked up a stone and tossed it into the woods.

"There must be hot places in the ground, and the water is heated as it flows," Thomas said. "It's still hot when it comes up through the ground. Rather interesting, isn't it? Ah, such is the wonder of nature." He turned and kissed her again. "I think *you're* a wonder of nature." After several minutes, the couples found themselves at the edge of a large pool.

"Sh-h-h, listen." Daren cocked an ear in the direction of a sound. They all stopped and strained their ears. They heard soft bubbling as water percolated into the spring. The foliage from the trees provided ample shade from the burning sun, and green, velvet moss wove a soft, springy carpet in and around jutting rocks that lined the spring's edge. From the sky, the shrill sound of a hawk filled the air.

"I can't wait to get in there." Daren dropped his bag, divesting himself of the loincloth.

"You and me both." Thomas stripped and padded to the edge of the spring where he dipped in his toe. "Boy, does this feel good!"

Daren came up behind him. "Was this a great idea or what?"

"Excellent as usual. I wish I'd thought of it myself." Thomas gave Daren's back a slap of approval. "Let's get in."

The girls watched from a distance, whispering as they admired the muscular ripples of thigh and buttock muscles of the men as they climbed over the rocks before slipping into the water.

"How is it?" Daria called out to the men.

"Hey, you girls come on in. It's great in here," Thomas waved them over. "Just be careful getting in. Use the rocks for support."

Daria and Rose tiptoed over the mossy patches. They crept over the rocks and sunk into liquid warmth. Rose settled in next to Daren, who encircled her in his arm, while Daria made her way to Thomas.

"How deep is this spring?" Daria moved her leg in different directions. "I can't find the bottom with my foot."

Thomas turned to Daren for an answer.

Daren shrugged. "I have no idea. Nobody's ever told me. At least we have enough rocks for a nice seating ledge, though." He closed his eyes and reclined back, sinking his body deeper into the water, which now reached just under his chin.

Rose broke the long silence and whispered in Daren's ear, "Is this a place where fairies dance?" She giggled and nipped his earlobe. He grabbed her arm and pulled her onto his lap, causing her to nearly slip off the ledge. She let out a startled little squeal.

He laughed and caught her quickly in his arms. "I don't know but there's a part of me that wants to dance."

She threw back her head and laughed. As she squirmed onto his lap and straddled her thighs around his waist, he slid in his erection with light thrusts of his hips. Daren supported her back with one hand and worked the tip of her breast with the other. Rose cupped his head in her hands and teased his mouth with her tongue. On a whim, she contracted and released her inner walls, squeezing and releasing his shaft with a firm, steady rhythm. Daren threw back his head and closed his eyes. His jaw tightened and his body tensed. In a few moments he opened his eyes and gave Rose a smile.

*   *   *

Across the spring Daria threw her head back in a loud moan as Thomas fingered through her wet folds. She dove under the water, placed her head between his legs, and took him into her mouth, sucking hard. On impulse, he broke free from her grasp, long enough to pull himself onto a large flat rock and settle back. She popped up out of the water, laughing as she straddled his hips. While her face dropped over his in an attempt to kiss his lips, his quick, agile fingers gently squeezed the tips of her nipples. He smiled; she giggled; her cleft grazed over the hard thickness between his thighs.

"Here, get up a minute." He jumped up and pulled her from the rock and led her to a mossy spot under a tree by the edge of the spring. "Hey, you guys want to switch up?" Thomas glanced from Daren to Rose.

Rose nodded and smiled.

"Yeah, that's fine with us." Daren grinned at Daria. "I want to check out those hot rings you've got."

"You come on over here then, Daren. You can play all day long if you want to." Daria plucked at her nipples with her fingers, and blew him a kiss.

When Daren and Rose reached the mossy spot, Thomas turned to Rose. "Come on, let's go somewhere else and leave these two alone. Daren, we'll be over there." He pointed to an area several yards away. Daren smiled and waved them off, nodding in acknowledgement.

"Alone at last." Daria gazed up at Daren with a smile as he sat down beside her. She reached up a slender finger and caressed his cheek. "I'm all yours."

"You're such a sweet one. "He licked at one of the nipples of her breast and played with the ring, making her moan. "These are great. I love them." He nipped at the other nipple, making her giggle.

"Daren, have you ever thought about getting that gorgeous cockhead of yours pierced?"

"Ah, a Prince Albert piercing. I think he started the trend, didn't he? And because the trousers of his day were made to fit tight, men got their piercing done so they could move their equipment aside and look nicer in their clothes."

"That's what I've read in historical writings. Whether or not it's true, I don't know. Either way, I still think you'd look good with one. Nice to know we women aren't the only ones who'll go out on a limb for fashion, huh?" Daria pulled him over and cupped his face in her hands. "I think you'd feel good and hot inside with something like that. I just know you'd rub me the right way."

"You don't think you'd like me just as I am? I'm hurt, you know." Daren turned his lips down and pretended to sniffle.

"I think you'll feel wonderful no matter what."

He smiled and moved in closer, pressing his lips over hers. With a gentle push, he slipped his tongue into her mouth; she kissed him with a tomboyish roughness. When the kiss ended, she smiled, stretched out, and opened her thighs.

Daren moved his head down and flicked his tongue over her clit. "You're such a treat, so sweet and moist, too." He dipped his tongue in deeper, working faster this time.

Daria lifted her chest and arched her back. "Yes … easy … that's good …" Her hips jerked, keeping time with each spasm that rolled inside.

"Good girl. Are you ready for me? Because I'm more than ready for you."

Daria nodded and stroked his hair. Daren placed himself between her thighs and readied himself for a swift insertion. The final move made her howl as her nether regions swallowed him to the hilt. He glided back and forth, pressed and pulled, his full tip grazing the sensitive area buried deep inside. His breaths became faster and shorter; his face flushed. She smiled up at him and, with a lusty gleam in her eye, squeezed her walls around him with such a grip that his shaft finally burst forth a load of thick, creamy semen.

"God, you're strong. Are you sure that sweet muff of yours doesn't have a nice set of teeth hiding in there?"

"I'm sure of one thing, Daren, you're as hot and fiery as your hair." She ran her hands over his head, winding her fingers within his thick waves. "And I like your hot-shot, bullet ramming me even better, even if you don't have yourself adorned with that sweet little extra we talked about earlier." She pulled his face down and kissed him. "Feel free to take aim and shoot me any time."

"I'm glad to oblige, ma'am," he said, trying to imitate his best western accent. "Thanks for the ride."

*   *   *

Thomas and Rose trailed back to the spot where they had first arrived. The sun peeked through the branches of the trees and enshrined the area in soft gold. He took her in his arms, held her close, and kissed her.

"I've missed you this afternoon." He stroked her cheek with a finger.

"Oh, really? Have you?" She gave him a sideways glance. "I would have thought you had other things to amuse you more."

Thomas looked at her a moment, puzzled. He shook his head lightly, dismissing her comment. "Nonsense." He pulled her down beside him on the ground and pushed her back. He rested easy on top of her supple body, shielding her face with his. "You are my crystal princess, after all. But I'm sorry."

"Sorry for what?"

"I didn't think about the jewelry causing you problems. I saw Joe before the game started, and he was giving you the eye. I prayed he wouldn't find you, but I heard you scream. Then

I saw you run away from him. I tried to yell, but things just happened so fast. Honestly, Rose, I nearly died with fright when you looked like you might jump off that cliff."

"Oh, I would have, rocks and all. Even if it killed me." She lifted her head and gave him a quick kiss.

"That's not funny, Rose. You really scared me." He peered down at her face and frowned at her poor taste in humor.

"I'm sorry, Thomas." Her smile faded. "Oh, you wouldn't miss me that much, would you?" The corners of her mouth twitched; her eyes sparkled.

With an impatient sigh, he rolled his eyes. "You don't think so? You silly girl, of course I would." He stared off in the distance, lost a moment in thought. "You know, Rose, though we haven't spent much time together during the last few years, just knowing you were around always gave me some comfort."

"Really, Thomas? I never knew that."

"Yes, really."

"You know what? Me, too."

He placed a soft kiss on her lips and stroked her hair with his fingers. On the top of each breast, he placed a kiss, savoring each peak on top. His tongue moved down over her abdomen, and just before he reached her willing cleft, he turned around and repositioned his hips over her head, his plump tip barely touching her mouth. Rose shot out her warm, pink tongue and licked the blossoming head bobbing over her lips, moving over the silky flesh with vigorous strokes. Thomas jerked at her touch. His lips came down on her, tasting the thick fluids, warm and sweet.

She opened her legs to the fullest and closed her eyes, ready for the gentle touch of his lips against her most sensitive parts. His hot breath hit her skin, and soft aches of pleasure mounted with each lick, thrust, and tug of his tongue and lips over the firm knot between her legs, searing her flesh with his caressing flames. Her fingers toyed with his sac, rolling each ball with a gentle squeeze. His body tensed, and he withdrew himself a little from her mouth.

Determined, she grabbed him, sinking him back down into

her mouth. Entrenching him in darkness, she nursed his shaft and tip, greedy, sucking hard, wanting more. Unable to contain himself, he lifted up and released warm, dripping streams of lust. With one last go, he focused on her clit, and within seconds, the tension that had coiled up within her, like a snake in hiding, struck out, sprang for freedom, and writhed out its pleasure with reckless abandon. Exhausted, he tumbled off and pulled her into his arms. Both lay breathless on the ground.

* * *

"Hey, guys, are you all ready to go back?" Daren called out as he and Daria made their way to where Rose and Thomas lay. "The sun's starting to set. We probably need to head on back to The House before it gets dark."

Thomas turned his eyes toward the sun. "Yeah, I think you're right. The game time is pretty much over. Let's get our loincloths back on and head back."

"Here, Rose, let me help you get this on." Daren pulled out her crystal bib and belt from his leather bag and refastened everything in place.

As they trudged through the woods, Thomas turned to his two friends. "Did you two enjoy yourselves while we were away?" Daria smiled up at Daren, who pulled her closer to him.

"We had a wonderful time, and I got to play with these sweet ringed tits, too." Daren paused long enough to kiss one of Daria's nipples.

Rose leaned toward Daria. "Tell me more about the rings you're wearing. I've never seen anyone with those before."

Daria smiled, studying her chest. "I got these here at The House. I've haven't had them too long. I didn't do it for pleasure and style, but more to satisfy the rebellious streak I have. My family would die if they knew I had these."

"Don't they hurt?"

"Believe it or not, no. Getting your tits pierced isn't as bad as you'd think, but having a terrific piercer who knows how to do it is the main thing."

"I don't know if I've ever known of anyone who has these. Is this a new fashion trend?"

"Actually, nipple piercing has been around for centuries, even longer." Daria turned to face Rose and continued the history lesson. "Women used to attach a decorative chain between the two rings and wear their gowns with the bust line so low, you would see their entire breasts. Of course this was all done among the societal elite as a fashion statement."

Rose continued staring at her, but remained silent.

"I'll say this," Daria said, lifting up and jiggling her ornate globes, "I would have stopped at nothing to have these done."

Chapter 5

LAUGHTER FROM DOWN THE HALL attracted Rose's attention, and she grabbed Thomas's hand, dragging him toward the noise as fast as her feet allowed. When sounds of mirth met her ears, she never missed a chance to witness the provenance of its source, hoping to catch some enticing action she may have missed before.

Upon finding the room, however, the scene of interest stunned her sensibilities, leaving her unsure whether to react with amusement or disgust. The occupants inside the room cared nothing for her opinion, engaging in their rowdy play as if their visitors didn't exist. The woman, attractive with a smooth complexion and light red hair cut into a shapely bob, straddled an attractive, muscular male with sandy-blond hair. Though her figure showed off curves in all the right places, her breasts struck Rose as the main focal point. They were swollen in size beyond any she'd ever seen, and her surprise came when the woman expressed her mammary fluid from a plump, red nipple. Her companion opened his mouth, hoping to catch the spray, but her precarious aim landed most of her contents on his face. They both roared with laughter. Rose stood watching in silence.

The lady now licked his face, lapping up the last milky drops. "Here, let's try this." She lowered an engorged mound, which he accepted in his mouth, sucking and pulling at the nipple with a new greed. The woman smiled. "There, is that good, precious? Are you getting enough? I love it when you go at me hard. It feels so good to unload this stuff." She stroked his hair, then reached between his thighs and surrounded the head of his shaft with her fingers, working around his head with a slow rhythm. Under her nimble touch, an erection bloomed, full, with pre-cum oozing from the top. At this moment she stopped short and glanced up at Rose and Thomas standing in the doorway.

"Hey, Thomas, you sweet thing! Why don't you come over here and see what mamma's got. Come on, I won't bite. It's fresh and warm, just the way you like it." She flashed him an alluring smile.

Ignoring Rose's look of dismay, Thomas grinned and headed toward the appetizing lady on the floor. "You don't have to ask me twice."

"Honey, there's some sweet stuff down below. Help yourself. I need a good tongue-lashing." The lady removed her breast from the blond man's mouth, and reclined on the floor, spreading her thighs apart.

"And a good tongue-lashing you'll get. Even more if I have something to do with it." Her companion chuckled and settled himself between her legs. He took a couple of his fingers and spread her lips apart and, with a flicking, wet tongue, started lapping at her wet flesh.

"Yeah—Oh—god, that feels so good," she said, eyes closed, spreading her thighs even wider. "Settle in, Thomas, like the good boy you are. You know the routine."

Thomas knelt down on the floor beside her and stretched himself out, placing his face over her breast. With a few playful licks of her nipple, he began sucking, swallowing her milk like one starved.

Rose's eyebrows shot up. What other routines did he know? She frowned, but the scene she witnessed held her in its own twisted grip, so she stared, paralyzed, unable—unwilling—to move.

The lady groaned as the blond man grasped her clit, sucking hard. He slid in two fingers, swirling her thick fluids in quick, circular motions. Rose leaned back against the door frame, listening to the faint sounds of soft swishing, accompanied by sighs of content.

"Oh, Thomas, you're a good boy." She smiled and closed her eyes again. "Yes, sweetheart, suck it good. Mamma's got plenty for her boy, yes she does."

"You're warm and tasty as always, Miranda." Thomas gave her ripe nipple a quick nip.

"Don't forget the other one, darling. We don't want any of the girls feeling lonely or ignored, do we?"

"Absolutely not!" Thomas nestled down further, snuggling

in closer as he took the nipple of the other breast in his mouth and continued consuming the new fluid she offered.

Miranda reached out and rubbed his back with affection. "M-m-m, there's nothing better than your sweet lips sucking away at my tits. You know to get a gal going." Before long she let out a shout. "Oh, Mike … god, yes…!" She tightened her jaw as her hips jerked with strong orgasmic contractions.

"Okay, Miranda. My turn now. I can't hold out any longer." Mike, a little out of breath, pressed his fat cock deep inside her, grunting as he moved, hips undulating faster. A few more staccato thrusts, he shuddered, unloading his thick, milky lust with a groan of relief.

All three stopped and looked at each other with a smile. Miranda let out a satisfied laugh. "God, you two were great!"

Rose cleared her throat and glared down at all three.

"I think it's time for me to go." Thomas smiled and stood up. "Thanks, Miranda. You too, Mike."

He sped down the hall and tried to catch up with Rose, who outpaced him by several steps. "Hey, what's the matter with you?"

"So you know the routine? Tell me, Thomas, do you indulge yourself so often that it's now routine for you? Is that it?"

"If I'm not mistaken, you were the one who couldn't wait to see what all the fuss was about. I followed you. Remember?"

Rose spun around and faced him, her eyes blazing. Thomas pulled her close and attempted to calm her with a kiss. The hard bulge between his thighs pressed against her, but his advances only fueled her anger. "How dare you! That's just … ugh!" She shuddered and pushed him away.

Thomas stifled a laugh, but said, in the most coaxing voice, "Oh, come on, Rose, don't be that way. It was all in fun." He made a move to take her in his arms once again.

"I said, stop it! Don't you come near me! Anyway, I have nothing to offer you. Sorry, I'm fresh out of milk." She whirled around again and continued down the hall.

* * *

Thomas, though somewhat amused by her outburst, decided this behavior needed to end. Her opinionated spirit always managed to fire up his lust. Besides, her little outburst served as a reminder that a good punishment always awaited the wayward admit. This time, his mind conjured up a clever one, which would no doubt cool her temper's fiery flames while serving to fan the flames in his loins. With a lunge, he jerked her close, picked her up, and tossed her over his shoulder.

"Put me down!" she screamed.

He paid no attention to her request and continued resolutely down the hallway.

"Thomas, do you need any help?" a staff member stepped out from behind the desk, her coworker trailing behind her.

"No, I'm fine, thanks. Not to worry, I'll fix her."

"Somebody's going to be in trouble!" The female desk attendant sang out the last words in jest to her male coworker, who stifled a laugh.

"Thomas knows how to handle you women." The gentleman grinned. "Trust me, he'll bring her down a notch or two."

When Thomas reached their room, he dumped Rose on the bed. "Enough of your impudence." In vain, she tried to scramble away, but he held her down with his weight. He grabbed her arms and placed them over her head. To her horror, she heard two loud clicks, finding herself cuffed to the bed.

"What are you doing?" Her voice filled with anger and panic.

"I didn't know you harbored a jealous streak, Rose." Thomas gave her a stern look.

With a light stroke of his chin, he stood and thought a moment, planning the particulars on how to proceed next. He knew his stalling only made her more impatient, and he took his time, gaining the upper hand while she waited, trembling. With a snap of his fingers, he crossed over to the chest of drawers and pulled out a towel and a large brass bowl with handles. The polished metal glinted in the sunlight and flashed sparkles of gold along the walls and ceiling.

"What are you going to do with that?" Rose's voice inched up several decibels. Thomas returned to the bed in silence, straddled her thighs, and untied the knot of her dress straps from behind her neck. He slipped off the dress and tossed it to the floor. The bright red material hit the carpet with a soft swish, leaving Rose on the bed, naked and vulnerable. He returned to the drawers and returned with a pair of cuffs, which he snapped on her wrists before releasing her from the bed.

"Just in case you decide to fight back or run away." His strong hands encircled her wrists, and he dragged her off the bed onto the floor, where he forced her to a kneeling position.

"Stop it! You're hurting me!" She cried, flinching at his touch.

"Nonsense, just do what I tell you to do, and don't fight with me anymore." Thomas spread her knees apart and placed the large brass bowl between them. "Now I need you to relieve yourself."

"Are you crazy?" She tried jerking herself free. "I can't go in there—right this minute—with you watching me!"

"You can, and you will." He glared down at her. Rose remained still for a moment. He leaned in close to her ear and, in a fierce whisper, said, "Do it now."

She stared straight ahead, angry, filled with a stubborn resolve to make no move.

"C'mon, Rose, don't be coy with me." He knelt on the floor behind her and, wrapping his arms around her waist, placed his hands on her lower abdomen. With a light pressure, he pushed against her.

"Ow, Thomas, that hurts." Her face contorted with discomfort.

"What's the matter? Mother Nature got you where it counts? She's cruel, you know."

Rose dropped her head but remained silent.

"Come on, Rose, make this easy for yourself. Do it now." His voice boomed with impatience. She twisted free from his grip, scrambling away, paying no attention to her cuffed wrists. Thomas smirked at her ludicrous attempts at escape and pulled her in place, giving her buttocks a good hard smack with his hand.

"Ow!" Rose howled in discomfort; tears sprang into her eyes.

"Yeah, I just love it when you pansy boys get tough. Sometimes these pampered little cunts need a good prick to keep them in line."

Thomas turned his eyes to the doorway and saw him lounging against the frame, the usual leer on his face. "Shut up, Joe! How long have you been standing there?"

"Long enough to know that when I see a bowl under a tight little pussy, I know there's some business about to be had." He gave a chuckle.

"Who let you out of your lair today?"

Joe threw back his head and gave a loud, hearty laugh. "Oh, I get around. I usually like the sight of liquid gold splashing out of a tight little cunt. Rather fun for me. I'd stick around to see your pretty princess pee, but I've got other fish to fry."

"Get out of here, then!" Thomas glanced up, grimacing. Joe gave another laugh and turned out of the room.

"Oh, god." Rose shuddered. "I hoped never to see him again."

"Forget him. My main concern is you. Now, let's go."

She struggled against his grip. "This is crazy, Thomas. Please, let me go!"

"Are you going to go now, or am I going to have to spank it out of you? You know I will, too." His grip tightened, and she let out a small whimper. He repositioned the bowl between her knees.

Silence.

Once again, he pressed his fingers above her pubic bone

and massaged with an even pressure.

She let out a cry. "Thomas, that's so uncomfortable."

"What's the matter? Is your cute little cunny bothering you? You've held out long enough, but you know how to fix this problem."

She whimpered louder.

"I'll wait here as long as you want, Rose, but I guarantee I'll outlast you." He moved his hands down between her legs, and slid in his fingers. With her moisture gathered on his fingertips, he massaged her clit, aggravating the sting even more. Rose gritted her teeth, screwed her eyes shut, and tightened her muscles.

"Just do it. Stop fighting. Let it go." Thomas brushed his lips against her ear, his finger working her sensitive knot even faster. She writhed, fought, stalled as his strokes grew harder and faster. She let out a sigh of defeat. With a moan, her inner hidden regions burst into contractions. Thomas held her tighter. The moment her spasms ceased, the stream came. In a gush, tinkling sounds emanated from the bowl as her water hit the hard metal below her. Thomas ran his hands through her hot fluids, his fingers warmed by the heat. "Just empty yourself. Let it all out." When her last drops plinked into the bowl, Thomas wiped his hand and then proceed to dry her off.

Rose opened her eyes, her face sullen. "Are we done yet?"

"Oh, no, dear, we're just beginning," Thomas chuckled in her ear. Rose rolled her eyes in disgust, widening them in surprise when he jerked her to her feet. He picked her up, tossed her on the bed once again, and cuffed her arms back into position.

"Thomas, please don't do anything more. Let me go," she pleaded.

He spread her legs apart and fastened each one in place with cuffs located on either side of the bed. The sight of her sweet, gaping sex made his flesh start to strain against his trousers. "You need to learn not to yell when you don't like something, and you surely must never shout at me and then walk away."

"I'm sorry I got mad at you. I won't do it again. If I promise to be good, will you let me go?"

Thomas refused to answer, neither convinced nor fooled by her change in attitude. "Too late, Rose. I'm on a roll, and you need to learn a few lessons in anger control. "He had no intention of hurting her, but enjoyed making her nervous and squirm a little. He walked over to the sink and washed his hands before moving over to the chest of drawers, where he retrieved lubricant, packets of cleanser, gloves, and a spare bag. From another drawer he selected two more items. He returned to the bed in silence, situated himself in a comfortable position, and placed his items, one by one, next to her open thighs.

"Thomas, what have you got?" Her voice trailed out, panic-stricken. "Can't you at least give me a hint?"

Silence.

"Thomas, please don't hurt me." Tears filled her eyes.

He didn't answer, but held up a sealed package, eyeing it with great interest.

"What's that silver metal thing?"

Thomas jerked his head away from his object of interest and turned to give her a long, hard stare before whisking the item away.

She sighed. "Does this all have to be a secret? Can't you just tell me what's going on?" She tugged at the bindings, straining her legs hard. Defeated, she blinked back tears, swallowed hard, and readjusted her head on the pillow.

He gently spread her apart, examined her, glanced back at the instruments beside him, and examined her again. "I wonder if this is a good size for you, or do I need a smaller one?" he said, posing the question more as an afterthought than as a direct question to her. His eyes lit up. "Yes, this larger one is best."

He smiled, satisfied his plan had come together, nice and easy the way he wanted. He liked the sight in front of him: exposed and helpless; her faced filled with fear and panic; the way her breasts, topped with fleshy nipples, heaved and called out to him when her hands were cuffed behind her head. He especially liked her pink, dripping nether regions, filled with more than one entryway into secret hidden places deep within her body.

However, something seemed amiss. The vision of her sprawled out on the bed before him needed one finishing touch. He thought a moment. He snapped his fingers again and got up from the bed. "Oh, I can't believe I almost forgot this one last thing," he said, chiding himself. He approached the chest of drawers and pulled out a ball-gag. When he returned to the bed, he inserted the gag in her mouth and tightened the straps behind her head. "There," he said, "something to help muffle your screams."

*   *   *

Rose pulled on the restraints that held her fast, unable to move. Tears returned, tumbling out of her eyes and sliding down into her hair. What on earth did he plan to do with her? He never seemed at a loss for wild ideas, and she never seemed able to conjure up a plan to beat him at his own game. With everything in place, Thomas began the proceedings. She heard the tearing sounds of packets being opened and gloves being snapped on. She gave a small jerk, as a cool gauze pad grazed her exposed flesh. Panic flared. As she bit down on the gag, she prayed and settled her head back into the pillow. Her body quivered, unable to relax. She chastised herself for becoming cross with him. Was it worth all this? She knew her temper sometimes came with a cost. She closed her eyes.

He selected his instrument of choice, opened the package, and slathered a generous amount of lubrication on its surface. Shocked, her eyes flew open. Her heart pounded so hard the drumming sounds filled her ears. She let out a muffled cry. A peppery sting from within announced the entry of a steel rod into that most private, tiny passage where her golden fluids of nature flowed, a place she had assumed to be the most hidden and protected of all. She battled against the restraints that held her tight. She bit down on the gag and shut her eyes tight again. If he would just please stop!

Under Thomas's skillful guidance, the heavy rod slipped down inside. Her delicate passageway opened up and hugged its steely invader like a long-lost friend. An incredible sense of fullness washed over her, and she began to relax. As Thomas moved the rod gently back and forth, tickling sensations permeated throughout her loins; she arched her back and let out a moan.

"It's like being made love to in a whole different place, isn't it?"

A soft hand encircled her chin, and she opened her eyes at the sound of a familiar, gentle, voice over her. John stared down at her, his eyes filled with their usual sparkle. He rubbed her cheek with a finger. When had he come in? Rose relaxed even more, comforted for some unexplained reason by his presence. The first time he'd seen her bare and vulnerable, she'd been embarrassed, but even then, something about him drew her in, a quality of authority that both intrigued and challenged her.

"Thomas, is it okay if I remove this now?" John pointed to the gag in her mouth.

"Oh, of course it is."

John caught hold of the straps, pulled the gag from her mouth, and tossed it on the bed beside the other supplies.

"Do you like this, Rose?" Thomas cast a smile in her direction and moved the rod once again.

"Yes—oh my god—what is that thing, anyway?" Rose dug her heels into the bed.

"It's a dilator," John said. "The movements inside create an incredible sensation of pleasure." He continued holding her face, looking at her tenderly. "Just lie back and relax. It's quite fun."

Rose closed her eyes and relaxed. A thickness filled her sex in response to the amorous kisses from her new metal friend. Within moments, the tickles near her pleasure spot sent out a wave of spasms as she climaxed with relief.

"Oh, you know what, Thomas, don't forget to make her sing," John gave Thomas a knowing wink.

Thomas laughed. "Right. We can't forget that. And I came prepared." He reached for a tuning fork. With a sharp blow of the tines against his hand, he brought the ends down on the exposed metal of the dilator.

Rose pressed her head into the pillow and squeezed her eyes shut. The vibrations from the tines rang out in her pelvic area. She let out a loud moan. John caught the nipple of one of her breasts and caressed the pink flesh between his thumb and forefinger. "How was that, sweetheart?" He leaned over her face and kissed her lips.

When the vibrations subsided, she sighed and beamed up at him. He settled himself on the bed beside her and took a nipple in his mouth, sucking firmly, alternating with a playful flick of his tongue. Rose tried to stroke his hair, but the cuffs held her back with a jingle of disapproval. John stopped and unfastened the straps. Free at last, she brought her hands down and ran her fingers through his thick waves as he suckled her once again.

For a brief moment, nobody else in the world existed but her and John, and his flesh against hers. "I'm glad you're here," Rose said, whispering in his ear. "I like having you near." She wanted to tell him how much she'd like to have his body deep inside hers, but she held back, hoping he could read her mind and be the initiator. Did he want her as much as she wanted him? She wondered.

John said nothing, but glanced over at her and smiled. Rose closed her eyes as Thomas kissed her internally with the dilator, a reminder of his presence. In one slow, smooth caress, she felt the rod slide out, and within a few seconds, Thomas's mouth lit on the swollen bump hidden in her cleft and teased the plump flesh with a fury. All the attention to her most sensitive parts drove her body into a stormy frenzy. Within a few moments, spasms of relief washed over her as both men succeeded in relieving the nagging, internal throb.

John took a deep breath, glanced at the pair and smiled. Rose caught a sadness lurking behind the sparkle in his eyes, something she found unfathomable, a paradox. He got up from the bed. "I've had a lovely time, but I do need to go." He gave Rose's lips a soft kiss and left the room, disappearing almost as quickly as he had appeared. His departure nudged a fleeting emotion of longing within her, as if he took a part of her with him, like a thief sneaking away gold with no intention of its return. When would she see him again?

*   *   *

Thomas remained silent, but the tender little scene he had just witnessed burned in his mind. Rose's words, the hunger in John's eyes, their closeness, all played over and over with a loud taunt. Perplexed and confused, Thomas suddenly found himself with the possibility of wanting her for himself. If so, to what extent? When had that happened? His fondness for her had remained constant through the years, true enough, but a compelling desire to seek her out never quite set in with him. Why? At this point, he knew one thing. His life at The House had provided him a certain stability, a predictable lifestyle, a means for satisfying his lustful appetites. Now her presence here challenged him, a knock at the door of dormant emotions he'd perhaps kept hidden and locked away.

First one, then the other, he unfastened the bindings from her legs and pulled her into his arms, his thickness hard against her. She opened her legs in an invitation to unite and, with eager anticipation, swallowed him whole as he pressed his way in without effort into total darkness. He took his time with her, ran his fingers over her satiny contours, stroked her golden tresses, explored the warm depths of her mouth with his tongue. In vain, he searched for an answer with each caress of her fingers, each moan, each sigh, each yielding movement of her body. Filled with lust and frustration, his loins cried out their thick tears, warm and streaming. Rose pulled Thomas into her arms and held him against her in a silent, thoughtful embrace.

Chapter 6

DAWN PEEKED THROUGH THE WINDOWS and illuminated the room with the soft, gray light of morning. Outside, birds sang, their day already in progress. Rose, wide awake, rested herself against Thomas's warm body. Naked, stretched out comfortably on his back, he lay fast asleep, legs slightly open, with one knee bent out. She loved watching him sleep, his usual commanding presence now replaced with one of sweetness and innocence. She snuggled up closer; he stirred. Between her fingers, she twirled a long pink feather, and began flicking the fluffy end over his stomach, under his arms, on his hips, and at last over the ripe, pink tip perched between his thighs. Thomas opened his eyes, blinking, a little dazed and disoriented. He looked over at her and smiled.

"You're awake early this morning," he whispered.

"Yeah, I couldn't sleep any longer." She flicked the feather over one of his nipples and stopped long enough to reach over and place a soft kiss on his lips. He said nothing, but stared and smiled at her. She moved her head between his legs and licked over the velvety, swollen flesh, which grew fuller with each hot, wet flick of her tongue over his curves and ridges. With his new erection, thick and full, he moved to take her in his arms, but stopped short, not quite able to reach her. The smile left his face. A rude jingling sound above his head made a startling announcement. Puzzled, he craned his neck to either side and discovered that both of his arms had been cuffed to the bed.

"Rose, what are you doing?"

"I'm bored." She stifled a quick yawn and got up from the bed, making her way to the chest of drawers. After pulling out some choice items, she returned, straddling his hips, while moving one of the cuffs so that his arms were crisscrossed. "I need you to get on your hands and knees."

"Excuse me?" He blinked at her, stunned.

"You heard me." Her voice rang out with stern authority. "I need you to get on your hands and knees, now. I'll help you roll over in the direction you need to go, so your arms are straight. Then you'll do what I tell you to do." Thomas continued staring up at her, dumbstruck. Rose placed her face close to his and said, enunciating each word, "I need you to move, this minute!" Thomas, without argument, rolled over on to his stomach and maneuvered himself up on all fours.

She smiled. "There, that's good." Leaning in close to his ear she whispered, "Now then, Thomas, it's time to start your happy day." Rose gave his buttocks a good, firm swat. She got off the bed and, standing in front of him, strapped on a phallus. In the dim light, he strained his eyes to determine its size.

"Oh, come on, Rose. Don't you think it's a bit early—?"

"Quiet! Or no lube for you." The sinister tone in her voice alarmed him a little.

He winced and hung his head. "Please be easy, is all I ask."

Rose wagged her head in front of his, her face filled with a taunting smile. "It's payback time for you, Thomas. You're not the only one who can plan a surprise sneak attack." She swatted his buttocks again and stepped back.

Smiling, she squeezed a generous amount of lubrication onto the phallus, which she admitted to herself *was* quite large. When she had requested this item earlier, the staff at the desk, a noted gleam in their eyes, had recommended the size. She climbed onto the bed behind him and opened his buttocks, aiming the tip at his anal entrance. With a thrust of her hips, she began impaling his backside, driving the phallus into his rectum.

Thomas gasped and twitched his hips. "Please go easy. This is a large size, even for me." He took several deep breaths to help calm the initial discomfort and relaxed his muscles. He sucked in his breath again as Rose pushed the phallus deeper inside. "Easy, please. God, you're splitting me apart!" He writhed in pain.

Her hips moved slowly at first, then faster, working the full length in and out against his prostate.

He let out a small groan. "Yes … much better. I think I'm getting used to the size." With a sigh, he dropped his head.

She reached around and cupped his shaft in one of her hands and worked his engorged tip with the fingers of her other hand, squeezing gently and massaging all around.

"Oh, god, Rose, please stop!" He begged. He gasped. "Please, I don't think I can take …" She ignored his pleas, smiling as she rode him hard from behind. After a few moments, the pressure in his pelvic area reached a point of no return, and with one last unmerciful thrust from her hips, he shot out jets of semen, thick streams pulsating onto the sheets in a little pool.

Barely able to catch his breath, he said, "Rose, really … I'm begging you … please stop! I'm d-done … I'm done now."

"Really?" The tone in her voice mocked him. She stopped and kissed the wet flesh of his back. The taste of salt stung her tongue when she licked her lips. "I don't believe you. I think you've got a little bit more of that fine, thick stuff in your sweet, juicy cock. It makes my pussy all wet inside just thinking about it. So I need you to let it all out, hard and good."

"What language! Are you practicing your dirty talk, Rose? You know that can be a turn-on." Thomas lifted his head and let out a chuckle.

"Quiet!" She delivered a swift blow to his buttocks again. Leaning over, she whispered in his ear, "So you like it when I talk dirty? Does it turn you on? I bet it makes your cock boil." She licked his ear and ended with a sharp bite on his earlobe, then swatted him again. "Okay, Thomas, rest time's over. Let's go. Let it all out hard and good like I told you to." She started in on him again, slower, easier.

"Oh, God! No!" He dropped his head down with a groan and heaved out the last bit of his fluids, thick drops sliding their way out, dripping and tumbling onto the bed.

"There, you are done now." She gave his back a few soft pats. He gasped and clinched his buttocks together as she withdrew the phallus. She caught hold of the cuff and crisscrossed it over the other arm. "Now roll over on your back."

"Aren't you done?" He frowned.

"Done? Oh, no. Actually, I'm just getting warmed up." Rose

yawned, stretching her arms to the ceiling. Thomas rolled his eyes and dug his head into the pillow. He tugged at the restraints. "What's the matter, Thomas? Cuffs get you down?" She grinned down at him.

"No. I love being tied down by a strong, powerful woman. It turns me on." He closed his eyes.

"Good. Glad you think so." She crawled off the bed, walked over to the chest of drawers again, and returned with another handful of unidentified items.

"Rose, what do you have in your pile of stash, honey?"

"Do you think that's something you need to know, or that I'm going to tell you?"

"Well, you seem to be full of surprises this morning. I just thought I'd see what you had. You don't have to hide anything. I'll play along with you, Rose, I really will."

"Good to know, but no deal. You don't fool me one bit, Thomas. Don't you get all casual with me. I know you better than that." She leaned over and whispered in his face, "You know what, else? I think you talk way too much, anyway." No sooner than he had opened his mouth to protest, she popped the ball-gag into his mouth and secured the straps behind his head. "There, *something to help muffle your screams*. Remember?"

*   *   *

As he heard Rose snapping on a pair of gloves, Thomas writhed under the bindings, his cries of protest in vain. Powerless to stop her, let alone call for help, he closed his eyes and prayed he'd survive without too much pain, or serious damage to his body. He caught his breath in horror. The touch of cool cleansing pads against the tip of his cock confirmed only one thing. His body was about to be the recipient of an intruding object, one delivered by unskilled hands.

"I think the large one will work for you just the same, don't you think, Thomas?"

Unable to answer, he opened his eyes and glared back.

"Oh, I'm sorry, I didn't hear you. Very well, the large one it is." Her fingers pried open his slit, and cold steel slipped inside. He closed his eyes once again while the weight of the rod worked itself deep into his passage with a gentle, persistent force. Much to his surprise, however, he discovered Rose displayed an uncanny skill in managing the rod as it traveled into his darkest center. He adjusted his head into the pillow and relaxed.

"How do you like this?" She moved the rod a little, ever so softly, back and forth against the area at his prostate. He stiffened his hips and closed his eyes tighter.

"Here, allow me." A familiar voice broke the silence in the room, and a pair of hands encircled hers.

"Huh?" Rose lifted her eyes in surprise. Thomas breathed a sigh of relief.

Daren stood, lording over both of them like a beautifully sculpted god. The rays of the morning sun, like a match, lit up the red waves of his hair. About his waist, he wore his usual loincloth. His golden eyes sparkled, and there was an easy smile on his face.

"Allow me," he said once again, and grasped the end of the rod. Thomas moaned with pleasure as Daren removed the steel rod, caressing the inside of his shaft until nothing remained but the fond memory of its hugs. "There, much better. He'll also be able to release himself without something in his way, won't you, Thomas?" Daren emphasized his last words a little louder. With a wicked, teasing look on his face, he squeezed and massaged the pink tip with his fingers. Then he rubbed and toyed with the tiny hole at the top before massaging the ridge right under his cap. "You like this, Thomas? Does it feel good to you?"

Thomas, with muffled cries from the gag, writhed under Daren's touch and shook his head frantically in protest.

Daren peered down at him in triumph. "My, you're such a big boy. I love watching you grow." His lips widened with a broad smile while he winked at Rose. "Don't worry about him, he's loving every minute of it." He chuckled. "Watch this." His other hand worked around Thomas's sac, and with light squeezes, he kneaded the plump balls gently with his fingertips. Thomas strained at the bindings. Daren's adept fingers proved merciless, and unable to ignore or remove himself from their stimulation, Thomas's body primed itself for release. He let out a muffled groan and unloaded himself, the milky white fluids dripping and landing into a tiny puddle on his stomach.

Daren reached down and swirled the pool of lust with a couple of long, slender fingers. He gathered up a small amount of the slick liquid and brought his fingers to the tip of his tongue. He smacked his lips, staring up at the ceiling a moment lost in thought. "You're rather tasty, Thomas. Oh, I almost forgot." He leaned over and released the gag.

"You bastard!" Thomas growled at his friend, giving him the evil eye.

"Oh, aren't you a hateful one." Daren narrowed his eyes in mock admonition. Without further notice, he leaned down and placed a lingering kiss on Thomas's lips, slipping his tongue in for a quick tour of his mouth. The metal cuffs jingled against the bed as Thomas tried to pull away again. Daren, finished with his playtime, reached over and released the cuffs. Thomas sat up, red-faced, and rubbed his mouth.

"You're a dog, Daren!" Thomas shook his head and let out a light laugh. He got up from the bed, stared hard at Rose, and walked to the chest of drawers. "I hope you like adventures, Rose, because I think you're in for one right now."

"Won't this be fun? I just love adventures, don't you?" Daren turned to Rose, clapped a little clap with his hands, and gazed at the ceiling with a blissful grin.

"Speak for yourself." Rose remained on the bed, a glum frown furrowed on her brow. No matter how she tried to stay ahead of her game, someone or something always stole her thunder.

Thomas rattled through the drawers and selected his supplies. "I think it's time we teach Rose that she can never have a one-up on us attendants, don't you, Daren?"

"Most definitely." He waggled a finger at Rose. "Special

moments aren't without consequences, you know."

"Well said, my friend." Thomas, supplies in tow, led the way out of the room. "Come on, Daren. Gather her up. We're tub-room bound."

She let out a shout as Daren's strong arms snatched her from the bed and flipped her over his shoulders. "Come, my sweet. Not to worry, we'll be gentle."

*   *   *

The old familiar wave of panic came over Rose once again. Now what were they going to do? Thomas led the way into the tub room, heading first towards the cabinets.

"Daren, let's place her over there." He pointed in the direction of the tub. "That way, we'll have easy access to water. Here, set up a soft area for her." He tossed several towels to his co-conspirator, who began spreading them out, one by one.

"Here, Rose, you'll need to lie down. This time, as a courtesy to you, your arms are free." Daren grinned graciously, and Rose, who knew better than to argue, allowed him to help her down.

"You spoil her too much, Daren, you know that?" Thomas came up to them, armed with new supplies and towels.

"That's not true. I hold my own with you, don't I Rose?"

"Yes, he does—that and more." Rose reclined back; her mood lightened just a little. Her uneasiness? Not so much.

Daren sat, and cradled her head between his hands and smoothed her cheeks with his fingers. "Rose, just try to remain calm. We aren't going to hurt you."

"What are you going to do, Daren? Can you at least give me a hint?"

"What? And spoil the fun? No, I'm sorry, we can't do that." He leaned over and kissed the pout on her lips. "You get too wound up. Relax and enjoy. That's my motto."

"You and your mottos. They don't help me much."

"Oh, that's because you dismiss them, my sweet." He placed

another kiss on her pouty lips, and managed to extract a giggle from her this time. "There, that's so much better, darling."

Thomas seated himself at her feet and, after setting up his supplies, spread her legs apart. "Rose, what I'm about to do is going to feel a little strange to you, but like most things we do around here, you won't feel any pain." She gave a start as he slipped a flexible tube within her rectal walls, the movement of which seemed more to irritate, rather than titillate. Her body tensed up and her eyes froze their gaze on the ceiling.

"Don't worry, Rose. You'll soon feel a total, cleansing relief." Daren stroked her tousled hair.

"You'll feel a cool liquid inside, so don't panic." Thomas lifted a bag of fluid, at which point the contents seeped their way into the dark depths of her body, instilling her with a certain fullness. She fidgeted a little.

"Why am I feeling so itchy, Thomas?" Her hips twitched, the tickling in her backside increasing.

"At times our body needs cleansing on the inside, just like our bath rituals cleanse us on the outside. We maintain overall vitality this way."

"Daren, is this true?" Rose wanted more than just Thomas's opinion.

"Of course, it's true. Why would we lie about something like this? Everything we do here in The House is in truth, no matter how enjoyable or odd it may seem."

"Okay, we're done with the bag." Thomas tapped her on the thigh. "Lie still, because I'm not quite done yet."

Daren leaned over her face. "Whatever you do, don't fight Thomas. You need to hold everything inside for a little bit."

"How am I going to do that when I already feel like …?" She frowned at little. The pressure building up inside her bottom made her wince.

"Hang on, Rose. I'm going to insert my finger …" With a smooth insertion of a gloved finger, Thomas entered her backside. "This will keep everything in place for a bit."

"Oh, god, Thomas, that feels so funny." She shifted to a

more comfortable position.

"You've experienced this before. Dr. James did the same thing to you during your exam, so this isn't new for you, exactly."

"I know you're up to no good, you two, so don't deny it."

Daren gave the top of one of her breasts a little tweak. "Rose, you're getting smarter all the time. You're right, there's more to come."

After a few minutes, she felt the fullness mounting even more. "Thomas, can't you do something for that irritating little itch?" She grimaced a little as he obliged by squeezing in a second finger and rubbing her walls with soft forward and backward strokes, followed by gentle rotations of his fingers. "There, that's better, somewhat. But you know what—" She cut herself off in mid-sentence, a powerful urge overtaking her. She tried to scurry up, but Daren held her down.

"Thomas, I believe she's ready." Daren glanced over at his friend. "I'd get everything situated if I were you."

"I think you're right." Thomas grabbed an extra-large, thick towel with his free hand and placed one side over her pubic area.

"Here, let me lift her up for you so you can finish." Daren removed himself from Rose's head and encircled his strong arms around her hips, lifting them enough for Thomas to work the remainder of the towel around her. As Thomas removed his fingers and secured everything in place, she felt an uncontrollable rush of fluids to her anal opening. She strained with all her might to maintain control, but her body rebelled. "Okay, I'll stand her up now."

"But Daren, if I stand up, I'll ..." Rose flushed with embarrassment; the thoughts of what was about to happen next made her cringe. With one easy lift, Daren pulled her to a standing position, while Thomas maintained a secure hold on the towel. Struggle though she may, her fight against nature ended with her loss, and her body released its inner contents. She closed her eyes to shut out her immediate surroundings, and wished with all her might to lose herself in the darkness. In one last act of defiance, her body pushed out every last vestige of waste, leaving her internally fresh and renewed.

"Good girl," said Thomas. "Daren, I'll remove this towel, and you can spray her off."

Daren nodded in affirmation.

Taking great care to avoid any spillage, Thomas removed the towel and gathered up all used supplies for their proper disposal.

"Okay, precious girl, let's finish this up." Daren placed a small, quick kiss on her lips before lifting her into the tub. She threw back her head and closed her eyes. The warm water from the sprayer hit her nether regions with a comforting stream, and she sighed with a newfound comfort, all itching and irritation removed.

"After I dry you off, we have one more thing to do." Daren ran the towel over remaining damp areas. Thomas stood before them and assisted Rose out of the tub and back on to the towels.

"We need you to kneel down on all fours." Thomas gave her a light push.

"What? What are you going to do now?" Rose glared.

"Just kneel down. That's all I'm asking you to do."

"Here, like this." Daren placed his hands on either side of her shoulders and gently pushed her down to her knees. He followed by placing himself in a supine position. "Place your legs outside mine. You'll be more comfortable that way. Now, you can lean over me, like this." He took her arms and placed them on either side of his shoulders. "Excellent. Just relax, because things will go much easier if you do."

"Daren's right, Rose. With what I'm going to do next, you can't fight me. If you thought the instillation was weird, the insertion of this plug will be stranger yet."

"Huh? Plug? What are you talking about?" She looked down at Daren in dismay.

"Remember the first room we saw when you arrived on

the ward after the admission process? The lady and gentleman, and what they were doing?"

"Oh, no!" Tears welled up in her eyes. She recalled the young gentleman straining and quivering as his mistress inserted a plug such as this. Sensing the fear in her voice, Thomas tried again to reassure her. "But Rose, don't you also remember how he liked the sensations? I'm sure you'll find this enjoyable. I'll be gentle. Here I go." She stared down at Daren.

"Deep breath for us, Rose." Daren held her face with a little more firmness, and tried to hold her gaze. "Just look at me."

Thomas grabbed a small steel, bullet-shaped bulb, flared out at the end, and entered its blunt tip into her orifice. With small, gentle pushes and twists, he attempted to bury the device to its appropriate depth.

"Ow, Thomas, that hurts!" Rose winced and tried to pull away, but Daren grabbed her arms and held her firm. The fullness of the plug, though not the largest, stretched her walls beyond their normal size, making her think she might really split apart.

"Calm down. Tensing up only makes matters worse." Daren reached up, guiding her face in front of his.

"The more you tighten up, the harder it is to insert this thing. Do what Daren tells you." Thomas pushed a little more. Terrified, Rose began to pant.

"Just take some deep breaths. Nice and easy. Follow me." Daren began an exercise of deep neutral breaths, rubbing her cheeks, encouraging her to concentrate and follow him. Rose said nothing, but swallowed, tried to blink back the tears, and focused on his face and the amber depths of his eyes.

"That's good. You're doing great. Nice and easy." She let out one loud gasp as Thomas finally drove the steel bullet home, as far as the device allowed. Her backside felt ready to explode, but as her walls acclimated to their new visitor, she discovered a new liking for the sensations of fullness.

"Are you done yet?" Breaths hitched in her throat.

"Yes, sweetheart, I'm done. Do you think you've learned

your lesson now? I don't think you'll try and outsmart me again, will you?"

"Yes, I've learned my lesson." Her face held a rather glum expression. "You're right, though. I never can seem to get the better of you no matter how hard I try."

Thomas smiled and rubbed her satiny buttocks with the palm of his hand and glanced at Daren. "I think we should let her relax just a little."

Daren nodded. He reached up and pulled her face close to his and buried his tongue into her mouth. Rose settled herself in his warm embrace, losing herself in a deep kiss. As his fullness pressed against her, an idea consumed her. Loosening herself from his grip, she turned her head toward the remaining supplies. She turned to him and smiled.

"You've been so sweet during this whole ordeal, I think you deserve a reward. What do you think?"

"A reward for me? I love rewards, just like adventures." His amber eyes blazed and his lips parted into a wide smile.

"Good. Lie back and enjoy. It's my turn, or should I say, your turn." Daren shifted into a more comfortable position, and Rose slipped on a glove.

"I'll say to you what you all say to me. Spread your legs apart."

He complied.

"I'll be gentle, too." She covered two fingers with lubricant and inserted them into his anus. Daren closed his eyes and sucked in his breath. She began moving her fingers around, taking turns with each one, stroking back and forth.

"Oh, Rose, I think you found the special spot." Daren smiled. "God, I love having the inside of my ass stroked. Your fingers are fantastic." His breathing became heavier. "Would you mind going a little faster in that area?"

"Of course. For you, I'll do anything," Rose said, her tone gushing and ingratiating. Her fingers moved faster. Daren's jaw tightened. She took up his blossoming cock between the fingers of her other hand and began working the tip, touching and massaging in all the right places. Daren groaned his face flushing. Rose kept on him, persistent.

He lifted his hips with each graze of her fingers against his prostate, and after a few more movements with her fingers, he finished his climax with a smile. "What a reward. Like I said earlier, I love them." He breathed in deep, easy breaths and blinked his eyes to refocus. "You were wonderful."

Rose removed the glove and, disregarding the milky puddle on his abdomen, settled on top of him once again. "I'm glad you enjoyed yourself." She ran her fingers through his hair and planted her lips on his for another lingering kiss.

After a moment, Thomas interrupted their little interlude. "Hey, guys, I'm still here, in case you've forgotten."

Rose turned her head back to see him perched on the edge of the tub. "Oh."

"Should I go and just leave the two of you alone?"

"Hey, buddy, you can come join us." A stony silence and a hard stare from Thomas made Daren check his mood. "You know what, you're right, we're done." The smile left his face, and in its place was a more somber expression. "We'll help you gather up the rest of these towels, and you two can head on back to your room."

"Hey, what about this—you know?" Rose tossed her head, pointing in reference to plug still lodged in her behind.

"You'll entertain your new friend until I decide he has to go." Thomas's tone held an edge of sternness, tinged with a hint of irritation.

Rose sensed a slight change in his demeanor, his mood and attitude a little different than usual. Unsure whether or not to challenge him, she decided to remain quiet and wait for a better time.

Chapter 7

AS THEY SETTLED DOWN together, Thomas cuddled Rose in his arms. During the walk back to their room, he decided to check his irritability for the moment; one question lurked in his mind, and he wanted an answer. He stroked her hair. "I have something to ask you."

Rose met his intent stare with a twinge of alarm. "What do you want to know?"

"Please, tell me how you learned to use the metal rods. You used a sound, by the way, which is used for men. You can hurt someone with those. But you were great. How come you were so good? There's no way you would have used them before."

Rose, silent and thoughtful, sank back against the warmth of his chest. She closed her eyes a moment while his finger gently caressed a nipple on one of her breasts. Her mind raced all the while as she mentally reorganized the events which transpired during the night before. Lucky for her, people kept all kinds of late-night hours in The House, and during the night, they proved themselves suitable and willing teachers. She collected her thoughts and recalled her story.

The previous night, still somewhat young, had presented her with an opportune moment to steal away from Thomas while he slept. An idea had been burning in her mind, and she needed some help on how reach a resolution. She'd slipped out of bed and made her way down the hallway, over to the beautiful marble staircase. Upon reaching the foot of the stairs, she'd turned left and headed towards the doctor's office. Rose had liked Dr. James from her first encounter with him. Not only did she find his face handsome, but his physique attracted her attention, too. She also admired his intelligence and compassion. He kept unusual hours, everyone knew, but he always made himself available for anyone, anytime, any reason. He would be the perfect person to understand her need and help her. With a pounding heart, she had knocked on the door and waited until he gave her an invitation to enter. Once she poked her head around the door, she stepped inside with a shy grin …

*   *   *

"Rose, how may I help you?" A warm smile lit up his face.

"Dr. James, if you have some time, I need your help with something."

"Are you okay? Nothing is wrong, is there?" His smile faded.

"Oh, no, not at all." Rose took a seat in front of his desk. "Can you teach me how to use the metal rods properly? You see, the other day, Thomas pulled a fast one on me and used these metal rods—a dilator, he called it—and now I just want to get back at him, like a surprise, you know."

Dr. James sat back in his chair, cleared his throat, and smiled a few seconds. Yes, the time had come at last. He'd found her a most tempting morsel from the moment he laid eyes on her. Though he usually didn't assist admits in "getting back" at their attendants, he didn't want to miss the opportunity to get to know her better, either. And her request presented him with the most golden of opportunities. Thomas, a seasoned attendant, would know how to manage her no matter what happened. At least this fresh young lady knew her limits, and such a cautious, wise person always earned his respect.

"Follow me back to the examination room so we can discuss this some more." He rose from his desk, ushered her into the room, and closed the door behind them. From a long counter against the wall, he retrieved a metal receptacle, lubrication, some packets of gloves, and cleanser. He also retrieved two sealed packages from a unit sitting on top of the counter. With a motion of his head, he invited Rose to accompany him to the exam table. He placed the sealed rods and other supplies on a tray adjacent to the table, taking great care to touch nothing.

Her eyes widened and filled with intense interest as he began peeling off his trousers and undergarments, exposing himself without shame, showing off a promising length and a luscious sac. In order to teach her the proper techniques she wished to learn, he placed himself on the exam table and reclined back, just enough to view himself with ease and maintain control of his instruments. He opened one of the sealed packets and dripped a generous amount of lubrication inside, taking care to leave the item untouched. He opened some cleansing packets, donned a pair of rubber gloves, and commenced cleansing the pink fleshy tip mounted on top of his, flaccid cock, while explaining the importance of using sterile technique.

"If you'll notice, Rose, I'm not hard."

"I see." She moved in closer. "Is that important, whether you're hard or not?"

"Yes. If your partner is hard, you shouldn't insert or remove the rod. Just so you know, this particular one I'm using is a little different from the dilator Thomas used with you."

"Oh." Rose studied him in detail, her heart racing in her chest. The doctor opened the package, exposing a silver rod, its steely surface flashing in the light. While he supported himself with one hand, he inserted one end of the rod with the other, using slow, deliberate movements, pulling his shaft over the cold, steel instrument. His hand controlled the speed, allowing the metal to glide down with precision. Rose watched his movements with fascination. "Now the rod is where it needs to be, and if you move it a little, I receive wonderful sensations, just as you did."

She nodded, remembering her experience. "This is wonderful!" She loved the way the hard metal lost itself in his body, sinking itself into dark, hidden depths in a smooth, controlled, effortless way, as the steely surface coaxed out shudders of pure delight.

"Now, Rose, it's your turn to do this on me so you know what to do."

"Huh?" Her head shot up in surprise.

Dr. James chuckled. "You came here, wanting me to help you, remember? What's the point if I let you walk out of here without doing this yourself?"

"I guess you're right." Rose blinked her eyes a little. "You made a good point, but I'm so scared I'll mess up and hurt you or something."

"You'll do a good job. Don't worry. I'll be here. I'm a doctor, remember?" He gave her a reassuring laugh. The more her eyes lingered over the vision of his impaled shaft, the steely end peeking out and taunting her, the more her lust grew. Fear began to dwindle just a little, and the idea of sinking this metal wand of delight into Thomas's delicate hole made her juices bubble. Dr. James slipped out the rod and placed it in the metal receptacle he had brought to the exam table.

The doctor repositioned himself. "Okay, Rose. Go ahead. Don't be nervous, but *do* be very gentle and careful."

With timid hands, she repeated the preparatory sequence she saw earlier. After placing the gloves on her hands, Rose took his magnificent pink head between her soft fingers and began cleansing the silky skin with great care.

This was the big moment. The wild beating of her heart filled her ears with a drum-like drone. Self-doubt crept into her head once again. She took a deep breath and strengthened her resolve. With trembling hands, she spread the tiny hole open and inserted the rod into the tip. The doctor closed his eyes and sucked in his breath as the heavy rod sank down, filling his shaft as her hands pulled, angled, and supported him in different directions. In a few seconds, all movements had ceased.

"Okay, now what do I do, Dr. James? Are you hurting anywhere?"

"Everything is perfect." His eyes narrowed, face constricted in pleasure. "This rod is a little larger in diameter, and has filled and stretched me every bit of the way down, nice and smooth the way it should. Now, I want you to move the end a little. Be easy, and no sudden jerks."

She followed his orders.

"Oh, Rose … god, this feels great. Gently … yes, that's it … Good girl." He sighed and smiled at her. "All I can say is you've got great hands."

Rose beamed with pride. "Whew, I'm just glad I didn't hurt you."

"I had no doubt you'd do a good job."

"Is this it, then?" Rose smiled and tickled him for a few more seconds, admiring the way she made him grind his hips and groan.

"You can take it out now. Nice and slow. I think you've got it." With a slow, gentle tug, she slid out the rod and placed it in the receptacle alongside the other.

The doctor took a moment to regain his composure and then cast her a lusty smile. "You know, there's nothing better than having your cock stroked with silky fingers and finally impaled with a rod by hands that know what to do."

"And I'll say that a lady enjoys nothing better than toying with a gorgeous one such as yours, and she likes it even better when she can make a man spark and sizzle inside." She stood close to the doctor and whispered in his ear, "A lady also likes her aching crotch stuffed and soothed by a nice fat cock, and the looks of yours make me ache." She landed a tiny kiss on his ear.

"Is your pretty little cunny hot, Rose? I'm game if you are."

She smiled and gently nipped the bottom of his chin. Between her legs, a hot fire raged.

"Come up here to me, then, and I'll quench that internal heat of yours."

Rose smiled, climbed on to the table, and straddled him with limber agility. The yawning cleft poised above him enticed his hands to work in a thumb. He at once began massaging the pink flesh with tender strokes before reaching in further and sinking a couple of fingers into slick, hot darkness. She closed her eyes and threw back her head; her abdomen jerked at the movements licking her insides. Catching sight of her flirty clit, he slipped out his fingers and caught the hard knot of flesh between his fluid-soaked fingers. His soft tugging and squeezing managed to work out a small moan from between her lips. He smiled and rubbed the back of her satiny buttocks with his free hand.

Without further encouragement, her hands cupped his velvety tip, and her nimble fingers teased his curves, followed by the pressing of her fingers with firm movements up and down along the swollen veins of a blooming shaft. Her tender ministrations worked up a hardness which caused him to fill and stand at attention.

"You really know how to make a man come with lightning speed, don't you? I'm nearly to the shooting point already." His face tightened from the pleasure and pain throbbing between his legs. She read in his eyes his desire and readiness to enter. Ready for his advances, she lifted up and mounted a beautiful, engorged cock, her juicy sex swallowing his total erection until the tip hit her back wall. With smooth, gliding strokes, her walls clamped down, hugging and licking the swollen flesh as she moved over him with an even rhythm. With each rise and fall, he lifted his hips up to meet hers, both coming together in sweet synchronicity.

"You feel so good." She threw back her head while she took him. "Nice, smooth, and hard." Her hips moved faster with each passing second, building up a fiery carnal storm. The harder she rode him, the harder he pressed on.

"Keep going, because I think I'm ready … now." Unable to contain himself any longer, the doctor's shaft erupted, releasing hot jets of passion, which set off paroxysms of contractions throughout her pelvic region. Rose glanced down at his handsome face. His full, inviting lips dared her to kiss them. She cradled his head while her fingers curled through thick salt and pepper hair. The scent of a clean, fragrant aftershave filled her nostrils as she moved her face down to dip her tongue inside his mouth. He teased back, her youthful breath filling his lungs, as his tongue stroked the inside of her mouth. Breathless, she sighed and settled down into his arms, feeling his heart pound against her chest.

Maturity and strength oozed from every part of him, creating an indescribable allure. This moment marked her first time communing physically with an older man, and she discovered an attraction to the comfort and sense of security offered within his enfolding arms. His breath now returned to a normal pace, while his strong hands stroked the curls in her hair.

"You did an amazing job." He gave her one more lingering, deep kiss and helped her down from the table. Rose watched him dress, searing each sight and curve of his body into her memory bank.

"Thank you again, Doctor. You've been a big help."

"Thomas will be in for a surprise, for sure. He's one lucky fellow." The doctor smiled.

Rose left the office and bounded upstairs to the wards. One more item of business on her mental to-do list required completion. Her reactions to an earlier experience had piqued her curiosity, and now she required closure. Based on staff suggestion, Rose had found herself standing in the entrance of that doorway, viewing an attendant and her admit resting on the bed.

*   *   *

"Oh, we don't mind letting you try at all!" The female attendant smiled at her from the bed.

At the sight of their engorged breasts, she knew the staff had selected well. The admit, a sporty looking girl with medium-length dark brown hair and full curves, reclined on the bed, supine, with her legs spread wide open, showing off a gaping, dripping wet sex. Her attendant, previously occupied with lavishing tender caresses to the willing cleft in front of her, beckoned Rose to enter the room. As she approached the bed, the admit had smiled, reached up for her own breast, and expressed a pale, yellowish fluid, while grinning with content.

"You need some relief, don't you, sweetie? "The attendant turned back to her charge. She cast her admit a fond look before reaching between her legs and inserting a long, slender finger. The admit arched her back, moaning and nodding in agreement. The attendant glanced up at Rose. "Melody and I need frequent relief. The build-up nearly kills you at times. I'm Audrey, by the way."

Rose took an immediate liking to Audrey, with her cheerful, reassuring attitude. She relaxed immediately. Audrey's face held a pleasing glow, and a head of closely cropped light-brown hair crowned a slender, curvy, figure.

"So you want to play with us, eh?" Audrey laughed, giving Melody a quick nod of approval. "I can sense you're not one of our persuasion, but that doesn't matter. We'll have fun, anyway. Come on, sit down right here." She patted the bed, and Rose sat down, awaiting further instructions. Her heart pounded, and her face flushed red from embarrassment. She knew Audrey spoke the truth about not being one of their kind, but no matter how hard she tried, the inability to erase the memory of Thomas's contented face stayed with her.

"First of all, let's remove your House attire." Audrey untied and removed Rose's dress. "Now I need you to get between Melody's legs. It's just easier that way for the first time." Melody looked up at her and smiled, spreading her legs wide to accommodate her. Rose flushed and started to move, but then hesitated. The other girls giggled, but Audrey directed her gently toward Melody. "Don't be shy, Rose, we don't bite, honey!" Rose took a deep breath, reminding herself once again why she wanted this experience. This was a good opportunity. She positioned herself between Melody's legs. As she leaned over, her long tresses fell against the girl's cheek.

In admiration, Melody reached up a hand to wind her fingers through the loose curls. "You have such gorgeous hair. I wish I could wear that length and look as beautiful as you do." After she smoothed a golden lock back in its place, she cupped Rose's face in her hands and guided her down to a plump, engorged breast.

"Here's what you do. Take all you can hold in your mouth." Melody lifted her breast to accommodate Rose. "Now just suck with a slight pulling motion, if you can. It can be a little tricky at first. If babies can do this, so can you." Rose, trying to dissipate her awkwardness, inhaled and took the full, plump nipple into her mouth. The fullness of the flesh enticed her to play a little, licking the plump bud with her tongue, teasing with a gentle nip and tug.

Now she understood why men liked this activity so much. She discovered that if she simply didn't think about it too much, her body relaxed better. Melody's hand smoothed her hair once again. "That's okay, honey, just take your time. You're doing fine." As Rose worked her mouth on the breast, the milk, warm and sweet, flowed without effort. Interesting. The taste wasn't bad at all. No wonder Thomas enjoyed himself. Once she emptied the first breast, Melody offered her the other. "Oh, you're good." Melody ran her fingers through Rose's hair. "Are you sure you haven't done this before?" she said with a wink.

"You're the first … that is if you're not counting when I was actually a baby." Rose stopped long enough to give her a light smile. As she enjoyed the nourishment, she felt Audrey slide two fingers deep inside her wet sex, massaging up and down against her slippery walls. A pink flush heated Rose's face, but she didn't balk. After all, the sensations made her hum with pleasure, even if it the touch didn't come from Thomas, Daren, or …

"Okay, honey, let's change positions." Audrey clapped her hands with a commanding air, beaming at both admits. Before she got up, Melody took Rose's face in her hands and gave her a kiss, slipping in her tongue for good measure. Startled, Rose flinched.

Audrey laughed and took Melody's place, positioning herself on her back. "Now it's my turn!" A triumphant smile brightened her face. "Oh, Melody, can you get our little friend out of the drawer over there, please?" With a mischievous smile, Melody slid off the bed and moved to a chest of drawers in one corner of the room. After rummaging around in one of the drawers, she brought out a phallus with straps on it.

"Great, now we have something to play with." Audrey winked at Rose, who stood rooted in place, blinking at both girls with astonishment. "Don't panic, Rose. I know you can use these quite well." She giggled at Melody, who threw her head back with laughter.

"We know you enjoy bopping the guys, but for a change, what about us girls?" Melody waved the phallus at Rose. "Come on over here and I'll help you step in." Rose hopped off the bed and moved toward Melody. The large shaft and tip, resting against her pubic area, flashed before her eyes as she glanced down. She shook her head at the sight. No matter how often she used these toys, the idea of a female sporting a penis between her legs never failed to strike a strange cord with her sensibilities. On the other hand, using a phallus filled her with a strong sense of power.

"Before we start on my top, I want you to go inside me first." Audrey settled back on the bed, spreading her legs open wide. "Don't worry, I'll help guide everything in." Rose, now in full swing with this game, positioned herself between Audrey's legs, opened her up with a couple of fingers, and aimed the tip at her bubbling entrance, ready to slide in.

"Oh, wait, I almost forgot about this." Melody sped over and placed a large amount of lubrication on the phallus before Rose went any further. "Wouldn't be much fun without this."

Audrey nodded. "True, but I'm wet enough, so it would have been okay. But thank you for thinking of my comfort, sweetie! That's why we get along so well together." She blew Melody a kiss and turned to Rose, "Go ahead, I'm ready now." She grabbed the end of the phallus and helped Rose guide the shaft deep inside her body. With a gentle, fluid motion, Rose slid in and out as Audrey smiled in approval.

"Oh … great! Keep going … nice and slow … you've got the idea. What a good girl." Rose settled into a good rhythm and continued at an even pace. After a few moments, she quickened her thrusts inside Audrey. The attendant moaned at intervals, her breath catching in her throat. Rose located the knot of flesh at the top of Audrey's sex. With even, circular motions and a firm pressure, Rose moved over the bump several times before bringing on a strong orgasm. Audrey let out light yelp, and Rose pulled out.

"God, you're good!" Audrey blinked several times, staring at the ceiling as she took a moment to catch her breath. "Now come here—no, wait. I have an idea." She got up from her position and, removing the phallus from Rose, indicated for her to lie supine on the bed. Melody retrieved a new phallus from the drawer and strapped the device in place. Rose, without further instructions, opened her legs wide in anticipation. Melody returned to the bed and took her position between Rose's legs and, with precision, inserted the toy inside her. With a gasp, Rose lifted her hips as the shaft slid into position. This one, larger in size than she'd held before, was covered with thick ridges, creating a pleasant internal vibration as Melody moved back and forth.

Audrey positioned herself at Rose's head, and placed an engorged breast into Rose's mouth. Rose accepted the plump, dripping nipple and sucked with a greedy vigor. Though pleasant, Audrey's fluids tasted a little different from Melody's. The warmth filled her throat, and after she suckled for a few minutes, she latched onto the other one. Audrey sighed with relief as both her breasts were emptied. She reached down, found Rose's clit, and began fingering the tip with fast circular motions. The grinding of the phallus within her walls, coupled with her clit being rocked back and forth, initiated a momentary pause. With a loud moan, her pelvic area rocked with strong contractions.

"Just let it all out, sweetie." Audrey stroked Rose's hair.

Rose lay there for a moment, breathing heavily as her spasms subsided. Audrey looked at Melody. "Let's do one more thing." She got up and placed herself over the bed, letting the backside of her bottom hang over the edge. "Okay, you know what to do, so give it to me good." Rose sat up in astonishment as she looked at the two girls before her.

Melody placed a large amount of lubrication on the phallus and, opening up Audrey's buttocks, pushed the full length deep into her backside. "Am I okay for you?" Melody moved slowly in and out. She reached around with her hands and squeezed Audrey's nipples, her hips undulating with a smooth speed.

"Oh, you're doing great, honey, just keep going." Audrey gasped as Melody rode her faster. Audrey reached an arm down between her legs and began fingering her own clit with frantic manipulations. In a few moments, she brought herself to orgasm, her hips shuddering in release. With a sigh of fatigue, she rested on the bed for a moment. After a few seconds, her head popped up, and she smiled at Rose. "Okay, your turn!"

Rose stared at her in amazement, unsure what "your turn" might mean. Audrey chuckled. "C'mon, give it to Melody. She likes to get it in the ass, don't you, honey?"

"Love it!" Melody wiggled her ass. Audrey retrieved the phallus Rose had worn the first time and handed it to her. Once she strapped the toy in place, she moved in close to Melody, who bent herself over the bed, her behind lifted, ready for the gear between Rose's legs. Audrey spread a generous amount of lubrication along the phallus, and Rose prepared to impale Melody. Her fingers spread apart the soft, smooth buttocks, and she pushed the tip of the phallus into the small anal opening, working it in little by little. Melody relaxed herself as Rose entered, gliding in the phallus to its hilt. As Rose moved back and forth, nice and easy, Melody groaned.

"God, that feels so good." She moaned with pleasure. "I love this. Go a little harder and faster." Rose wrapped an arm around Melody's waist and found her clit, which she maneuvered with her other hand. With rapid motions, Rose strummed away inside Melody's walls, back and forth. Melody twitched her hips, her thighs quivering. She sucked in her breath, picking up the occasional grunt where she left off. She'd grasped her own nipples, squeezing them, milk dripping between her fingers. With a few more thrusts from Rose, she climaxed with a gasp, rocking her hips back and forth with staccato jerks. When Melody's climax subsided, all three girls collapsed on the bed, laughing.

After a few moments of idle conversation, Rose got up. "I've got to go. If Thomas wakes up, and I'm gone, he'll have it in for me. I've had a good time, though." She slipped into her dress.

"We've enjoyed it too, honey. Hope we've helped." Audrey helped tie the dress straps behind Rose's neck.

"More than you can imagine. Thank you." She smiled and gave them both a kiss before heading back to her ward. A few good hours of sleep remained, and she intended to enjoy every minute of them.

*   *   *

When Rose finished telling him the story of her visit with Audrey and Melody, Thomas threw back his head and laughed so hard he nearly cried. "So we guys win out, huh?"

"Yes, you do. It was fun in its own way, and they were really sweet; but I prefer having a man beside, and inside, me. That's why I didn't return to the woman you were with. I just didn't think she would go for another female."

Thomas recovered his composure and asked in a serious tone, "But, Rose, you seemed so angry when you saw me with Miranda. Whatever possessed you to change your mind?"

Rose scratched her head and thought for a moment. "I had a long mental wrestling match with myself. To me, a mother's milk belongs to her baby, not used for fun and games with other people. I saw mothers as off-limits sexually, untouchable. Of course it dawned on me that they still want as much fun as everyone else. So I decided to take the plunge, experience the taste. I mean, while I'm here, why not? Besides, you did mention that no one would ever know except the people involved here."

"True. If you want to try something new, better do it while you're in The House. It's a safe place for trying new things. And we all strictly adhere to confidentiality."

Rose gazed down at the bed, running her fingers in slow circles. "I have one other thing to confess."

"What's that, sweetheart?" Thomas picked up a small lock of her hair, watching it fall as he released it.

"I think the other problem I had was jealousy. Daria has those audacious nipple rings, Miranda has milk. You men seemed to fawn all over them more than … I just don't feel like I have much to offer in the way of …" She pursed her lips and made a vague gesture.

Thomas's mouth dropped open. "You've got to be kidding me."

Silence.

He hugged her closer. "I never knew you felt insecure before. When we've been at parties together, all the guys seemed to ogle you, fighting to get a shot at you. And they sure weren't going after nipple rings and milk." He smiled down at her. "Let me tell you something. You're perfect being you, all anyone needs. Nobody judges you here based on little extra add-ons. One day you'll no doubt be a mother, so you'll have what Miranda has. As far as piercings go, you can get those anytime you want."

Rose thought a few seconds. "I guess that's true enough. Well, I have a question for you then." She pulled herself up and looked him right in the eyes. "What's your … 'persuasion … as they call it? I saw what Daren did to you."

Thomas pulled her closer to him. "Rose, let me put it to you this way. Daren and I basically prefer females, but as you've seen, others prefer a partner of their own gender. Sometimes things around here get a little strange, and I personally can tolerate some limited male sexual contact, such as what Daren did, but nothing more. He's similar to me, though he's one of those people who pushes the envelope. There are times when we guys just get silly, and I have to tell you, as unusual as Daren is, he's a great guy and a top-notch attendant. But you already know his ways. You've experienced him for yourself. I'd trust him with anything."

"Oh, I couldn't agree more."

Thomas glanced at her with a smile and placed a kiss on her lips. "So now that we've had this purging of souls, there's one more thing I need to do." He got up off the bed and went to the drawers again. "By the way, I need you to get on all fours.

I'm going to remove the plug now."

"Will this hurt, Thomas?"

"I'll be as easy as I can. Sometimes they can be a little stubborn." She flipped herself over, somewhat apprehensive. "Okay, here I go."

She gave a jump as his hand gripped and began removing the plug, with gentle twists and tugs.

"Ow!" She whimpered, pulling away with discomfort. He stopped for a moment, applied lubrication to the fingers of one hand, and inserted them inside her slit. From inside her depths, he moved his fingers along her walls with a soft, gliding pressure, feeling the stiff outline of the device as he slid back and forth, hoping his strokes effected release.

"Rose, take some even, deep breaths, sweetheart." He removed his fingers from inside her inner passage and began rubbing outside her anal opening, coaxing her muscles to release the object inside her. Rose gave one last mental and physical attempt at total relaxation, which resulted in the steely object's release into his hand.

As she tried to scramble away, he grabbed her. "Oh, don't move. You're not going anywhere."

"I thought we were done." Rose's face clouded in dismay.

"Not so fast. I'm not through with you yet." He gave a light pop on the rear. "Get back here."

Rose let out a huff of disgust, as he placed her in position in front of him. She felt him open her buttocks up once again and press his cockhead against her anal opening.

"Oh, god!" She gasped as he slowly pushed himself inside. "Ow, Thomas, that hurts!"

"Calm down. I'll try to go easy on you."

"Can't we save this for some other time?"

"There's no time like the present, my dear, and I intend to have you now." She let out another whimper as he tried to work himself inside by degrees, slowly pushing deeper into her rectum. Though he tried to be easy, her body screamed as though she were being ripped apart; her breathing became labored. He stopped a moment before he continued again. Rose let out one last gasp as he finally buried his full length. He remained there for a few seconds so she could acclimate to his size, rubbing the side of her thigh with the hope of comforting her more. As he began to move in and out with a slow motion, she let out a soft moan. The discomfort soon gave way to pleasure as he filled her up, rubbing and hitting just the right place to make her climax. He alternated with undulations of his hips, stroking the wet bundle of nerves tucked away in her cleft. She dropped her head, letting him work the inside of her. Her hips shuddered as he coaxed out a climax. A few more pumps and he released himself, shooting out thick jets of lust. "Good?" he asked, rubbing her buttocks.

"Yeah, I'm good." She turned, bringing herself to a kneeling position, her face meeting his.

"So … what did you think?"

"Not bad. Took some getting used to, but you feel good inside, like you always do." She smiled at him, her eyes taking on a lusty shine. An unexplained, strange, hot feeling came over her.

"You like me inside you?" he whispered softly in her ear.

Her arms wound around his neck. "I do, Thomas, I really do. I like the way you fill me up, nice and deep. I like my pussy milking your juicy cock and swallowing your thick cum, too." She licked his earlobe with a hot, moist stroke.

"Um, Rose, what's come over you?" Thomas sensed a flush creeping over his face; his eyes glazed with a new lust. The pounding of his heart grew louder; the rise between his legs grew harder.

"You know what else?"

"What?" He held her in his arms, face close to hers.

"I'm glad you're the first to take everything from me. I'm glad it's you. I like giving everything to you first."

"Really, Rose? Are you sure?" He leaned in closer and dropped his face over hers and gazed into her eyes. "Are you really sure?"

She didn't answer, but reached up and pulled him closer so his lips touched hers. She'd truly meant everything she said. That much she knew for certain. But she didn't want to think about emotions, what-ifs, or what might be. At this moment she wanted only to drown in his kiss, forget about answers to questions she didn't quite understand. He reached down and massaged one of the nipples on her breast, squeezing the red nub before taking it into his mouth, where he sucked and licked with a vengeance. Rose dropped down and reclined herself on the bed and opened her legs wide, indicating a desire to be filled.

He inserted his fingers, rubbing her walls firmly, feeling the thickness of her fluids. He scooped up a generous amount of her release and worked her clit, sliding his fingers back and forth and around over the tip. The knot at the top of her sex ached, and she lay there, open and willing while his fingers worked, and the sparkle in his eyes held her mesmerized. In a moment, she gave a small shout as he brought her to orgasm. He re-positioned himself so his shaft lay between her breasts. His hands squeezed the mounds of flesh together, hugging him in a firm grip while his hips worked to release a milky thickness on her chest.

She reached into his warm pool with a finger and brought her hand to her lips. "Daren's right, Thomas, you are rather tasty, if I say so myself." She looked up at him and smiled. Thomas laughed and placed another kiss on her lips. He settled back down on the bed and cradled her into his arms. Somewhere deep inside, though, a sense of uncertainty lingered in his heart.

Chapter 8

"OH, THIS SOUNDS pretty interesting." Rose reclined easily against the large pillows placed on the floor, her legs spread open, as Thomas lounged between them, rubbing the inside of her warm, moist core with a careless motion of his finger.

"Yeah, this is a pretty interesting game, because neither admit nor attendant knows with whom they'll pair up. At least with a tag game, you can tell beforehand if you want to tag someone or not."

"I remember playing this game when we were young: the boys tried to steal a kiss from a girl they liked, or a girl from a boy they liked. The game seemed innocent enough, though."

"This isn't played exactly like you remember it." He carelessly slid his finger in deeper, swirling her fluids. Rose threw back her head and closed her eyes a moment as he wagged his finger to and fro inside her center of joy. Between her thighs a thickness gathered. She enjoyed these moments of pleasant conversation with him; she especially enjoyed the attention he lavished on her naughty bits. Her eyes strayed over to the silky, pink bulb between his thighs. The tip of his cock reminded her of a tight, curled up rosebud before it was about to bloom. She laughed at herself, at the ridiculous notion of comparing the tip of a man to a flower. Where did she come up with such analogies? At the ridiculousness of it, she chose to keep her humorous, creative imaginings to herself.

"So how does this game work, Thomas? Tell me more." She opened her legs wider, silently signaling him to continue with his tender caresses.

"Here are the rules. After all the attendants have created a special message on a slip of paper, we'll all go down to the mailboxes on the first floor and select a box at random. We just slip our note in a box, and the postmaster locks each one when we're done. When the admits go down after us, they select a box at random, and follow the directions in the note. Once you find the sender of your message, well … anything goes."

"How will we know which box is appropriate for our

taste?"

"Easy enough. You see, each attendant's box will be labeled with a sticker. The traditional male and female signs will be used: the circle with an arrow for guys, and the circle and cross for girls. Then, either a yellow dot or multi-colored dot will be used to denote gender preferences. Similar to the tag game we played a few weeks ago."

"Oh, good." She clapped her hands with enthusiasm. We did have fun during the last game, didn't we?"

He smiled at her. "I think you'll enjoy this game, too. We attendants have to get creative in how to spend the day. We want a good time with our new admit, so there should be thought in creating the setting and whatnot."

"What do you have planned, Thomas? Can you give me a little hint?"

"I'm not telling you! You could coincidentally choose my box, you know."

"Yes, I guess so."

"This isn't like the other game, when we weren't allowed to tag our own admit. We at least saw them first. This particular game is totally random, or blind, I should say, so you might select anybody, or get me."

"Or get Joe! Oh, gosh, I hope my luck holds out better. I don't ever want to be near him again … for any reason." She shook the unpleasant thought from her mind. "You know what, for some reason or another, I have a sense this time will be different. I think I'll get someone with a fun sense of adventure. I just feel it in my bones."

"Yes, we know your bones never lie." He grinned, wiggling his finger faster again.

"Don't tease about my intuition, Thomas, I take it seriously.

"And you should, sweetheart. You know we play this game in two weeks. At least I'll have some time to come up with a message and get the things I need for the day."

"And all we admits have to do is wait like children

anticipating Christmas. What a hard thing to do."

Thomas crawled up from between her legs and leaned over to place a kiss on her pretty, pink lips. "You'll be just fine, but no cheating or trying to find out what I'm going to do. Do you hear me?" He rolled her over, just enough to give her a quick, firm swat on her backside.

"Ow! That hurt. You're mean!" She laughed and tried to scurry away from his quick hand, but he caught her in his arms and placed another longer kiss on her lips. His fingers exploring her nether regions always made her lusty. The sliding motion of his fingers over her swollen, slippery walls always made his cock throb. Thus, they ended up in a quick round of lovemaking right then and there on the floor.

*   *   *

Up to the very day, Thomas was still working on his message. Finally he said, "Whew, I'm done, and today's the day. I may have finished my message at the last minute, but it's done, nonetheless." He put his pen down and rubbed his eyes.

"So what does your message say?" Rose came up behind him and tried to peek at the note, but he snatched his hand away.

"Rose, you've been trying to get the information out of me for the last two weeks. When are you going to give up?"

"Never." She stuck her tongue out, wrinkling her nose at him. "I must admit, though, you're pretty clever at hiding things."

"You've kept me on my toes."

"Good. Somebody has to, and it might as well be me." She kissed his cheek.

"Well, we have just enough time to get ready. So let's go do that thing we do."

"I do love our bath rituals, Thomas," she said as they walked to the tub room hand in hand.

"We've finally created our own ritual, haven't we? But we'll need to hurry. We have little time left." He turned on the water and stepped in. She climbed in after him.

"I'll get your back if you get mine. It's hard to reach back there," she said.

After a few minutes, he said, "Okay, Rose, I think we got everything. Sorry, no naughty stuff this time, we're on a time crunch."

Once they reached the room Rose said, "Thomas, can I wear my crystal outfit again?"

"Of course you can, sweetheart. Since someone else won't be choosing you first, I see no problem." He went over to one of the drawers and retrieved the jeweled outfit from its velvet box. He snapped everything in place and stood back, surveying her. "Let's leave your hair down for a different look this time, and I'll leave off the leash."

"Great idea." She twirled around in front of the window. "How do I look?"

Thomas moved over to where she stood, took her in his arms, and kissed her. "You're always radiant, whether you wear crystals or not."

John's voice came over the loud speaker. The game was about to begin. "Well, here I go. I'll be back in a few minutes." He turned out of the room and disappeared down the hallway.

Rose paced the floor in their room, heart pounding with excitement. Who would she pick? How would it go? Would she enjoy him? Would he like her? And would Thomas like his new admit for the day—better than he liked her? There she went, thinking all those thoughts again. She took a deep breath.

After several minutes, Thomas returned. "We're done. Admits will be next, and then time for the fun stuff."

"Did you see anyone deliver a message in a box that I should pick?"

"Rose, you never give up, do you?"

"Oh, please, Thomas, I want someone really good … like you." She bounced on the balls of her feet and wrung her hands.

"There would be no guarantee you'd get my box. Everybody runs at once. It's a madhouse, so there's just no way."

He stopped himself short and just laughed at her. "You'll be fine. You know how to handle yourself. Just have a great time, that's all."

Once again, over the loudspeaker, John gave the order for all the admits to report to the mail area. Rose sucked in her breath and made her way to the door, resolved to deal with anything that came her way.

"Good luck, Rose, if I don't see you this afternoon." Thomas gave her a quick kiss.

She turned and gave him one last hopeful look before making her way down the hallway and stairs. The crystal chandelier overhead and her own shimmering drops nearly rivaled each other in their flashing beauty. Even the stone goddesses on either side of the landing couldn't put her to shame, and they seemed to hail her beauty as she arrived in their presence.

Rose joined the group of admits milling around the mailboxes, as they waited for the command to select a box. She waved back at Daria, who'd smiled and waved in recognition.

"Hey, honey!" Rose gave a small jump as a female gave her a quick kiss on her face, nearly missing her lips.

"Hi, Melody!" Rose gave her a warm smile and a hug. "Are you ready for this game?"

"Oh, you bet I am. I just love suspense, you know. And you know what, don't be afraid to try something new and choose a different type of box, if you know what I mean." She gave Rose a wink and turned on her heel to talk to someone else. Rose laughed as she left, knowing full well what she meant. Rose shook her head. That would be a little too much suspense for her taste.

After several minutes, the command was given, and the admits made a rush for the mailboxes. Rose nearly toppled over as the crowd jostled her from one side to the other in a frenzied rush to select what they considered the choicest box. She squeezed herself through the crowd, pushing her way toward the huge display of glass boxes. In a state of confusion, she studied their glass fronts framed with ornately etched brass. One by one, the boxes became empty. A twinge of panic set in, and she threw up her hands in dismay; they all looked the same to her. She scanned the boxes again, spying the color of pretty pink paper in box number sixty-nine. Intrigued, she opened the tiny door and carefully pulled out the note. A soft floral fragrance filled her nostrils. She lifted the paper to her nose and took a sniff. How interesting and creative! The writer had put some thought into presenting the message. She opened up the note and read:

Within the heart still waters run deep. Inside dark caverns, the fairies sleep. Come to Earth's chamber and spend the day. In nature and shadows, we'll frolic and play.

What a darling little poem. And just where was this earthy chamber? Was it real or just a metaphor?

"I need you to follow me." A familiar masculine voice spoke behind her, and a hand secured her wrist.

Rose lifted her head and met a pair of dark, sparkling eyes staring down at her, a knowing smile crossing a handsome face.

"Why, you know who it is, John?"

"As a matter of fact, I do. I have to escort you to his location."

Rose looked around her. She didn't remember seeing anyone else being led away. Everyone else seemed to have read their notes, gotten the room numbers from the note, and raced off to find the new attendant for the day. Why did she need an escort? How strange this writer of poetic messages must be. "Can you at least give me a hint?" she smiled slyly, batting her eyelashes, hoping for at least a little clue.

"Not on your life! I've been instructed and sworn to utmost secrecy not to reveal any more to you. You think you can just persuade me with that pretty little smile of yours to give my friend away?"

"Well, a girl's gotta try, don't you think?"

John gave a merry laugh. "Let's go. It's a little bit of a

walk from here." He wrapped her arm around his and led her back down the hallway and out the front door of The House to the outside grounds.

* * *

The bright sun greeted them, floating high in a periwinkle blue sky, while fluffy cotton-like clouds meandered their way to unknown destinations. Birds sang their shrill tunes and flitted about the branches of the trees, stopping to jump down and preen their feathers in the birdbaths scattered throughout the gardens. Rose loved the grounds here, the beautifully manicured gardens, looking as if they had just jumped off a storybook page and landed right where they were. The forest was even better, having an almost magical feel, with gigantic trees, leafy slopes, mossy hills, and the occasional winding brook that seemed to pop up and surprise you.

They were going a different route from the one that led to the waterfall and the hot springs. John walked beside her, his strong hands holding hers in a soft grasp. They crunched through the leaves and twigs on the trails leading them to their desired destination. Secretly, Rose found herself wanting him in more ways than a light, exploring touch of a finger, or lips upon sensitive areas of her flesh. She wanted him, all of him, inside her.

But she found the yearning for him went much deeper than just holding his cock inside her. She felt drawn to him in some unexplained way, something stronger than her relationship with Thomas. Her feelings for Thomas may have blossomed into adoration of some kind, a kindred spirit for all time, but somehow she couldn't quite see herself with him as easily as she imagined herself and John.

She'd kept these thoughts to herself, mainly because he'd seemed detached overall from House activities, showing up sporadically, it seemed, when the time suited him. When he came around, the world seemed brighter, safer. Little did anyone know that her dreams at night were filled with visions of their bodies intertwined, lips on lips, his cock buried deep inside her, filling her with his lust and passion. Could he ever share the same desire?

As they trudged deeper into the woods, Rose finally broke the silence. "John, where exactly are we going? Can you at least tell me that?"

"No, I cannot! You are a persistent little thing, aren't you?"

"Thomas says the same thing, just this morning, as a matter of fact."

John smiled at her, but then came to a sudden stop.

Rose looked up at him in surprise. "What's wrong? Why are we stopping?"

John took her head in his hands and leaned down, giving her a deep, soft kiss. To her surprise, and dismay, he stopped and started walking again, as if the whole motion had been a mere afterthought. Puzzled, Rose grabbed his hand and pulled him back. She stared up at him. "Why did you do that?"

He stared her square in the eye. "I just wanted to, that's all. You look so pretty when you move, so light, so sure of yourself. I couldn't resist the temptation."

"Why did you really stop, John?" Her eyes met his, and she stood still, her jaw set. "I'd like an answer, if you don't mind."

"Really, is that so?" He stepped back away from her. "Did Thomas fail to tell you that you're a demanding little thing, too? I'm shocked you'd speak to me this way."

Rose dropped her head, face flushed with embarrassment. "I'm sorry."

John continued, "Besides, what if I don't want to give you an answer? I'm the steward here, and you're an admit. Isn't that enough?" He cocked his head at her and chuckled.

Rose blinked and swallowed hard, saying nothing for a second. His comment stung as a slap on the wrist, a rebuke for her impertinence, but somewhere in the depths of his eyes, she viewed more than his simple answer, sensed something deeper. Deep in her gut, she *knew* there was more. Did he want her as much as she wanted him, after all? In a bold move, she reached up, and pulled his face down on hers, plunging in her tongue, greedily stealing another kiss from his lips. Her hands ran through the thick locks of his hair and she pressed her body against his. No matter how he tried to hide, she knew for certain the hardness between his thighs couldn't lie.

When her hand slid down to trace the outline of his cock, John grabbed her by the wrists and gently pulled away. He took a deep breath and said in a soft voice, "The day is getting on, Rose, and you have a young gentleman who desperately wants your company. We need to go on."

Disappointed by his reaction, Rose's face flushed with shame, and she bit her lower lip, trying to hold back the sting of tears. In order to maintain some last shred of dignity, she gave him a polite smile, allowing him to take her hand in his once again. As they walked, she chided herself for coming on too strong, too forceful. She could try her will with Thomas or other attendants. That's what she was supposed to do during her training at The House, practice what she learned. John was a different situation; he was management staff. Had she challenged him wrongly when she should have just kept quiet? Maybe he called the shots, period. They continued their walk in silence, but an occasional view of John's face, like one in deep thought, still convinced her he was hiding something from her.

*   *   *

The cave loomed before them, a large gaping hole in the earth. They had made their way out of the woods, up a small hill, and into a rocky clearing. A small stream gurgled outside the opening and wandered off into the woods.

"We're here." John stopped just short of the cave entrance.

"So this is where I'll be today?" Rose stared in

amazement at the size of the entrance. "I didn't know there was a cave here. Nobody ever mentioned it to me."

"You don't hear many people talk about it at The House. It's almost like a well-kept secret. I'm not sure why, either, because this cave is such an interesting place. Well, what are we waiting for? Let's go on in." He took her hand and led her inside. The brightness of the sun faded away and the temperature became cooler as they made their way deeper into the interior. Long, solid columns of stone burst forth from out of the ground, and many more like these dangled from the rocky ceiling above. Tiny pebbles and small rocks littered the ground and scattered out from beneath their feet as they walked. As Rose's eyes adjusted to the dimness, she made out several pathways lined with small lamps. She raised her head and viewed larger lights placed sporadically throughout the entire cave, giving the overall environment a soft glow.

"How interesting. There's electricity in here?"

"The House directors put lights in here several years ago so this place could be used more easily. Imagine how dark it would be in here without lighting."

She reached out her hand and rubbed the stone walls as they passed. Once they reached a certain point inside the cave, John led her through a stone archway and into another room, also lit by lamps. In the distance, Rose saw a stone bridge that climbed upwards to a dark opening in the rocks. She strained her eyes. Did this cave have other rooms? Her mood brightened. But the last surprise shimmered several feet away to her right.

"There's a lake in here?" Unable to resist the temptation, she sped over to the water's edge, careful not to trip over a stone or catch her foot in a hole, and dipped her hand into the ice-cold water.

John came up beside her. "It's a fascinating lake, isn't it? We really don't know how big or deep it is, or where the water starts."

"A very mysterious place, it seems." Rose breathed in, looking around in awe.

"Yes, very much so. Let's head back over here." John took her hand in his, leading her away from the lake and back across the room to a small alcove.

"I just love the stone." Rose stroked one of the hard fingers projecting from a niche. John quickly took her in his arms and turned her back against the wall. The click of each cuff around her wrist seemed to echo throughout the room as he snapped them into place, securing her to the wall.

Her jaw dropped open and her eyes filled with alarm. "What are you doing?"

"I've been told to prepare you," John lifted his head, scrutinizing her, a light smile on his lips. Rose stood there, confused.

How had she missed these sizable rings bolted deep into the rock? "What a smart idea, the House directors putting something like this in here." She tugged at the cuffs, grimacing.

"We never leave any stone unturned."

"Very funny. This isn't the best time for jokes."

"Oh, maybe not for you, but not bad for me." John patted her cheek and smiled. "Everything seems tight enough. I don't think you can get away, at least." He stood still a moment and looked around him. "There's one more thing. Oh, yes, here it is." He reached behind some rocks near one of the bolts and pulled out a blindfold.

"Oh, John, please don't. I hate those things." She stamped a foot.

"Sorry, Rose, I can't do that. I have my instructions, you know."

"Who cares about silly instructions? Just don't follow them." She frowned at him, exasperated.

"I'm surprised at you! You think I don't follow orders?"

"You're the boss, aren't you? You told me so yourself earlier. You don't have to follow anyone else's orders."

John gave a loud, hearty laugh. "I'm not the boss of you today, Rose, not by a long shot." He studied her a moment, the smile fading from his face. He sighed. "You know what, you've been rather tricky today."

"In what way?" Irritation welled up inside. Her pride still smarted from their earlier encounter. Why didn't men just play nicely, and dispense with all the secrecy?

"Your tone of voice is not very ladylike," John chided. He continued studying her, walking back and forth. Rose averted his stare and dropped her gaze to the ground. "Let me see, you first asked me to reveal whose box you got, then you tried to get me to tell you where we were going, you demanded answers, and finally stole a kiss from me."

"Oh, stop, I get it." At the moment, she didn't care if she sounded snappy.

He stole in closer to her and moved a finger over one of her pink nipples, ending with a gentle squeeze.

She lifted up her head with a start. A nagging throb filled the area between her thighs. He was even more handsome when he seemed cross. His mirthful expression gave him an amiable look. The muscles bulging through his clothing drove her to distraction, inflaming the urge to rip the fabric right off him. Nothing would have pleased her more than to suck that stiff cock and relieve him of every drop of cum he possessed.

As if reading her thoughts, He slipped the blindfold in the waist of his trousers. With a swift move of one hand, he pushed the crystals of her belt aside and plunged a couple of long, slender fingers deep into her sex, sliding easily over her walls. Her hips writhed with his touch. He smiled. "Excellent, your attendant will be pleased, at least. I know for certain he likes his girls wet and ready, but I'm not done with you yet." He wrapped his hands around her, knelt down before her, and buried his tongue into her cleft.

Rose pulled on the restraints. Her knees weakened. "John, please." She struggled to stand, gritting her teeth for control. He said nothing but continued moving his tongue over her wet flesh. His hands held her tighter. She closed her eyes and cried out as his mouth came down over her clit and sucked hard.

Just as her body prepared for orgasm, he stopped, looked

up at her, and smiled. "There's a lesson for you."

"Oh, you're horrible." Rose groaned, twisting in pain. "You did that on purpose, didn't you?" The throb, hammering between her thighs, made her eyes water. Or did she want to cry? John whipped out the blindfold and placed it around her eyes, securing the ends in a tight knot behind her head.

"Now you're on your own." He turned and started to leave, but in an afterthought, he whirled around and added, "Oh, by the way, I wouldn't be fooled by pretty poetry and sweet perfumed paper. You're going to need all the luck you can get this afternoon."

Rose's heart stopped a moment. What did he mean? A cry caught in her throat as she called out to him, but the sound of rapid footsteps signaled his exit out of the cave. How frustrating. If only she didn't have the cursed blindfold around her eyes!

*   *   *

An overwhelming silence filled the cave, with the occasional breeze for a whispering companion. Rose turned her ears and listened. Light footsteps padded in her direction. As they moved toward her, the pounding of her heart kept time with each soft thud against the ground. The footsteps stopped a few inches in front of her, and the warmth from an unknown body made her tingle. Her ears picked up the rhythm of soft breathing. A dull drone sounded in her ears, and her skin stung with needle-like pricks, all in response to a new fear. To her relief, the visitor released her from the cuffs, but not for long. Two strong arms forced her around to face the wall and cuffed her back into place. Dizzy and disoriented, she staggered.

"Who's there?" she called out in a loud voice. Instead of an answer, much to her horror, a hand inserted a gag in her mouth and secured it around her head. Her heart sank; it was that cursed ball-gag she hated so much. John's words rang true. Luck didn't grace her with favors today. Blindfolds and gags had never struck her fancy for intimate trysts. The pretty poem on pink perfumed paper, the walk with John, the fascinating cave with its mysterious rooms and lake, all posed as mere illusions. Her hopes for a fun-filled day faded fast, and she blinked hard to keep the tears at bay. What more would happen?

Deft, cool fingers unfastened her jeweled bib, followed by the crystal belt. Without her jewelry, the cool air hitting her skin reminded her of her nakedness. She shivered and her teeth chattered. All movement stopped, and stillness settled over the room. Somewhere in the distance, she detected the sound of dripping water from the stone ceiling as droplets splattered against the rocks below. From behind her came a rustling sound, and her heart raced.

She cringed with dread, and her skin grew clammy. Strong fingers spread her buttocks open, and she cried out with a muffled shout. Cold steel inched its way into her backside with concentrated precision. Tremors ran through her legs, and her hips jerked harder. Cold, crawling sensations, from what seemed to be the ball end of an unknown device, traveled up inside her body, causing her to recoil against the rude invasion. After a moment, though, she found these movements heightening her pleasure, with an internal tickle each time she moved.

The stranger brought two leads of rope under and around her arms, wrapped them back around her chest, and ended by tying the ends to the device. She sensed this cold, metal toy was a hook, and no matter which way she moved, the hook inside her moved, too. Other than the embarrassment of being trapped like a fish on a line, the pleasure inside her created a delicious erotic fullness in her sex. Unseen fingers slid their way deep inside her and rubbed her walls while moving the hook at the same time. She bit down hard on the ball gag and pumped her hips hard and fast, not caring how she looked in front of her new companion. The fullness in her clit produced a fierce ache between her legs, and all she desperately craved now was relief. No such luck; the fingers stopped. Even through the gag she could not help but suppress a frustrated sigh.

"Impatient, are we?" the voice said.

Rose's heart jumped. She knew that voice, loved that voice. Familiar hands removed the gag and blindfold, followed by the wrist cuffs.

"Daren!" She could hardly believe her luck. The cave ambience created a perfect setting for his wild nature, or for his wardrobe, the usual loincloth.

He smiled at her. "I'm happy to see you, too." She flung her arms around him and held him tightly to her. He gave her a deep, passionate kiss, running his fingers through her golden tresses. Much to her embarrassment, she found herself grinding against his thighs. The tickling of the hook inside her drove her mad, and the hard bulge between his legs enticed her further.

"So you like this?" A satisfied smile crossed his face, and he reached behind her and tugged at the rope again, making her squirm.

"Daren, you're wicked. Are you going to keep me—um—hooked this way the whole time?"

"I'll keep you hooked long enough." Backing off, he studied her with great care and deliberation. He peered off in the distance. "Let's go this way."

*   *   *

Daren latched on to the ropes around her body and led her in the direction of the stone bridge.

"We're going to the room up there?" She pointed in its direction.

"Yes. We'll have a good time in there."

"All I know is, no matter where we end up today, I'll be with you, and we'll have a great time."

"You're a sweet one, Rose." Daren stopped to give her a quick kiss. When they reached the end, she stopped short, allowing him to enter first. He knew these rooms. No reason for taking a chance on falling down a black hole or twisting an ankle.

At last he found a brass chain and gave a light tug. Lamps

hidden among the rocks illuminated the room, casting beams of light across the walls. This room, small and bare, showcased embedded rocks poking their heads out of the earthen walls. The floor appeared to be compressed clay. In the middle of the room, lay a soft, forest green coverlet, complete with Daren's black leather bag. He led her to the coverlet and indicated for her to kneel down. No sooner than he'd reclined on his back, Rose seized the moment she'd been waiting for, and straddled his thighs to tackle the loincloth. With eager hands and hungry eyes, she peeled back the cloth, exposing all of him; but in the dim light, a glint of silver caught her attention.

She leaned in and, upon closer inspection, discovered an amethyst jeweled scroll perched on top, the steel post lost deep inside his shaft. Small chains attached the ornate cap to a ring that fit snugly under the ridge of his head, anchoring the device in place. Filled with awe, she stared at the strange beauty and creativity of this device and couldn't resist moving her soft, delicate fingertips over his tip, feeling the smooth texture beneath her fingers. With one finger she rubbed over the jeweled scroll in his orifice, feeling the gem in the center, cold, hard, and smooth against the pad of her finger. She grasped the scroll between her thumb and forefinger and wiggled the rod in and out about an inch or two. Daren closed his eyes, shifted himself into a more comfortable position, and sighed, enjoying the movements inside his shaft.

For a few minutes, she entertained herself, plucking up and releasing the jeweled rod, mesmerized by its sliding back in place, teasing him on the inside. She eyed his sac and gave each springy ball a soft squeeze. For a moment she felt at a loss on what to do next.

Out of the corner of her eye, she spied the black bag. What did he bring today? Reaching over, she grabbed the leather strap, opened the flap, and rummaged around inside. At the bottom, she located an amber bottle. Into her cupped hand, she poured a soft, green oil. An earthy smell wafted into her nostrils when she rubbed her hands together, and her fingers began to tingle with a soft warmth. She slipped her hand under his sac and rubbed the oil into his skin, softly squeezing and massaging each of the spongy contents inside.

A tickling sensation filled her bottom, and she discovered Daren grinning at her. His hands worked the ropes with a light tug, building up her climax just as surely as she was building his. She applied more oil, and her hands coursed over his pubic bone, followed by circular movements to the inside of his thighs. He lay back, surrendering to the moment as her hands tended to the sensitive areas of his flesh.

"You're wonderful, Rose." He rested his hands behind his head. "Where did you learn this kind of touch?"

"Oh, a fantastic teacher taught me." She had to admit the techniques learned from Thomas now served her well.

Daren closed his eyes and arched his back. The nipples on his chest hardened as Rose worked the pink flesh between her agile fingers. The delicate curve in his mouth depicted a smile of pleasure and trust. She adored the way he surrendered, his body accepting every motion of her hands against his skin. On impulse, she leaned over him and placed a soft kiss on his lips. He opened his mouth, and she pushed her tongue inside, teasing him back. He took one of her breasts in his hands and worked over the soft skin with his fingers. The force of his erection didn't go unnoticed. She stopped and caught a glance of the jeweled scroll rising out of his opening as the pressure built up inside his cock.

"I want in, Rose. Please, let me in." His eyes blazed with a lusty ache.

With the irresistible, pleading look he gave her, temptation won out. She removed the ring from the tip of his cock. No longer anchored by its chains, Rose pleasured him one last time, moving the jeweled top up and down. He sucked in his breath, swallowed hard, and closed his eyes.

She dropped her face close to his. "Do you like it when I do that?"

He blinked, lifting his hips as she toyed with him. "Oh

yes, but I don't know how much longer I can last." With a smooth, easy tug, she removed the rod and straddled him. Warmth washed over her as Daren's body merged with hers. The movement of the steel rod in her backside and the fullness in her nether regions worked in tandem, igniting an explosion of sensual bliss in her pelvic region. She threw her head back as the two of them moved in a controlled, steady rhythm.

Daren stifled a groan as she worked her hips, rising and falling, sure and steady. Her walls contracted and relaxed around him, and within moments, she extracted a deluge of emissions. He remained silent but fixed his gaze on her.

In the pink glow of the lights, Rose stretched her supple body, striking magnificent poses as she arched her back. She fluffed the golden strands of her hair, cupped her breasts, and squeezed the tips with her thumb and forefinger. Her rapid breathing had subsided, and once composed, she leaned over to kiss his lips.

He sat up. "I think we can remove this now." Kneeling behind her, he unfastened the rope from the eye of the hook.

Rose squinted, tightening her buttocks as Daren slid the hook out of her body. "You know what, Daren, I almost hate to lose that thing."

"It's great , isn't it? I thought you might like it once you got used to the feeling."

"Hey, do I get to use something like this on you?" She faced him, lips curled in an eager grin.

"Oh, I don't know, Rose. You're not interested in that, are you?"

The coy tone in his voice excited her. She made a quick dive for the black bag and prowled a moment. "This will work!" With a triumphant smile, she threw her hand up, waving a large strap-on phallus. "But I need one more thing." She dug into the bag again. "Here it is." Lubrication in hand, she turned to him, ordering in a commanding tone, "Okay, Daren, down you go. You'll like this better than fingers." She gave his shoulders a firm push, but his knees remained glued to the ground, and he continued looking at her as if he didn't comprehend.

"Let's go! Now!" She popped his buttocks, snapping him out of his momentary reverie. He shimmied his hips a second and laughed, but bent over and placed his hands in front of him.

"Go easy, please." He glanced over his shoulder. "By the way, I think your fingers are wonderful."

Rose strapped on the phallus, applying lubrication over the shaft and head. She knelt and positioned herself behind him, aiming at his entrance. Her soft hands rested on either side of his waist, and with a small, controlled push, she entered the head of the phallus into his backside. Daren twitched as his body accepted her thrusts. With smooth undulations, she glided the phallus in and out, the tip hitting him in just the right place. He let out a small grunt. With the established rhythm set in motion, she reached around his waist and grabbed his head between her fingers.

He gritted his teeth. "Boy, you know just where to touch a guy." He grew harder in her hands. As she continued with earnest thrusts, fingering his tip, his breathing grew frantic, and his cheeks flamed a bright scarlet. The groans grew louder, more earnest.

"You okay?" She viewed him, worry growing steadier each second. He didn't look well.

"Yeah, I'm fine." He let out a gasp. "Oh, god, Rose ...!" He dropped his head down on the coverlet, struggling to hold himself up.

"Daren, maybe I need to stop just a minute." Concerned, she stopped and moved her fingers softly over his back while he caught his breath. As she pulled herself free, he quivered, letting out a soft moan. She unstrapped the phallus and tossed it to the side of the coverlet. "You know what, let's let your body rest a bit. I don't want you passing out on me or something horrible like that. Come here." She stretched out on her back and cradled him in her arms. Her fingers strayed through the thick, wavy flames of his hair. "There, I think that's much better." A maternal instinct washed over her, creating a desire to offer peace, comfort, and protection to the small boy she sensed within him. She held his head tighter to her chest.

He lifted his head up a little and gave her a sheepish grin. "Sorry, I think all the build-up got the better of me. It always does. You might say it's my Achilles's heel."

She reached up and caressed his cheek. "That's okay. You don't need to worry about anything, but you scared me. Are you sure you're okay?" She smiled at him, stroking her fingers over the curves of his back and over strong muscles protruding beneath his smooth skin. His eyes glowed, sparkling like pools of liquid amber.

"I'm fine now. You really know how to get a guy going, that's all I have to say. Damn, your hands are good!" With a soft chuckle, he moved to kiss her on the neck. From his fiery locks, she caught a soft whiff of spicy cologne, a strange, pleasant scent which fanned her internal lust. Her fingernails grazed over the curves and muscles of his buttocks. He shimmied his hips and ground himself against her.

"God, Rose, that feels so good. Those nails of yours give me the shivers—makes me want to give a good long howl." At the same moment, he lifted himself up on his hands and knees, stretched his body, and threw his head back in a hyperextended position toward the ceiling.

His quick movements startled her, and she tensed. With anticipation she waited for him to do something next, something strange and characteristic of his nature. Her imagination ran wild. What would he do? What if he morphed into some strange animal? What if he let out a howl? How would such a noise sound echoing throughout the cave? She stifled a giggle. "Are you going to do it, Daren?"

"Do what?" He stared down at her, puzzled. "Howl?"

She nodded.

He shrugged. "I was only stretching a little, that's all." After digesting her question a few more seconds, he threw his head back and laughed.

Rose, overcome by a strange sense of humor, closed her

eyes, opened her mouth, and from the depths of her throat, let out a shrill howl that filled the room.

Startled, Daren's jaw dropped in utter amazement. When her unexpected fit subsided, he burst out in a rolling fit of laughter. She gave a small squeal as he nipped her on the neck. His moist mouth and hard teeth against her sensitive flesh, combined with his tickling fingers in her sides, sent her writhing with laughter.

In a moment, his lips met hers in a passionate, greedy kiss. The staunch erection between his muscular thighs played inside her wet cleft. She took his cock in her hands. Each tweak of her fingers resulted in more pre-cum pooling in his slit. Without further word or warning, his ejaculate fell in a small, warm puddle on her abdomen. With a flick of his tongue, he gathered up his own lust and, to her surprise, offered her a load by passing the contents between her open lips. She sucked and licked off the remnants of his passion, a thick film of saltiness filling her mouth.

"I love the taste of your magic potion." She pulled his face over hers, kissing the tip of his nose. "And it's okay if you don't change into anything weird."

"My magic potion? And just what do you imagine me changing into?"

"I don't know. Just crazy thoughts going through my head, I guess."

"You know what needs to change, though? The scenery, that's what. There's more to this cave than just this room."

"Doesn't surprise me. Tell me about the lake. I think it's just fascinating." Rose's eyes lit up.

"Let's go, then. Let's pick up everything we have here and get moving, because we're going on a little ride. I have another place to show you."

Chapter 9

ROSE AND DAREN made their way out of the room and over the bridge. A few yards beyond the bridge found them at the lake's edge.

"We need to go on around this lake to the back side over there." He pointed a finger to the far side. Rose squinted her eyes in the direction he indicated, barely noting what looked like a large cutout in the stone, showing nothing but inky blackness beyond the opening. She guessed the lake continued into another room. The sheer darkness set off a wave of nerves, while at the same time, nudging a sense of adventure. She trusted Daren, his sense of direction, and knowledge about this place. Besides, anywhere else they could kick up the lust would only give her another notch in her experience of strange places and wild ramblings. She scolded herself for not keeping a diary of all this, a memento for future reference, something to tell her children in her old age.

"Are we going through that opening there?" She craned her neck, gazing off in the distance.

"That's exactly where we'll be going. There's a small dry area where we can rest—or play, rather." He looked at her now and smiled. "The rest of the lake goes under the rock walls." He took her hand and led the way to the back side of the cave, where they found a small rowboat anchored to a stone post.

"Nice. We're going on a boat ride. How exciting!" She clapped her hands.

"So you don't make it a habit of spending your time in caves with lakes, I see?" Daren carelessly tossed the coverlet and leather bag into one end of the boat. Rose accepted his hand as he assisted her onto the seat behind the middle one. "Careful. Don't slip or fall. We don't need that much excitement." He climbed in, settled himself on the middle seat, and took up the paddles. With slow, hard strokes, he rowed toward the direction of the opening in the rock wall. The soft breezed kissed Rose's body as they glided along the water. She turned her head right and left, craning her neck to see everything that passed by.

The opening into the next room was several yards away, and Daren rowed to the nearest side wall. He reached over and pulled another chain. Rose's mouth flew open in awe. The room filled with a soft glow. The lake glittered all around them, and across the large cavern, she saw the surrounding walls. How difficult to imagine the water continuing its journey deep into the earth, where no eyes had ever peered before. On the opposite side, she made out a dry shelf of land.

When they reached the other side of the cave, Daren tied the boat to another rock post before tossing out their supplies onto a rock slab. He and Rose pulled themselves out of the boat and on to the rocky ground beneath them. This room, similar to the other, consisted mostly of large, smooth flat stones and boulders.

"Here, help me spread this cover out," Daren said. He rolled up one end of the coverlet, creating the semblance of a soft pillow. "There, this should do the trick." He stood up and inspected his work with satisfaction before picking up the leather bag. After seating himself, he motioned for Rose to join him.

"It's a little chilly in here." She snuggled close. Even in the cool air, his skin radiated uncommon warmth. The cold stones under the soft coverlet greeted her naked flesh with a biting chill.

"You'll warm up soon enough. I'll see to that." Daren worked himself in between her legs. His body warmed her, instilling a sense of safety. His tongue burned hot against her flesh as he moved it over once side of her neck, coursing over her chest, lighting on one of her nipples. Her temperature shot up, along with a throbbing in her clit. He slid his slender fingers deep into sex. He smiled, giving her a knowing look.

From the leather bag, he pulled out a neatly bundled towel.

"I have a little treat for you." He unwound the towel before revealing a small glass phallus in the motif of a snake, complete with a curvy body covered with small bumps. The vibrant colors in the glass flashed as beams of light caught the smooth surface.

"How cute!" Rose sat up and stared in wide-eyed disbelief at the object before her. "I've never seen anything like that before."

"I call her Sissy." He raised the phallus to his lips, plastering a small kiss on its shiny surface. "She's a sweet little pet, requires little care, and she doesn't bite." Daren peered at Rose. "Just lie back. Sissy wants to play a little."

Rose smiled, resting her head into the makeshift pillow at the head of the coverlet, legs apart as she opened herself up for the glass snake. Daren's gentle fingers spread her lips apart and slid the it inside her with a smooth push.

"That's so … wow, that feels …" Her hips arched and undulated up and down as she felt the phallus slide in and out, the bumps teasing her walls, the curves stretching her wider. "Daren, that feels so good!" She gasped as he moved the phallus in and out. "Keep moving. Go a little faster!" Her eyes closed, and her hips moved quicker.

"You like Sissy, then?" He gave the phallus a few gentle twists. "I thought you two would get on nicely." With nimble fingers, he worked the tip of her clit, preparing her body for an orgasmic frenzy. Rose let out a small whimper, vocal releases matching the hard and fast pumping movements of her hips as he brought out a strong climax. When the spasms died down, Daren removed the phallus and rubbed the top of it in her cleft, running the bumps on the glass over her sensitive clit. Her arousal soared higher, and she squeezed her own nipples, heightening the sensation even more.

Daren watched her with a smile of approval. After some time, he stopped moving the phallus. "Here, let's change positions a moment."

"Please don't stop. You guys always do this to me, all of you."

"Well, aren't we meanies," Daren said, cooing in her ear. "Rose, did you ever think that just looking at you makes us … well, ache—and ache hard." He added, "I lay awake at night jerking myself off while I think about you."

She gave an exasperated motion with her eyes. "That can't possibly be true. I think you just exaggerate."

"You think I'm kidding you?"

"I think you guys say things all the time that you don't mean. That's just your way, it seems to me."

"And you don't think you girls do the same? Well, just for sauciness, I think I'll sit here and let you suffer." He sat up cross-legged and folded his arms against his chest.

"Oh, Daren, please don't do that."

He continued sitting and staring at her, stopping on occasion to survey the ceiling.

She pumped her hips a little, hoping he'd finish her off. "Please … do something … anything!"

Still no answer; still no movement.

"Okay then, I believe you, but please don't stop."

"I think there could be bats in here, don't you, Rose? I sometimes think I see one, but I can't be sure." His eyes drifted up to the ceiling again. "Have you seen a bat up close before? I have, and they're really kind of cute." He glanced over at her and grinned, before focusing upward.

Rose, in no mood to discuss flying rodents, gave up in frustration and disgust. "Fine, I can take care of myself. I don't need you guys, anyway." She repositioned herself, stretched out a little more, and began plucking at the tips of her breasts, pulling and letting the plump flesh snap back in place. Her eyes still closed, she reached one hand down between her open legs, lighting on the top of her clit. With delicate, even strokes, she moved over the wet, slippery surface. "Oh, yeah, this feels good. So wet and sensitive." She sighed, gave a little groan, and arched her pelvic region a little. "You know what, Daren, when I'm aroused, I can take my own tip betweeen my fingers and squeeze and tug … like this, and …" She let out a light moan. "I love playing with my clit. It feels so good. That's the reason I got sent here …"

"Enough! I can't watch this anymore." He grabbed her wrists. She opened her eyes and saw Daren poised over her, eyes blazing, face flushed. "You're killing me here, Rose. You win, okay?" He broke out into his customary bright smile. "But let's try this, if you don't mind." He flipped himself so his bobbing erection landed over her lips.

"Terrific, Daren, does this mean your magic wand is mine?"

"You bet it is, and all the magic potion you want." With a soft grunt, he sank himself into her hot, wet mouth. She sucked his head and licked his cock, feeling the engorged veins underneath his taut skin. Daren leaned over her full, pink sex and pulled her outside lips apart. True to her word, he glimpsed her clit peeking its way out, inviting him to play. He dropped his head and unloaded the fullness of his soft, wet tongue, rubbing with unmerciful strokes. Her legs opened wider and her hips rose to meet his engaging mouth. Daren took the plump, wet flesh between his lips and sucked hard, the sharp pinch causing her to wince. If not for his own fullness occupying her mouth, she would have cried out; but only a soft squeak left her throat. A few more licks and some draws on her clit sent her body writhing in a feverish orgasm. She dutifully continued working on him, lashing her tongue against him, squeezing his balls. A few more swirls of her tongue, and she drew out liquid magic.

"That was great." Daren turned around and cuddled her up in his arms, his body warm and strong spooned against hers. He placed a kiss on her soft cheek and stroked her hair back in place.

"I was wondering, Daren, don't you have an admit of your own? I've never seen you with one."

"Yeah, I have my own admits. I just don't have one at the moment. The young lady who was mine left The House not too long ago, just before you came, I believe."

"Do you like being at The House?"

"You bet I do. There's nothing like being here. I have a lusty nature, which suits this place. The House and I were made for each other."

"You know what I've noticed about you?" She turned

and faced him, caressing his cheek. "Your attention to detail is amazing. You think of everything, like what to bring to a game or an outing, where the setting will be, how to entice someone. It's like each piece of the event means so much to you, like writing that cute little poem I got out of your mailbox. Why is that?"

He paused and thought a moment. "I've never thought about it before, but I guess you're right. Perhaps I'm a romantic at heart. You see, up until a few years ago my family and I traveled to faraway places, and during my travels, I learned the arts of love and various lovemaking practices. The first time a lady introduced me to sexual pleasures, I was hooked from that point on."

"What kind of different things did you learn in other places that you couldn't learn in our country?"

Daren sat up continuing his story. "You see, Rose, during my travels I learned that some cultures use pleasure gardens. These gardens are created for sensual activities, and are sculpted and designed with that specific purpose in mind. In these gardens, I learned how to touch the body and stimulate sensitive areas, how fragrance works to create arousal, and many unusual positions used during lovemaking. We don't have that here—other than at The House, of course."

"How interesting. I've never heard of such a thing. What do these gardens look like?"

He stroked his chin and thought a minute, trying to collect the memories in his mind. "They remind me of the gardens scattered throughout the grounds of The House. They're aesthetically pleasing, with fountains everywhere, soft grassy areas, stone sculptures, hidden places for privacy, colorful flowers, and shrub bushes trimmed into interesting shapes."

Rose nodded. "Okay, so tell me about your first experience. Was it in a pleasure garden?" She smiled at him, weaving her fingers through his fiery hair.

"Believe it or not, yes." Daren stared off in the distance and recounted his story. "I remember her, Anala. Her name meant 'fiery,' and her lovemaking lived up to its meaning. Her skin, was darker than yours, and flawless. Her black hair fell in soft waves around her shoulders. I loved her eyes. They looked so sexy, bright and eager when she smiled. And I adored her accent.

"While we were together, she taught me a lot. Some of what I learned, I still use on my admits. She'd seen me walking around, probably with a curious look on my face. She walked over to me, and we struck up a conversation. Finally, she told me she worked in these gardens, and wanted to show what went on. I didn't have to think too much before jumping on her offer. I'd already seen enough to get a vague idea. She was hot, and if there was a way I could sink my cock inside her, I wanted a shot."

"She sounds interesting, Daren. So what happened next after she talked to you?"

"We made a date. She suggested coming back just before sunset when the air was a little cooler. I had a hard time getting through the rest of the day, and even slipped into a bathroom for a few minutes to give my cock a good fix. When I came back, she had changed clothes, dressed in a sari that hugged her body and was transparent enough to show her breasts tucked up in a gold-embroidered brasserie. Because of the clever design of the sari, it accented the pelvic area without giving anything away. For a moment I thought she'd transported me to another world. My cock felt like it would explode."

"Do you think I'd look good in a sari? Sorry, I didn't mean to interrupt. I just think the clothing seems pretty."

"You'd be divine and dazzling." Daren leaned down long enough to kiss her lips.

"But go on. This is getting good."

"Anyway, we went to a private spot hedged all around in thick shrubs. These hedges were at least six feet tall. A large tree stood in the middle, and the grass was soft and green. When we sat down, she asked me what I knew about women, and had I ever been with one, did I ever … you know … play with myself."

"I remember that routine." Rose giggled at the memory of her intake exam. "But I'm sorry, I digress. Continue your story, Daren."

Daren cleared his throat and continued. "I told her honestly that I hadn't been all the way with a lady before, but I did spend times alone, milking my cock while thinking about women. She finally took off her sari. What a body of a goddess! Her dusky skin was prettier than I'd remembered earlier, and I couldn't stop staring at her tops and hips. I grew hard. All I wanted to do was grab her right then and there and go at it. She gently helped me out of my clothes, unbuttoning and removing each piece until we stood facing each other, naked."

"Were you as embarrassed at that point as I was?" Rose said, interjecting again.

"Absolutely." Daren laughed. "I don't think there's much difference between men and women when you're not wearing clothes, and you're in front of someone of the opposite sex for the first time."

"That's good to know. You men seem so cocky, like you have it all together."

"Trust me, Rose, that's not a bit true." His last remark contained a hint of sternness. "But back to the story. She told me to lie back on the grass, stretch out, and get comfortable, which I did with gusto. Staring up at a clear, blue sky, I couldn't wait for what she'd do next. For the next several minutes, she rubbed her silky fingers all over me. She paid attention to my nipples, squeezing and rubbing them. She moved to the inside of my legs, and landed on my swollen cock, which threatened to kill me if we didn't do something soon. I think she read my mind, because she took my cockhead in her mouth and went at it. I thought I'd entered another dimension. I nearly rose off the ground, but she continued flicking her tongue, hitting me in all the right places, nearly setting me off.

"She took one hand and worked my balls like her life depended on it. I thought I'd melt into the ground right then and there. I thought if she didn't stop, I cut loose right then and there.

I tingled all over, could barely catch my breath, and my eyes were suddenly out of focus. Then it came, the spasms, that moment when you feel paralyzed and you're happy about it. I shot out stronger than I ever had before. I could tell by the look on her face she was pretty proud of herself. I was proud I'd had my moment with her. She straddled my hips and leaned over to kiss me. I went for it. I cupped one of her breasts and played, squeezing the skin, flicking and pinching the nipple, nice and easy so I wouldn't hurt her. The feel of her was like leavened dough, soft and springy."

"Now I'll never be able to see bread quite the same way again, Daren, with such a description as that. She sounds delicious." Rose gave him a sly smile.

Daren sighed, a slight frown on his face. "Rose, do you have to keep throwing in your zingers? Do you want to listen to this or not?"

"No, I love the story. I really do love the story."

He glanced down at her hands. "And for godsakes, stop playing with yourself. You're driving me crazy."

"Sorry. It's just that when Thomas and I are talking he always throws in an added treat."

"Well, I guess I can't be outdone by old Thomas, now, can I? Trust me, I can pacify that sweet quim of yours with no problem." He repositioned himself between her open thighs and plunged in a couple of fingers. "Seems like I got you going."

"Yes, as always!" She blew him kiss. "Now go on. I want to hear the rest of what happened."

Daren continued his monologue. "I played with her breasts a few minutes longer, while she toyed with my cock and balls. When she was ready, I watched as she spread her legs apart, with no shame whatsoever, and reached between her thighs. Her fingers touched on something I didn't yet understand, and I looked at her closer for a better view. She said to go ahead and touch her, so I spread her apart. With a slender finger, she worked her clit, round and round and round. She told me I could try, and I worked the plump, springy knot until she gave a little cry. She tossed her head back and forth a little, shut her eyes, and clenched her fists, her hips pumping in time to an internal rhythm I didn't understand yet, either; but I think I was beginning to catch on.

"Then it happened. She pulled me over her, and I positioned myself between her legs. I went in nice and smooth, while she guided me. She'd been with a lot of men, so her core held all of me without a problem. I loved the way she felt inside, her walls hugging around my cock, wet and hot. Natural instinct took over, and I didn't think much after that. I let myself go, passing in and out of her like a well-oiled piston. Her eyes had glazed over, and her smile looked like someone daydreaming. Our breathing matched, fast and even. I'd finally settled into a good rhythm, and discovered I'd sped up the more urgent I got. She'd begun panting a little, letting out a tiny cry every now and then. I knew I wasn't hurting her because she opened up more like she couldn't get enough. My balls ached harder than they'd ever ached. My thighs hurt; I had that funny, fuzzy vision again; and it's like I wasn't a part of the present world anymore. I made one last thrust and unloaded inside of her. It was then I felt her contractions tugging on my length. From the look of her, she'd climaxed too. When we finished, we cuddled up on the ground and fell asleep. That night, we slept under the stars. At times, we engaged in a few more rounds of lovemaking. When I woke up just before sunrise, she was gone."

Rose lifted herself up on her elbows, eyebrows raised in surprise. "She left? Just like that? That's not good. I'd be mad, if I'd been you."

Daren eased Rose back down on the coverlet. "I wasn't angry at all. I understood her place in those gardens, and I knew she'd completed what she wanted to do. And I admit, I am grateful for her tender initiation."

"Did you ever see her again?"

"No. I simply got dressed and stole out of the garden, but I left a much wiser person. So when you ask me why I do the things I do, this is the reason why. Much of what you see going on at The House is what I learned abroad. I think those special touches make a worthwhile difference in the intimate experience you'll have with someone."

"Hey, Daren, you know what? I think you're a true romantic, after all."

Daren smiled and stroked her hair. "I have a feeling it's getting late. I think we better head back to The House."

They picked up their belongings, and carried them back to the boat. Daren took up the oars and rowed back to the front room leading out of the cave. When they reached the lake's edge, he assisted her out of the boat and retrieved their items. "We have to get one more thing before we leave. I nearly forgot about it." The crystal jewelry, still in its same place, flashed in the lights. Daren reached down to pick everything up and placed them back on her body. "There, it's all back on, now." He finished hooking the clasp on her belt, turning her around to face him.

Rose threw her arms around his neck and kissed him. "I had fun, Daren. You're wonderful as always." She peered up into his eyes. "I think it would be fun to do something in a garden sometime."

"Maybe you will. When you do, think of me." Taking her hand in his, he led her out of the cave, and the couple made their way back to The House just as the sun started to set.

Chapter 10

ON THIS DAY, Rose found herself full of wanderlust, and with Thomas's blessing, she headed for the grounds surrounding The House, hoping to entertain herself with something fun, sensual or otherwise. Though she enjoyed Thomas's company, she liked having a small number of hours to herself on occasion. With twitching anticipation and speedy feet, she ran down the marble staircase, oblivious to anyone or any distraction along her way. She loved traveling the staircase; she loved this particular place in The House most of all, because she felt like a princess as she moved over the stone steps, bathing in the rainbow flashes cast off from the great crystal chandelier above.

Taking a right turn at the foot of the stairs, she headed down the hallway. Nearing the end, she discovered John's office door closed up tight. Rose lowered her head for a harder look at the bottom. No light, which meant he'd left The House. Where could he be today? Puzzled, a deluge of questions flooded her brain. Somehow his absence gnawed at her, enveloping her in a strange, sudden sense of loss and emptiness. He'd always been around, showing up in the most unusual places, at the most opportune times for her, and his tender engagements had won her over. Not once had the idea ever occurred to her he might have a life outside The House. What if he had a lover? The thought horrified her. Why did he need another when he could have her? Maybe she should have taken more initiative, but their interlude during the walk to the cave had set her nerves a little on edge. Better to let him come find her. After all, he'd succeeded in putting her in her place.

She shook her head to collect her wits, and continued out a side door leading to the outside world. The sun's rays hit her, hot and bright, and she skipped into the world of nature until she found herself immersed in the forest. A soft breeze blew, scattering the fragrance of wildflowers into the air. Rose inhaled and sniffed the scents. Several trails wound through the grounds, and one looked as appealing as the next. Unfamiliarity and too many choices left her in a quandary, so she picked one at random, not worrying too much where the path might lead.

Within a few moments, after rounding a bend, a small cottage came into view. A trimmed lawn and tidy rows of flowers and shrubs outlined the front. What a surprise to stumble upon a scene so quaint! There were no stories she remembered hearing about other dwellings on the grounds, and the look of this one reminded her of those she read about in fairy tales. Who lived here? What would she find on the other side?

Astonished at her own boldness, Rose wandered off the main path and on to a trail leading to the house. Only the hum of insects shrilled through the air, and the warm heat of the sun kissed her skin. She kept trudging down the trail and spied a small side window. Tempted as she was to peek inside, she decided to keep walking. What if she got caught snooping? How would she tell someone her idle curiosity had gotten the better of her good sense? The trail led to the back of the cottage, but the sound of distant tinkling caught her attention. Someone must live here, then. She strained her ears and tried to locate the direction of the sound.

She crept forward and saw a wooden fence with an open gate. Getting up her last nerve, she passed through and found herself in a quaint garden, filled with wild flowers, varieties of herbs nestled in their beds, and pruned shrubs. A small, gurgling creek ran through the middle. What a charming and soothing place to lose yourself. Again, the soft sound of chimes filled the air. She craned her neck in the direction of the sound and spied them in the far corner of the garden. Without another thought, her footsteps flew across the stepping stones, across a small wooden bridge arching over the creek, and over to the area where she spied the object making the noise. She blinked several times, not sure if her eyes were playing tricks on her.

The wind chimes consisted of a long-haired siren riding on top of a large winged penis. Beneath the large shaft, a smaller penis emerged. From the wings and penile tips hung chains holding cast metal cutouts in the shape of breasts. Smaller bells pierced the tip of each nipple. When the wind blew, all the bells and breasts clinked against each other, filling the air with an enchanting, chiming music.

"You like my tiny tinkles?"

As the voice cut the air, Rose jumped, letting out a small shriek. A hard bulge pressed against her backside, and two hands clamped over her breasts, holding her fast. The two hands turned her around to face their owner.

"John!"

"Caught you looking!" His smile beamed as radiant as the sun, and his eyes contained their customary sparkle, his personal trademark.

"I thought I was alone."

"I was over there." John pointed to a large cluster of vines. "No wonder you didn't see me."

After she recovered from her shock, she broke down in a fit of giggles. "I think your tiny tinkles are titillating," she said, trying her hand at alliteration.

"I think you're rather titillating yourself." John leaned over and gave her a soft kiss. "What are you doing here by yourself?"

"Thomas gave me a few hours to myself."

"How generous of him. I'm surprised he ever lets you out of his sight."

Rose laughed. "Believe it or not, he lets me off my leash every now and then."

"If I had you on my leash, I'd never let you go. Ever." John held her close and gazed into her eyes.

"Is that so? I'm not so sure I believe you." She stared at him a moment and continued, "You were a mean tease on our way to the cave, by the way. I've been meaning to come and give you a good scolding, but—"

"But what? Thomas's leash kept you from it?" John threw back his head and laughed.

"No, silly, but you scared me, trying to make it look like I'd be spending the day with someone mean and hateful."

"Sorry, Daren made me swear not to blow his cover. But weren't you happy with him? I heard you had a good time."

She'd thrown caution to the wind at this point. The way his eyes fairly made love to her, the way he held her said enough. It was now or never. She could toughen up and take a chance with him, or play it nice and hope for the best. Her gut said to go for it.

"Daren's fantastic, but you're still a bad boy for trying to trick me, and I do mean to make you pay." John let out a playful sigh. "Well, if I have to be scolded or punished by anyone, you would be my pick." He smiled at her once again and gave her a quick kiss on the tip of her nose.

"Really, now? You better be sure because you might get what you wish for." Rose lifted up an eyebrow and cast him a sly glance. "I at least respect a man who knows what he wants." Her hand strayed over one of his buttocks and delivered a light squeeze followed by a light swat.

"Trust me, Rose, I am a man who knows what he wants."

"Good. So are you admitting you were naughty and a good scolding would set you straight?"

"Definitely. I'm not sure where my manners wandered off to that day, but naughty boys do need to be taught a lesson."

"Well, since I'm here, and my time this afternoon is limited, why don't we start your payback now?"

He stood there a moment, taking in her words. Finally he bowed his head. "No time like the present. Your wish is my command."

* * *

An iron trellis had caught her attention earlier while she had been admiring the chimes, and now the vision of John tied to the bars, naked and under her command, filled her with a sense of power she wanted to use. Whether it was too much heat from the sun or knowing she and John were alone, she couldn't tell. But a new confidence welled up from some unknown place inside her, and she aimed to play it for all it was worth.

"Very well, then, let's get started." She reached up, untied the straps from her dress, and removed them from their loops. Next she reached for the bottom hem of her dress and peeled the garment off her body. John stood there in wide-eyed amazement. "Come here." She pointed to the trellis.

Hypnotized, John followed her command and moved toward the trellis positioned against the wall of the garden.

"I need you to strip this instant."

John stared at her a moment, but responded to her commands with flushed cheeks, pulling off each article of clothing and tossing it to the ground. "You know, it's been a while since someone as lovely as yourself made me follow orders."

"Well, it's time to end your dry spell, wouldn't you agree?"

"Oh, yes. I'm looking forward to it." He smiled and waited for her next command. Rose turned his back against the bars and used the straps of her dress to tie his hands over his head, fastening them tight. "Good, you won't be going anywhere fast." She stepped back to make sure he stood just where she wanted him. As she viewed him for the first time without clothing, his body took her breath away. His heavy breathing accented the muscles in his chest, and his strong skeletal frame displayed the fine contouring of a well-developed man. A full sac hung between a pair of strapping thighs, and a thick cock with a glistening head stood at attention.

"My, my, aren't you a pretty toy to play with." Rose administered a light swat to his shaft and watched his full, pink tip bob back and forth. Her hands cupped his sac, and the soft pads of her fingers squeezed and massaged with a concentrated tenderness. He closed his eyes and sighed. Struck with an idea, she stopped and glanced over at the creek. She turned around, crossed over to the edge, and dipped a hand into the icy liquid. Yes, the water was freezing, even on a warm day. Perfect, just what she wanted. When painful cold became unbearable, she headed over back to John.

His eyes narrowed. Rose parted his buttocks and entered two slender fingers into his backside. He jumped and winced with a start at the touch of her cold fingers sliding inside him. Her fingers moved up and down his walls and managed to hit his sensitive areas with perfect precision. He opened his mouth and let out a soft groan. Just when he seemed the most ecstatic, Rose stopped. His eyes popped open and he flashed her a look of dismay.

"Welcome to my world, John." Her eyes flashed as a teasing smile crossed her lips. "Hurts, doesn't it? You men always do this to me, so it's time for payback."

"Come on, Rose, we men aren't that bad, are we? Can't you at least cut me a break this once?"

"What? And make it all better for you? I don't think so. Not right now, anyway." She looked up for a moment. The sun cast hot rays throughout the garden, and her body felt moist from the heat. "You know what, though? I'm rather thirsty. It's warm out here, don't you think? I'm sure you have something nice and cool inside to reward a girl's hard work." She whirled around and sped across the bridge, toward the back entrance of the cottage. In mid-stride, she stopped and called back, "Can I bring you anything? Oh, you know what, on second thought, you look fine to me right now." She gave a careless shrug and strode off once again.

When Rose opened the back door of the cottage, cool, refreshing air hit her skin. She walked in and noted the simple, quaint decor. A small wooden table and chairs stood in front of her to the left, and a cupboard lined the wall next to it. To the left of the cupboard she discovered a small kitchen area. A brocade sofa graced the right-hand side of the room and faced a stone fireplace that lined the right wall. Wooden bookshelves framed each side of the fireplace and supported numerous volumes of books.

Time for that drink she wanted. She turned around and slipped into the kitchen, where she soon found several glass containers holding various fluids. Two green bottles attracted her attention, and she pulled them out and placed them on the table. They looked just like soda bottles. There had to be something good in them. Where to next? To the right of the back entrance she discovered the wooden staircase leading to the upper level. Perhaps John kept some playthings upstairs? Though she felt like an intruder, she wanted to see what this cottage looked like, and where John obviously spent his free time when he wasn't at The House. She moved up the stairs cautiously, the wooden joints sounding off soft creaks with each step.

When she reached the top, she noted only a modest linen cupboard to the right at the end of a small hall, and the bedroom to the left. She turned and entered the bedroom, which also contained the bathroom. A large wooden box rested at the foot of the bed. Not one to waste time, she opened the heavy lid and exposed an eye-watering collection of leather cuffs, phalluses, and lubrication. Excellent! Now, what to choose remained the big question. She reached inside and, after rummaging through the contents, chose a tube of lubrication and a small phallus with a slight curvature at the tip. Perfect! Just what she wanted. Satisfied she hurried downstairs with her toys, picked up the bottles on the table, and scurried outside to the garden where John awaited.

*   *   *

John glanced up at the sound of footsteps.

"Fancy meeting you here." She dangled the toys and bottles from each hand.

"Very funny." He grimaced and glanced down at the objects she held. A new smile lit his face, and the old sparkle danced in his eyes. He continued watching as Rose scrutinized him, licking her lips while she decided how to proceed next. The sight of the toy in her hand stiffened his cock. Deciding to break the silence first, he said, "So did you find something to quench your thirst? You sure took your time in there. The day's getting on, you know."

"Really? Did I make you wait too long? I feel like maybe I'm holding you up. I think I should untie you and go on back to The House so you get on with whatever you were doing before I arrived."

Alarmed, he scrambled for words. "You'd leave and not make me do penance? What about payback? I mean, how heartless of me to have teased you in the cave."

"Are you sure you're up to it? Do you really want it?"

"Please stay. Yes, I really want it. Give it to me, Rose." Of course he didn't want her to leave. She needed to stay longer and play. At this point, he wanted to overtake her, explore every curve, every sensitive area, and her leaving robbed him of that chance.

A smile twitched across her lips. "Well, since I took my time just a few minutes ago, I'll not waste any more because your time is now at hand." She brandished the bottles at him like one heading up a battle brigade, and placed them, along with the phallus, on the ground.

As she moved in closer, his eyes met hers. The tips of her breasts pressed against his chest, encouraging the throb between his thighs. She lifted up her head and placed her lips on his, filling him with a deep, tender kiss, ending with a sharp little bite on each of his nipples. His breathing increased. The urge to consume her rose stronger. She slipped down on her knees, facing his engorged shaft. She licked the tip of her tongue in his slit, tasting the tiny, salty pool gathering at the top. John closed his eyes a moment, trying with all his might to contain himself and his will to spend. As she continued to take all of him in her mouth, he became frantic inside, filled with a desperate need to create some sort of distraction.

Just as her jaws and tongue began sucking and licking, he blurted out, "Rose, did you say something earlier about being thirsty? You're turning red from the heat."

She stopped her work and peered up, eyes glinting. A frown clouded her face as she collected her thoughts. "What if I did say something about wanting a drink?"

"Well, I think you might quench that thirst of yours with one of those bottles you have, instead of leaving them on the ground. They're getting warm out here in the sun, and you went to all that trouble."

"You know what, perhaps you can drink one first. I did bring enough for both of us." She jumped up, leaning in close to his face, a sardonic smile on her lips. Her eyes narrowed into slits before softening into a lusty gleam. "You know what," she said in her most seductive voice, "you're pretty hot yourself." Her mouth opened and she flicked out her tongue to lick the side of his cheek. John's heart pounded harder. Her cockiness had proved a bit bolder than he'd bargained for. He licked his lips, and his mind raced for way to placate her. "But Rose, you're my mistress today, and it would be rude of me to sip first."

She fell back a little, studying him. "You make a good point," she noted. He waited with baited breath for her to crack open a bottle top and pour the contents down her pretty throat, but met with disappointment. "You're right. I am your mistress today, and so I'll drink when I'm ready. And I'll be ready when I'm through with you first."

Great, his luck seemed in danger of slipping away. With this behavior, he believed aggravating or reasoning with her may be his undoing. He gathered up his energy and stood with a new resolve. "Very well, Mistress, as you wish." He bowed his head low.

"There. Such an answer from you is more suitable." Rose grabbed up the phallus and applied a thick coating of lubrication over the surface. "Time to finish my job here." John closed his eyes, opening himself up for the invasion, his heart pounding and thrilling with anticipation. With a steady hand, she opened up his buttocks once again and inserted the phallus into his anus.

The initial sting quickly turned into gliding bliss as the shaft slipped in and filled him up, the curved tip hitting the sweet spot deep inside his body. Rose passed the device in and out, the grinding rhythm prodding him to an aching fullness. The hard ache in his cock nearly drove him mad. The vision of her alone always drummed up a healthy dose of lust. At nights, alone in his bed, he often fingered himself to raging erections, finishing himself off with thoughts of her. His aching balls reminded him he was near the spilling point once again, and he nearly broke down and begged for release.

Nothing but disappointment and frustration awaited him. She brought the movements of the phallus to an abrupt halt and removed the device, giving it a light toss on the ground. "You know what, I think I'll have that drink now."

John sucked in his breath through clenched teeth. "Yes, what a wonderful idea." The old ache between his thighs nearly split him apart, but the knowledge of imminent freedom and control subdued the frustration overcoming him. Luck crept within in his grasp once again. He chuckled to himself. No doubt this young lady before him thought herself smart enough to get one over on him, but he knew better. Patience and discretion, two of his favorite virtues, usually served him well in situations such as this one, and now they would pay off to his advantage. He watched her with great interest.

Rose snapped the top off a bottle and sipped some of the liquid inside. John waited as she swallowed down the contents. She jerked her head up in surprise and blinked her eyes. He smiled. She shrugged and sat down on a large, flat rock, continuing to nurse the green bottle. Several minutes passed before she held an empty container in her hand. Her mood sobered up a moment. "John, this stuff tastes funny. Sort of earthy, and my mouth feels cool and tingly. What is it, exactly?"

He shrugged. "Only a homemade concoction of mine. I created the drink using an old family recipe."

"An old family recipe? What's in it?" She cast him a wary look.

"I can't tell you that. My family, as did our ancestors before us, guards the formula like it's gold."

"What nonsense. This stuff can't be *that* special." Rose reached up and rubbed her head. "God, I feel woozy." She started fanning herself with her hand. "Maybe the heat is getting to me after all." She shook her head. "Now my whole body feels funny. I'm starting to tingle in the strangest places." She twitched, plucked at her nipples, and repositioned herself on the rock. "You know, John," she said, stretching her neck from side to side, "I must say this drink is rather relaxing. I almost feel like I'm dreaming. Very good stuff here."

"Are you okay?" John asked, trying to keep a straight face.

"Sure, why wouldn't I be?" She smiled over at him.

"You seem a little—oh, I don't know—out of character or … distracted! That's it, distracted. Why don't you untie me so I can help you."

"I'm fine, really … but then again …" She looked around a moment. Then she glanced back at him. "You think you can help me? Because I'm feeling rather … well you know …" She turned her eyes back at him and fluttered her lashes.

"I guarantee I can make you feel much better. Go ahead and untie me, and I'll come take care of you." He took a most ingratiating tone, hoping she'd give in and untie him. His efforts were rewarded.

"Well, you're not much use tied up anyway." She sighed, drew herself up, and walked toward him. The straps fell to the ground as she untied the knots. He stooped down to pick them up and when he stood up, she plastered her breasts and wet crotch against his skin. Her hands entwined themselves around his neck, and her fingers lost themselves in his thick locks. Without further distraction, he grabbed her wrists, placed them above her head, and tied them together with the straps. She staggered just a little, but managed to remain standing. He smiled. So far everything succeeded just as he'd hoped.

Her eyes rolled up. Noting the bindings around her hands, she searched his face with a glazed stare. "Are you going to take me now?" Her body pressed harder against his.

John lifted her face to his, and gave her a deep kiss, teasing the top of her lip with his wet tongue. "I'd love nothing better than to take you totally and completely, Rose." Finally he spoke the truth without fear, without holding back, and the thoughts of his heart came tumbling out in an emotional avalanche. He stared into her face. "Taking you has been a fantasy of mine since the day you graced the steps of The House. Little do you know, I've spent days, hours waiting for this moment, waiting for the right time. I'm tired of being careful, trying to find delicate ways of handling my feelings whenever I see you. Your coming into my garden today didn't happen by coincidence. I think it's fate, you and me here alone today. And by god, I aim to make it worth both our whiles.

"Oh, please do—and be quick about it!" Rose tried to sound cross, but her bite on his earlobe disarmed her tone.

He picked her up in his arms and carried her over to one of the larger trees and placed her on a cool patch of green, shielding them both from the glare of the sun. Rose stretched herself out, oblivious to the bound hands above her head. The sun's rays stealing through the branches highlighted the soft curves of her delicate figure. As he viewed her, bound and willing, John played with the notion of tantalizing her willing body, showing no mercy, until her earnest pleading to stop satisfied him. However, his internal cravings and lusty desire acted with a voice of their own, leaving him weak. "You know this will be our first time, don't you?" Rose gave him a shy smile. She spread her thighs apart, inviting him to keep true to his word. John bit his lip, ready to pounce. The moist feminine bits before him flirted with his self-control, but he managed to hold himself in check, and let out a soft chuckle.

"Yes, you're right, sweetheart, this is our first time." He smoothed a lock of her hair back in place, viewing the seductive pink nipples on each breast. He placed a tender kiss on her lips, moving his finger over the curve of one of her breasts, ending with a smart squeeze of the nipple. She opened herself wider, enticing him to enter.

Watching her obvious internal pain reminded him of his restored power, and he took even greater pride in knowing her relief depended on him. He smiled down and responded with a soft lick on the outer rim of her ear. Her fingers twitched, and she remained silent. He caressed the tops of her breasts, pausing to sample, with a full draw from his lips, each full peak. As his tongue continued down her body, the heat of is breath trailing over her flesh, she closed her eyes and clenched her jaw, attempting to stifle an occasional whimper.

At last he trailed down to the hollow of her stomach, stopping to play in her navel, the perspiration leaving a salty residue on his tongue. His mouth finished the exploration of her body by licking and sucking the slippery clit between her thighs, the soft brush of his mustache grazing the sensitive tip as he lapped at her fluids. As his movements caused an aching crescendo within her, she opened her mouth and cried out her release. John smiled with satisfaction, watching her hips jerk. With a shift of his body, he prepared himself for a full merger with hers.

"Are you ready, Rose, for real, this time?" He smiled down at her, aiming the head of his cock at her entrance.

"Yes." She opened her eyes, flashes of blue shining upon his face. "I've been waiting, too."

"Here goes." John placed his hands on either side of her shoulders, raised himself up, and pushed his way in, slipping in his thick length. She continued staring up at him, never once removing her eyes from his. She yielded to his advances, reveling in the act of being filled and invaded as he pressed forward with each determined thrust.

Once he tapped her back wall, he readied himself for release, passing in and out, gliding with deliberate, smooth movements. As the pressure mounted, his engorged tip throbbing, he moved with earnest, staccato thrusts. His mind slipped into another dimension, and his thoughts fixed on nothing but the sensation of his cock moving inside a tight sheath. The ache in his balls had reached a crescendo. He closed his eyes for the finish. Within a few seconds, he climaxed, giving himself over to spasms and a heavenly release. Rose smiled as her muscular walls contracted against him, swallowing the thick warmth filling her dark center. He leaned down and kissed her, slipping his wet tongue into the depths of her willing mouth. After a few moments, he released the bindings from her wrists, and the pair stretched out under the shade of the large tree.

"John, I have a question for you." Rose, lost in thought, stared out over the garden, off into the woods beyond.

"What, sweetheart?"

"Where on earth did you ever find those unusual wind chimes? I've never seen anything so strange before."

He grinned at her. "More than likely you won't see any others like the one I have. You see, the chimes were given to me as a gift before I accepted the position as steward of The House."

"Who gave them to you?"

"A young lady from abroad whose family signed her in for treatment. As my admit, I taught her all about the fine arts of lovemaking. Her way of saying thank you came in the form of the chimes, which she gave me after leaving The House. The story goes like this. There once was a craftsman in her homeland who became well-known for building chimes like these. This particular style, which was originally concocted by ancient craftsmen, was perhaps created and forged as whimsy pieces for those who wanted to show a naughty sense of humor. Oh, and one other thing, legend tells when two people make love near the chimes, each is destined to find their true love in the near future. I don't know whether or not the legend is true, but she mentioned this at the end of her story."

Rose nodded. "I'm like you. Not sure about the legend part of it." But I agree you're a naughty boy, and you deserved the gift, no doubt." She reached over, and placed a kiss on his cheek.

"I think you're the naughty one, the way you try to seduce me with your moves. You think I don't catch the way you flirt?"

Rose let out a careless laugh. "I hardly guessed you cared. You always take your time, or leave me hanging, like you did in the cave."

"I do care. I pay attention more than you give me credit for doing."

She rolled around, placed her head in his lap, and looked up at him. "John, tell me about the cottage here. I always see you in The House. I guess I never thought about where you go when you're off duty."

"This cottage is used as the steward's quarters. You're right. When I'm not working and need some time off, I stay here. Did you treat yourself to the grand tour when you went in earlier?"

A pink blush splashed across Rose's cheeks. She averted her eyes in embarrassment. "I did. Just a little. I didn't prowl too much. I did see the box at the foot of your bed, as you can tell."

"The place is small, just enough for one person, so you can't prowl through much." He sighed and squinted at the late-afternoon sun. Small beads of perspiration covered his forehead, and his cheeks flushed from the heat. "I don't know about you, but as much as I love my garden, I'd like some cooler air. Come on inside." His thighs shifted beneath her head, and Rose sat up, pulling herself to a standing position. They both picked up their clothing, the phallus, and the green bottles, and Rose trailed along behind him as he led the way back to the cottage.

"Ah, this is much better." John breathed in the cool air. He turned around and smiled at Rose, took up their possessions, and disposed of them in a special, designated place. He placed the remaining bottle back in the kitchen.

The volumes of books attracted Rose's attention, and she stood before them reviewing the titles on the spines. "I didn't know you liked reading so much." She reached out to finger a large tome with a glossy dust jacket and fancy lettering.

"I'm an avid reader when I find the time." John sauntered over, wrapped his arms around her waist, pulling her against him.

"This one seems rather interesting." She pulled out a small volume and opened the pages. "I see these strange positions everywhere, on the door frames of The House, from people in their rooms."

"The Kama Sutra. It's an old collection of teachings on the art of lovemaking. Have you not ever read this?"

"Are you kidding? My parents would never allow a book like this in our house."

"Oh, of course not." John said nothing more, but brushed his finger against an open page. "The teachings say we must learn about the ways of desire, and understand how this particular emotion works. Once we accept the fact that we need physical pleasure and become comfortable with our sexuality, we grow and know ourselves in the best possible way. We establish a foundation that launches us to the next level in our growth."

Rose cocked her head in thought. "Really? Interesting. I've never given it all much thought, but I guess it's true. We're not normally taught those sorts of things, are we?"

"Unfortunately, no." He became silent. As he rested his chin on the top of her head, he pulled her closer.

She turned around and asked, "So how many of these positions have you tried?"

He closed his eyes, laughing. "Would you believe me if I told you I've tried all of them, and I'm pretty good?"

"Yes, as a matter of fact I would."

Rose lifted her eyes to his. Soft and kind, they penetrated the depths of her soul, searching for an answer to a mysterious question he seemed hesitant to ask. The neat, trimmed mustache above his mouth highlighted the pink fullness of his lips, and Rose found herself wanting to kiss those lips just as she did when she first laid eyes on them. Within his embrace, she found a comfort much different from the ordinary familiarity she experienced with others. Perhaps his maturity and self-assured manner projected a sense of security. His calm and collected attitude, not to mention his lovemaking skills, won her respect and admiration.

She replaced the book back on the shelf, and faced him once again. Her arms wound around his neck, and she pulled his head down toward her face. Their lips met, and both found themselves in a passionate embrace, their kisses eager and deep. His hands warmed her as he ran his palms down the length of her sides, over her lower back, and down the curves of her buttocks, playing over her skin, supple and smooth. She caught the scent of earthy perspiration from his hair. Her heart pounded harder as he held her close. A desire to remain connected became so strong, the thought of ever letting him go filled her with an immediate emptiness.

He peered down at her and smiled. "Let's go upstairs and clean up a bit."

Rose's eyes lit up. "I think that's a great idea." She slipped her hand in his, and he led her up the stairs, through the bedroom, and into the bathroom.

*　*　*

The room, though tiny, showed off clean, white tiles on the floor and walls. A simple mirror crowned a neat porcelain sink on the right-hand wall, and a shower area filled the left-hand corner.

"Don't you have a tub?"

"No. This space is comfortable, but not designed for permanent living. You have just enough for basic needs. No other objects of distraction—except for you right now." He smiled and kissed her forehead. He walked to the shower, twisted the knobs, and adjusted the water until the temperature suited him. "Come," he said pulling her toward him, "won't you join me?"

She snuggled in his arms and rested her head against his chest, feeling the rise and fall in tandem with his breathing. She smiled, enjoying the warmth of the shower against her skin. After a moment, he reached for the fragrant bar of soap resting in the dish and began lathering his face.

Rose couldn't help but admire again his muscular, handsome frame glistening in the water. But the mound of flesh fluttering between his thighs attracted her attention most of all.

With a burst of enthusiasm, she robbed him of the bar of soap, lathered her hands, and massaged the suds over him, caressing each bit with tender attention. She smiled as his cock swelled between her fingers. While she touched those most sensitive areas of his body, she discovered a certain excitement with him, much different from her bath rituals with Thomas. Her body tingled whenever he came near. A strong, invisible magnet seemed to draw her to him, and she remained helpless against its force. John sped through the remainder of their shower and shut the water off with a rush.

"Here, let me help you." Rose grabbed a plushy towel from the rack and dried his back.

"Now it's your turn." John snatched the other towel. "You know what, even with wet, limp hair, you're still charming!" He stopped a moment. "In all honestly, you're truly beautiful."

"Nothing like a bath to make things look better, eh?"

"Here we go!" He flashed her a quick grin and, hoisting her up in his muscular arms, threw her over his shoulders. Once they reached the bedroom, he tumbled her on to the bed, where she hit the soft covers with a giggle and a thud. She flipped over on her back and flopped down, settling into the crisp sheets. In an instant, her whole mood changed, as if a magic wand waved its starry tip, releasing the spell of sleep. Her lashes fell, and she drifted off into the world of dreams. John stood there in disbelief, a raging fire still burning within him. He let out a soft chuckle, shaking his head as he crawled into bed beside her.

*   *   *

During the night, Rose awoke with a start. Sitting up in bed, she glanced toward the window. The full moon hung high in the sky against a backdrop of sparkling stars. She looked around the room in momentary confusion, trying to reorient herself. This setting didn't resemble her room in The House. Outside, only the sound of chirping crickets filled the air. She viewed her bed companion expecting to find Thomas, only to discover John stretched out in a peaceful easy sleep. Rose settled back down between the sheets.

For a long time she remained still, listening to his soft, even breathing, staring at him, thinking how much his presence filled her with comfort and a deep sense of normalcy, like they belonged together. But what about Thomas? He'd be worried about her. Did he know where she was? Filled with a sudden grip of panic, she pulled herself out of bed and stole around the room until she found her clothes.

"Rose, what's wrong?" John sat up and rubbed his eyes.

"I'm sorry, I stayed longer than I'd planned to. Thomas will be mad at me for not coming back."

"It's the middle of the night, and it's dark outside. How do you think you'll find your way back?"

She stopped. The thought never occurred to her. Even with the light of the moon, she doubted she could pick up the trail again.

"Come back over here and get in bed. Besides, I've already notified Thomas. He knows you're here."

"Won't he be mad, though?"

John shook his head, puzzled. "Rose, I'm the steward, Thomas's boss. He has no power over me, whatsoever."

She dropped her dress back to the floor and stood next to the bed. "You're right. I keep forgetting." She smiled and slid in next to him, but not without a strong twinge of guilt. "I guess confusion got the better of me. I've been asleep for a long time, haven't I?"

"You and me both, dear. In the morning, I'll go back with you to The House. Now let's get back to sleep." John took her in his arms, and both finished out the night together until the early morning sun peeked through the window.

Chapter 11

THE DINING ROOM HUMMED with activity as attendants and their admits engaged in finishing up their midday repast. Thomas glanced over, spying an admit reclining on her back, legs spread wide open. Between her plump thighs, an attractive chestnut-haired male attendant busied himself, sucking hard in order to fish out an unidentified morsel hidden deep inside. The admit, straining her loins, let out a stifled giggle as her attendant met with success.

In one corner, a female admit straddled herself over the head of her attendant while engrossed in the act of squeezing copious amounts of thick, sweet cream in over his engorged shaft. She added a finishing touch by landing a fat, juicy, red cherry on top. Her attendant busied himself at the other end with inserting tiny slices of fruit deep inside her, picking up select choices from the collection resting on top of his chest. The attractive, auburn-haired admit giggled and wriggled her hips at intervals as the attendant, with adept fingers, slid the slippery bites inside, one piece at a time.

"Ready?" called the attendant to the stuffed admit. He slipped in the last piece and teased her buttocks with a quick tickle of his fingertips.

"I am. Are you?" She twisted her head, craning her neck to catch his expression, but his fingers playing inside her wet cleft gave her the answer she required. "Here goes—"

As she dipped her head down to lick the cream off his loaded cock, she lowered her hips over his open mouth as his eager tongue flicked back and forth. With a little heave, she released the succulent treats, which burst forth, one at a time, landing in the attendant's mouth as he controlled the arrival and consumption of each piece with astute oral skill. His hips writhed as the admit continued licking and stroking him with her tongue, sucking long and hard to clean off every vestige of cream. When she finished her carnal dessert, the attendant delivered a thick, cream of his own making, his emissions shooting in rhythmic spurts into the air. Pleased with her work, the girl laughed and plucked up the stranded cherry between her teeth, turned around, and dropped the plump, ripe delicacy into his mouth.

"Ah, never a dull moment at mealtimes." Thomas smiled as he turned back and faced Rose. While he had spent his time gawking at his comrades' activities, Rose had entertained herself, turning her chest into a tasty, tempting confection. He rewarded her efforts and licked one of her smothered breasts, dripping with pink frosting. "Mmmm, you're tasty as usual." He smacked his lips and made a nosedive for the other breast, removing the sweet spread with zesty flicks of his tongue. She let out a small squeal of delight while he finished off his treat, pulling hard on her nipple, catching the full, pink flesh between his lips. "There—I'm done now."

"You still have some frosting on your mouth ... here!" Thomas remained still, as she licked off the fluffy compound.

"Did you get every bit?" He tried to sound serious, but the twinkle in his eye gave him away. "And ... let's not forget these." Thomas picked up one of the tall beverage glasses resting beside them and placed the cold drink in her hand. Rose took a few sips and placed the glass back down on the floor. He frowned. "What's the matter, don't you like the taste?"

"Oh, there's nothing wrong with the taste, Thomas. I just don't want anymore. I'm not very thirsty right now." Her eyes wandered about the room once more, trying to determine if her repertoire needed any new additions in the way of new physical tricks or positions. Mealtimes at The House always lent themselves to more creative debauchery, and she didn't want to miss any of the action.

Thomas, not one to be put off, interrupted her scouting attempts. "Rose, I normally don't order you to eat or drink everything we put in front of you, but this time I insist. You need to finish the whole glass." He picked up the container and held the straw in front of her lips. "Now drink," he commanded.

"Thomas, I don't see the point in ..." She started to protest, a twinge of irritation bubbling up inside, but his authority over her kept the heat in check.

"Do as I say—NOW! I'm not asking again."

From experience, she knew that tone in his voice meant business, and arguing only wasted time. Better to dispense with reasoning and drink up before his patience wore thin. Besides, she didn't want to create a scene in the dining room with a petty fight.

"Fine, then." With a pout on her face, she accepted the glass and began gulping down the liquid, hoping her obedience appealed to the better side of his nature. "What's so important about this stuff, anyway?" She wrinkled her brow, studying the contents and stirring them with her straw.

"I just want you hydrated and healthy. We're pretty active around here, you know. And besides, you don't drink enough fluids to suit me." His mood softened, and the tone in his voice became more amiable. The sapphire pools in his eyes twinkled in approval. "Is that so?" She stared up at him, refusing to accept his answer as truth. The quick change in attitude, along with the casual, caring tone in his voice, didn't fool her; something deeper always lurked behind his requests. Why should this time be any different?

After finishing the drink, she flipped over on her stomach, resting her chin in her hands. At this moment, a wave of calm stole over her body, as if invisible fingers massaged her mind and muscles, relaxing each fiber and nerve into a more peaceful state. Possessed with an irresistible urge, she blurted out a question she'd wanted to ask for quite some time.

"Thomas, I've been meaning to ask you something, and I hope you can give me an answer."

"I'll try. What do you want to know?"

"Does the food we eat here contain special ingredients of any kind?"

"Special ingredients? What exactly do you mean?" Thomas swizzled the inside of his glass, a blank expression on his face.

"Well, you know, stuff like you throw in our bath water. Take look at everybody around us and the crazy things they do. You and I do them, too."

He studied his glass in silence for a moment, lost in thought, tracing the rim in steady, circular motions with a forefinger. His face flushed; he twitched his shoulders and moved his head from side to side, as if trying to relieve a sudden catch in his neck. After a few seconds passed, he finally swallowed, licked his lips, and shook his head. "No special spices or foods I'm aware of."

Rose studied his face, but his composure remained steady and unnerved.

"Why?" His gaze met hers. "Has the food ever made you feel strange in any way? If so, you've never told me." He cleared his throat and sat up in a cross-legged position, scrutinizing Rose's reactions.

"No, I don't recall any strange sensations as such—or none that stand out, I guess. But the whole atmosphere here is full of wild behavior, day in and day out, all the time."

"I do agree with your comment. House directors designed the program to encourage freedom in sensual expression. Our job as attendants is to help keep things exciting. You're not telling me you're bored here, are you?" A teasing smile lit up his face, and his eyes sparkled.

"Not at all," Rose said, shaking her wavy locks. Her eyes now glowed, and a sheepish smile crossed her lips. "I must admit, I kind of like being here." She let out a tiny snicker. "Father would kill me if he knew. Serves him right for sending me here, don't you think?" She sniffed and tossed her head in mock indignation.

"Personally, I think he made a wise choice. We get great results here. Our methods are unconventional, but we believe in exploring the ways of the flesh to the fullest degree. If you can't accept your own sexual nature and enjoy basic pleasure, your spirit remains trapped in continual shame, even subconsciously. The view of the world and personal relationships become inhibited and stunted." The former levity in Thomas's voice faded, and his attitude took on a more solemn demeanor.

"Thomas, do you think it's possible Father already knew

what goes on here? Do you even think it's possible he was an admit here at one time? Or Mother?"

Thomas frowned. "What a question! I doubt any father would willingly send his daughter to The House. Parents have a hard enough time with their own sexuality, let alone view their offspring as sexual beings, too. And besides, even if it were true, I can pretty much guarantee neither your father nor your mother would ever tell you they were admits here."

"But, Thomas, you could find out. I know you could persuade John to go through old records." Rose looked up at him and smiled. "Wouldn't it be interesting to know if Mother and Father were involved in a sordid past?" She giggled, then shuddered. "But on the other hand, the idea strikes me as both interesting and sickening at the same time, don't you think? Maybe it's better if you don't try to find out."

He took her head in his hands and placed a tender kiss on her lips. "Rose, now you do sound crazy. I'm not doing that. Come on, let's go clean up. We're a sticky mess." Thomas took Rose's outstretched arms and pulled her to her feet. Turning out of the dining room, they left the noisy crowd behind.

*   *   *

Rose started to turn down another side hallway when Thomas grabbed her arm and jerked her back in place. "Just where do you think you're going?"

Her face flushed a rosy red as she tried in vain to pull away. "I just need to take care of some things first before we wash off. Do you have a problem with that?"

"Whatever you need to do, you can do in front of me. You don't just run off on your own."

She shifted from one foot to the other. "Come on Thomas." She clenched her fists, trying to control her rising irritation. "You never mind if I take care of some things in private. What's the big deal now?" A deluge of angry words nearly fell from her lips. Luckily for Thomas, the aftereffects of the drink helped her maintain some semblance of control.

"You always ask me for permission first, unless you decide to go sneaking off like you do sometimes."

"I don't sneak off that much. Only one time, if I remember."

"If I know you, Rose, I'm sure you'll run off again. You have this way about you—a problem with authority, I'd say."

"Thomas, I really need to …" With an urgent tug, she tried to pull away from him again.

His eyes lit up, and the corners of his mouth twitched into a smile. "I know what you need, and trust me, I'm going to take care of you." His hold on her arm tightened, making her wince with discomfort.

He pulled her along at an even faster pace, and in a few seconds, they found themselves in a vacant tub room. The rays from the afternoon sun flowed through the window, casting a warm light throughout the room. One of the bars from the screen in the corner flexed its muscle of steel, shooting off a blinding glint from the surface. Thomas strolled over to the cabinet and removed some towels and a pair of cuffs.

"Thomas, do we have to use those?" She bounced lightly on the balls of her feet, desperation mounting.

"Yes, we must use 'those'." He turned back to her with an expression of disapproval. "Do you always have to question everything I do with you?" He studied her distress a moment before rummaging through the cabinet for supplies. "Come over here first. Now you're going to learn how we use these iron bars. Heaven knows you've asked me about them a hundred times."

As he cuffed her arms to the bars, she jumped at the cold touch of steel against her back. With mild trepidation, she watched while he placed towels on the floor. What crazy activity did he have in mind now? "Now, I need you to lie down on your back." She glared at him a second but, without a word, did as he instructed.

He assisted her to the floor, stretched her arms over her head, and replaced the cuffs. To her, the sound of snapping locks always held such an air of finality, as if she may never be free again. Thomas looked down at her and smiled. With the palm of his hand, he moved over her lower abdomen, studying this part of her with care. She closed her eyes. The warmth from his hand offered some comfort to the ache in her pubic area. "Hang in there with me a little longer," he whispered. "I'll be back in just a minute." As he stood up, Rose opened her mouth to protest. Too late. He disappeared out of the room, leaving her in solitude.

She lay there in silence, entertaining herself by studying the tile work crisscrossing in artful patterns across the ceiling. The House contained beautiful architectural designs, continually amazing her at every turn. However the raging fire burning in her lower abdomen spoiled her appreciation of anything beautiful at the moment.

Outside the window a bird sang a merry twitter, mocking her lack of freedom, the lack of control. Time seemed to tick on forever, but in reality, only a few moments elapsed before Thomas returned, carrying a bag filled with liquid. He stopped by the cabinet, rustled through the drawers for another handful of supplies, and finally settled himself down to a kneeling position beside her. In a neat, semicircle, he placed each item within easy reach.

"Okay, Rose, I know you've waited long enough. I need you to bend your knees and spread your thighs open for me." He smoothed her hair back as she executed his request, exposing a glossy sex.

"What are you going to do this time, Thomas?" Her mind whirled with a mix of curiosity, excitement, and a little anxiety. "You won't hurt me, will you?"

He smiled down at her, his eyes softening with kindness. "Sweetheart, have I ever hurt you?"

"No, but I can never be sure when my good luck may run out." She shot him a small grin.

"How can I say this? You've been through the most intense activities as my admit. Everything else we do may be different or unusual, but not hard or painful. Pain is not my style. I thought you understood that by now."

Rose remained silent.

"Okay, I'm going to help you now." He reached over and began opening all the packages, adding lubrication where needed, and finished by filling up a large syringe with a clear liquid from a glass vial. Rose heard the familiar snap of gloves and felt the cleansing pads brush against her folds as Thomas wiped her with care. She turned her head and saw him lifting a brown, floppy rubber tube, one end dripping with a lubricating gel. A smaller extension of this tube branched off near the end.

"What is that thing you have?" Her eyes widened in surprise and her heart began to pound. "I've never seen such a thing before."

"We call this a catheter. Something to help you find relief. Here I go." Spreading her apart, he inserted the end into her small private passage, the same place where he once passed the steel rods. Her body relaxed as the tube slipped inside, filling her in a softer manner. As he pushed the end into her bladder, Rose winced a bit, feeling a sudden urge to relieve herself. Thomas moved a small clamp over the tube before grabbing the syringe and pushing the contents into the smaller tube extension. "Now I've inflated a small balloon with some sterile water to keep all this in place for a bit." He tore off a small piece of tape and tacked the end of the catheter to her inner thigh. "I'll help you up now," he said, unsnapping the cuffs.

"But Thomas, aren't you going to …?"

"I'll take care of you, Rose, but on my terms, not yours." He pulled her on to her feet, and snapped her wrists to the bars once again. His eyes now filled with new lust. His voice dropped to a low pitch as he lifted her chin with his finger. "Now tell me why you tried to get away from me earlier."

She didn't answer.

"Tell me, Rose, why were you so eager to get away from me this afternoon?"

In anger, she flared back. "Oh, Thomas, you know perfectly well why— I'm not saying anything else." She clammed up and became sullen.

"Is your sweet little crotch stinging? Is that the problem?" He pressed up against her, his shaft and tip growing full as they lodged in her slit. Using one of his hands, he applied a light pressure over the bulge in her lower abdomen.

She whimpered in discomfort. "You like making me squirm don't you?" She twisted her body and pulled at the bars. The internal stinging became sharper by the minute.

He whispered in her ear. "Yes, actually I do." His tongue flicked against her earlobe and coursed its way down her neck. She closed her eyes as the moisture from his mouth caressed her skin, his hot breath sending her heart racing. His fingers played over her breasts, squeezing her nipples with a sharp pinch. Deep inside, she burned for want of relief. With mixed emotions, she decided she both loved and hated him when he teased her like this, enjoying his merciless torture as much as wishing him to cease. She let out a soft moan as he continued to move his hand over her flesh, landing a fingertip on top of her clit.

"Oh, Thomas … please …" She shifted her body again to lessen the ache.

"In just a minute … just a minute longer," he breathed in her ear. As he rested his head against hers, he massaged her clit. The warmth from his finger licked her hot spot like flaming tongues of fire, sending a searing heat ripping throughout her pelvic area.

"I don't think I can hold on anymore." She gasped, her knees ready to collapse.

"Oh, but you can. You have no choice, really. I have your body under my complete control. You can't even—well—I have everything shut off. There's no chance in your …" His lips covered hers, locking them both in a deep kiss. His finger continued to work her clit until he succeeded in sending her into a frenzy of spasms. Her buttocks hit the bars as she pumped her hips and tried to pull away; she let out a small shout. Her eyes brimmed over with tears, more from impatience than pain. The lusty glaze left Thomas's eyes, the spell of the moment broken by her cries. He reached down to the inside of her thigh and shifted the clip. Gazing down in horror, she witnessed a golden stream running down her leg and draining on to the floor. Secured to the bars of the screen and unable to move, the warmth of her own fluids against her skin created an uncanny, startling awareness of helplessness, a glaring reminder of her dependence on Thomas, even to the point of elimination.

"Do you feel better now?" He ran a finger over her flushed cheek.

"Much better." She gazed down at the puddle on the floor. "I didn't think I could take much more." She shook her head. "You do know how to push the limits don't you?"

He stroked her cheek. "Yes, I do push the limits, but never to the point you'll be physically harmed. Anyway, you'll end up a better person for it."

"I highly doubt all this will make me a better person." She turned up her nose.

He unfastened her wrists and held her close in his arms. "Rose, you will be a better person, trust me." His lips pressed against hers for another kiss, his tongue flirting with hers. When this kiss ended, his eyes viewed the space between her legs. "I need you to lie down."

"Aren't we done here with all this? I'm sure you can take this thing out with me standing up." The serious expression on his face told her otherwise, and she allowed him to assist her to the floor once more.

"Do you have to be somewhere? For one who's not in charge, you sure like to call the shots, don't you? You're so impatient at times, and you get a little irritable and fussy, too."

"You think so? I guess I've not thought about my moods." His comments caught her off guard. "Do you think others feel the same way?"

"I'm not sure. All depends on how you act around them. Remember, I'm not with you all the time. When you're with me, I just want you to relax and enjoy yourself. You won't be here forever, you know."

Thomas attached a small bag of fluid to the end of the catheter. "I'm going to fill you up again, but you won't be waiting like you did just a few seconds ago, I promise." As he held up the bag to instill the fluid, Rose experienced the fullness growing in her pubic area, accompanied by a light cool, tingling sensation. When the bag was empty, he deflated the balloon and removed the catheter. "Good, we're done now."

Rose, taking a notion, sprang up on her knees and pushed Thomas down to the floor. She placed her thighs over his and pinned him down with her hands. "By the way, you're right. I like being in charge sometimes, but you men make it rather difficult around here." His laugh faded as she pressed a kiss into his willing lips. As much as those deep blue eyes tempted her to lose herself in their cobalt depths, she deferred.

As she settled herself on top of him, she caught his swollen shaft, and ground against him, riding up and down in a smooth, easy rhythm. The longer she pressed and glided over his flesh, the more she burned, the intensity inching higher by degrees. She came to an abrupt halt, and their eyes locked. Her mind raced, her eyes flared, and a knowing grin spread across her mouth.

Thomas returned the grin as if reading her mind. "Just do it, Rose. Let go. It's okay." With this unexpected permission, she required no further encouragement, but knew the next step required concentration and a strong will.

"Are you sure?"

He nodded.

She positioned her hands on either side of Thomas's shoulders and hovered her hips low over his, barely grazing his cock. The old vision of the waterfall deep in the forest flashed in her mind once again and played its familiar song. With a deep breath, she closed her eyes and relaxed her muscles. In a torrent, she drenched all of him, her fluids trickling down the folds of his thighs, over his balls, and into the crease of his buttocks.

"Release every bit." His eyes contained a fiery, lusty glaze, and his hands played over her backside.

In one last effort, she strained to empty out the last drops from deep inside her body. "Now I feel better." She bent over him and pasted her lips on the side of his neck, tasting a tinge of salt from his sweat. Her nose inhaled the musky scent of his hair as her fingers ran through his soft, short locks.

"Turnabout, fair play." His words rang out loud and clear, jarring the silence between them. She stopped and stared down at him in surprise. He licked his lips, and the fire in his eyes grew stronger.

"What do you mean?"

"You know me, and I mean what I say."

She narrowed her eyes at him. "What now?"

*　*　*

With a swift and agile maneuver, he caught her in his arms, rolled over, and flipped her over on her back, pinning her down between his thighs. "Now it's my turn, and I intend to enjoy myself now."

"What, you didn't enjoy yourself before? Really? I thought you always made sure you pleasured yourself at all cost, even at my expense."

Thomas's eyes flared at her remark, and leaning over her face, he gave her pouty, pink lower lip a sharp nip. "You saucy girl." With a swat of his hand, he popped the outside of one of her thighs with a resounding smack.

"Ow!" She writhed under him, her skin tingling. "Thomas, I only meant to tease. I didn't mean anything by what I said."

"Then why did you say it, then?" His face fell in close to hers, their noses almost touching.

"I don't know, I guess I wasn't thinking. It just slipped out." She turned her head away, hoping to avoid antagonizing him further, only to have his hand propel her head back into position so their eyes met once again.

"Rose, it's high time you learn to speak the truth inside

you. Stop saying things in the heat of a moment." The sparring between them soared his lust, creating a need for release. Without another word or thought of penetration, he repositioned his legs and pushed her thighs apart. With a few seconds of working his cockhead, he pumped warm jets of passion into the open folds between her legs. The intense blue of his eyes held her captive, and this time she succumbed to their magnetic pull. She locked her gaze on his as his fluids pulsed against her sensitive parts.

"Turnabout, fair play, Rose." He smiled down at her once again. With this last comment, he rained down a cleansing shower of gold, washing off the remnants of his lust within her. She closed her eyes. His cascade of fluids felt hot pattering against her private lips, filling and flowing into her hidden regions.

She giggled and pulled his head down over hers. "You're always full of surprises. I never know what you'll do next."

He didn't answer, but he placed a tender kiss on her lips, his demeanor softening. "I'm a hard taskmaster, Rose." With a sigh, he lowered his head and placed another much softer bite on her lips.

"I have a question for you, Thomas."

"What's that, sweetheart?"

"What did you mean about my being a better person with all this stuff?"

Thomas thought for a moment. "The different activities we do here aren't only for sensual exploration and personal discovery, but an opportunity for trust-building. That's all I meant."

Rose said nothing, but tucked his comment away in her memory for further consideration.

Chapter 12

ROSE HEARD THE SNAPPING of cuffs around her thighs. A strap around her hips anchored her to the table. Her arms, stretched over her head, were bound together at the wrists and tethered to something unseen underneath. A pair of hands shifted the metal plates housing her thighs far apart, spreading her open to such a degree she felt the rush of cool air against her hidden, feminine bits. She winced and stared at the ceiling, overcome with an unexplained sense of shame and indecency, her nakedness and vulnerability a brutal reminder of her choice to make a pact with the devil. And the devil always got his due.

Trapped down below in the bowels of The House, she almost reconsidered, wishing for the safety and warmth of the upper wards instead of remaining in the cold, sterile environment of the isolation chambers. But a burning desire for a favor compelled her to toss aside reason and subject herself to him with humility. With a strong resolve, she decided to endure whatever he dished out. After all, she didn't make her decision on a whim, but had pondered her desire for a long time, weighing the pros and cons.

"Well, well, Princess, so you come here wanting me to help you?" Joe ran his hands down the length of her torso, pausing to pinch and grind her nipples between his thumb and forefinger. "It must be my lucky day. Like I said earlier, no problem. But why me? And let's be honest, I know you don't like me very much." He waited for an answer.

Rose licked her lips and tried to think of how to handle such a pointed question. What if he decided not to grant her request based on her answer? Mustering up the last remnants of her confidence, she said, "I've heard countless people here at The House tell me that you're the most skilled piercer, and what I want done is in a very sensitive place."

"Ah, yes, so true. But you ran away from me during our last encounter, and I haven't forgotten the nasty bite you gave me. A little gift to remember you by. Now all of a sudden you trust me with a very delicate procedure? I still don't get it."

Damn him! Did an interrogation come with this deal, too? Impatient, she turned her head toward Joe. "Look, I'm sorry about last time. The truth is, when I want something done, I want it done right and by the best person."

"Well, aren't you a bold lady all of a sudden, not like the screaming fiend I met the first time." He stroked his chin and narrowed his eyes. "But you've forgiven me, and I think I can forgive you, too—but at a price—and my fees are high."

"Fine, I'll do whatever you want." Rose turned her eyes up in disgust and resumed staring at the ceiling. "Can we at least get on with this?"

Joe arched is eyebrows in surprise. "For such a pampered puss, you're a mouthy little thing, aren't you? And from what I can see right now, I'm not sure you're in the best position to be calling the shots here. But I'll overlook this error out of … generosity." He smirked and delivered a sharp pinch to the outside lip of her sex, grinning when she winced in discomfort. "First I need to do a total examination. This is my standard procedure I do with everyone, so don't think I'm picking on you."

"Fine, get on with it, then." Rose sighed and tried to appear relaxed and in control while stretched out on the devil's altar.

Joe chuckled and shook his head. "You fascinate me, Princess. For a girl who's bound and helpless, you're still stubborn enough to give orders. That's okay, though. Your manners don't bother me in the least. Trust me, I have ways to shut you up. We'll see who bosses whom." He strode over to a set of cabinets and soon returned to the table with all his instruments. Rose felt his warm fingers spread her apart. She flinched at the insertion of a cold, steely instrument under her clitoral hood. Her jaw clenched. It became clear to her his total exam started from bottom to top. Joe lifted the blunted end of a thin rod and stretched her skin first to one side, then the other, before grazing the instrument gently over her clit. His fingers retracted the hood, exposing the tiny glans, engorged, pert, and stiff. Nice!

"Has anybody ever said you have a plump, juicy clit?

They're rare, you know. I don't get much of a chance to handle one so squeezably tempting as yours." Taking the entire tip between his fingertips, he squeezed and tugged it gently.

Rose shut her eyes and tried to stifle a moan. Had it not been for the strap holding her, she would have writhed her hips off the table. Her whole crotch throbbed and her heart pounded. She gritted her teeth. "What about the area we discussed earlier? Will you do what I asked or not?"

"Well, Princess, of course." He delivered a sharp pinch to each nipple. "I always like to see if there are other areas I can use as a backdrop for my handiwork. I'm always in search of new ideas."

"What I'm asking you to do is not new, from what I hear, so don't get any other thoughts in your head."

"Princess, you never stop do you?" He leaned over her face and smiled, his eyes dark and piercing. "But you know what, I like a girl who knows what she wants, so if you're ready to pay up, I'm ready to deliver."

The prospect both excited her and filled her with a certain dread. At this point, the idea of backing out didn't sound appealing, either. Besides, she hadn't decided to navigate the lonely, creepy hallways down here, in search of the devil's lair, for nothing. She hadn't made lightly the decision to keep her intent a secret from Thomas, who didn't know she was here. Even Daren, whom she adored, didn't suspect anything, though she knew he would have loved the idea. Rose drew in a deep breath. "Fine, do it, then."

Joe stood over her. "You know, Princess, I usually like my fun hard, mean, and nasty, but for you, I'll make an exception, since you made it clear last time you prefer a milder flavor. Consider yourself fortunate, because I don't usually mix with your type." He opened a small drawer built into the side of the exam table and pulled out a gag. "I'm sure your princes upstairs have at least introduced you to this." He waved the gag in front of her eyes, making sure she caught the sight of the red ball and dangling straps. Without another word, he inserted the ball in her mouth and secured the straps behind her head.

"Now, Princess, let's begin." Joe smiled and leaned over close.

*   *   *

Rose said nothing, but prepared herself for the worst. She closed her eyes and bit down on the gag. As he drew near, she almost believed his hot breath scorched her skin. He started with the peak of one of her breasts, first grasping the flesh between his lips and sucking hard, then ending with a sharp nip. She let out a small squeak and tried to twist her chest away from his grip.

"Nice and easy now, Princess. You won't be getting away quite so easily this time. But I must admit, you have a great set of perky tits, and they'll be golden when I'm done." He moved his head over her other breast and repeated the same movements, but ended with a harder bite. Rose let out a groan. He ran his tongue over her abdomen and paused to lap at her navel for a few seconds.

The queer tickling sensations nearly drove her mad. She strained against the bindings, a fullness gathering between her thighs. He knew how to whet her sexual appetite. His fingers parted her open, and he flicked his hot, wet tongue, fast and furious, over her clit, sucking her so hard he wrung ecstatic cries from her throat. In one final move, he took the pink tip between his teeth and gently grazed over the wet flesh. A muffled scream caught in her throat, and her body rolled with spasms. The metal plates sounded off a light rattle as her hips pumped, their rhythm matching each orgasmic contraction. His lips teasing her flesh turned out better than she'd bargained for; she rather liked him sucking her in such a sensitive place. Inside her core, she sensed her fluids roiling.

Joe leered up at her. "I bet those pansy princes upstairs have never gotten a rise out of you the way I just did. Isn't that right, Princess?"

Rose said nothing, but prayed her panting breath and

glistening eyes didn't betray her too much.

"Yep, I thought so." He smiled. "You can't hide your pleasure from me. I know that lusty bitch-in-heat look when I see it. Now I just pleasured you, so I think it's only fair that you pleasure me in return, don't you agree? Just nibbling that sweet little clit of yours set my cock on fire, and I think your wet little pussy will do a nice job of making me explode." He unsnapped his trousers, revealing a stiff shaft wagging a shapely cockhead. "Okay, Princess, I'm coming in, and I want your pussy to suck me hard, like it's starving for food." He drove himself deep into her dark channel with a smooth thrust, hitting just the right place. Through the gag came a series of stifled groans. He pulled out, just enough to keep his tip lodged in her entrance, and slammed into her once again.

His measured thrusts, plunging into her depths, set her inner core on fire. His ample head tormented her sweet spot. He knew how to get the better of her, and he knew she knew it. She took some deep breaths and tried to focus on something else in the room to distract her, to stall her body from coming too soon. If she'd harbored an ounce more of bravery, she'd give it all up and let him have his way with her, allowing him to indulge in some twisted fantasies of his own.

He ended his maneuvers with sharp, quick thrusts and climaxed hard, pouring himself into her dark regions. "You like this, Princess?" His voice came out raspy from the height of pleasure. "Do you like my fat cock in your tight little pussy? Feels good, doesn't it?"

Rose, straining against the bindings, her moans stifled by the gag, only blinked and tried to lift her hips against the strap. To her surprise, she found herself opening her legs wider.

Joe smiled and reached up to pinch a nipple. "I see your little twat wants some more. See, I'm not so bad, am I, Princess? But I still have some thick stuff in that cock of mine, and I aim to give it all to you, so don't worry about getting shortchanged." He unfastened all the straps, released her hands, and repositioned her over the exam table, exposing her backside.

Rose gasped through the gag and bit down hard. The remnants of his lust ran in thick streams down her leg.

"You know what, Princess," he said, "I'll at least lube up a little for you. You've been a good tight one, and you've held all the goodies my cock offered you." He opened a side drawer once again and grabbed a tube of lubrication.

In the next moment, she closed her eyes and tried with all her might to relax. His last entry inside had sent her body climaxing harder than she'd ever done. This new invasion had to be at least as good. She felt her buttocks being parted, and the stinging and burning bolted up through her backside as he pushed his way in, straining his body hard against hers. With deep breaths and clenched fists, she accepted his advances until he had buried himself up to his hilt. His tip hit a sensitive spot, and the undulations of his hips, coupled with the fullness within her walls, increased the ache raging inside. To torment her more, he reached around and worked her clit with a merciless vigor, squeezing the plump flesh for good measure. Within moments, she climaxed again in spite of herself, groaning and clamping her teeth on the gag. She finally decided she rather liked his nasty devil's spear, impaling her with sharp precision. For a little, she'd beg for more if she could. However, she decided to keep this dirty little secret to herself.

"There, Princess," he said, gasping a little, "you're a thief, you know that? You've stolen every last ounce I have." He swatted her on the buttocks. "But I have to say, I liked your dripping, wet pussy the most. There's nothing I like better than a dripping, wet one. I like my girls good and wet, you know." He gave the large lips of her nether regions another firm pinch and delivered another good hard smack to her buttocks. The sting radiated through her, and to make matters worse, he pinched the area with his thumb and forefinger, enhancing the burning even more. She winced and gave a little cry as he placed her back on the table and refastened everything in place once again.

He removed the gag and leered into her face. "Well, how did you like all that? Did you enjoy yourself? I know I sure did.

Did you like my fat, juicy cock inside you? Did it fill you all the way up? Did you like my fat snake in that tight little snatch of yours? *Did you?*" He brought his face down over hers, nearly touching her. "Answer me!"

Rose scowled. "Yes, Joe."

"Good" He ground her nipple between his fingers. "That's good, because I think you'll like this, too."

He left the room, passed through a door leading into an adjoining chamber, and returned wheeling in a cart carrying a large item with a cover over it.

Rose's heart pounded even harder this time. God, would this ever end?

He walked over to her gaping slit and inserted three fingers inside, stretching her open. "Yes, I think this will work quite nicely. You know, Princess, I'm glad you said you liked my snake in your pussy, because I have a special treat for you." Removing the cover, Rose, to her horror, viewed the contents of a large glass cage. A long snake rested inside, coiled in comfort around a piece of driftwood. Joe reached in and gently removed the animal from its resting place.

Too numb and shocked to even scream, Rose shut her eyes and dropped her head back on the table in dismay.

"What, no prince to come and rescue you? I'm so sorry," Joe said, jeering. "But don't be afraid, Princess. My pet won't bite." He turned his attention back to the reptile and cooed, "You're harmless, really, aren't you? Are you going to play with us today? Yes, you are." Joe stroked the snake as it wound itself around his arm, the forked tongue flicking in and out of its mouth, the tapered head showing off tiny eyes sparkling like two beads of onyx. He placed the snake, head down, between her breasts.

Rose, with sobs catching in her throat, tried to contain herself. Joe looked at her and smiled an evil grin before reaching down to work both nipples of her breast between his fingers. Rose tensed up as he began to squeeze and work the plump, pink flesh. His sharp pinches caused her to writhe in pain. The snake lifted its head and began slithering its way down her chest, over her abdomen, and down between her legs, dragging its body over her clit. With a new fullness in her pubic area, she closed her eyes and swallowed hard. Before the animal finished curling around her thigh, Joe stopped the work on her breasts and took up the snake with one of his hands. He passed the tail over her clit and vaginal orifice. The fullness inside her grew stronger, and much to her shame, she tried to arch her hips up toward him.

"That's it, Princess, just relax. Open your pussy up nice and wide for us. That's a good girl. Our friend won't hurt you," Joe said in a reassuring whisper. His fingers found their way into her entrance, and as he spread her open, he began sliding the tail deep inside her. Numb with fear, thinking she must surely be dreaming, she stared at the ceiling and tried to catch her breath. In vain, she tried to dissociate herself from this surreal moment, but the strange new fullness, cool and smooth, inside her loins teased her in a different way and pumped up her arousal to a new level.

"Oh, yes, your hot little pussy will warm our friend's tail, won't it, sweetie girl?" Joe aimed his words at the snake while his sure hand finished filling her up. When he had placed as much of the tail inside her as she could safely and physically hold, he released his fingers, letting her walls secure its new contents. "There, you like my snake deep inside you?" He rubbed her abdomen a few seconds, then patted it softly. "I knew you would. There's nothing like the sensations of a good snake in the cradle. Now I need you to do something for me." He eyed her slyly. "My friend and I want to see you work. Your pussy doesn't get a free lunch, you know." Joe moved over her and unfastened one of her hands.

Rose just glared at him in disbelief.

He continued, "So I need you to take that free hand of yours and work that clit like you've never worked it before."

Rose remained dumbfounded, not quite believing him.

"I said work that clit of yours. Work it good and hard." With that last comment, he gave her crotch a sound, hard pinch that made her cry out. "You'll be crying a lot harder if you don't do what I tell you to do. So get started and be quick about it. We haven't got all day, and I can give you what you came for."

Rose, still scowling at him, decided to get this whole business over with. Besides, a dull pleasure ache had managed to sneak up on her and now waged a war inside her. With her free hand she found the pert little bump between her legs and began moving her finger in slow, circular motions.

"That's a good girl." Joe watched with great interest. "You just keep going because I want to see you get off on my pet. I want that twat of yours to hug and kiss my friend like a real long-lost pal."

Rose closed her eyes, trying too hard not to think, and kept working herself until a fullness gathered at her tip. For the moment she concentrated on nothing else but the smooth pad of her finger against her own wet flesh. Each complete, circular motion of her fingertip brought her to the brink of relief. Within seconds, her interior burst into spasms, and a flood of contractions consumed the reptilian penis inside her. The snake, stimulated by her movements around its tail, began slithering out, coiling itself around Joe's hands. Her hips jerked while her spasms played out. She dropped her head back on the table, exhausted.

*   *   *

"Good girl. Now we're done." Joe replaced the snake back in its cage and rolled the cart over to one corner of the room before walking over to a small sink with cabinets overhead.

From his movements, Rose gathered he was cleaning himself up. When he finished, he pulled four small towels out of a cabinet, dampening them in water and adding a generous amount of cleanser to two of them. He returned to the table and began cleansing her sex with great care, rubbing through every fold. She relaxed for the first time and enjoyed the warmth of the towel against her skin. He paid special attention to the cleansing of her clit, which nearly sent her over the edge again. After drying her off, he cleansed her breasts, paying close attention to the nipples. As wild and fearsome as he had seemed in the beginning, his demeanor now took on a different quality, as if someone had flipped a switch, turning on a new character. Any fear she had experienced earlier vanished along with the last shudders of her climax. She still marveled at his attractive hands smooth fingers, well-shaped and strong, suited for steady, accurate work.

He leaned over and spoke to her, his voice calm and gentle. "Look, do you still want me to go through with this? I've got you prepared if you're ready. But I am giving you a chance to change your mind if you want."

"Of course." This whole ordeal had been exhausting, but her determination remained. "Why would I not go through with it? I came to see you for this, and I intend for you to do it." She hadn't gone through hell with the devil for nothing. Now it was his turn to hold up his end of the bargain.

"Fine, then. But before I start, I want to tell you something else, too. I love what I do here. And you came to the right person for this job. I'm swift and precise. Any discomfort will be minimal. I'm the best there is, and when I'm done, you'll be glad you came. Now, I want you to lie back, try to relax, and we'll be done in a few minutes." His finger gently swept away a free strand of hair that had fallen over her face.

He pulled a stool over beside her chest. Her heart started pounding at the sound of him snapping on his gloves. Then came the cool damp, cleansing pads across her skin. The big moment had arrived. She felt him grasp one of her nipples with steel forceps. With clenched fists and baited breath, she braced herself for the worst, wincing at the quick prick of her tender flesh. She took several deep breaths, forcing herself to relax.

"I'm going to thread the ring through, and then I'll do the other side. You're doing good, though." He handled her with great care, and proceeded to the other breast.

"Are you okay?" Joe glanced up at her. "The worst is over."

"I'm fine," Rose said. "You're right, it wasn't as bad as

I thought it might be."

He finished threading the last ring and fastened it in place. "That's all, Princess, you're done." He grinned at her and removed his gloves. "I'll unfasten you, and then I'm going to let you rest a little."

To her surprise, he scooped her up in his arms and carried her into the adjoining chamber, where he placed her on a bed. Like the upper wards, the head and footboards were constructed of iron, outfitted with the same tools of bondage. Except for a few cages housing reptiles, the overall look of his room didn't differ too much from hers.

She glanced at him. "Thank you. You did a good job." Taking a moment to catch a view of her chest, she smiled. "They look good, don't they?"

"Fantastic, if I say so myself. Of course you're a striking lady who wears them." His face, for the first time, struck her as rugged and handsome, as it brightened with a soft, warm smile. On impulse, she reached up and brought his face down close to hers. Joe took her head in his hands and placed a kiss on her lips. He slipped in his tongue, which Rose accepted, sucking and caressing it softly with her own.

He straddled her body, clenching her between a set of powerful thighs. The full mound of flesh flashing before her eyes tempted her fingers to grasp the pink head and softly stroke the velvety flesh and all its curvatures. She fingered open the slit at the top and found the opening unusually large. Perplexed, she stopped a moment.

"Have you ever seen anything that big before? I'm rather proud because I worked to get it that way."

"Really?" Rose cut a quizzical eye up at his smiling face. "I've never seen anything like this on—"

"I'm telling you, Princess, you're not dealing with a pansy boy here. But you know what, I've got another treat for you." He slipped off the bed and walked over to a drawer across the room. When he returned he placed a small amber bottle and a pack of rubber gloves on the bed. "Here, put one of these on."

Rose slipped on one of the gloves.

"Now I'm going to add this." Joe tipped a bottle of liquid over her pinky, and an odor of peppermint filled the air. "Here's what I want you to do next. Simply stick your small finger inside. Be gentle and no rushing. Go nice and slow. Believe it or not, this is one thing I like to feel every bit that I can." He reclined on the bed and made himself comfortable. His plump tip rested easily between his thighs, waiting for her advances.

"Are you sure? I've never done this before. Are you sure I won't hurt you?"

"You may not have a chance to do this again, because there's not many people around here like me. You're about to experience something unique. Now no more talking. I need you to finger fuck me good."

"Is that what you call it?" Rose widened her eyes and then took a deep breath. "Here I go. Nice and easy." She took his tip in one hand and gently inserted her gloved pinky into his opening, sliding in with gentle movements until his shaft swallowed both joints.

"That's it, Princess, nice and smooth," he said with a sigh.

She slid her finger in and out, caressing the inside of his shaft with slow, deliberate strokes, his hidden walls hugging her as if they never wanted her to leave. Every movement of her finger grazing against his interior pulled out sighs and groans from his throat, which filled her with pride and delight, not to mention a sense of power. Rose discovered she adored pleasuring him this way far better than using sounds or dilators, which seemed so cold and distant in comparison. Invading him with her finger created a type of bond rivaled only by traditional intercourse. The more she stroked his flesh, the more she became infused with a strong desire to overtake his body and rule his senses.

*   *   *

Joe relaxed and closed his eyes. The oil on the glove now penetrated his skin and lit a cool fire inside. The stinging fullness made his juices bubble. He shifted into a more comfortable position and lightly threw his arms over his head, stretching himself out in total comfort and bliss, ready to surrender himself to his beautiful invader. But the sudden snap of cuffs around his wrists jolted him out of his comfort zone. He opened his eyes and saw Rose staring down at him, her face covered with a lusty smile. Her eyes blazed with a strange fire he found a little unsettling, but intriguing at the same time. His shaft, now cold and empty, longed to have her inside again. He squinted at her, puzzled. "What are you doing?"

Rose said nothing.

Joe tugged on the cuffs and then smiled. "So have you got some new mischief on your mind, Princess? I love a woman who's a mischievous wench. I wouldn't have thought you had it in you." He gave a light sardonic chuckle.

"I've got plenty on my mind, Joe, and I guarantee you'll hear me out." Her voice came out low and seductive. "And if you don't play your cards right, you'll be my wench, without a doubt." She peeled off the old glove and replaced the remaining one on her slender hand. Smiling, she covered her fingers with a new application of liquid from the bottle. "Did you like me finger fucking you, Joe?"

He smiled, but said nothing.

"Do you want me to do it again? Do you like my finger toying with you, filing you up?"

"Yes, Princess, I do." His eyes glazed into a dreamy stare.

"Good. I'll finger you again, Joe, and I'll wring the cries out of you. But before I do, there is one thing I'm just dying to tell you."

"What do you want to tell me?" He barely whispered. He ached for her hands, throbbed at the thought of her slender finger plunging into his shaft and filling him with carnal bliss. She straddled his hips and reached down between his thighs. His eyes locked on the ceiling, and a stifled groan slipped out between clenched teeth. His body stiffened at the chokehold around his sac, the constriction orbiting him into a new state of ecstasy.

"In case you didn't know," Rose said, peering into his face, "princes are quite valiant, brave, and strong, not the flowers you think they are."

Her grip tightened around him, and he let out a gasp. "You've got quite a hand on you there, Princess." His breathing became more labored. He swallowed hard and tried to calm the heat building up within him. Her new commanding nature instilled in him excitement and helplessness, the usual feelings when cuffed and at the mercy of someone new.

"Yes, I do have quite a grip. At least that's what I've been told by more than one prince. I'm wondering, though, if I should just crush you and let those sweet little marshmallows of yours wither away and die, or should I show you mercy and release you?" Maintaining her hold, she fingered open his slit.

"But you know what, I think you've gotten me addicted to torturing your sweet, little shaft. I love how you swallow me, how smooth and warm you are, how sensitive and fragile you are, too." She pressed in the tip of her middle finger and felt his walls start to swallow her.

Joe groaned again, squeezing his eyes shut a moment. His loins boiled and threatened to erupt if she didn't stop tormenting him, but he knew her hold on him controlled that, too.

"I'll need to decide soon what to do with you, because I know you won't last forever." She smiled at him while gently working her entire finger into his hidden depths. Her finger teased him, licked his flesh, and filled him in a way that made him want to cry out. He took a deep breath and maintained control.

"Princess, I don't think I can hold on much longer. I'm ready to shoot out everything I have inside me. And your grip is cracking my nuts like nobody's business."

"Interesting. I've never been referred to as a nutcracker

before, but I'll take your comment as a compliment." To his surprise, she dropped her head and clamped her teeth over his sac, biting hard enough to elicit a shout of pain.

"Don't worry, Joe, you're not bleeding, and there is still a little time left. If you want to save yourself, you have to acknowledge this one thing so you never, ever forget it." She slipped her finger out and moved her face over his.

"What do you want me to say? I'll say it. No problem." He blinked in pain. "God, you're killing me."

Rose took his chin in her hand and, placing her face close to his, said, "Tell me that princes are strong and brave."

"What? You're kidding me, right?"

"Tick-tock, Joe." She tightened her hand around his jaw and gave his balls a firm tug. "Tell me that princes are strong and brave. Do it!" She tugged again. Pain shot throughout his pelvic region, a dull ache settled in. At the mercy of her hands, he gasped, trying to tolerate the discomfort, which he mostly found to his liking. His vision became a little fuzzy, and he tried to find his voice. "Say it, Joe, if you want to keep these fluffy little darlings of yours."

He grimaced. This princess—or this terrible *femme fatale*—won hands down. Unbelievable. His respect for Thomas soared; he'd trained this girl well. "Okay, Princess, I admit that princes are strong and brave."

"Say it again. I want to hear you one more time. And say it like you mean it.

"Princes are strong and brave," he said louder, straining against the cuffs. He gritted his teeth again. How he hated saying this, even in play. He always thought the males in the upper wards were too soft for his taste.

"Very good. And one more thing, tell me you'll never forget it."

Joe blinked his eyes a few times and then stared at her. This lady proved herself a relentless taskmaster. "Princes are strong and brave, and I'll never forget it. Really, Princess, I won't. That's a promise."

"Excellent. That's more like it." She loosened her grip and massaged him gently, working to increase the circulation, especially at the top near the base of his shaft. "There now, that wasn't so hard, was it?" Rose smiled. His lips tempted her, and she dropped a soft kiss on them. "Are you still dying to fire your shots, as you called them earlier?"

He nodded. His mouth twitched into a faint smile; his eyes still glazed from her hard squeezes.

"Good. I'll help you load up." She took his length in his hands and continued working the stiff erection looming in front of her. With one last move, she worked the tip of her tongue into his pink head and licked and pushed as far as she could. As she pinched and stroked around the ridge, she wiggled and wagged her tongue against his sensitive walls, nearly driving him blind with bliss.

"Princess, I'm ready to blow." Joe closed his eyes and tensed his hips. Rose felt his balls pulsate against her fingers, and removing her tongue, she swallowed every thick, creamy drop he pushed out.

She sat up, wiping her lower lip with the tip of her finger. "There, now we're done." After uncuffing his wrists, she delivered him one last kiss, sinking her tongue into the warmth of his mouth. Joe sucked the wet flesh, tasting the saltiness of his own ejaculate. He explored her willing mouth with no fear of biting pain this time. When they finished he caught his breath and continued to stare up at her in silence.

"So how was it?" She traced around his ear with her finger.

"Princess, what can I say? You're a damn good fuck. Absolutely incredible."

"What would you like to do now?" Rose smiled, and swayed from side to side over his thighs, eyeing him with lust.

"I've got itchy fingers now." He smiled. "Hand me that bottle."

Rose smiled and reclined on the bed. Joe leaned over her and rubbed her thigh. She bent her knees and spread herself open.

"More willing this time, aren't you?" he said with a wink, enjoying the vision of her, open enough to glimpse her pink folds.

She closed her eyes and sighed. Joe watched as he slid his fingers deep inside her. He knew the pleasure of the cool oil as it burned against her slick walls. With clenched teeth, she stifled the urge to moan. He said nothing, preferring to bask in silence, wanting to hear nothing but breathing and the sound of his fingers swishing in her thick fluids. He'd turned the palm of his hand up, working his fingers in deliberate, forward strokes that soon sent her body into a fit of hot release. She opened her eyes, locked them on the ceiling, and concentrated on nothing but his touch and the jerking of her hips.

"That's good, Princess. Just hug and kiss my fingers. It's okay. You have a nice bite inside there, too, you know." With his other hand he worked her clit, tugging and rubbing with a slow, steady rhythm.

"Joe!" Rose cried out and arched her back, gasping. Another round of spasms overtook her, and she lost herself in the internal pleasure pain.

"I knew you still had a little more bite in there. Good, huh?"

Rose relaxed a moment and closed her eyes.

"Princess, as much as I hate to end our fun here, I can just bet your prince—who's strong and brave, I might add—will be looking for you. If I know you, I'm sure you didn't tell him about coming down here."

Rose laughed. "You're right, I didn't tell him. He doesn't have a clue. I just said something about needing some fresh air and time alone."

"Let's go back to my work room and get you dressed. And one more thing, I'm glad you had the guts to come and see me."

"Joe, what can I say? I respect a person who's a master at their craft." She wrapped her arms around him and whispered in his ear, "And you are a master." Joe chuckled and gave her one last, lingering kiss.

*   *   *

Rose headed back upstairs. Smug and proud, she barely felt the cold, hard floor tiles beneath her feet. The long line of rooms, which appeared to go on forever, caught her interest for the first time, and she wondered what lurked behind each closed door as she passed.

She also tried coming up with ways to tell Thomas her secret. What would he do or say once he found out? Standing with her back to one of the doors, she rehearsed several options in her mind. How desolate it was down here. She strained her ears. Other than the droning of a distant generator, the halls remained quiet. For all its outward appearance of solitude, Rose experienced a sudden uneasiness, a suspicion she might not be the only one traveling through the ghostly bowels of The House. She shook her head, hoping to shake off her premonition as mere foolishness, and pulled herself away from the door, intent on picking up her pace once she started again.

The clap of a hand over her mouth and another surrounding her waist paralyzed her with fear. Her blood ran cold, and she struggled as she found herself pulled into the room behind her.

"So this is where you go for fresh air and alone-time, is it? We've been waiting for you." Thomas moved in front of her, his faced clouded in a mix of disapproval and concern.

Rose managed to turn around in the arms holding her captive and discovered John behind her, his face solemn. His eyes didn't flash with their usual sparkle, but stared at her with a stony hardness she'd never seen before. Her body grew hot with fear, and a clammy sweat crept over her skin. She took a deep breath, gulping down some fresh air. Words stuck in her throat, though she wanted to appease them with an answer of some kind.

"What did he do to you?" Thomas glared at her.

Rose stared at the ground, saying nothing.

John released his grip and stood back a moment, running his gaze up and down. He spoke with quiet authority. "Remove your dress, Rose."

On the verge of tears, his request fueled her anger. Why did she always have to answer to these men and account for every action or decision? Her feet remained anchored to the floor and her arms hung like heavy weights by her side.

"Did you hear me? I said remove your dress, and do it *now*." John's voice grew a bit louder and now contained a pinch of irritation. Rose looked at Thomas, who continued to staring at her. He made no move to intervene, and his silence indicated she needed to do what John asked.

She sighed, humiliation now slinking its hot fingers around her, and pulled her dress over the top of her head. Thomas's eyes widened as he reached over and snatched the garment from her hands, leaving her stripped and exposed. He gave John a surprised stare, but said nothing.

"Let's see what we have here." John turned her around little by little, scrutinizing every detail of her body. He shrugged. "Nice rings for such sweet little cherries you have. Do you like them?"

Rose said nothing.

"Answer me, Rose. Your secret's out now. You don't need to hide anymore."

She swallowed, her face void of emotion. "Yes, I do like them. I wouldn't have gone to see Joe if I didn't want him to do this for me."

"What else did he do for you?" John glanced at Thomas. "Come hold her for a moment."

Rose closed her eyes. Thomas caught her arms from underneath and pinned her against his hard chest. The heat from his body warmed her bare skin.

John dropped to his knees and faced Rose's bare sex. His hot breath hit her cleft and permeated her skin. He reached up toward her lips and prepared to spread them apart.

"You won't find anything down there, John, in case you're interested. He didn't go that far."

"I'll have a look anyway, if you don't mind. I always make it a point to check things out for myself." John grinned up at her. "You won't think too ill of me will you?" The old sparkle crept back in his eyes, and he focused again on the area between her legs.

Rose caught her breath; Thomas's grip tightened around her arms. Her hips tensed up as John's warm fingers found their way into her hidden folds and soon worked themselves inside her. The grazing of his finger over her clit set off a blaze of lust, and she strained against Thomas's grasp.

"You have quite a prominent fun button, Rose. Did Joe do anything like this by any chance?" He retracted her hood and tweaked the pert flesh between his thumb and forefinger.

"John ... please ... no ..." She tried twisting herself away, but ended up pumping her hips. A throb pounded between her thighs, and her cries encouraged him to work her harder, faster. "I'm begging you, please ..." If Thomas hadn't held her close, she would have collapsed to the floor. John's grasp on her most sensitive part, though gentle, sent bolts of heat coursing through her. The old pleasure ache filled her core; her buttocks clenched. With one loud cry, she pressed against his hands as her hips shuddered. She dropped her head, catching her breath.

"There, you can't say I left you wanting this time. Thomas, you can let her go now. I've got her." He stood up and cupped her head in his hands. She lifted her eyes and saw the same haunting stare he gave her when they were alone in the cottage. He pulled her face up to his and placed a kiss on her lips. The close proximity of his body radiated a sensual energy so strong, its overwhelming strength nearly sent her swooning. Her arms wound around his waist and she hung on tight, wishing his kiss would last forever.

The sound of Thomas shifting his position broke the spell, and John's kiss came to an end. He pulled himself away. "She's all yours, Thomas. I think she'll be fine." He turned around and slipped out the door.

"Here's your dress. You can put it back on again." Thomas reached out and handed the garment back to Rose. His face remained solemn. A distant mood pervaded his entire being. "Let's go back upstairs." He entwined his fingers around hers as they left the room.

*   *   *

Later that night, after he and Rose retired for the day, Thomas lay lost in thought, his mind racing with unanswered questions. He stared up at the ceiling, unblinking, twiddling his thumbs.

"Thomas, what's wrong with you?" Rose turned over and faced him, stroking his hair. "You've been acting strange since we left from downstairs."

"Have I?" He hoped he sounded casual, but with the emotions broiling inside, he wasn't so sure. "I'm sorry, I didn't know I was acting funny."

"You've seemed rather preoccupied or something. I can't figure out what's wrong with you right now."

"Rose, nothing's wrong." He continued eyeing the ceiling.

"Well, I have a question. How did you and John find out about me and Joe?"

Thomas turned his head toward hers. "John is all over this place. He'll turn up when you least expect him to. During his rounds, he saw you down the hall and knew where you were going. When he made it to Joe's rooms, the door was shut, but he heard your voices through the door. He went back to his office and let me know. Then we both knew, so we headed on back downstairs and waited and waited."

"Why do I have to report everything I do to you guys? Can't I have at least a little bit of privacy, do what I want to do for a change?"

He lifted himself up on one elbow, and cupped one of her

breasts in his hand, stroking the satiny flesh between his fingers. "There's very little privacy in the world, unless you want to live in total isolation from humanity. In any relationship, Rose, there's accountability for actions and decisions. You can't just think of yourself. There's another person involved when you're with someone else."

She grimaced, "I guess that's true. And no, I don't think I want to live in total isolation, bored out of my mind, either."

"I have a question for you now." Thomas pursed his lips. "I've been keeping it to myself for quite a while."

"What's the question, Thomas? Will this be something that's a trick question, or one that I can't answer very well?"

"Do you trust me?"

"What? That's a crazy question. Of course I trust you." Rose sat up. "What made you ask such a thing?"

"You run away from me at times; you challenge everything I do with you; you didn't tell me you wanted to see Joe; and John told me about your getting up in the middle of the night at the cottage. He said you were afraid I'd be angry at you."

Rose said nothing, but blinked at him in disbelief.

"Besides, I see the way you treat the others. You tell Daren you'll do anything for him. And with John, even more so. Don't think I don't notice the way he looks at you, the way he kisses you, the way he touches you. You seem drawn to him. You show others a gentle behavior that you don't show me. You once said you were glad to give everything to me first, but I'm not so sure I believe you. I don't think you thought much about what you said when you told me."

Rose rubbed her head. "Oh dear, Thomas, I don't know what to say. I never knew you felt all these things. Why didn't you say something sooner? We could have talked about it."

"I don't know. I think I wanted to make sure my imagination wasn't running amok, but as time ticked on, I knew I needed to get to the bottom of everything." He reached over and rubbed her arm.

She sat there a few moments before dropping back down

beside him. "I think you're right. We've known each other almost all our lives. Maybe I take our friendship for granted. I never meant to hurt you, that's for sure. To answer your question, yes, I do trust you. I do feel secure when I'm with you. But sometimes your commanding presence and stern manner throw me off. I adore you, but you scare me, too. You seem so strong, forceful, like nothing can ever stop you."

Thomas smiled. "Really? I didn't think you saw me that way."

"And besides, I think I'm just a questioning and suspicious person by nature, which creates lots of problems for me, as you can guess."

"And what about John?"

She rubbed her eyes with a weary hand. "You're right, he does have a pull on me. He did from the beginning. I don't know how to explain it. Whether there's anything more, I have no idea. I haven't given it all much thought, to be honest with you. But if it's all the same to you, he can be a tough taskmaster just like you."

Thomas gazed at her, noting the intensity of her face, the way she fidgeted at the mention of John. As much as he hated to admit it, part of him felt some relief. Were they truly at the same place at the same time, harboring a certain love and respect but nothing beyond that? He rubbed a finger over her cheek. "Don't know about you, but I think we still need to talk more about all this. Not tonight, but definitely tomorrow. Let's get some sleep." Thomas reached over and switched off the light.

Chapter 13

"ROSE, YOU'RE UP LATE. What's going on?" John looked up from his ledger and smiled. The knock at the door had startled him; her presence startled him more.

"I couldn't sleep. I brought us a midnight snack. Thought you might be hungry. What are you working on so late?"

"Just some paperwork for The House. I must admit I've gotten a little behind. Come on in." He sat back in his chair, motioning for her to enter. The fruit on the small tray she carried seemed appetizing enough, but the hunger he felt didn't require food. Since her visit at the cottage, he had thought of no one else. Visions of her filled his head, creating in him a mad obsession, threatening to derail his very existence.

Rose crept into the office, her eyes roving all around. "I've always liked your office, John. I like the atmosphere in here, the high ceilings, even the glow of that gorgeous lamp you have on your desk. No wonder you don't mind staying. You have a lot of books here, too, just like at the cottage. And where did you get some of these unusual figurines and knickknacks on your shelves?" She picked up an ivory netsuke carving depicting two figures making love and ran her finger over the cool, smooth surface.

"I've done a little traveling in my day, so I picked up various and sundry souvenirs along the way. Like the wind chimes, some of these items are also gifts from past admits."

"Those admits must have loved you a lot. They sure seem to like giving you tokens of their affection."

John laughed, all the while thinking how much he liked her willing, adventuresome spirit. With her, he never knew quite what to expect. Trying to gain an upper hand proved a challenge against her bold and naughty ways. Why was she really here? "Yes, I like tokens of affection. They're all as unique as the ladies who gave them to me." He got up from behind the desk and closed the door. "Let's just sit here on the floor." He took the tray from her while she sat down. When he situated himself and the tray beside her, she selected an apple slice and bit down on it daintily, while he pulled off a grape and popped it into his mouth. He closed his eyes for a moment, savoring the juicy, soft flesh.

"John, are you happy being the steward here? I mean, did you enjoy being an attendant like Thomas?" Rose gave him an inquisitive look.

He thought for a moment before answering. "Yes, as a matter of fact I liked being an attendant. To be honest with you, I've always had a strong drive, even when I was an older child. I never could figure out where it came from, but it was there. That's why I came here to begin with. This place gave me an opportunity to indulge myself without feeling guilty or thinking there was something wrong with me. I jumped at the chance."

Suddenly he looked directly at Rose and added, "But things change with time, I guess. Lately, I've grown bored with whimsical affairs and meaningless encounters. At this point in my life, I'm wanting more, wanting something more enduring. I guess I'm ready to move on. I want a family of my own. I want to own land and a home, and find a different job." He stopped to read her reaction.

Rose said nothing at first, but kept her gaze on his, listening to every word. When he finished, she averted her eyes and looked down at the fruit. "I can understand that."

John continued. "Being a steward allows me to have some distance from the intense work of an attendant, while still giving me a chance to have pleasure at my choosing. You see, now I choose the people instead of having people assigned to me."

Rose nodded, grabbing another slice of apple.

"What about you? What do you want out of life, Rose?" John's eyes focused on her.

She stared at the fruit, wide-eyed, and finally cleared her throat. "Well, I think what you're wanting sounds really nice. It's what most people want." She smiled and trailed off, saying nothing more.

"Why did you come here tonight?" he asked, lifting up her chin with his finger so their eyes now met.

She blushed and sat up straight, trying to formulate her words. "You know what, John, I really do understand what you said earlier. Since I've been here, I've realized that I have different feelings with different people. Some stir up certain things in me, while others don't."

"How do I affect you, Rose? I want to know. And besides, you still haven't answered my question." His voice had dropped to nearly a whisper as he leaned in toward her, running his finger through a stray lock of her hair.

Looking down modestly, but with conviction, she answered, "John, I'm not the greatest at talking about feelings. Thomas has been trying to get me to talk, just like you, right before I came down here, actually."

John bristled at the sound of Thomas's name. Did they both want this woman? His jaw clenched. He needed the truth more than ever, and he aimed to get it tonight.

Rose continued. "All this 'I want to know' chitchat makes me uncomfortable, but I'll tell you this, I came here tonight because I wanted to see you. I just wanted your company, that's all."

"That's all? Is that it?" He wasn't fooled by her casual answer; her demeanor suggested differently. His instincts told him she had come to him for a reason, one she hesitated to tell. He pressed harder. "Somehow, Rose, I have a sneaking suspicion there's more to this than you let on. I need you to tell me the truth because it's important to me. Why have you come here tonight?"

She swallowed hard and poured out her words like a heavy rain. "The truth is there is an attraction I've had for you the moment I first saw you. The feelings are so deep I have trouble finding words to describe them. I like your maturity, your confidence. I like the way you smile and the way your eyes sparkle when you're teasing me. I don't know, you weave a magic spell that draws me in. I'm more comfortable and secure with you than with anyone I've ever been with—including Thomas—and he and I have known each other a long time, if you didn't know already."

John remained silent, his eyes steady. Inside his chest, his heart nearly exploded as emotions washed over him.

"When we spent the night together in your cottage, the whole situation struck me as normal, like we …"

"Like we belong together?" John said, with a soft smile.

Rose dropped her head and fidgeted with a grape, trying to wrest it free from the stem.

John reached over and placed his hand over hers, stopping her war with the fruit. He looked at her and smiled. His eyes flashed with triumph. Sitting up on both knees, he took her head in his hands, placing a soft, lingering kiss on her lips. He took her in his arms and positioned her onto her back. She lifted up in compliance as he pushed her dress up and softly spread her legs open. He could see the hint of her folds, glistening wet.

He slipped his fingers deep inside. Her thigh quivered as he stroked up and down, her warm fluids covering his fingers. She lay back, closed her eyes, and yielded to his touch. He spread her sex apart and brought his soft mouth down over her clit, teasing out the tip, smooth and firm, licking with a quick, circular motion. Out of the corner of his eye he caught the vision of her fists clenching as she exploded with a rush of orgasmic waves. He moved his tongue to the entrance of her passage and tasted her, thick and sweet.

Rose lay there a few more moments before sitting up and removing his face. She got up on her knees, and placed him firmly but gently on his back and then turned around, situating her hips over his head. John, surprised by her actions, allowed her to continue. He heard her hands moving through something unseen. He didn't remember anything else but the tray of fruit in her hands. How had she managed to hide something else from him?

He smiled. "Sweetheart, what are you doing?"

"Sh-h-h, it's my turn." She turned around and smiled back at him. "Here, pacify yourself a moment." She lowered her hips over his mouth. With renewed energy, he began fingering inside her again, and finally pulled her open, glossing his tongue over her clit.

Rose selected her supplies and placed them out in front of her in a hurry. She unsnapped his trousers and wrapped her hands around his velvety smooth cockhead, and leaning down further, took it fully into her mouth, tracing its shape with her tongue.

"Oh that's great. Yes … push harder at the top … that's good." He let up on Rose and closed his eyes, giving himself over to her movements. But the sounds of paper tearing and the snapping on of gloves disrupted his moment of surrender. The work on his tip stopped, and now he felt something rather cool against his skin. All of a sudden his eyes flew open. He caught his breath and winced with a twinge of discomfort. He sensed something cold, hard, and intrusive pressing its way into his soft opening.

His eyes glazed over as he felt a rod sliding gently into his body, hugging and licking him internally, like a snake with a rounded-end tongue, slithering into a small tunnel, forging forward, filling and opening him up by degrees. He swallowed hard. His heart pounded, but he commanded himself to relax. It had been a long time since his body experienced an invasion such as this, and taking soft, deep breaths, he allowed Rose to slide the rod back and forth inside him, feeling it graze his hidden walls, creating silky sensations that soon became too delicious to describe. He reached his hands up and rubbed her buttocks with his fingers as she kept her attention on the rod. After a few moments, she slipped it out with great care.

"How was that?" Rose asked.

"Incredible. God, you're good."

"Excellent, but I'm not done yet. I'm using something different this time. An open wand for your hot shaft, which means you can come with no interference from me."

He relaxed while she inserted the wand. "Oh, that's a tight one. Easy does it." He closed his eyes, tensing with a little discomfort. With a gentle persistence, she tenderly coaxed it into his body. When she had inserted the device in all the way, she slipped the ring over his cockhead to hold it in place.

"I'm done. Are you okay?"

"I'm good. It's tight, but I like it pretty well so far."

She stroked his cock, followed by squeezing the sac between his legs. His flesh hardened each time she licked around his head and under the ridge. She moved her tongue over the taut flesh of his cock, ending with the sucking of his tip. He let out a moan, his emissions bubbling up from deep within his loins. His balls ached, and the warmth of her mouth on him riled up the frenzy inside. He let out a cry, tensing his hips. Rose came down on top of the wand and consumed all of him, squeezing his balls and working his cock a little more to get every drop. She turned around and delivered a kiss on his lips and slipped in her tongue. As she explored his mouth, he tasted his own ejaculate, salty and slick. He always found the texture of his own lust rather interesting, never quite sure how to judge the taste.

He pulled her down on top of him and cradled her in his arms. She nestled her head against his neck, and they both rested a moment, catching their breaths. As they cuddled together for a while, he grew restless. His pubic area burned, and he lay there for a moment distracted, not wanting to ruin the mood with any unnecessary activity.

"What's wrong, John? You look uncomfortable all of a sudden." Rose grinned. "Is the fruit getting to you?"

He chuckled a moment before answering, a little embarrassed by the inconvenience of nature. "Did you plan this, Rose?"

"Not exactly. I have no control over some things," she said, trying to look innocent enough.

"Well, then, you're right." He sighed and threw up his hands in defeat. "I need to go, if you know what I mean."

She smiled. "No need to worry; I've got just the thing for you." She pulled some items from the bag she brought. John sat up and opened his mouth in surprise, speechless with her choice of supplies.

Rose waved a small package in front of him. "I think I

can help you with this problem."

"You're simply amazing. I don't know what to say."

"Don't say anything. Just lie back and relax. I'll take care of you." Rose pushed him softly back down on the floor. She gently removed the hollow wand he still wore, and placed it in a spare bag along with the other used instruments. Donning gloves and going through proper cleansing procedures, she introduced the catheter into his bladder. John lay back and enjoyed the sensations of the soft tube sliding inside, filling him up where the rod used to be. He winced a little, feeling a sudden urge to relieve himself as she completed her insertion.

"Much better, I must admit."

"Good. I don't want you uncomfortable." Rose kissed his cheek.

He ran his fingers through her hair. "Although I must admit this whole thing feels a little strange, relieving myself with you watching me." He caught a glimpse of his fluids draining in the bag.

She leaned over and kissed his lips. "It's okay. You're with me." After a moment she clamped off the catheter and slowly removed it. "There, I think you're done." John closed his eyes, feeling the tube slipping out, its internal kisses giving way to sensations of emptiness. Rose set everything aside and began stroking him again. Looking down at him tenderly, she whispered, "I have something else for you, too."

John sat up, alarmed. "You've done some major things here already, so what else could you possibly think of?"

"No need to worry. You're right, the big stuff is done, but I have a token for you." She held before his eyes a large golden ring that looked, in fact, like a miniature crown. "Somehow I don't think you'll be keeping this on a shelf in your office. At least I hope not."

"You've got to be kidding me! This is incredible!" John gasped. He broke out laughing and fell back down on the floor, clapping his hands in approval. "God, I love it!"

"I hoped you'd be surprised." Rose chuckled.

"What are you waiting for? Put it on me." John stretched

out while she took up his tip, slipping on the ring, securing it snugly under the ridge. "Now, there's your crowning glory." She gave his head a soft pinch, and rested down beside him.

"Rose, I ... "He pulled her over on top of him, giving her a long, deep kiss. His hands reached down and, catching the bottom of her dress, slipped it all the way off over her head. Laying her on her back again, he selected a full, plump nipple, licking and toying with the ring. She opened her legs, and John willingly obliged. He slid his fingers inside, feeling her moisture. Rose reached up to stroke his hair.

"Good?" John worked his long smooth fingers against her walls.

"I love feeling you inside me, John. I wish you'd never stop." She let out a little moan when his finger tip hit her in just the right place.

After gathering some of her moisture on his fingers, he softly withdrew and smothered her clit with circular caresses.

Rose arched her back and moaned, "Oh, John, please, no teasing! I want you inside." Her voice rang out in desperation.

He smiled and whispered in her ear, "Do you like it when I do that, Rose? Does the hurt feel so good that it's unbearable?" He leaned down and kissed her. The heat from her breath sent a surge throughout his body. "You're empty right now, but you want me to fill you up, don't you?" His fingers swirled around in a thicker pool, her hidden center crying as much on the inside as she seemed to cry out to him on the outside.

"John, please ... inside ... no teasing ..." Her eyes glazed over and she tried to catch her breath.

He didn't wish to keep her wanting, though teasing her a little bit amused him. But her eyes and the look on her face told him what he needed to do—and quickly. He pushed himself inside, filling her up. He moved in and out with smooth thrusts; her body relaxed under his weight. He paused a moment and kissed her neck.

"Thank you." She looked up at him with a grateful smile and ran her fingers through the soft locks of his hair. His movements came faster, his breathing more labored. She closed her eyes, settling her head back firmly against the floor, willing and ready. She bloomed like a flower beneath him, opening herself up to his advances. He glided like a well-oiled machine, steady, smooth, not stopping for anything. He slipped out of the present moment, basking in nothing but the feel of her internal walls clenching his cock with a sure grip, The deepest part of her wanted him, even more than Thomas, and for this union of their bodies, this blending of heart and soul, he moved in and out of her with mindful gratitude. He pressed against her, letting out a small grunt. She accepted the full release of his passion. John said nothing, but stroked her face with his hand.

"Stay with me a while longer." He removed himself and resnapped his trousers; Rose busied herself with slipping her dress back on. He reclined back on the floor again and snuggled her in his arms. His finger strayed over one of her nipples and lingered there, tracing the outline of the ring through her dress.

"Seems you like them as much as Daren does."

"So tell me, Rose, why did you decide to have this done? I never thought of you as one who is—how to say this—? So nonconformist."

"I've seen Daria with hers, and I guess I wanted some, too. The guys seemed to love them, and I know she did. She said she would have stopped nothing to have them done."

"You got those sweet fruits of yours pricked because of Daria?"

"She told me the social elite did this to make a fashion statement. Did you know that, John?" She rubbed the top of her dress. "Now all I need is a decorative chain of some kind, maybe one with jewels or something."

He chuckled and kissed her on the cheek. "We'll have to make sure you have one, then. One with fiery diamonds to match your strong spirit." He stopped, catching himself before he said any more, catching himself before his emotions betrayed him.

*   *   *

Rose dropped her eyes from his gaze. Her cheeks flushed at his words. She wanted to change the subject. "Thomas said you saw me going into Joe's place, and then you told him about it. Why did you do that?"

John cupped her chin in his hand and lowered his head to kiss her lips. "We worry about you, that's all."

"He's good at what he does, you know. He did a good job."

"What price did you have to pay? And you know what I mean by that question."

"He's not quite so bad." Rose grinned at the memory of it all, her little secret.

"I think a lot of his style is just a front."

"Just a front? He's a bull, I'd say. But you're right, he follows the rules and I've heard his skills are top-notch." He kept his eyes on Rose. "So tell me, how did you handle his animal ways?"

She smiled, eyes twinkling, and let out a small chuckle. "Let's just say I ended up taking the bull by the balls. I fixed him in the end. Surprised me and him."

John raised his eyebrows. "You got him by the balls?" He laughed again. "Can I ask for details?"

"Um, no, you don't need to ask. Just trust me on this one. Believe it or not, I can handle myself."

"You may be able to hold your own, but you'll always be my little flower, Rose." John, ready to kiss her again, stopped in midaction. He swallowed, caught his breath, and stroked her hair.

Rose felt another flush covering her face. This time his words fell over her like an avalanche, shaking her emotional foundation. She wanted to stay with him forever, never leave his sight, but the conversation, his words, knocked on the door of her heart too hard, and part of her wanted to run and hide a little longer. "I think I need to go back upstairs. If Thomas finds out I've sneaked away, he'll be worried."

"He should worry. I would too, if I were in his position."

John smiled. "I'm glad you came down tonight. Maybe we can do this again?"

"I don't see why not. I'd like it also." She pulled herself up, gathered up her bag and the empty tray, and headed back to the upper ward.

*   *   *

"Where have you been?" Thomas fired off his question as soon as she settled back down into bed.

"Nowhere, really. I couldn't sleep and just wandered out and about for a few moments to get a little fresh air. I'm sorry I woke you up." Rose reached over and stroked the head of his cock, hoping to stop his questions. To her surprise, he caught her hand and gently removed her fingers.

"You're lying, Rose. I know better. Where did you go?"

She said nothing, but stared up at the ceiling, overcome by a sense of guilt.

"I knew it. You went to see John, didn't you? He's been around here late at night. Don't think I don't know."

She grimaced with disgust, hoping the light from the hallway didn't show her face too much. "Yes," she said, exasperation taking over her mood, "I did go see him. You're right, he was working late, so I just stuck my head through the door and said hello."

"Another lie. You've been gone for more than just a few moments."

"Do you time everything I do?" Her voice filled with irritation and impatience.

"While you're here, I'm responsible for you. Your whereabouts and safety are my concern. Did you forget?"

"Thomas, are you okay? You sound mad, almost angry, and you're acting a little odd these days. What's wrong with you?" She sat up and faced his outstretched body. "We're friends, so you can tell me what's going on. Please talk to me." Much to her surprise, when she reached out and ran her hand over his stomach, his body stiffened. To her alarm and disappointment, he said nothing, but turned over and fell fast asleep.

Rose's heart pounded. Things had taken a different turn lately, and she didn't understand why, let alone what to do. His behavior struck her as unusual, not the carefree attitude he possessed most of the time she'd known him. Seized by a cold grip of panic she'd never experienced before, she shivered. A tidal wave of isolation crushed her senses so strongly her heart nearly broke. No matter what happened, she never wanted to lose their friendship or the closeness they shared. Friends mattered. They were as important as lovers.

She lay back down, falling into a sleep filled with fitful dreams.

Chapter 14

ROSE AWOKE BEFORE BREAKFAST, alone in an empty bed. Though the last few days with Thomas had maintained some semblance of its old normalcy, the new divide widening between them glared at her with unkind eyes.

She slipped on her dress and walked out to the main desk. "Do either of you know where Thomas went? He's not with me."

"I think he's in the common room at the end of the hall." The attractive female attendant behind the desk smiled, pointing in the proper direction.

"Thank you." Rose started off in the direction of the common room. Never once, since her admission to The House had she awakened without Thomas beside her, his warm body ready for hers, ready to play and explore. To her dismay she heard sounds of laughter in the distance. When she reached the entrance, she discovered Thomas and Daria, the only occupants, stretched out in the far left corner of the room. Rose hung back a moment, watching.

"You always feel so good, Thomas. I always like sneaking in a roll with you when we get the chance." Daria reached up and ran her fingers through his hair.

"You and me both, sweet girl." Thomas dropped a quick kiss on her lips. "I've got to unload, though. My dick's about to explode."

"Let Old Dick rip away is all I have to say." Daria dug her head into the carpet and stretched her arms over her head, legs thrown open wide and ready for Thomas's advances. He plunged in, moving with quick thrusts, grunting at intervals. After a few undulations and a couple of hip-twists, he paused, shuddering.

Daria cooed, "Just the way I like you, Thomas, nice and hot, like the spicy, sizzlin' man you are." She pulled his face down and gave him a noisy kiss that filled the room.

Rose glanced back down the hall to make sure no one else had heard. Red-faced, she turned back to view the room again.

"Hey, honey!" Daria waved from the corner.

Startled, Rose found herself caught, and no way out. "I'm sorry, I was looking for Thomas. I didn't mean to interrupt."

"Come on over here a minute." Daria waved Rose over. "I heard you got some new trinkets for those cute little tits of yours."

Rose, somewhat encouraged by Thomas's smile, walked over to the corner. "Let's see."

"What?" Rose's face turned a deeper red. "Oh, you know what these look like. You don't want to see mine."

"I want to see them on you. I insist." Daria sat up while Thomas disengaged, quickly snapping up his trousers.

"Let Daria see. She didn't believe me when I told her." He reached over and, before Rose could stop him, untied the straps and pulled the dress down over her top.

"Nice! I never guessed you had it in you. I told you to get the best one there is, and Joe's the man." As Daria admired Rose's full, adorned mounds, she plucked away at her own ringed peaks, much more for the benefit of Thomas's lustful gaze.

Rose nodded. "Um, yes, he's a good one. I'm glad I followed your advice on getting someone skilled." She pulled her dress back up, turned to Thomas. "I'll just head on back to our room and get ready for breakfast, unless you have other plans already." Without waiting for his reply, Rose nodded to Daria, and turned on her heel.

*　*　*

Time rolled in slow motion with each step she took, dragging her down, little by little. Rose, with a heavy heart, reached her room and sat at the foot of the bed, her back to the door, trying in desperation to find calm somewhere in the messy tangled thoughts jumbling in her head. Numbness seeped through every muscle in her body, and she wished for nothing more than an ability to vanish, to disappear into some black hole or realm far from The House. She jerked her head up at the touch of a pair of warm, strong hands around her shoulders.

Thomas sat down behind her and pulled her into his arms. "Like I said the other night, we need to talk a little more."

"Oh, Thomas, I'm fine—you're fine ... It's okay, really."

"Rose, stop putting on such a tough front. I think we're both a little confused right now, and we need to resolve this if we're going to continue forward."

"Continue forward? What do you mean?" Rose somehow became more aware of the hardness and warmth of his chest than ever before. His voice sounded more clear and strong than ever before. This whole moment seemed to take on a different meaning than ever before. All her senses seemed heightened, focused on this one moment, the here and now within his embrace. Whether or not she liked talking about feelings, he was right. This needless tension between them required resolution. She had to trust that honesty would keep them whole and strong for the rest of their lives, regardless what the future held for either one.

"What do you want? I need you to tell me." Thomas rested his cheek against hers.

"I'm not sure." She fidgeted, not wanting to bring the subject of John into the discussion. The thought of it scared her.

"Now's not the time to run and hide. I need you to talk to me. Our friendship ... relationship ... whatever, depends on it." Thomas's voice remained soft and kind, not drenched in the steely tone like the other night.

"I don't know, Thomas." Rose flinched, not sure how to start. "I think we've always enjoyed a strong friendship that's managed to endure throughout the years, whether we've spent lots of time together or not. But I think our time here has changed things for us, and not in a bad way, either." She turned around and faced him. He moved to the head of the bed, pulling her with him, and stretched out on his side.

"Tell me more about how our time here has changed us."

His stare bore a hole through her, but a tender finger moved against her cheek.

"You asked me not too long ago if I truly meant what I said about giving you everything first. The truth is, yes, I do mean what I say. No matter whatever happens to us in the future, I will always be glad you were the first. I wouldn't trade the experience for anything in the world. You did an amazing job in sticking right by me every step of the way. You've helped me understand myself much better, and I think I'll be able to view things differently in the future, thanks to you."

"What about John?"

"What about Daria?"

"Now Rose, that's not fair." Thomas turned his head toward the ceiling and chuckled.

"Yes, it is fair and you know it, so I'll come clean. When I saw you with Daria a few minutes ago, I understood then how you must have felt when you found out I was spending the night with John. And I heard what she said about sneaking in moments to spend time with you. As you told me one time, 'Turn about, fair play.' And like Daria with you, I stole in a moment with John the other night."

He swallowed and licked his lips before answering. "Could it be we've found ourselves, at the same place at the same time?" He smiled and kissed her.

"You might be right." She laughed and shook her head. "I never saw us as anything more than friends, and our coming together like this shook everything up. We've done a whole lot more than what friends normally do." She stared across the room. "Of all things, I never dreamt we'd be having a conversation like this one."

"Me neither, but that's okay. Your being here has made me think about things in my life, too, Rose, so don't feel bad or guilty. And let me add that doing things in the safety of a solid friendship is a good way to have experiences and not get your heart broken, usually." He rubbed his lower lip. "Maybe this whole thing needed to happen, to both of us." He repositioned himself on his back. "But I think it's become clear that you and I truly have our sights on other people, and our agreement on that makes things easier. I'll say this, go with your instinct, no matter what. Will you at least promise me that?" He turned his head and smiled.

"I promise you I will. And promise me you'll do the same." Rose, suddenly filled with her old sense of naughtiness, sat up and straddled herself over his thighs. Leaning over his face, she said, "You know what, Thomas, I think we're the type who will endure regardless, no matter what happens. I just feel it in my bones."

"And we know your bones don't lie!" He gave her a soft nip on the tip of her nose before ending with a kiss.

Unable to ignore any longer the hard mound between his thighs, an irresistible temptation pressing against her sex, she made a dive for his trousers. With fingers flying, she unsnapped the front panel to reveal a beautiful, engorged shaft, ripe and sweet for swallowing. She lifted up the bottom of her dress, and glided on …

*   *   *

"Thomas, can you come out here, please?" The attendant working the desk poked her head in the doorway and motioned for him to come out. "We need to see you right away."

"Sure." Thomas headed out behind her. Later he returned with a bag in his hand.

"What have you got, Thomas?" Rose glanced in his direction. "You were gone long enough." She sat up, wrapping an arm around him as he sat down next to her. "Why do you have such a sad look on your face? Is everything okay?"

He remained silent, shaking his head, staring off in space.

"What's wrong? Please tell me." Rose tugged on his arm. "And what's that bag in your hand for?"

"Rose, I don't know how to tell you this, but your father

is on his way to pick you up right now. I have to get you ready for discharge."

She blinked in disbelief. "What? Are you sure? Who told you that?" Her heart pounded. Unable to sit still at this announcement, she began pacing the floor. "This can't be true. Can you at least check again, and make sure you didn't hear something wrong?"

"Rose, I've already checked more than once. I even talked to John. He said your father called him. Coming from John, the information is the most accurate you'll ever get."

"Oh, this is awful." Rose sat down on the bed again, wringing her hands, tears welling up in her eyes. "But I don't want to go." She stood up again, a new anger rolling over her in hot, nasty waves. "I won't go. I'll run way. I'll run off into the woods and hide. Nobody will find me. If I start now, I'll get a head start. You won't tell anyone, will you, Thomas, if I run and hide away somewhere? Then I can come back later this evening, and Father will be gone."

Thomas gave her a rueful smile. "As creative as you think you sound right now, the whole idea is crazy. You can't run and hide. Did you ever stop to think your Father would have us tear this place apart to find you?"

"He's the one who sent me here in the first place. It would only serve him right for doing such a mean, horrid thing to his little girl. And I am his little girl, aren't I?"

"Rose, stop for a minute! Listen to yourself." Thomas threw up a hand to interject. "Just stop. First of all, you are not a little girl anymore, whether you like it or not—whether he likes it or not. And another thing, he sent you here with the best intentions. After your experience here, do you now disagree with what he did?" Thomas caught her as she paced by, pulled her on the bed, and hugged her close. "Do you disagree with what he did?"

She sighed and tried to choke back the tears. "I guess not."

"You guess not? You're not sure? Is that what I'm

hearing you say now?"

Rose scowled at him. "Oh, Thomas, of course you know I wouldn't trade my experience here for anything. Though you have to admit The House's method of treatment would make him or anyone do more than raise an eyebrow." She now grinned a little.

"Well, yes, you do have a point there, but we know the treatment worked. All he needs to see is how much better you are. Can't you at least do that, Rose, show him how much better you are?"

"I guess so, but oh, how I hate to go. For some reason, the thought of leaving never occurred to me. But I guess things can't last forever, can they?"

"Of course not, sweetheart, but our friendship and experience together will always last. You know that, don't you?"

She nodded and rested her head on his shoulder.

"Now come on. I don't like this any better than you do, but we need to get you dressed."

*   *   *

"Uh-oh, street clothes can only mean one thing. You're leaving us, aren't you?" Daren stopped in the doorway and leaned against the wooden frame. The bright sunlight through the windows lit his hair in a fiery blaze.

"Daren, I'll miss you as badly as Thomas." Rose walked over and took him in her arms. "I do adore you so much." She smiled up into his face and, for the last time, beheld his golden eyes, soft and kind, but with a glint of sadness.

He lifted her face and gave her a long, deep kiss. "I'll miss you, too, Rose. I think you're one in a million." She ran her fingers through his hair and gave him one last long hug before he quietly turned out of the doorway.

She turned around and faced Thomas. "Well, sweetheart, this is it," he said. "This is good-bye. For obvious reasons, I can't escort you downstairs, but you and I both know you have the way to John's office memorized." He lifted her chin and peered into her eyes. "I've enjoyed every minute with you, Rose. Being with you has changed me forever, made me think, and I thank you."

"Same here." Her eyes swept around the room once more, attempting to burn the images into her memory forever. "I'll miss this place, the beauty here, the people." With a heavy heart, she walked to the doorway. Before she turned out, Thomas grabbed her arm and moved in for one last kiss. Rose made a mental note of every detail, his soft mouth, his warmth, his strength, his smell, the softness of his hair, the beating of his heart against hers. "Good-bye, Thomas." She left the room and made her way to the marble staircase.

How she hated her clothes as she walked. They held her in a tight grip, threatening to choke the very life out of her. On the landing, she surveyed the entire lobby, finally turning her eyes upward to catch the last rainbow flashes from the great crystal chandelier. With slow, deliberate steps, she made her way down to the bottom. No more imagining herself as royalty in a magnificent palace.

"Well, well, Princess, so this is farewell." A hand grasped hers and assisted her down from the last remaining step on to the main floor. "As we say here at The House, 'street clothes can only mean one thing.'"

She smiled lightly. "Yes, Joe, that's what I've heard."

He continued to hold her hand, his grip warm but firm, his eyes on her, intent and steady.

"I'm going to miss being here, but you know what, as strange as this may sound, I'll miss you, too. I know one thing for sure, I'll never forget you."

"Ah, Princess," Joe said, a sparkle in his eye, "likewise. But one thing you should never forget is that you, like princes, are strong and brave."

Rose laughed.

"So just remember that one thing. Even in today's age, there are men who love a strong woman." He winked and squeezed her hand and headed up the stairs. She stood watching him until he reached the top and disappeared into the upper corridors of The House, those same corridors that had served as her home for a while.

Rose turned toward the right hallway, took a deep breath, and lifted her head and shoulders. With one last effort, she headed toward the office.

"Here she is at last." John stood up from behind the desk. "We were beginning to wonder if you'd run away."

Rose entered the room, a forced smile on her lips. Her father and mother stood up from their chairs, and her mother held out her arms. "I see you've come, too, Mother," she said, giving her a hug.

"Oh, darling, we've missed you so much. I told your father I couldn't bear waiting alone at home while he came for you."

"The house has been too quiet with just the two of us, Rose, and we agreed you needed to come home." Mr. Barweather gave her a hug and kiss on the forehead. "It's time for you to come home now."

"We have your travel bag here, and we're ready to leave if you are, dear." Rose's mother picked up the bag and moved toward the door.

Rose caught sight of John leaning against the front of his desk. She fought hard to contain her tears. Though his face held a soft, thoughtful grin, the old sparkle in his eyes seemed a bit subdued. Too numb to move, she remained rooted to the floor, a dazed expression on her face.

John cleared his throat and came toward her. "Rose, you were a model patient. We wish you the best of luck at home." He reached for her hand and patted it. She detected a stiffness in his voice, and his formality showed nothing of the familiarity they'd shared.

"Thank you for all you've done." Her voice came out raspy as she fought the sting of tears. "I learned a lot." She stared at the ground, barely mumbling her words, unable to meet his gaze.

He shook her hand lightly in response and released his hold. "I hope all of you have a safe trip home." He waved to her parents, who waited patiently by the door. Mr. Barweather nodded in acknowledgement, and the family exited the office.

*   *   *

With a wistful gaze through the back window of the car, Rose stared after The House and grounds until they faded from sight. The ride home seemed to last forever, and she wished for its end. She listened to her parents make small talk with a mild interest, only answering when spoken to. Though the day beamed sunny and beautiful, Rose's mood reflected a raging thunderstorm pounding away inside her heart. Just as scared as she'd been when driving to The House, she was now equally sad upon leaving it and the life she'd grown to love. If only her parents would change their minds and turn around.

But the rolling hills and countryside soon gave way to the sights and sounds of the city, and before long, her old neighborhood crept into view. Her heart sank; she really was coming home—for good.

"We're here." Mr. Barweather turned and gave his daughter a big smile. "Rose, your room is the same way you left it. Nothing has changed while you've been gone." He hugged her close and opened the front door.

She passed through into the entrance hall, surprised how the walls seemed to cave in on her, rendering her nearly claustrophobic. The old familiarity of home did little to warm her soul, its decor and atmosphere striking her as foreign, as if she had never lived here before. With heavy steps, she plodded up to her room. All her old things—her bed, her bureau, tiny trinkets and mementos—seemed to stare back at her as if she were a stranger in their midst. The afternoon sun peeked through her window, and she walked over and peered out, viewing the trees and flowers outside.

"Darling, are you all right?"

She turned around at the sound of her mother's voice. "Yes, I'm fine. Why?"

Her mother placed the travel bag on the floor and wrapped her hands around her daughter's shoulders. "You've hardly said two words since we left The House. Your father and I thought you'd be desperate to come home. You pitched such a fit about going there to start with."

"Oh, Mother, I've been away for a while. I just need to get used to everything again."

"That makes perfectly good sense, dear. Just rest. Dinner will be ready in a few hours, and we're serving your favorite dishes. I have the best china and silverware set out in your honor. I know how you enjoy a pretty table, just like I do." Her mother gave her a kiss on the cheek and left the room. Rose smiled. Did she even remember how to use utensils?

Dinner passed with light, pleasant conversation with her parents, along with a few family members and friends who had come to celebrate her return home. Rose discovered she still possessed a knack for handling utensils, and her good manners had managed to stay with her. For all the pleasantries exchanged, she found the conversation stiff, the mannerisms of everyone forced and mechanical. When the last person waved good night, she headed off to bed.

"Sleep well, dear. You'll enjoy sleeping in your own bed again." Her mother kissed her forehead.

Rose went up to her room and shut the door, turning the lock with a twist of her finger. She stripped off her clothes and tossed them on a chair. Standing there naked in the lamplight, her eyes fell to her chest where the two metal rings flashed their steely bits at her, their presence her only link to a fading past which slipped away minute by minute, leaving nothing but a ghostly figment in her mind.

After some consideration, she decided to forego sleeping nude and slipped on a nightgown for modesty's sake. She switched off the light and crawled into bed. Darkness closed in on her, trapping her like a gnat in a web, unable to escape.

Outside she heard nothing but the crickets chirping their nighttime songs. The light of the full moon bathed the room in cool shades of silver. Solitude hit her like a rude slap on the face, and now a deluge of tears stung her eyes. How she missed Thomas! Her body ached to have him near, to hear his soft breathing next to her, to spoon her body against his solid, warm back. He'd probably sleep with Daria tonight, or some other admit. Tears came hotter and faster, and her chest heaved out soft sobs. She clapped her hands over her mouth in an effort to silence herself. What if her parents heard? How would she explain her crying spell if they asked?

She threw the covers back, got out of bed, and stood in front of the window. As she stared into the night sky, she remembered her time with John at the cottage, how she'd teased him, how he'd consummated his desire for her, the last time they'd spent together in his office. One memory of him led to another until, overwhelmed with strong emotions, she broke down in a fit of silent tears. Exhausted and drained, she finally slipped back into bed and fell into a deep, dreamless sleep.

*　*　*

"Rose, I'm worried about you." Mr. Barweather entered the room and sat on the bed beside her. Rose, pretending to read, looked up at him over her book and said nothing. "You've been home a few weeks, and you're moping around here like you've lost your best friend or something. You don't smile much, you're withdrawn, you're weepy all the time, and overall you seem like a total wreck. What's wrong with you?"

"I don't understand. I'm fine. At least I think so." Rose tried to sound casual, hoping her father accepted her answer as the truth.

"I think you're lying, Rose. You're a pretty opinionated girl, and it's not like you to keep your mouth shut for so long." He leaned in close and whispered, "What did they do to you there? It must have been something awful, because you've been acting funny since you've come home. You can talk to me. I'm your father, for godsakes."

"They were very kind. Don't worry so much." She smiled and patted his hand, praying he'd now leave her in peace.

"All I can say is you sure don't look like old Willie Strumpkin or Thelma Starnsby when they came home. This is all just dreadful!" He shook his head and left the room.

Rose tried to bury her head in the book and concentrate on the words, but found, to her dismay, she'd been holding the pages upside down the whole time. She threw the book on the bed in defeat. As much as she hated to admit it, her father was right. Ever since her arrival back home, depression held her down with its hateful, weighty fingers. Fresh air always did her some good, and she decided to take advantage of the beautiful garden behind the house.

"Mother, I'm going outside. I want to see what's new out back."

"I think that's a wonderful idea, dear. You need some sun. You've been looking rather pale since you've come home."

"I think a sniff of your roses and gardenias is just what I need." She smiled and gave her mother a kiss on the cheek, then left by way of the back door in the kitchen. The soft breeze hit her skin and the sun began to warm her spirit a little. She watched the butterflies as they floated and landed on the choicest flowers, lingering to drink the soothing nectar. She always loved a romp in the garden. Her mother had hired a horticulturist, and they had gone great lengths to create an intriguing, meandering layout, which included a small gazebo that sat at the far corner across from a regal oak tree.

She made her rounds, dipping her nose into a host of open blooms, and finally trudged over to the gazebo. Disillusioned and unable to liven her own mood, even while immersed in the beauty of her mother's garden, she began to wonder how she'd ever return to her former contentment. Her father was right; her situation was dreadful. How did dull Willie Strumpkin and the prim and proper Thelma Starnsby adjust to life after The House?

Just when her despair seemed to have sunk to the lowest level, she caught the sound of a woman's voice singing out her name.

"You-u-u-u ho-o-o-o-o! Ro-o-o-o-se!"

"Mrs. Starnsby!" Rose jumped to her feet and ran to the gate to meet the slender, older lady, who stood on the other side, frantically waving a handkerchief, smiling all the while. The breeze had caught up her hat and cocked the headdress to one side of her head, giving her an overall rather comical look.

Rose stifled the urge to laugh. "I was just thinking about you. Come on in." She lifted the latch and allowed her visitor to pass through. "Would you like to join me in the gazebo? It's much cooler in the shade."

"I would love nothing better." Thelma Starnsby readjusted her hat and followed her hostess. In a few moments, they were resting comfortably on the benches. "What a lovely place you have here. I know your mother has such a way with flowers and plants." Mrs. Starnsby craned her neck in all directions, making sure she saw everything. On occasion, she'd sniff the breeze. "What a fresh, earthy scent. I bet you enjoy spending hours out here."

"You'd think so, but I'm not feeling very spry or happy these days, if you can believe that."

The lady leaned forward and said in a low voice, "Rumor has it that you're feeling rather down, crying and spending far too much time by yourself. I went to visit my cousin, who lives within walking distance from here, and while I was in the neighborhood, I felt it my duty to come by and see you."

"Rumors? And just what have you heard?" Alarmed, Rose sat up straight and turned to face Mrs. Starnsby, a twinge of panic welling up inside. Yes, she felt miserable, but she preferred to keep her feelings, and her affairs, private.

"As you can guess, some secrets don't keep themselves well, and I had heard that you'd returned from a stay at The House." She gave Rose a wink and a pat on the shoulder

"From what I've been told, you had a much easier time when you came home. Why am I having so much trouble?"

"Dear," she said, taking Rose's hand in hers, "what people don't know is that my beloved Harry and I had been giving each other the eye for quite some time before I went to The House. You see, he appeared to have designs on me, the way he flirted and carried on, but the way he dragged his feet, never letting me know one way or the other if we'd ever be together, nearly got the better of my sanity. Why, I finally couldn't take it anymore … and well … I broke down. And I'm sure you know the rest."

"No, I don't know the rest, Mrs. Starnsby. What I'd like to know is how you handled coming back home alone."

"Darling, that's quite a simple answer. You see, by the time I left The House, I had concocted a plan, thinking this last effort would surely help him make up his mind about us … or not."

Rose leaned in closer, intrigued. "So what did you do? You won him over."

"I invited him to dinner one night, preparing a meal like they serve at The House. One thing led to another … and you can guess the rest.

Laughing, Rose nodded. "Yes, I can!" But after a brief moment, she frowned. "Unfortunately, I don't have designs on anyone, nor does anyone have such notions on me." She kicked at the floorboards with a toe, staring out the gazebo, her former dismal mood settling over her again.

"Nonsense, dear. You're quite a beauty, and a delightful person. I'm sure someone has their heart set on you. I just feel it. So don't worry your pretty head to death any longer." Mrs. Starnsby picked up the pocket watch about her waist and glanced at the time. "Oh, would you look at the time. I have to get back home." She stood up to leave. "My dear, I bid you adieu. I'll show myself out. You just sit here and think about what I've told you." She headed out of the gazebo, trotted over the stepping stones, and out the gate. Rose waved back at Mrs. Starnsby's fluttering handkerchief, her last good-bye, before she continued down the sidewalk and vanished from sight.

Rose sat in the gazebo a while longer, mulling over her previous conversation. Though Mrs. Starnsby found her happiness, she wasn't exactly sure when or if she'd ever find that elusive commodity herself. Overcome with boredom and more despair, she shook herself from her reverie, heading over to the oak tree, where she stood for a while beneath its large, leafy branches. She stared out across the opposite side of the garden and started daydreaming again.

"Oh!" She gave a small shriek and jumped, as a pair of arms cinched around her waist, pulling her against a tall, strong body. When she managed to turn around, she clapped her hands over her mouth, and her eyes welled up with tears.

"Have you missed me?"

"John!" Rose stood staring at him, dumbfounded.

He glanced around the garden and finally said with a smile, "I see you don't have any tiny tinkles yourself. That's too bad. I kind of like their spirited chimes myself."

Silence.

"Are you okay, Rose, you're usually not so quiet. Did I come at a bad time?" With a laugh, he pulled her hands down from her face and kissed her, running his warm tongue against the roof of her mouth, sending a familiar warmth flaming throughout her body.

She closed her eyes and lost herself in his kiss and embrace. When they finished, she opened her eyes and stared up at him. "You're still here."

"Of course, why wouldn't I be?"

"I just didn't want this to be a dream, that's all."

"No, sweetheart, you're not dreaming; and I'm still here."

"Not to sound rude or anything, but exactly why are you here?"

John laughed. "I hear you've not been yourself since you left us, and I decided to come see for myself."

"Who told you that?" Rose bristled with a surge of indignation. Why couldn't people mind their own business instead of hers?

"Your father, of course. Who else?" John held her face in

his hands and peered down into her eyes. "He's worried about you. He called me and told me all about what's happened since you've come home, and wanted to know what on earth we did to upset you so much." He chuckled and added, "You know, most people who leave The House are usually pretty happy, or else they stay on as staff." He kissed the tip of her nose and smiled, his eyes resuming their old sparkle.

"How's Thomas?"

"Wonderful. I see him and Daria together much of the time. An interesting pair, I must admit. She's such a brazen girl, but he seems to rather like her bold nature."

"Good." Rose felt a bit surprised at her sense of relief. "I'm glad to hear it. I thought he'd taken a fancy to her, myself. I saw them together in the common room the day I left." She dropped her gaze, focusing on the green grass under the tree. Words failed her.

John lifted her chin with his finger. "I have a question for you. Even if your father had never contacted me, I still intended to come here and ask it."

"What is it? Are you okay?" Rose stared back at him, puzzled.

He pulled away for a moment, not sure how to begin. For the first time Rose saw him flush, and wondered at his show of uncertainty.

"It's okay, John, you can ask me anything." She took his hand in hers and gave it a small squeeze. "Please tell me."

"I don't know how to say this, but—I love you, Rose. I think I loved you the moment we met. Your leaving nearly tore my heart out, but I had to maintain a front for the sake of your parents. I hope you haven't held my coldness that day against me."

"For heaven's sake, of course not. I knew we couldn't let on in front of them. Remember, I agreed to House rules. All things must be kept confidential. And don't think Father hasn't already pressed me to tell what happened there." She stopped a moment, the earlier part of his words still playing in her ears.

With a smile she gazed up at him and said, "The truth is I love you, too. And to be honest with you, I think Thomas saw it way before I admitted it to myself."

John reached over and took her in his arms. "Remember our last conversation in my office before you left?"

Rose flushed and nodded.

"I said I wanted more out of life than just working at The House. I meant what I said. A few days after you left, a favorite uncle of mine contacted me and offered me a home and a position in the family business." John paused a moment.

"He sounds like a nice man, and a caring uncle. Did you take him up on his offer?"

"I did. I resigned from my position at The House, and have been working with him since then. But what I want to know, Rose, is this: will you marry me and be my wife?"

She stood there blinking up at him, saying nothing. A sudden roar filled her ears like the rushing sound of waves on the sea, and she staggered back a few steps trying to steady herself. John caught her and held her tight to keep her from falling. "So will you? Are you giving me a yes or no?"

Her heart pounding so loud she hardly heard herself, she looked up into his eyes and said, "Yes, I will! Of course I will!"

John leaned down and kissed her again. "You won't ever have to spend another night alone, Rose. I know that feeling, and I don't like it one bit."

She laughed. "You don't have to tell me twice. My first night home just about killed me. I thought I'd lose my mind."

"I'll do everything in my power to make you happy. You know that, don't you?"

"Of course. I'll do the same. It's a two-way street, you know. At least that's what I learned from my time at The House."

"Oh, I have something for you, a small token." John reached into his pocket and pulled out a long silver chain interspersed with gems. He dangled the link before her eyes. "What do you think? Would you wear it?"

"It's rather long for a bracelet." She examined the piece closely. "I think my wrist is too small, but it's beautiful just the same."

John threw back his head, laughing. "This is not a bracelet." He cast her knowing glance and continued smiling.

She frowned a moment, trying to think. "Oh, my god, you didn't! It's a chain for my … ! She flashed him a big smile. "So when do I get to wear it?"

"I say there's no time like the present. We seem well-hidden behind this tree, and I'm pretty fast with my hands."

She pressed in close. "Go ahead, I dare you."

With eager hands, John unbuttoned her blouse, smiling wider as her breasts came into full view, bearing their two glistening rings. He worked the ends, fastening the chain between the rings. He stood back a moment to savor the view.

"How do I look?" Rose turned a little from side to side.

"Magnificent as always." His eyes gleamed. Unable to resist, he placed a soft kiss on top of each peak before buttoning up her blouse. "Good, only you and I know about this. Nothing shows through the material."

"Now I have a question." Rose tugged on his trousers and pulled him close. She unfastened the fly, happy with the view of a soft, plump button resting between his thighs. A second once-over confirmed a ring of gold resting underneath the ridge of his tip.

"I've never removed it since the last night we spent together." He squirmed a little and wriggled his hips. "Rose, no teasing. Those fingers of yours will be the death of me, and I know there's nowhere here to hide for long." He gave her a kiss, just long enough for her to finger him for a few more seconds, before he pulled away and refastened his trousers. "Let's go. We need to tell your parents. I want you as quickly as possible, so there's no time to lose."

"I think we'll find them in the sitting room. They usually like to spend time in there, Mother sewing, Father reading or going over his financial ledgers." Rose wrapped her arm through his and led the way.

*   *   *

"Mother, Father, we have something to tell you." Rose led the way into the sitting room. Her mother looked up from her sewing, and Mr. Barweather glanced up from a paper he had been grumbling over.

"Well, John," he said, getting up from his desk, "did you finally figure out what's wrong with Rose? Because we, for the life of us, can't figure it out ourselves."

"Mr. Barweather, as a matter of fact, I do know what's wrong with her."

"Well, let's have it, man, what the devil is wrong?" He and Rose's mother both stood and waited for the answer.

"It seems to me," John said, taking time to formulate his words, "that your sweet Rose is sick."

"Sick? Exactly what do you mean?" Mr. Barweather frowned as he walked over to John. Rose's mother dropped her sewing, joining her husband. "And I need you to be honest with us. Whatever sickness she has, we're prepared to fight it to the utmost with every resource we have." He pounded a fist into the palm of his other hand.

John sighed, trying to appear serious, while Rose gathered every resource within her to stifle a giggle. "I have discovered that your daughter is in fact … lovesick."

Her parents turned to stare at each other before turning back to John. "Did we hear you say 'lovesick'?" Rose's mother said. "Surely you can't be serious."

"Yes, you did, and yes, I am." John maintained a straight face.

"And just what do you propose we do about this, John?" Mr. Barweather stood with a dumbfounded expression on his face.

"Well, for someone who is lovesick, I suggest you find them a suitable mate, and I have someone in mind."

"And just who might that be?" Mrs. Barweather moved closer next to Rose. "We would only approve if the gentleman was proper, and promised to treat our daughter like the real lady she is."

"Ah, Mr. and Mrs. Barweather, I promise to treat Rose like the princess she truly is. I love her from the bottom of my heart, and I can't live another day without her. Truly, I think we're both lovesick. Our marriage is the only suitable solution."

Mr. Barweather threw back his head and laughed. "John, John," he said between fits of laughter, "you really had us going." He patted John's back, trying to catch his breath. "There's nothing I like better than a man with a sense of humor. Heaven knows we need some of that around here."

"What do you say? May I have Rose's hand in marriage?"

"Oh, but of course you can. We think you'd make Rose a wonderful husband, and no doubt you understand her far better than we do." Mr. Barweather shook John's hand and patted him on the back some more. "John, welcome to the family."

*   *   *

Two weeks later, after a simple wedding ceremony held in the Barweather garden, Rose viewed her new home for the first time. "What a beautiful Victorian house, John." Standing at a large iron-gated entrance, she stood in awe of the graceful structure at the end of the drive.

"Beautiful, isn't it? And wouldn't you know it's not too far from The House." He put his arm around Rose and kissed the top of her head.

"From the look of this place, we have our own pleasure grounds. You did mention this was an estate, yes?"

"I did. Thanks to Uncle Henry, he's giving us this property. He and Aunt Nora never had children of their own, but he made quite a bit of money in his day and accumulated all kinds of property. He wanted to give his favorite nephew a proper wedding gift. At least that's what he told me."

"It's the most proper place I've ever seen." Rose turned

her head back and admired her new home once again. "But I want to know something, is it haunted, are there any fun spooks lurking around inside?" She giggled and pressed against him.

"You have such an imagination. During the short time I've been here, I've yet to see any spooks." He smiled down at her. "But the house does have a couple of new occupants. Let's get on down the drive and go inside and have a look."

When they arrived, John took out a key and unlocked the large door.

"Oh, John, I love this. And look at the magnificent winding staircase over there." Rose stepped over the threshold and into a grand entrance hall, gliding over the dark, polished wooden floor, eyeing every aspect of architecture and furnishings.

"They aren't marble, but I hope you'll feel like my princess every time you move over them."

"You know I will. And, oh, what darling little kittens." She stooped down to stroke two little balls of fluff mewing at her feet.

"These are the two additional occupants, a wedding gift from Thomas. He told me you were quite fond of cats."

Rose widened her eyes, remembering her first time in the tub room with Thomas, when she'd promised to be his best kitty. "Um, yes, that's true. I like cats a lot, especially when they purr."

"You'll have more than enough time to check out the rest of this place. You're my bride, my wife, and mistress of not only my heart, but this place." He took her arm and pulled her to her feet, breaking up her interlude with the cats. "I want to show you our bedroom. I'm sure we'll spend lots of time there."

They crossed the entrance hall, and Rose felt like a princess again as they climbed the stairs up to a large hallway with four rooms, two on either side. "Our master bedroom is at the end of the hall on the left. I like the privacy. I just know you'll like it." He plucked the sleeve of her dress and led her to the end of the hall.

"What an amazing room." Rose scanned her surroundings. "I like the crystal chandelier over our bed. It reminds me of a smaller version of the one at The House. I always loved that chandelier." Her eyes roved over the ornate armoire in one corner and the two night stands on either side of the four-poster bed. She admired the needlepoint rugs on the carpet. "I especially like the fact we have a fireplace in this room. Now I get to bask in front of the flames with you." He smiled and kissed her on the forehead. "But what's in the box here at the foot of the bed?"

"Oh, just a few odds and ends, some little extras." John's eyes took on a mischievous glow. "Well, go on, have a peep inside."

Rose opened the heavy, wooden lid and peered inside, finding all sorts of cuffs, phalluses, and even a small compartment containing lubrication and other sensual oils. Smaller boxes held rods, wands, and other pleasure toys. She laughed, shaking the golden ringlets on her head. "No bedroom is complete without a specialty box. I pity those who don't have one."

"What do you say we take a moment and play?" John came up to her side, pulling her into his arms.

"I'm all yours, totally and completely, forever and always." Rose pulled his head down and kissed him. The bulge between his thighs teased her, sending a throbbing ache to the top of her sex.

He unbuttoned his shirt. "Before we start, I'm going to open the window and let in some fresh air. By the way, our room overlooks the garden."

"How nice." Rose slipped off her shoes and stockings. "I love gardens. I'm sure this place has a nice one."

"It's very nice. I took the liberty of checking it out thoroughly once I moved in and began setting everything up." He slipped off his shoes and socks, and unfastened his trousers, letting them slide to the floor before kicking them off.

Rose now stood before him, every vestige of clothing in a heap by the foot of the bed. The silver chain resting between her breasts sparkled in the sunlight. John came up to her, eyes glowing, and pulled her into his arms. His length, full and hard, pressed into her with more determination. His chest heaved with anticipation, and she sensed a look of pride on his face. "I guess we need to turn the covers down." She grabbed a corner of the cover at the head of the bed. Clean white linens lined the mattress. John picked her up in his arms and placed her on the bed. "First time as man and wife, Rose." His face hinted with urgency. Her eyes gleamed with the pleasure pain of lust as she opened her thighs. Happy he didn't insist on cuffs, she wrapped her arms around his neck, pulling his face over hers. Her mouth covered his with the softest kiss; her eyes closed at the touch of his flesh against hers. She let out a soft gasp; her nether regions accepted him as he impaled her with sure, tender thrusts, filling her with a warmth and fullness, nearly taking her breath away.

She hung on tight as he glided back and forth, in and out, in a slow, gentle rhythm. Her eyes flew open and locked with his, her smile of approval encouraging him in every way. In a few moments, her walls wrung out the very liquid soul from his loins. And through the open window, borne on the waves of the afternoon breeze, the sound of chimes tinkled in the distance.

Read on for a sneak peek of more hot new titles from Scarlet Darkwood.

Bonus Chapter: Mistress of The House
Chapter 1

THELMA STARNSBY slipped the brown leather bag over her shoulder and turned around to give The House one last hard stare. The ornate building seemed to stare back, as its methodical chevron-shaped architecture sprawled across a massive expanse of velvety green grass. Most avoided thinking about the local asylum, viewing it with horror. But for the past few months, her stay here had provided the opportunity to learn one other truth about this place, one the public would shudder even to think about. Unlike them, however, she had quickly embraced the treatment, reveling in their methods of healing.

She turned around to open the car door, settling herself in the front passenger seat of a handsome 1926 Chrysler Imperial E-80. Once she had adjusted herself, placing the bag beside her feet, she pulled her cloche hat lower over her eyes, wishing to remain inconspicuous during the drive home. The driver, provided as a courtesy of The House, shut the door and returned to the other side, sliding into the driver's seat.

"Where to, lady?" A broad smile lit up his handsome face, as he started the car.

She smiled back, not without some wistfulness, knowing this might be the last time she'd ever find herself surrounded by the most handsome people on earth, all collected in one place. "6969 Chastity Lane."

The young man's smile faded, his expression turning into one of disbelief. "Chastity Lane, is it? Is that a real address, or are you just toying with me?"

"Oh, no, it's my real address." She lifted her hand to her mouth and stifled a snicker. "Not so fitting after a stay here, don't you think?"

"I should say so." He chuckled, slowly pulling out of the drive. "You'll give that street a whole new meaning, altogether."

"Trust me, I already have a plan to make that happen." Thelma grinned and closed her eyes.

Yes, she had concocted a plan, all right, using all the

wisdom garnered from her stay at The House; the plan incorporated her intense training in pleasures of the flesh, along with a last-ditch effort to get Harry Wisenburg to marry her. After a little over a year of their having spent time with each other, she'd grown tired of waiting; something had to give. Many would consider her method most unorthodox, even damning to her soul; but secretly, she damned society for squashing sexuality, man's most basic nature. Worse yet, she damned them for placing women in a status not much above that of animals: mere property. But she rested a little easier these days, aware of the new crusade young women had lately begun to lead, trying in desperation to rid themselves of the shackles wielded by old, patriarchal domination.

"So what's a dame like you gonna do once you're home? And I must admit, for an older broad, you're sure a looker: nice hair, slender figure, not to mention some great fronts." The driver whistled, giving her a quick, approving wink, and then turned his attention back to the road.

With a wrinkle of her nose, she sniffed in disgust. "Yes, what to do once I'm home? I'll be trying to get my life going forward again, instead of stalling out like it did before." She shook her head a little. "Geez, I thought life was about over for me, at my age, but it's not. Why it's just beginning, really!"

Before her admission to The House, her last statement would have rung in her ears as a loud lie. In fact, the miserable, helpless feeling of life passing her by had almost became the final nail in the coffin of her lonely existence, causing her to spiral out of control into an emotional breakdown.

"You don't say so! Really?"

"Trust me, most of you think life is for the young, but, as I've just learned during my stay at The House, it's just not so."

"Tell me something, if you don't mind me being so bold to ask." The driver's face showed sincere interest, and he wiggled a little to get more comfortable in the seat as he drove the distance from the countryside where The House stood, hidden from public view, to the populated town where Thelma lived. "What brought a pretty little thing like you to The House? You know, once everybody finds out where you've been, they'll think you're just a crazy old bat!"

"Will you please stop calling me old?" She reached over and swatted him on the thigh. "If we weren't driving, and in another location, I'd strip those breeches off you and swat that mighty fine rump of yours."

"Ah, my rump couldn't be swatted by any finer a lady than yourself." The warm grin filled his face, while a light flush colored his cheeks.

"As for being called crazy, I think it's funny most people think The House is just the loony bin."

"Well, it is, at least one side of it, anyway." He patted her on the knee. "But from the sound of you, the staff on the naughty side taught you a lot, didn't they?"

Thelma stretched her shapely legs as best she could. The car began to feel a bit cramped, and the road to her house still stretched out several more miles. "Yes, they did, lucky me!"

"Yeah, you were lucky. Better for you to end up on the naughty side, after all. They have lots of wicked fun over there." He turned his head toward her and lowered his voice. "I know, because I've walked through those halls and peeked in the rooms."

She laughed. "I'm sure you have, given the fact there are no doors to those rooms. You got yourself quite an eyeful, didn't you?"

"Oh, baby, what I'd give to …" He shook his head. "Enough about my being a Peeping Tom. So how'd you get to the good side, that's what I wanna know?"

She shrugged. "I was feeling out of sorts, frustrated at life to the point I nearly lost my mind, so my doctor recommended it. He's a good friend of Dr. James, the House physician."

"You don't say!" The driver stared straight ahead, tapping his fingers on the wheel. "They must be some mighty interesting cohorts, Dr. James working at The House, and his friend recommending you to come. Makes you kind of think, you know."

"Good point. As a matter of fact, I never would have described Dr. McGuiness as a sensual type, now that I think about it. He's always so stuffy and straightlaced when I see him. I wonder if, behind closed doors, he's anything like his buddy!"

Thelma's mind flashed back to her first encounter with the handsome Dr. James. Rules of The House dictated that every patient, or "admit" as they were called, undergo a physical exam before participating in the House program. And yes, Dr. James knew how to perform a thorough physical exam, in every sense of the word, using his fingers to rub, explore, and tweak all the right sensitive places. She took in a gulp of air, exhaling little by little, trying to dull the beginnings of a new ache looming between her thighs.

The driver shifted in his seat. "I know you want this kept secret and all, but what are you going to tell everyone when you get home? People are nosy, you know."

"I have that story planned too." She threw back her head and laughed. "I'm a teacher by occupation, and before I left I made up this story about going off to do some temporary teaching in another city. They'll just think I've come back, that's all."

He nodded and clicked his tongue. "Good way to do it. Keeps 'em minding their own business, and it's a believable story."

Even Harry had believed her. She smiled, remembering the sadness in his eyes when she told him of her leaving. He seemed heartbroken, wanting to know the address where he could send letters, reminding her of his undying devotion. But she made enough excuses, and finally convinced him he didn't need to engage in letter-writing, since she'd only be gone for a short while.

Thelma closed her eyes for a moment, feeling the hum of the car as it moved on down the road. All this nervous-breakdown nonsense she blamed on Harry, for dragging his feet on popping the question, all the while flirting with her nonstop. How he'd carried on, crooning away about how her eyes lit him on fire, how her smile made his heart flutter, how her very presence filled him with purpose, giving him every reason in the world to get out of bed every morning.

She pursed her lips and patted the leather bag, nearly laughing out loud. How quick he'd be willing to get out of bed once she'd had her way with him remained the big question. Yes, he might have every reason to stay in bed!

After a few moments of driving in silence, the driver tapped her on the knee. "You got a special someone in your life you can practice on when you get back?"

"Um, I think I do, and if this doesn't do the trick to get him to propose marriage, then I guess I'll be doomed to spend the rest of my life alone."

"You ever been married?"

Thelma winced. She didn't talk to a lot of people about her past, which was frankly a humiliating one. "Only for a brief time. I was eighteen, and we were married just a few months before he suddenly left: no word, no warning, just up and left. I finally got a letter from him telling me that he just wasn't ready for marriage." She took a deep breath and continued. "I never saw him again, and in order to not seem like used goods, I've always told everyone that my spouse died of an illness."

"Yeah, like I said before, keeps 'em minding their own business." The driver turned and smiled at her. "But I just know a bewitching dame like yourself won't be alone much longer, I just feel it. And with what you know about men, you'll bring any one of 'em down to their knees, begging you to never let 'em go!"

"I'm hoping so … I'm hoping so." Though she felt armed and ready for her next set of battles, a twinge of doubt still tugged at her. What if Harry wasn't the type to fall to his knees … for anybody? After all, his wife's death several years ago hit him hard; he'd never seemed inclined to marry again.

The car sped through town, and after some longer roads

and a few turns, they headed into an old neighborhood filled with ornate, well-maintained Victorian homes. He nodded and gave a light whistle. "You live in a nice place, gal." His head moved back and forth, surveying the fine houses, each perched on a neatly manicured lawn. "You got money or something?"

"Well, just what I inherited from my parents. I live in the same house I grew up in."

"I see. Nothing wrong with that." He turned the car to the right. "I bet the man you have your eye on has money too? I mean, you people seem to stick together, you know."

Thelma smiled. "Yes, we do, don't we? And yes, he's done quite well for himself." She turned her head toward the driver. "You know, he only lives a couple of blocks from me, and walks over to my house a lot if he's out and about, or just wants to drop by."

"You don't say. Well, now that's pretty handy, especially if both of you are wanting a quick little something-something." He clicked his tongue again a few times and nodded, smiling. "Hey, lady, I think we're almost at your place."

"Yes, turn right there, the road on the left."

"So this is Chastity Lane … which will soon be known as Lover's Lane, yeah?"

"I'm praying so. Oh, please drive on around the house. I'll go in through the back door, just in case. I don't feel like getting any of my neighbors stirred up. They're nice, but I just want some time to get used to being back home again."

"I understand." He brought the car to a halt next to the back door. "Hang on, I'll help you out." He climbed out of the car and headed toward Thelma's side.

She grabbed up the leather bag and swung her legs out of the car.

"I see they fixed you up a goodie bag." He smiled and quirked an eyebrow up and down.

"Yes, and I intend to use everything in here." As her feet hit the stone drive, she pulled herself out of the vehicle and threw the bag over her shoulder. "I've got it from here. I don't have anything else with me. My doctor told me to leave everything at home."

"Well, The House provided everything you needed and then some." The driver tipped his hat and made his way around the car. Before he got in, he turned around to face Thelma one last time. "Hey, doll, just remember one thing. A girl who is chaste will never be chased. I really suggest you use everything in that bag. And if you want my advice, I'd be quick about it too!" He gave her a farewell salute, slipped inside the car, and slammed the door shut. With a few maneuvers, he turned around and headed back down the driveway before he sped out of sight, taking away with him her last tangible connection with The House.

Thelma smiled and reached in her pocket for the key. With a quick twist, she opened the door and stepped inside her home, her world, the real world, where life didn't flow with any predictable routine with adoring attendants who only cared only for your comfort … and pleasure. With a breath of relief, she found the house had remained the same as she'd left it, with everything in neat order and all furniture covered in large sheets to keep out some of the dust.

She'd chosen not to have anyone check on her place, which might have proven a foolhardy decision, but considering where she'd spent her time away, this choice had seemed the most prudent for privacy. One by one, she began lifting off the sheets, uncovering a magnificent collection of Victorian furniture. A stale odor reached her nostrils, and to freshen up the air, she moved around the room, opening up the windows. Within minutes, the fresh scent of flowers and grass filled the downstairs.

After moving through the kitchen and dining room, she crossed over the hallway to the large living room, where she removed more sheets and opened up windows. The dark, cold fireplace still smelled of burned wood, yet in her mind's eye, she beheld a future of roaring fires and intimate moments she planned to have with Harry. But her heart beat faster at the sight of a wooden door on the opposite side of the room. On the other side of the wall was a room, one which might have been used by others as a private study or office. Thelma, however, had decided long ago her home had needed another bedroom on the lower level instead.

After much daydreaming during her time at The House, she'd already determined how this room might now figure in her plans to win over her beloved Harry. Giving the leather bag a fond pat, she walked over to the door and slipped into the room. Perfect! She'd even had a small bathroom added for convenience. Her eyes scanned over the simple iron bed, a small nightstand and lamp resting beside it. On the opposite wall, in one corner, stood a chest of drawers.

Other than a dainty overhead light, the room, almost coincidentally, reminded her of the one she and her attendant had shared at The House. A simple room, but one where a lusty couple could indulge in sexual pleasure. She let out a laugh. At least this room included a door for privacy, a stark contrast to the doorless rooms at The House.

The bag slipped from her shoulder and slid to the floor. With a quick grasp of the strap, she picked it up and walked over to the chest of drawers. From her "goodie bag," as the driver had called it, she pulled out containers of lubricant and vials of scented oils. After placing these inside the drawers, she pulled out a strap-on phallus, some cuffs, a blindfold, and a ball-gag, which were her favorite items. She kissed each one, remembering fondly how her attendant had introduced these toys to her, and placed them in their own special drawer.

Thelma finally turned out of the room, shutting the door behind her. After exiting the living room, she stepped into the hallway and turned left, where she climbed the stairs to her own bedroom. At the top of the steps, she turned right into a large master room. The spaciousness took her breath away, after having spent time in a much smaller and modest room at The House; but the feeling of isolation and loneliness hit her the hardest.

As she stood in her own bedroom, silence came crashing

down against her ears. No sounds of lusty moans, no flirtatious giggles, and no clinking of metal cuffs against iron bars. The other three remaining bedrooms, meanwhile, were devoid of naked bodies entwined in passionate embraces, or tongues and fingers of the occupants exploring moist nether regions or stimulating sensitive areas of the flesh.

She slipped out of her clothes and changed into a comfortable robe before heading off downstairs to make something to eat. Tomorrow, she'd uncover the furniture in the other upstairs rooms, and give her whole house a good, general airing out. In the coming week, she'd have her house back to its former beauty. As she sat at the table, sipping a cup of tea, her thoughts turned to thinking of ways to get Harry to propose. At thirty-eight years of age, Thelma knew little time remained before spinsterhood might be her lot in life. At forty-three years of age, Harry still looked good, and he'd been widowed long enough, in her opinion. The intense sexual training she'd received during her stay at The House gave her a strong advantage over most women, who merely played a passive role during lovemaking sessions with their husbands.

Passivity remained a thing of the past for Thelma, and she knew from this point forward, if Harry spent any time with her, he was about to learn a thing or two; no woman around stood a chance against her. Swallowing the last bite of her sandwich, she got up from the table and made her way to the living room again. Along the right side of the wall, opposite the fireplace, stood a studio upright piano, which had been her mother's. She sat on the stool, opened up the lid, and began stroking the keys. Music somehow relieved her of stress, and for quite a while she played, stopping at times to think about Harry, imagining how his soft flesh, instead of these hard, ivory keys, might feel beneath her fingers.

He'd be surprised to see her. Or would he? Had he forgotten her already? A chill ran up and down her spine. Out of sight, out of mind, she'd always heard. Perhaps instead, absence made his heart grow fonder? One thing remained certain, she'd find out soon.

The afternoon sun faded away to darkness of night. Tired and weary, Thelma returned upstairs, slipped on a nightgown, and crawled into bed, settling into the sheets. Wearing a nightgown felt strange after an extended period of sleeping nude. For a while she tossed and turned, thinking just how to spend her first day home tomorrow. The bed felt cold. How odd to spend a night alone, and not in the company of an attractive man. Bedtime at The House had given everyone an even greater excuse for cuddling, fondling, and checking out dark, sensitive areas with flicking tongues and sly fingers.

At long last she rolled over and closed her eyes, trying to force herself to fall sleep. If she played her cards right, she'd never have to sleep another night alone. Her eyes closed, and she fell into a deep sleep.

About The Author

Scarlet Darkwood wields a mighty pen, or at the very least, delivers mighty punches to the computer keys when she's typing furiously on a story. She likes dark and twisted, and the weirder, the better.

Always preferring avant garde themes, her stories take the reader on unusual adventures, exploring the darker parts of the human psyche as she whips out cunning prose wrapped in provocative themes. Sometimes she veers from her beaten path and takes a happy-go-lucky romp in the brighter sides of life, kicking up her style into sharp, snappy dialogue and clever descriptions.

Writing in several genres unleashes her imagination so she never grows bored. From a young age, she's enjoyed writing and keeping diaries, but didn't start creating novels until 2012. She's a Southern girl who lives in Tennessee and enjoys the beauty of the mountains. She lives in Nashville with her spouse and two rambunctious kitties.

For more information about the latest concerning Scarlet and her work, sign up for her newsletter: http://eepurl.com/Rt5HP

You can visit her BLOG at: www.scarletdarkwood.com

Follow her on Google+ at: http://google.com/+ScarletDarkwood

Follow her on Twitter at: http://twitter.com/ScarletDarkwood

Follow her on FaceBook: http://www.facebook.com/scarletdarkwoodauthor

Check Out Scarlet's Other Works

Erotica:
Pleasure House
Dance of Desire

Supernatural Romance
Words We Never Speak

Erotic Romance:
Master of The House
Mistress of The House

Erotic Shorts:
Hard Way In
Fun with Dick and Peter
Naughty and Nice

If you have any questions, comments or suggestions, you can reach the author at: sdarkwood@gmail.com